KENNETH KAPPELMANN

The DRAGON UNKNOWN

HIDDEN MAGIC VOLUME II

The final approval lies with the author.

This is a work of fiction. All names, characters, places, and incidents either are the product of the author's imagination or are used fictitiously. Any resemblance to actual persons, living or dead, or actual events is purely coincidental.

Print ISBN: 978-1-61296-848-3
PUBLISHED BY BLACK ROSE WRITING
www.blackrosewriting.com

BLACK ROSE writing™

ISBN: 978-1-61296-848-3
PUBLISHED BY BLACK ROSE WRITING
www.blackrosewriting.com

Printed in the United States of America
Suggested retail price $ 24.95

The Dragon Unknown is printed in Adobe Caslon Pro

PART I

For
Keith Kappelmann
and
in loving memory of
Carol Kappelmann

PART II

For my sisters, Jean, Mary, and Kim; and my brother
(in-law but brother nonetheless), Calvin.

In memory of Mark Allen Selbee (1969–2014)

PART II

The DRAGON UNKNOWN

PART I

PROLOGUE

✤

Schram Starland, prince of the human city of Toopek, thought about the last three years of his life. He had gone from a human youth walking with his canok friend to an elf-human magician providing leadership over the world. He had lost much—his lifelong friend Kirven, his mother and father; new friends had died and new relationships made. He had married his love and seen love grow in those around him.

Their trek to save Troyf had been successful for now. The prophecy Kirven had created had been fulfilled by what Schram believed was how his friend had designed it. Schram was tall, strong, and powerful, but was he powerful enough to defeat the black dragon, Slayne, and his magical wrath? With his companions, Stepha, Princess of the Flyer Elves and wife to Schram; Maldor, the young human-built maneth (large creatures with a lion mane) thrown into Batt Line Leadership and currently captured by Slayne; Jermys, the dwarf who lost his twin brother in the final battle with Kirven; Krirtie, the fiery human girl who was in love with Maldor; and Fehr, the bandicoot rat with a habit of getting into trouble but a critical piece nonetheless. They had found the source of the evil and struck hard against its offensive.

However, Slayne, the evil black dragon believed to be behind this dragon offensive still lived. He has captured Maldor in their pursuit to obtain the weapons of the Ring of Ku. The maneths and elves have moved to support Toopek, for they all know if Toopek falls, their chance of winning this war is low. Geoff, King of the Maneths, is overseeing Toopek while Madeiris, King of the Elves is supporting both the maneth homeland and Toopek while still

9

holding Elvinott against all forces as Schram and his companions still try to find the solution to defeat Slayne.

Fate has taken them far, but what does fate have to do with the future? What has happened to Schram's mother, not seen since Toopek was originally attacked so long ago? How can they save Maldor and how can they obtain and harness the powers of the weapons of the Ring and the Staff of Anbari? They have only begun to understand the powers held deep within Krirtie's scimitar, Jermys's hatchet, Stepha's bow, and the hammer that had become affixed into Maldor's arm, perhaps protecting them both from the evil clutches of the black dragon. Where should Schram begin, and who can he trust in these very dangerous times, and how can he learn about the powers of his staff, the simple branch obtained in Anbari's Dominion? What does it mean, and who can teach him? All these questions must be answered before the hidden magic may finally be revealed.

The Masquerade

S chram did not know exactly what to expect as he approached
his longtime friend's door. They had only been back in Toopek
just over a week and already all of the companions, except Krirtie
and himself, had departed to prepare for the first unified offensive
against the dragon forces. Since their return, Krirtie had remained
in her family's old house, spending her free time by herself as she
fought to work through her hardships, giving her presence only
to bid farewell to those she had fought beside for so long. Schram
only hoped the news he brought could break down some of the
shell she had built around herself, for he did not want to leave her
in this state. However, the time to act was soon approaching, and it
was his job to lead the maneth troops through Elvinott. He knew
that he must speak with her today.

Slowly, he raised his hand and began to knock, gripping his
magical staff, the Staff of Anbari, tightly with his other. He was
greeted with silence and proceeded to pound harder, although he
knew the first had been heard clearly. Again, no sound was returned,
and giving a slight sigh, the human-turned-elf magician said in a
raised but gentle tone, "Krirtie, it is Schram. Please open the door."

He waited patiently as he heard the shuffling of various papers
depicting of someone rising from a seat, knocking whatever they
had been working on to the floor. His elven ears heard footsteps
slowly walking toward the door, then the soft, cracked voice of
his lifelong friend. "Go away, Schram! I do not wish to speak to
anyone, including you."

His head dropped, letting his long black hair fall about his
shoulders. "Please, Krirtie, I bring news which I think you might

find valuable. Besides, if you don't open the door, I shall enter by my own resources, and you know what a mess I can make going that route," although they both knew in moments Schram could have the door swing harmlessly open with only a short incantation.

With a loud snap, the bolt holding it closed popped back, and slowly the large wooden door swung ajar. A deep musty odor bit Schram's acute elven sensing nose causing the magician to take a step back while the stale air from inside was quickly replaced with that from the summer afternoon. He wore a broad smile in spite of the smell and the worn expression of his friend. Her hair was tangled and not well kept, with as much dirt spread across her face as appeared to be in the front room of her house. The armor she had worn so proudly for nearly the past two years remained stacked beside the door while her brilliantly curved and glistening scimitar sat against a chair Schram assumed she had just come from.

Her voice was dry and spoke of many sleepless nights. "Come on in. I suppose you would only make more of a mess if you used your *other resources* to force entry."

"I don't think more of a mess is possible."

She shot a daggered stare back toward him questionably. "What?"

Schram smiled in return but did not repeat himself. She already gave the distinct impression she was not pleased to see him, and he did not wish to make matters worse. He opened his arms and replied, "Are you not even interested in my news?"

She returned with a quick hug of her own. "If you brought the news I desire, you would have kicked the door in to tell me. I know you well enough to know that you cannot keep good news a secret too long. I suspect you are here to bid me farewell and give your love as the others have already done."

Schram frowned as he felt the pain she was still feeling over her losses. She made her way over all the rubble to again sit in the chair next to her sword and pick up a book that had remained open to where she had left off when he had knocked. Schram glanced around the small room to see that his first impression was correct—this house was in shambles. Books and papers lay scattered anywhere they could find a spot to rest, along with enough other garbage to keep a wandering bandicoot busy for weeks. His expression must have told his feelings, as Krirtie added, "I haven't had a chance to clean in a while."

The magician smiled. "Pay it no mind. I am used to it when I come to visit here." He paused to let his comment sink in. Then he added, shaking his head, "Yes, the Waywards were never known for their cleanliness."

Krirtie's frown began to turn slightly upward as she heaved her book at him. "Watch your mouth, Schram, or so help me I shall make you clean this place on your hands and knees."

Schram caught the book before it struck him in the stomach, laughing slightly when he saw the redness in his friend's face. "There, I told Jermys I could make you smile. That dwarf is buying the first round of ales." His speech stopped when he began to inspect the book she had been reading. "*The Legend of Draag*? This book is nothing more than a fable. It is based more on one elf's mystic dreams than true reality. What is going through that mind of yours now, Krirtie?"

His tone had become much more serious, and the smile that had begun to form on Krirtie's face as quickly vanished. "In less than two years, I learned to love another like I have never loved before. I always believed you would be the one who would capture my heart for good, but when I met Maldor, my whole life changed." Schram set his staff to the side and moved over to sit next to the girl who had a large tear forming in her eye. Her voice cracked slightly as she continued. "More than once he risked everything to save me, and for what? To end up prisoner in some forgotten caverns facing the wrath of a crazed dragon magi." She put her hands on Schram's knee and her voice became much stronger. "I have taken every book from our libraries regarding the subject, whether fiction or fact. I will find a way to help him, for he is all I have left."

Schram put his hands over the girl's, and his expression told her he understood. Gently he pulled her close. "Krirtie, I know of the feelings you hold for Maldor, and I carry similar feelings for Stepha. However, to attempt to help him on your own would be foolish, only resulting in your capture or even worse, death. How do you think that would make Maldor feel? Also, you are by no means alone. When Maldor was taken from us, our entire group was struck deeply. None have forgotten what that maneth did for us, and in time, we will all go back to help him, that much I promise."

Krirtie looked up, still crying. "But Maldor doesn't have any time. Each day more of his life fades as Slayne slowly wins over his plight for the hammer. If we don't act soon, Maldor will die."

He sighed deeply, then continued in a voice that hinted at pleading. "How about this? I will take care of my business at the canok homeland, then return to meet you at Elvinott, and we will discuss a possible rescue effort."

Her face showed surprise when she said, "You wish me to accompany you to Elvinott to aid in the elves' attempt to retake their forests?"

"I wouldn't think of going without you. Besides, your mother is not comfortable around the elves and dwarves. I think she would prefer your company."

"My mother! Where is she?"

Schram smiled broadly as the now-excited woman was on her feet and standing over him. "Jermys and Madeiris happened upon a small group of renegade humans trying to make it back to Toopek. They had fled at various times and subsequently been captured by goblin armies. All the men had been killed, but some of the women were spared. This group broke free from their captors sometime ago and has since been wandering aimlessly, trying to avoid recapture. Your mother saw the elven party traveling through the forest and made her presence known, speaking to the two she recognized, Stepha and Madeiris. They felt it better to take her on to Feldschlosschen rather than let her party risk returning to

Toopek. Although our surrounding forests are fairly safe, you can never be sure."

"Oh, Schram," she exclaimed, falling into his arms. "Thank you. Thank you very much. This is the best news I have heard in longer than I can remember."

He pushed the woman back a little and added softly, "Now, I haven't seen her, of course, but remember all she has been through. I am sure much has happened to her in the past eighteen months, and I don't want you to have false expectations."

Her smile faded. "I know, Schram, but the point is, she lives. I still do have a family."

He lifted her aside and then rose, retrieving his magical staff in the process. "I trust you will be ready to leave at first light tomorrow?"

She stood on her toes and kissed her childhood friend on his cheek. "I am ready now, you fool magician."

He shrugged a little, pressing his lips into an odd smirk before adding, "I would not want my mother returning to this mess, but I guess for Waywards, this is clean."

He shut the door quickly before hearing another large book strike hard behind him. He briefly twisted his lips into a smile, as he knew he could clean that mess in only seconds with a simple spell, but also feeling it would do Krirtie good to do it herself. He hurried off, remembering he too had much to do before tomorrow, including talking to Geoff and Alan regarding the safety of Toopek.

⸎

"I can't believe you are erecting a second wall around the entire city," said Schram, looking over the top view drawing of Toopek that Geoff had prepared.

The maneth appeared concerned. "It's all right, isn't it? I mean, this is a human city. It is not really my place to enforce—"

He was cut off by Schram's raised hand. "You have guarded this city better than anyone else could have hoped to do. It is our city, and if you feel this will help protect it, then by all means, do it."

Geoff smiled. "Good, it should be completed in less than a month. And look here"—he pointed to another spot on the map—"all the buildings that remain standing are reinforced and in key positions to defend, in the unlikely event both the walls are breached. I think by hiding bowmen on the rooftops, we will be able to hold against any ground assault the goblin and dark dwarf armies can throw at us."

"The problem lies with them damn flying beasts," echoed Captain Maximus Pete's rough voice from the side as he guzzled a mug of ale. "Those dragons ol rip this town apart sure as I'm the ugliest captain in the Toopekian fleet."

"Aye," said Geoff, "the dragons present a problem."

Schram stepped forward. "I will create a magical barrier over the city, but it will, by no means, be safe from penetration. The dark magic the young dragons wield will break through soon after encountering it. However, if there is an all-out attack, it might give you a little extra time to create a possible defense, or if necessary, provide the time to gain a retreat for some."

There was a brief silence as the assembled leaders thought about the prince's talk of retreat. Geoff then smiled and said, "Don't you worry, Schram. We'll hold this city." He slapped Alan Grove, the third lieutenant who now was leader over the human forces, on the back, and in a strong and defiant voice continued. "This human and his men fight like none I have ever seen before, and besides, we don't have anywhere to run. Assuming the attack strikes here first, we could fall back to Empor and then Drynak, but after that, where do we run to? Furthermore, what kind of defense could we put forward at Drynak? It's nothing more than a desert town as it is. We'd be no more than targets on an open pond in that pathetic city. No, we will fight to the end here and possibly take a good number of them bastards with us."

Pete gave an affirmative nod, filling another ale for himself in the process. Schram's face did not show the enthusiasm that the pirate's did, as he contemplated the thought of Toopek being a city under constant war and possibly becoming the first of the fronts to reach a point that it must fight to the death. His thoughts showed clearly in the lines on his face, but he spoke with the energy of one confident and sure. "Assuming our troops with the elven and dwarven armies are successful, Elvinott will again be in our hands and another possible escape route if the situation dictates as such. Also, perhaps I can come up with some other defense against the dragons when I consult with the canoks. Their knowledge is much more extensive than mine. If there are other possibilities, they will know them."

"Are you sure they'll help you?" asked the huge maneth, now joining Pete with a drink. "The canoks are still not considered survivors from the first dragon attacks 200 years ago."

"I am sure, for I bring them an offer they cannot refuse."

Geoff smiled and passed an ale over to the human. "I hope you are right, for Toopek's sake."

⚬⚬⚬

The plans were clear. March a direct course toward Elvinott. If they met with any goblin interference, they were to be killed on the spot. Word of their movement behind the force holding the elves and dwarves at bay in Feldschlosschen had to be kept secret. Schram had assembled about 200 humans and maneths to tip the scales against the dragon armies at Elvinott, but if it was going to be enough, he did not know.

He had chosen a route to take them deep into the mountains, well around the goblin-held town of Lawren. He toyed with the idea of going through the small outpost in an attempt to put it back under human rule, but he could not afford the time or the risk should a warning of their movements spread. All reports from the town was that it was business as usual there, regardless of who claimed leadership. And of what Schram knew about Lawren from his past visits, he could only assume this to be true.

It was still hours before dawn, and even leaving at this hour, the best time they could hope to arrive in Elvinott would be late tomorrow. Schram greeted Krirtie pleasantly as she appeared next to him in her full armor with her magnificent curved scimitar at her side. She returned with a smile, though most of her attention was drawn to the farewells from various friends and, of course, Geoff. He added a few extra words meant only for Krirtie's ears, and Schram assumed they had been in reference to their mutual friend, Maldor.

The large King of the Maneths and now leader of Toopek moved over and faced the human prince. The two did not speak but only gripped each other in a powerful embrace, their words spoken clearly with their eyes. The two parted, and Schram gave the motion with his staff to depart, followed by an echoing roar and cheer from the accompanying maneth and human guards respectively. As they reached the first glade just outside the city boundaries, Schram turned around with Krirtie to take a final look at their homeland before it drifted out of their sight. A slight red haze showed like a shell stretching from city wall to city wall but only apparent to the magician who had created it. Schram pulled his human friend close. "I wonder when we shall return this time?"

She sighed slightly. "I hope when it is all over." There was a pause before she added, "And I hope we will not be alone."

Schram smiled as they turned and moved to again walk at the lead, but the frown, which slowly grew on his face, told that he believed Krirtie's statement would not become true. He did not know from where it originated or what exactly it meant, but he had an overwhelming fear that his lifelong friend would never see her homeland again.

They walked steadily for a long time, completely free of any interference. Schram pushed his party onward, but his instincts were telling him that something was not right. It was just past noon when they stopped. "What do you think, Krirtie?"

"I don't know, Schram," she replied, looking around. "If these are all there are, it will not be a problem. We could silence these twenty trolls in only moments. However, it's more likely that they are not alone, and if a search party should wander back to a slaughtered camp, our presence and movements would definitely become common knowledge."

"I agree," he replied, motioning to a nearby maneth guard. "Meris, spread the word for everyone to sit down tight and keep their ears open. If fighting breaks out, tell the company to sweep the forest looking for strays."

The maneth, who is actually the current head of the Dimat line, though all are fighters now, nodded and began to relay the orders when Schram caught him again. "Also, take a small party out and see if there is a way around this camp."

Again he gave an affirmative nod and quickly departed. Schram knelt next to Krirtie as they both peered through some tree cover at the trolls camped before them. Krirtie whispered, "It is funny that they sit so calmly while a force ten times their size watches them unnoticed."

"*Unnerving* is the word I would have chosen. Trolls are by no means the dragon army's finest, but they are also not ones to have an isolated party of this size alone in the woods. I don't like this at all."

The entire party sat motionless for several hours as they waited for the search party to report. It had taken much longer than Schram had expected, but since there was no change in the troll camp in front of them, he decided to hold his position until he was forced to act. There was some commotion at the back of the lines that drew his attention, and he quickly moved to investigate. His run was greeted by Meris coming at a full sprint back to him. The maneth was white as a ghost and panting heavily by the time they reached each other, and after he took a brief drink of water, he said, "Trouble, sir. We made a path southerly through the mountains thinking we had found a new line to take to Elvinott. However, after about a mile, we came across another group similar to this one in size. We continued southerly and then came upon our worst fear—a huge troll outpost. It is well hidden in the trees, which is probably why none of our scouts or flyers have come across it before, but trust in the knowledge that it is there, and their numbers are great. These forests are thick back here."

Schram looked disturbed as Krirtie joined his side. "How many?"

"We couldn't be sure, at least 400, not counting those camped in the smaller parties."

The magician slumped. "Damn! I knew it just didn't feel right not running into any resistance until now. Slayne probably has these mountains planted thick with these parties, guessing what our plans would be. He found the perfect use for his near-useless troops—an alarm."

Meris raised a hand so he could continue. "There is more, which is why we had to return at such a quick pace." Schram's frown became even more grave as he knew what was coming next. "A group of about five trolls snuck up behind us as we looked over the camp. We were caught by surprise, but their inferior fighting abilities proved no match for ours. However, none were sure, but I think one could have fled. We might have set off their"—he paused then added—"alarm, as you call it."

Krirtie interrupted. "Now we have no choice, Schram. We have to go through them here or return to Toopek and get word to Feldschlosschen that we could not make it."

His expression did not change. "No, we won't retreat. We will never have a better opportunity to retake Elvinott. Some of us have to get through." He turned to Meris. "How far is the outpost?"

Meris replaced his maneth club he had been carrying since his return, then replied, "One mile to the first camp and another to the main outpost."

"Good, then we might have enough time." He turned back to Krirtie. "Gather up the eighteen best human fighters we have with us. Meris, lead a group of about five maneths back to the nearest troll camp and keep watch over it, for I believe if the main camp does know of our presence, they will continue backtracking in pursuit, alerting that camp rather than following your trail exactly. Keep a close eye over them, because this is what I have planned."

"They never knew what hit 'em," said Krirtie, pulling her troll armor over her head.

Schram motioned to the other humans Krirtie had selected to join her in changing armor. "Help move these bodies into the trees, and I will prepare them as is required," he shouted as he hurriedly ripped the dead troll's armor free and launched his bloodied body into some nearby brush."

One of the humans approached him. "Prince Schram, this troll's armor is too damaged to even think about wearing."

Schram frowned, both from his address as "prince" and the news the man brought. "Here, our numbers are already too thin. Use this armor and I will find another answer."

The human busily switched into the troll gear Schram had recovered and joined the other humans, all now almost completely "trolled" over. Schram caught Krirtie's worried gaze and then began chanting softly to himself. The woman stared at her longtime friend, watching alongside the frozen gazes of the other guards as Schram's face suddenly began to lose its shape and character. His body began to shorten and become fatter, with his green-brown elven skin turning a deep black. His nose grew long and bent downward at its tip while most of his muscles moved to better position themselves as rolls of fat folding over his troll-like boots. His armor lost its elven shine to be replaced with the dull, black dents common to the other trolls. Schram fell to his knees. The only feature depicting that he was the Prince of Toopek was his long jet black hair pushing from beneath his helmet, and the long wooden staff he had become known to carry held tightly by his side.

"Schram," hollered Krirtie while she watched the magician collapse to the ground.

He looked hazily toward the girl. "Quiet please, I am all right. I just did not realize how much it would take out of me, or even if I could do it. Tell the others we are in position. If we have been discovered, Meris will be returning shortly, and stopping to chat will not be an option. We must be prepared."

Krirtie moved to relay the message, clanging uncomfortably as she fought to adjust to her new armor. Schram groggily rose to his feet, and he knew if what he had planned was to work, he would have to fight through his weariness and act like a troll in pursuit. He gave one more incantation, and his staff took the form of a curved, black sword.

Maneths and humans, 170 of them, sat patiently about 500 yards northwest of the masqueraded troll party, while two parties of five maneths each had left on their own. One was Meris's group, who went to watch the troll camp to the south, whereas the other took off at the fastest pace possible to warn Geoff that a force of over 500 trolls could be closing in on Toopek—that is, if Schram's plan was successful.

An uneasy silence seduced the entire forest before the loud maneth roar burst through the air.

"That's the signal!" Schram hollered. "You all know what to do, and remember, we are trolls, so hide your faces. If discovered, you are on your own."

There were mixed sounds through the group when Schram waved his sword, and the twenty humans fell into the trees behind him. They shouted and cursed in the best troll voices they could muster with the few key phrases Schram had taught them as they fell into pursuit behind the thunder of maneth and human footfalls tearing a mean path through the underbrush toward Toopek.

They had gone less than half a mile when Schram could see their party growing larger from the other trolls joining in the chase. In all the wild confusion, he could not tell his party from the real ones. He only hoped that feeling would be equal in reverse. Furthermore, he hoped all would be able to stay near the rear guard and turn around when the time was right.

"You there," echoed a raspy troll voice from behind. "Were you the leader at the north point that alerted them?"

Schram had trouble understanding all the linguistics, but he thought he had gotten the main idea. He stopped his slow pursuit to turn and face the troll who had spoken. "Aye, do you have a problem with my actions?" he asked in return, raising his sword slightly to show displeasure at being questioned.

His tone was condescending and hard, trying to equal the other troll's displeasure with the situation. Thankfully his voice had become altered with his physique, so the approaching troll was completely fooled by Schram's appearance. However, since the troll had his sword drawn and his eyes locked in a displeasing stare, Schram knew his effective magic would help him little except to die looking and sounding like a troll. If not for his quick reflexes, his head would have been removed without another word spoken. The surprised look from the troll that had attacked turned to that of fear when he was on his back with Schram's sword tip to his throat.

Fire beat down from his eyes as he roared at the now-humbled troll leader. "Attack me, you swine! I shall slit your throat for having the thought."

The fear in the troll's eyes was matched only by that in his voice. "I am Garschmidt. Highest ranking troll. Why do I not recognize you?" He paused for Schram to answer, then added, "You know I was only following our master's orders. You know he said only to keep any troops back, not pursue."

Schram smiled, letting a ball of saliva drip between his lips to strike the troll in his forebrow. "My men saw the party and knew with your aid, we could easily smother them." He pressed his foot deeply into the captive's chest, causing him to gargle up some slop. "They numbered less than one hundred. Think how pleased our master will be when we tell him we single-handedly crushed the offensive."

The troll's eyes seemed to brighten as Schram's plan for bettering their position with their master appealed to him. He pushed Schram's foot aside and sharing a crooked smile, adding, "Yes, I believe you are right. We will crush the rebels then return to our post and send word to Slayne himself." He laughed deeply and leaned closer. "We will be well rewarded."

Garschmidt was now on his feet hollering at any guards around him to follow. Schram suggested he scout the area to gather more troops, but the lead troll would hear nothing of it, grabbing the human and pulling him along beside him.

They ran for some time, and although Schram tried to keep an eye out for any of his camouflaged friends, he found locating them an impossible task. The longer he remained with the trolls, the more danger he was in, as Toopek may be poised for a defense that would include defending against who he appeared to be. Suddenly, a scuffle broke out between two trolls that had bumped each other during the chase. The commotion grew drawing Garschmidt's attention. The troll approached the two fighting and in one swift motion beheaded them both. He turned back to Schram for approval and saw that Schram was gone.

⚭

"I hear something coming," said Krirtie softly.

"I told you we should have left while we had the chance," replied one of the guards. "Now the troops have started to return."

"Be quiet!" she exclaimed as they all now heard a twig snap, followed by the worst chirp of a yellow-bellied ingle fly any had ever heard.

"Schram?" she whispered outwardly toward the sound.

The magician burst through the trees, almost knocking his friend over as he came. "Krirtie, what are you doing saying my name? What if I had been a stray troll party? With that comment, you could have alerted the whole forest to your presence."

The girl appeared stung. "Well, what the hell kind of call signal was that? You sounded like a female bandicoot giving birth."

"As if you couldn't tell, whistling through these god-awful troll lips is not the easiest thing I have ever tried to do."

Both seemed to be growing in anger and defensiveness until one of the other guards interjected. "You know, you both are making enough noise now to wake the dead, let alone alert a nearby troll detachment."

Schram froze on the guard and then his look gradually softened. "You are correct." He turned to Krirtie. "How many more of our team still need to return?"

She glared. "Including you, that makes twenty here." There was a moment of silence, then she added sarcastically, "Some of us felt that hurrying back to the rendezvous point was important."

Schram recognized her tone and gave a quick smile. "I am sorry for everything. However, I was, shall I say, unavoidably detained."

She grinned in return. "I saw you get stopped by that other troll, but I couldn't help as I was pushed along with the troll assault. It took all my strength just to work my way to the side and slowly drift back."

Schram threw his blubbery black arm around the girl. "Tell me about it." He turned to the group. "Come on, we should hopefully now have a clear path to Elvinott. If we move through the night without making camp, then we should be able to reach the safety of its forests by early afternoon."

There were mixed emotions stirring among the men, and it brought about a comment from Dolf Stollman, the largest of the humans chosen. He stood nearly Schram's size and build before the magician's magical metamorphosis to the troll, and now the human appeared completely out of place as his troll armor did not nearly cover his body. Dolf said, "I do not feel any pleasure in the idea of running through this jungle throughout the night, but compared to the choice of mixing with the troll parties again, I shall run for a week. I now understand why you wanted only humans for this part of the task. I am over a foot shorter than most of the maneths, and I still stuck out like a stray bandicoot at a tigon banquet when we mixed with the trolls. Several glanced at me questionably when they passed by, and I can only imagine how they would have treated a maneth. However, coming to the point of my comments, would it be all right to ditch this garb now, for the discomfort is unforgiving?"

Schram smiled. "Relax, friends. We only have to wear this armor another day, and we shouldn't have any more troll entanglements. However, just in case, I will take the lead, as I believe I would be more convincing in a confrontation, but if weapons are drawn, no troll can be allowed to escape. We are only twenty, and we have to make it through. Even in these small numbers, we will be a major force against the goblin armies at Feldschlosschen. Let's move."

There was a scattering of waving swords and cheers when Krirtie grabbed Schram's arm. "I will take the rear and try to cover some of our trail." Schram nodded affirmatively and she added, "Oh, and Schram, is there any customary procedures for elves to break a joining?"

He raised one of his thick eyebrows. "A separation? It is written, but never has one occurred. Why do you ask?"

"I just wanted to know if Stepha would have something to fall back on when she sees you." She laughed heartily. "I used to think how bizarre your ears looked after you began to become more elf-like." She paused while her smile grew even greater. "But that troll nose?"

She continued laughing now, with several of those nearby not hiding that they had overheard and were finding the same humor. Her laughter did not cease or even lessen as she headed to take her place at the rear, snickers from each guard echoing as her comments were passed. Schram glared momentarily and then smiled as he too thought about the reaction of the Princess of the Flyer Elves if she was to see her husband looking as such. With a slight chuckle of his own, he disappeared into the brush with a line of human trolls at his heels.

⚭

They traveled throughout the night, and as Schram had hoped, they had not encountered any troll resistance. By the time they reached Elvinott, most of the magical physique Schram had induced upon himself had been worn away by the enchantment of the wood. He turned to his weary companion now standing next to him and said, "You see, now there is nothing for Stepha to see."

Krirtie grinned briefly, but her attention was drawn to the faces of those they traveled with. She pointed, "Look at their eyes as they behold the beauty captured with this forest. They look like children looking upon a mound of the sweetest chocolates Gnausanne has to offer."

"Don't laugh too hard," replied Schram as he reached his hand into the wondrous fountain of the princess to scoop up a mouthful of water. "It was not so long ago that the young woman standing before me now wore that same look of amazement. It is said that to look upon the trees of Elvinott, any evil mind would turn good. If their expressions"—he motioned to the eighteen humans still dressed as trolls—"are any example, then it must be true, and those trolls are on our side."

She smiled again. "I will always believe this to be the most beautiful place on all of Troyf."

"Then you feel as I do." The two hugged, and then Schram turned to speak to the spellbound men behind him. His speech momentarily broke them from their trance. "Men, please deposit your armor into the waters of the fountain. You will be given more when we continue after we eat and rest."

With that, he turned and headed toward the king's castle, the most magnificent oak in the forest with a huge castle carved into its base. The men behind were stunned, both from the idea of depositing their black and dented armor in such a beautiful fountain and from the idea of continuing their trek after dinner; but when they witnessed Krirtie's armor splash briefly into the water to be replaced with brilliant flashes of all colors on the spectrum and appear on its surface as shiny, newly forged armor bearing the crest of Toopek, all concerns for the journey were quickly forgotten.

Each man was proudly wearing their new armor when Schram returned, himself carrying only a shield bearing the colors and markings of Elvinott and his marvelous wooden staff. The chatter and conversation that had been taking place quickly dissolved, leaving the large human-elf looking down over his resting army of twenty. He gazed up into the dark sky and peered at the explosion of stars across the forest's roof, absorbing the silence and peace he heard as if it was a song. The calmness in his eyes seemed to be a drug affecting those around as all reveled in this moment of pure serenity.

Softly, Schram turned his head downward and spoke. "My friends, let me extend my apologies for having to push you so hard these last two days, and my appreciation for how well you performed. However, even as I speak now, I can only assume Slayne is moving what troops he can over to reinforce his barrier between here and Feldschlosschen. With this in mind, we have to continue on tonight so we will be in position for an early strike tomorrow morning. I know we are all tired, but since only twenty of us were able to make it through, we must attack before the reinforcements arrive. If we make good time through the forest, we can still catch five or six hours of sleep before dawn, and also, there is safety in these forests, so we will have nothing to fear as we travel."

His last statements seemed to pacify those on the verge of falling off as he spoke, and gradually the entire group stood and continued behind their leader.

The Separation

Even leaving at dawn from the Elvinott forest border, they still had over three hours of traveling to reach where Madeiris had said the goblin armies were massed, and that was assuming they would not meet with any other resistance. Since they were no longer under the elves' protective enchantment, dragon troops could be placed anywhere along their path, which would slow their journey.

However, Schram felt lucky to have made it this far only running into two small goblin parties, which were both possibly considered deserters. He looked across the large glade that nearly six months ago had been the sight of a fierce battle when the fleeing elves had met a battalion of dragon forces being led by one large blue dragon. Schram looked to where the blue had fallen beneath the wrath of Jermys Ironshield's fierce hatchet, and a deep sadness fell over him. He thought of Draketon, the large red dragon that helped them in the Black Pool of the South Sea, and the promise he made to him. Hopefully Schram could keep that promise and only a very few more dragons would be needlessly killed in this war, though he knew one which must. Yet, as he looked across the now-busy and -filled glade, he did not see how this situation would allow it. Whether all three dragons had been there the whole time was now beside the point. The fact was that now they not only were facing nearly a thousand goblin and troll armies, but they had the support of three large and seemingly mature and very powerful dragons. Schram saw the confident expressions of his twenty soldiers quickly begin to fade as they too witnessed what stood before them.

Schram gathered his troops into a small semicircle as he quietly spoke. "I know it does not seem likely as you look across this glade that our mission has any chance of success. However, remember that the elves and dwarves have nearly twice that number ready to tear down upon them at our signal." He paused while he prayed in his mind that this really was the case, and the dwarves and elves really were there waiting. "Furthermore, I will make it appear with a display to make the gods proud that we are in much greater numbers than we actually are. But once again, I am not a fool or a leader to force any man to his death. The chance of success is not great, and if anyone would rather retreat to Elvinott, then I will harbor no bad feelings and apologize for not being able to accompany them in their return." There was an ominous silence as each turned their heads to see the other's reactions. He waited several moments before continuing. "Fine, and thank you all, and may all our gods be with us. On my signal, we attack."

Several dropped their heads in final prayers while Schram moved back to where he could watch what was occurring across the clearing. Krirtie came over to join him. Softly, she said, "Schram, I just wanted you to know that I have always loved you and regardless of what happens, you will always be my greatest friend."

The human magician was quite taken by the words and rose to face the hard but sensitive girl before him. Her eyes spoke of confidence, but Schram could feel the fear within her. Placing a hand on her shoulder, he replied, "Krirtie, you know I feel the same toward you. You were my only human friend in Toopek when nobody else would even talk to me. You were the first human who did not look at me as some sort of alien from the elves. I was young, and I did not know at the time exactly how important your actions would prove to be to me, but know this, they were more important than I could ever put into words." They embraced tightly, and he knew they needed to clear their heads before they could effectively mount an attack.

When they separated, Schram stared into Krirtie's eyes and added, "An old friend used to say the same thing to me every time I left his homeland—'Schram, don't lose your head, and you won't lose your head.' He meant it to be funny, but as with most of what he said, there was a great deal of wisdom behind his words." He smiled. "You are a powerful woman and a great warrior. Trust in your actions and the sword by your side, for I know then that you will act bravely and always be victorious. Don't fall into simple traps because they appear the easy answer, for usually the easy way is the wrong way."

He removed his hand and looked over his small army, motioning for her to go to the far side away from the dragons. As she positioned herself, she thought about all she had heard and knew that his message was meant for a time other than the present. She made herself a mental note to explore his words later as all the explosions and noise taking place now brought reality upon the whole group. Schram had given his signal.

He had sent a barrage of energy pulses throughout the group, ending with his total force being directed toward the three dragons. Commotion ensued everywhere as his tiny force attacked from the trees, screaming and ranting as if they brought several thousand soldiers. The goblin armies that had been focused toward the dwarven mines spun to greet the onslaught of attackers, and as the humans drew near, none knew if the elf and dwarven cavalry were going to be present or not; and if you could read anything from their fierce attack, they didn't care. Suddenly, the sky erupted with elven arrows, and the lines of goblins preparing to meet the human force fell face down, arrows protruding from their backs.

Schram sent bolt after bolt toward the dragons, but as he had feared, these beasts were stronger than those he had faced in the past, and quickly two moved from his attack, leaving only one faced off against the magician, essentially buying the magician's time so the others could defend and attack those around. Schram created a barrier of energy around him, which allowed all attacks upon him to be easily discarded so he could concentrate on the dragons. The one he now faced had created a similar shell around itself, and the two locked magic as each attempted to break through the other's defenses. An overpowering screech was heard to his side, but Schram could not turn his head to see what had happened. All he knew was one of the other dragons was screaming its wicked roar in anger, the source driving it to that being unknown.

Stepha lay on the ground, her magical bow knocked to her side as the beast she had just wounded deeply howled at her, swinging its talons, trying to grab the elf who had inflicted so much pain, but being met with a human woman's sword between them. This dragon, though younger, had a similar barrier surrounding his blue body, but it seemed nonexistent to the blade of Krirtie's scimitar and the arrows from Stepha's bow. Krirtie stood strong between the two, swinging her sword wildly, trying to give the elf princess enough time to recover. She could feel her arms starting to tire when another screech broke through the glade, and blue blood flowed profusely around the arrow lodged fatally in the dragon's breast. Krirtie began to fall to her knees only to be grabbed by Stepha, who drew her sword to block a goblin attacking the human from her side. Krirtie quickly recovered from her momentary lapse, and the goblin attacker was almost as soon dead.

Everywhere they turned, another goblin party was preparing to attack. "They seem to be coming out of the cracks in the soil," hollered one human before feeling the point of a goblin dagger break through his armor, striking a death blow to his back. The other dragon, a huge green, which was the largest of the three, had moved to battle a party of dwarves, who were being savagely slaughtered by the beast. Flames erupted across the glade as elves, dwarves, and goblins alike screamed helplessly while their bodies were engulfed by fire. Elves sent repeated bowfire into the dragon's belly, but the arrows only seemed to strike and then bounce aside, only harming whom they fell toward. More fire blew in waves, flooding the clearing with enough heat and smoke to melt the strongest of steel.

The dragon became entranced by the screams and pain he was causing to those he had been taught were his enemy. Jermys spotted his opportunity and attacked, swinging his magical Hatchet of Claude at the green's glowing enchanted barrier. There was a flash of brilliant light as the two forces met, and the strike caused the dragon to roar in pain, though his armor he called skin was not broken. His magical barrier shifted in intensity, becoming thick in the area where the dwarf was madly striking him. The dragon arched his head downward, bellowing a deep laugh, which rocked the dwarf back nearly pushing him to the ground.

Fear filled Jermys's eyes. For the first time, his hatchet was not powerful enough to strike the beasts he had so often been able to bring down at will. Fire dripped from the green dragon's nostrils, dropping like balls of lava scorching whatever they struck. The beast arched his neck and sent a sheet of fire point blank upon Jermys, who stood with his hatchet raised. There was a roar louder than any clap of thunder Troyf had ever heard when the beast felt the point of Stepha's arrow into its back and Krirtie's sword cutting deep into its neck. The dragon shifted its protective barrier to face Krirtie and Stepha as green blood flowed across the scorched ground. He was totally lost when the hatchet bit his neck. Jermys' last thought was how he was not cooked with the ground around him, but the problem was, he had no answer. Krirtie stepped forward and swung her blade downward, silencing the dragon for good.

The fighting across the glade remained fierce, with heavy losses occurring on both sides. Schram and the remaining dragon, a brilliant red, were held locked tightly in their battles of wills. Several large parties of elves had been moved through the lines, and it became apparent to Stepha and Krirtie that the plan was beginning to turn successful. The noise of the fighting grew to an apex until the last dragon let out a roar, as if something had opened its chest and pulled its heart out while it remained beating. Many in the glade swung their heads to where the beast was struggling to stand. All fighting halted when they witnessed what had happened and what was approaching. Stepha ran over to help Schram make it back to his feet from where he had been thrown when his opponent had been struck. Both their eyes grew wide when the huge blue landed next to the red and its rider climbed from its back.

"Greetings, Schram, my son. It has been a while."

"Yes it has, man who was once my father," responded Schram as he took a step toward the dragon lord.

The dragon lord's laughter seemed to strike Schram deeply as it pierced the silence that had seduced the glade. All waited patiently to see what this new encounter could mean, except Jermys, who motioned for more elves to seize this opportunity and slip through the lines. The dragon lord looked around, his ever-present robe still in place, but his hood was absent and the reptilian tail showed clearly from his back.

His eyes burned ice into each individual but froze on Krirtie like fire. His voice was raspy and completely foreign from the man he used to be. "I am pleased we meet again, Krirtie. I was deeply angered when you murdered my comrade, your father."

The human woman stood strong, though the memory of killing her father at the confrontation at Eltak struck her deeply, as was intended. Schram spoke, trying to bring the attention back upon him. "Her father has found peace and been welcomed to the afterlife—something you may never find yourself."

The once King of Toopek ignored his son's statement and moved to stand in front of the girl. "The one you know as Maldor is close to meeting your father." Krirtie's eyes swung to greet Keith Starland's, and they met like two fireballs colliding at the speed of light. "Yes, girl," he added slowly, "soon he will die, even possibly before my return."

The pain and anger was clear as it boiled within her, but Krirtie surprised even Schram when she replied, "What makes you so sure you are going to leave this glade?"

The dragon lord laughed and turned, pointing his finger toward the human known as Dolf Stollman. A beam of light shot at the bewildered man and suddenly the spot he stood was empty. He turned back to Krirtie. "Because nobody will ever be able to defeat me or those who stand at my side."

Schram immediately pointed his staff toward his father but then suddenly swung it back to the dragon he had previously fought that now seemed fully recovered. With a similar flash of light, the large red vanished. The magician swung to face the deep, angered expression of his former father. "He was a fool to keep his guard lowered. He should have known I would have realized you would be prepared for my attack."

Isolated scuffles began breaking out as elven arrows began dropping goblins who also had dropped their guard during this unique break in fighting. The dragon lord's stare bit through Schram with hatred. Suddenly, his face dropped, and Schram could feel the presence of magical hands prying into his mind before protection could be erected. Schram's father wore an expression of complete disbelief, which seemed to be shared by the dragon he had previously ridden. Schram had quickly blocked the mind search, but whatever he had exposed to the ones before him put extreme fear and amazement in their eyes.

The dragon lord moved over to stand beside his mount while sending telepathic messages to his dragon troops. The goblins quickly began backing away from the fighting, many fleeing in whatever direction they could. The stunned gazes of the allied forces only remained frozen, completely confused about what was taking place. However, none of their looks compared to that which Schram wore.

The dragon lord leaped onto his dragon's back. "You are full of surprises, my son, though I no longer am sure that is the case. We give you Elvinott, for I must talk with Slayne. I don't think even he has considered this." With that, the dragon spread its huge wings and lifted them into the air, quickly disappearing over the horizon.

Many dwarves and elves gave a slight pursuit behind the fleeing goblins, but the more important matters of moving the elves back to their home took precedence, making any pursuits short-lived chases serving only to assure the goblins were indeed retreating.

"What the hell was that?" asked Fehr. "Why did they leave?"

All eyes fell to Schram. "I don't know, my friends. I don't know."

Though the answer was not what they wanted to hear, they all accepted it for the time. Krirtie seemed the most disturbed but held her tongue.

Schram and Krirtie joined Stepha in the elves' return to their homeland. Jermys remained in Feldschlosschen to help restore order to the dwarven lands, but not before he had a chance to greet those and bid them farewell and safety for their journeys ahead. Also, he again extended the welcome arms of Feldschlosschen and Antaag, should their paths ever bring them near, and added his support if his help was ever desired.

Schram knew Jermys to be as honorable as any on Troyf. If he was needed, he would be there, no questions asked. He was one of the companions who had done it all, and now he proudly carried one of the weapons of the Ring of Ku—the Hatchet of Claude. Like the scimitar by Krirtie's side and the magical bow on Stepha's back, Schram knew the weapons of the ring were key to their success. He only worried about the remaining one, the one tightly tied to their lost maneth friend.

Schram bid Jermys farewell and sent his best to Fehr, to the grumbles from the dwarf who said the rat had been tearing up his mines worse than any of the goblin attacks could dream to. Schram smiled and waved but once again felt sad about leaving his friends behind.

"Really, Krirtie, I don't know," he shouted. "Believe me, I wish I did, but I am as much at a loss as you."

Krirtie frowned. "You better not be holding out on us, Schram Starland, or so help me, I'll…"

Stepha raised a hand, halting the girl before she could continue. "Really, Krirtie, the look in his eye should tell you he does not know what the dragon lord meant. Let him be for a while, it has been too long a day to end it fighting." She turned to Schram. "Clear your mind, my husband. I know he searched your mind and more than that, I know he found something within you that scared him. Try to find it, for I am certain it is important."

Krirtie quickly calmed and added to both of them. "I'm sorry. I should have known better." Both nodded appreciatively as she turned to Stepha to continue. "I never had a chance to thank you for saving me from the dragon and then the goblin attack that followed."

Stepha looked surprised. "It is I who should be thanking you. If you had not acted so quickly, the dragon would have snared me quick as anything. You saved my life, and I hope someday I can repay the favor."

Krirtie only bowed her head slightly while Schram sat up, both stunned and worried about the discussion of events he had just heard. He started to speak, but the elf princess cut him off. "This is not the time for painful discussions of war. Though many lost their lives, and this saddens us all deeply, we were victorious and my—our people are home. We will have celebrations this night."

Schram pulled his beloved close and held her tightly as the door to the great hall of the king's castle slowly was pushed ajar. A tall muscular figure broke through the opening to stand before the small group. "I have been looking all over for you three!"

"Madeiris!" cried Stepha with tears filling her eyes as she leaped to her brother's arms.

"Greetings, King," said Schram, also rising to stand beside the elf.

Madeiris grinned. "*King* sounds as proper from your mouth as it would from mine in reference to you."

Schram smiled as he too hugged the elf. "Well said, brother, well said."

"And you," Madeiris began looking toward Krirtie, who had moved closer. "I have someone I think you might be interested in seeing." He motioned to a guard in the hallway, and in a moment the guard and another figure entered.

"Mother!" cried Krirtie, tears now filling her eyes as they met each other in a tight embrace.

The festivities, though clouded with the thoughts of those who gave everything to make this plight possible, continued, and an essence of cheer was carried to all of their hearts. It was late in the night when all finally retired, but that night carried something with it that none in the forest had felt for a long, long time. All slept with a calming peace surrounding them and the ones they loved.

⚭

"Damn, Schram, I swear you can move giving less sound than the most gentle of elves."

"From you, Madeiris, I take that as the greatest compliment." He looked across the peaceful glade where the elf king sat alone. "What brings you out so early this morn?"

Madeiris leaned back and said, "For the first time in too long I was allowed to sleep in our forests, a feat my father—and you—made possible. I could sleep here every night if given the opportunity."

The human smiled and sat down beside his friend. "Don't leave yourself or any of the elves out of your memory. Many died in this most wondrous effort, and its success is attributed to what everyone gave for it."

"Trust in the knowledge that I will never forget what the humans, maneths, dwarves, and the elves gave of themselves..." His voice trailed off then he added, "But just looking at the faces of those throughout Elvinott last night"—he paused as he fought for the proper thought and finally added—"I know my father would be proud."

"Aye," replied Schram with a sigh. "That much is certain. You returned the elves to their home." He put his hand on Madeiris's shoulder. "You should be proud as well."

The elf smiled in return, but his eyes told that he knew why the magician had searched for him so early this morning. Softly, he added, "Do you leave today, my friend?"

Schram sat back, letting his long black hair fall down below his shoulders, revealing the tips of his brownish-green pointed elven ears that had begun to develop during his training of the Ring of Ku. His look was long and distant, and all he answered was, "Yes, I must."

There was a long silence as both individuals seemed to be trying to gather up all the peace and serenity they could before they shuffled back to the reality of the period. Madeiris finally rose and brushed himself off. "I assumed last night that you would be leaving soon. After our discussions last week in Toopek, your plans have been completely clear, although my stubborn-headed sister has been prying at me since then to try to convince you to take her with you." Schram smiled as he knew what the elf king had been going through regarding his sister. However, his decisions had not changed, although Stepha had not kept her desires to join him a secret. Schram wondered if his ears were still red from her verbal assault.

Madeiris grinned slightly as he seemed to read his friend's thoughts. "I told her it would be your decision, and I see in your face that she did not agree with it."

He put his arm around the king's shoulder as they began to walk back. Softly, almost to himself, he added, "To say the least, old friend."

⟨ɷ⟩

"Yes, go," replied the king, sending an elven guard running to the forest.

"What is it?" asked Stepha as she and Schram approached, the human well packed with provisions Madeiris had ordered prepared for him.

"It is nothing much," replied the king. "I sent scouts out last night to investigate the trails between here and Toopek. The first flyers just returned saying that trolls were scattered in small bands throughout the Toopekian mountain forests. It seems Geoff had a surprise waiting for them as you hoped he would."

Schram replied, "That is the best news I have heard today. I knew he would be ready for them. I only hope Slayne doesn't wish to retaliate against the city right away, for I am not sure he could handle an all-out offensive against him yet." He paused, thought a bit more, then added, "But if anyone could, Geoff would be the one."

"Aye," added Madeiris, "but don't worry too much about Toopek. My elven reinforcements will be there in another day. Any attack will be met with a strong defense."

He smiled broadly now as he took the elf king's hand. "Thank you, my friend and brother."

The king bowed his head, followed by a strong embrace. "I will leave you now and let others bid their leave, but know that my thoughts go with you, wherever your path takes you. Take care, Schramilis, and know that you always have a home among the trees."

"You take care as well, Madeiritilantilis Malis, and thank you."

The king left, leaving Schram beside Krirtie and Stepha, the elf moving aside to let the human woman have her old friend for a time.

"Hurry back, Schram. We all need you with us."

"I will, Krirtie, but like I said before, trust in yourself and you will always do fine. Also, tell your mother I send my love. It was nice to see her again, especially since she seemed so well."

"I will tell her." She smiled, and before departing added, "And don't worry, I shall keep my head about me."

Schram smiled briefly and then turned to Stepha. He could already see tears forming in her large green elven eyes. The two said nothing at first and only fell into each other's arms. Schram set his pack down upon the only piece of armor he was going to carry—a delicately shaped shield with intricate artwork etched into it depicting both his Toopekian crest and the colors and symbols recognizable only to elves. It was a gift from the elf he now held tightly. Next to it, he rested his magical staff, though it looked to be nothing more than a fallen branch from one of the magnificent trees they now stood beneath.

Schram gently pushed the woman back, letting his hand fall into hers, matching their elven Rings of Joining to cross backs. "I love you, Stephanatilantilis, now as much as ever. No matter what distances separate us, we will always be together, and soon no distances will remain."

I love you too, Schramilis, and I understand what you do and why you must go alone, but that does not make it easier. I shall wait for your return, standing by my brother as princess over Elvinott."

The two gripped each other once more and then parted, Schram slowly moving to gather that which he was carrying with him. Giving one more kiss to Stepha and wave to those who looked on from the city, he disappeared into the trees.

Large rolling tears now streaked the elf's cheeks as she turned to head back to the city. Nearly halfway back, she was greeted by Krirtie, who said, "Stepha, I know this is not a good time, but we have to talk, for it is a matter of life and death."

⚬⚬⚬⚬

"You sap-bellied dragon lover, this is preposterous!"

"Then stay here, you no-good flee blanket!" answered Jermys.

"Use your head, Jermys. We need help if we are going to help Maldor. Damn, you need help for even thinking about it. Let's get Schram and Stepha. They will give aid, and you know Krirtie would be willing to try, assuming she hasn't already left." He paused as a fearsome frown grew across his face, sending a tight, beaten edge to his words. "Damn it, put that hideous pipe away and listen to me!"

Fehr was now yelling, and the agitation building on the dwarf's face was not hidden. "No! You listen to me, gar bait! King Kapmann at Antaag has a ship leaving tomorrow for Gnausanne. He said we could take it on as far as we needed to. If the currents and winds are in our favor, that means we could conceivably go all the way to Draag in only days. Schram himself said Slayne had some new plan cooking. He definitely would not expect a rescue attempt to take place at his stronghold. With only two of us, we have a better chance of slipping in unnoticed, and who knows, maybe when Maldor is with us, we will be able to do some real damage at the heart of the enemy." He paused and then added, more softly, "And think of the story it would make."

The rat's eyes began to glow but quickly faded as he contemplated the entire plan. "You mean you want to just sail down the Draag River completely unnoticed, then go walking randomly through the caverns and save Maldor, and then complete the journey with a surprise attack?"

Jermys grinned. "Yes!"

Fehr began cursing irately in every language he knew, ending with some choice words of ancient dwarven. Jermys now smiled even more broadly. "So you will be joining me then?"

"Yes, someone has to keep you out of trouble." The rat went mumbling off, still cursing every other word.

The dwarf yelled to his back. "Hurry, friend. We'll leave as soon as you are ready. And the correct pronunciation is 'hevenslen.'"

"'Asshole' is how Schram says it."

⁓⁓⁓

"This will truly prove to be a first," said Fehr as the two traveled through the mine tunnel under the river connecting the two dwarven cities of Feldschlosschen and Antaag.

"What's that, a dwarf teaming with a vile rat?" asked Jermys, smiling.

Fehr's lips formed a tight frown. "No, a rat joining with Jermys Ironshield, Great Sea Captain of the South. What color was it you turned when we were sailing the South Sea with Captain Pete? Green? Blue? Or was it a mixture of both? Did you turn elven on us?"

The dwarf's face was devoid of pleasure as he thought about the past journeys he had taken by boat. He glared at Fehr. "King Kapmann has assured me this boat is quite large and will sail the roughest waters as if it were a spring day."

"What difference does that make?" chattered the rat, his face blushing beneath his fur. "Even if we sink, it wouldn't matter because you are such an excellent swimmer." His laughs began to echo off the cavern walls. "Remember when we first left the port of Icly. We were tugging you behind like we were using you for bait, though nothing would dare bite your nasty skin."

"Shut up, you damn thief! I swear I'll cut your pathetic tail off and feed it to you for dinner if you speak one more word!"

Fehr appeared stung as the dwarf stared down upon him and was about to speak, but then held his words as Jermys continued. "And besides, with all the weight and size you've put on, I do not think you'd be too buoyant yourself nowadays. I am just glad you can walk on your own because I was not about to lift your chunk of a body now."

Fehr was steamed. "I knew you could not resist attacking my weight. It did not take you long before you had to..." He paused and his face softened. "I do miss the days with Krirtie and how she would carry me everywhere we went. However, any weight I *might* have added is due to that dwarven food you have been stuffing down me lately. All you guys do is eat and smoke."

"Stuffing! I never saw you turn down a meal, much less not have between-meal snacks on top of it. Yes, I've seen and heard you creeping the hallways at night, and the cooks have watched you pick their locks on the food cabinets. That is why we added those new locks."

Fehr smiled. "Yes, those new ones took almost thirty seconds to get through, truly worth their weight in gold."

"They were when you consider all the food hidden in storage behind them was, shall we say, enchanted with a special sauce."

Jermys was talking over the laughter in the corridor as the rat's smile vanished. "What are you talking about, dwarven scum?"

Jermys's potbelly jumped irregularly. He was so pleased with what he was about to say. He faced the now-white-with-anger rat and replied, "To put it most simply, if anyone is to be green on our voyage, it will not be me."

Fehr appeared somewhere between disbelief and total confusion. He stared hard at the dwarf but knew that he was not bluffing. His laughter was too pure and his expression too pleased with the success of his plan. "I will get you for this, dwarf. If anything should happen to me, I will get you for this, and trust you will not be so pleased with the result."

Strange garbled noises echoed through the hallway as Jermys simply smiled and shook his head. The only words that were issued was a simple statement between gags. "Zule tanka dvarpha."

Jermys's jaw dropped as he absorbed the ancient dwarven language being used so graphically and directed toward him. The green rat slowly made his way back to the dwarf but only stared hard at him, not able to truly speak.

Jermys raised his hand and motioned the rat forward. "Hush now, we are about to enter the king's chambers, and I don't want your lunch spread across his throne. Your sickness has slowed us down enough already."

"You should have thought of that before you poisoned my food. I'll be lucky to stay on my feet before King Kapmann, much less control my overactive stomach." He completed his comment with a high-pitched belch to make a pirate proud. The Antaagian dwarves leading them now glared down in disgust. No dwarf but Jermys greeted rats as friends, but because of who Jermys was, Fehr had to be accepted. Still, Antaag was nearly totally against the newfound relations. Though Fehr was the only one who had ever made any contact with the taller, potbellied dwarves of Antaag, he was enough to completely halt any further exploration of the idea.

Jermys began to enter the large throne room depicting King Kapmann's royal chamber when he stopped and whispered something to the lead dwarf. With a slight chuckle, the dwarf agreed and let Jermys pass. As Fehr pushed his way through, he was greeted with dwarven axes and a slamming door. "Jermys asked that we keep you busy while he talks with the king. I think we can find some light work that someone of your size could handle." Laughter filled the hall as one of the dwarves scooped the rodent from the ground and carried his long-faced body toward the river. Fehr, in his sickened state, could do nothing but close his eyes and concentrate on his stomach, helpless to prevent whatever was about to happen.

"Is the ship ready?" asked Jermys, ignoring all formalities of speaking to a king as his adherence to customs had become somewhat desensitized with his close relationship with King Krystof of Feldschlosschen.

Kapmann looked noticeably disturbed by the blatant disregard of policy but answered the question put forth. "Yes, Jermys, the ship is ready."

Jermys frowned. "I am sorry if my abrupt words offend you, King Kapmann, but I have much on my mind and little time to resolve it. This voyage is sudden and I am second-guessing my judgment regarding it."

Kapmann rose. "You have not told me your destination or plans at all. You have expected me to fulfill your every wish without regard for policy or order." Kapmann was becoming even more noticeably disturbed, and then suddenly his expression relaxed. "I see you still carry the Hatchet of Claude by your side. In this I know your actions must be true and probably very dangerous.

Perhaps the fewer who know of your plans, the safer you will be. Your raft is ready, my friend, and you two can leave when you are prepared. The guards will help you load should you require aid." He paused then added, "Good luck, wherever your path takes you."

Jermys had heard all that had been said, and although something seemed strange about Kapmann, discovering what all was going on in his mind would have to wait until the key thing he heard was clearly resolved. "Raft? Shouldn't there be a large crew of some kind for such a large ship?"

Kapmann shook his head. "I am sorry. I thought word had been passed to you already. Gnausanne needed a shipment of minerals immediately, so the ship I originally planned for you to use left yesterday. However, it is not a problem, as I set aside another boat for you that you will be able to have totally at your disposal for as long as you will need it. Your party will be the only cargo, so it should better fit into your plans as well."

Jermys's heart sunk as the vision of the large sea liner was replaced with a picture of a bathtub with a sheet for a sail. Fehr was going to have his revenge, he was sure of it.

Seeing his displeasure, Kapmann added, "I hope this is all right. It is really the only boat I could spare. I thought you would be pleased."

Jermys forced a smile. "Thank you, King Kapmann. It is just my head and belly both prefer a larger, smooth-riding ship that tosses waves, not a small one that gets tossed by them."

The king laughed and slapped the dwarf on the back. "I sometimes forget you Feldschlosschen dwarves don't take to the water well. Here"—he reached beneath his long white beard and pulled out a small pouch—"some of my special mix of tobac. It will make your ride more pleasant."

Jermys's face lit up as he reached out to grab the small bag. "Perhaps you would like a smudge now, before I leave."

"Aye, Jermys, it's a right, nice time for a smoke."

He pulled out his long, delicately carved wooden pipe that hooked downward nearly twelve inches before turning back up to open into a small cup. The two sat back as a strange green haze began to fill the room being accompanied by an ear-to-ear grin across both their faces.

A New Direction

❧

"I am sorry that I could not speak with you earlier, Krirtie, but there were matters with Elvinott I had to see to immediately regarding the flyer scouts that were returning. What is it that could be so important as you implied earlier?" Stepha began shaking out her wings in the fountain as she inquisitively gazed toward the human girl who stood with a worried and impatient look about her.

Krirtie replied, "I want to ask your help in something I have planned, but I want to emphasize that there is no obligation."

Stepha stepped out of the fountain bath while Krirtie struggled to find her next words. She was intrigued with her serious tone but had no idea where it was going. She placed her hand on her shoulder. "Come on, Krirtie, tell me what troubles you so."

She giggled slightly. "You sound just like my mother."

Stepha too smiled. "Is that what this is about, your mother? Well, I think it is wonderful that you have found..."

Krirtie raised her hand. "No, my mother is a more-than-welcome sight, but she left a short while ago with the elf party heading for Toopek. This is over a completely different matter, and I guess the easiest thing to do is simply spit it out." She paused and moved with Stepha at her side to sit on the edge of the fountain. "I am going to Draag to find Maldor."

Her mouth fell wide open to join her eyes in disbelief. "Krirtie, that is crazy! Going in alone would not help Maldor, it would only get you both captured." She avoided speaking of the possibility of death in elven fashion, but she knew that it was a more likely possibility. "Schram will be back soon, and we will all go to help him. Only then can we hope to save Maldor from the evil clutches of the dragons." She paused, then added in a softer tone, "We all miss him dearly, for he is as much a part of our family as anyone, but we have to act in a way with the best possibility to help him. You know he would not wish us to risk even the slightest chances of harm in his rescue. You know if anything happens to you, he will be destroyed."

"No! I feel Maldor's time grows shorter by the day. You heard what the dragon lord said about him. He may be facing death as we speak."

"Those were just words to scare you," replied the elf as she placed her arm around the trembling woman. "Do not fall into his trap. We must wait for Schram."

Krirtie's face grew long. "I cannot wait for him, and I don't believe he wanted me to. Could you wait if it were Schram who was being held?"

She stared at the elf, hoping to gain some support, but she quickly realized she would not be finding any there. Stepha replied, "If I believed in what he fought for, I would wait. Also, it is ridiculous if you think Schram wanted you to go. He made it abundantly clear to me before he left that he would speak to the canoks and then return, unless his business took him elsewhere first. Then, when he returned, we will assault Draag with whatever it takes to save Maldor."

Krirtie, with tears now falling helplessly across her cheeks, pushed herself up. Her voice cracked under the stress and emotion, but she knew she had to force her words out. Stepha was her only chance. She knew she could not do this alone. "What if he can't return right away? We both know what he has before him. It may take time, and time is the one luxury Maldor is without. Stepha, I came back to ask you to accompany me because your aid would be extremely valuable. However, if you refuse, I will still go."

She put her face into her hands, and when Stepha rose to comfort her, she turned and disappeared into the nearby forest. The city of trees, with all its beauty and excitement, gave no cure for the pain Stepha was feeling. She turned and stared at the wondrous statue of the Princess of the Flyer Elves, her long golden hair falling down the intricate carvings making up her wings and back. As the water from the fountain trickled down the face of the statue, so did it down the one it was modeled after.

With a long sigh, she glanced to where Krirtie had disappeared, and seeing no sign of the girl, she turned and headed toward the castle. She knew the only one who might be able to make some sense of this was her brother, if she could be lucky enough to find him.

❧

"Madeiris, are you here?"

The elf nearly jumped from his seat as he swung and faced the girl whose entrance had gone completely unobserved. "Martak, sis, you about shook my heart free from my body." His shocked expression calmed when he noticed the stress in her eyes, and he added, "Please sit here by the fire. It seems you have much on your mind, and even if I am not as wise as many kings before me, perhaps as a big brother I can find some answers."

Stepha moved over and sat next to her brother in front of the fire in the great hall. To her left rested the large wall plate tablet depicting the treaty between the elves and the humans, drawn up in the wake of Schram's kidnapping by Hoangis over twenty-six years ago. A sadness filled her eyes as she thought about her now-distant husband. Her loneliness and longing for his presence were evident in her actions, but she knew there were matters at hand that had to be discussed. She cleared her mind and concentrated on her reasons for coming before Madeiris with her troubles.

She placed her hand on her brother's as it rested on his knee and said, "Madeiris, I have much that sits poorly within me at this time, but what I wish to discuss with you is something I do not believe even you have considered."

50

The elven king seemed intrigued with his sister's statement and used her pause in speech to add, "I can see whatever it is troubles you gravely, and I hope I may hold the answers and wisdom you desire."

She smiled and continued her thought. "I must leave with Krirtie tomorrow."

Madeiris's head tilted slightly in surprise, and he placed his free hand to his chin. "Where must you go on such short notice, and why does it involve Krirtie? In the past you two have accompanied others on very dangerous treks; I don't want you now getting into something that might be too much for you both to handle alone."

Stepha appeared offended and agitated, but before she could respond, Madeiris added, "Do not think I don't have total and complete confidence in your abilities. I know you are both incredible warriors, but I also know how your minds work, and I have seen that look in your eyes before. If what I suspect is true, where you plan to go may be more than even your abilities are prepared to handle."

Stepha shook her head. "I fear that what you suspect *is* what I have in mind, but my reasons for such a dangerous journey are unknown to you. We have to go to Draag and attempt to find and save Maldor."

Madeiris stood. "Out of the question! I discussed this possibility at length with Schram prior to his leave, and he made it adamantly clear that by no means was anyone to attempt such a plan. His reasons were well-said and not open for negotiation."

Stepha joined her brother, both of them standing and showing great determination in their faces. "Krirtie carries Maldor's child."

"What? She told you this? How can it be? They have been apart so long."

No, she did not have to tell me. You know as well as I that an elf who is close to one can sense these things. And you also know maneth young are carried for up to two years. I believe Krirtie is starting to feel the burden of the life within her, and she will stop at nothing to attempt to save him. Without my help, she won't have a chance at Draag."

"No, even with your help you both won't have a chance. There has got to be another way." Madeiris began pacing around the room, searching his mind for any answers he could find. "Send for Krirtie. I want to speak to her myself. Possibly I will be able to make you both understand what our options are, and that a futile rescue attempt is not one of them."

Stepha smiled. "I have sent for her already, for I knew you would wish it."

"Fine. Perhaps you also know what I should say to a stubborn-headed sister and her bull-headed human friend." His voice was clearly showing the burdens he now had resting on his shoulders. Leader over a nation at war with forces of evil, architect for rebuilding a society, and big brother to a powerful and confident sister all rolled up into one young elf.

Stepha smiled again. "Consider my other option is to follow my husband." She paused then added, "But Schram would strip the green from your skin should you allow that action. Therefore, now I am giving you another choice."

Madeiris smiled in return to the comment as he pictured Schram's face should Stepha's suggestion be brought to light. "Yes, Schram would not stop with my skin. However, offering me the better of two evils is not an acceptable answer."

His comment was cut short as an elven guard appeared in the doorway, his face showing a strange unknown distress. "Pardon my interruption, King Madeiris, but the princess asked me to locate the human woman. I found her trail. Attempts to cover it had been made, but I could follow it easily enough. She appeared to have stopped briefly, backtracked, and then turned and continued southwesterly. I felt I should check here before forcing her to return, but her pace is such that only a flyer could reach her before she leaves our forest, and I could not even guarantee that."

Madeiris frowned. "Southwesterly? What city would she come to first, assuming her course stayed as such?"

Stepha stepped forward. "She does not know the woods well. She most likely is attempting to reach Feldschlosschen and seek the aid of Jermys. However, if the direction is as he says, she will be well west of the dwarven cities."

"That she will be," added the guard.

The king sat back against the long table, which was placed in the center of the room. He looked toward the two in the room as they peered back awaiting his command or blessing, depending upon who was to be spoken to first. His lips began to turn slightly upward as he focused his eyes on his sister. "Go catch her and lead her to Feldschlosschen. If Jermys accompanies you and Krystof will give his blessing, then you have mine as well." She grinned and was nearly out the door when he called her back. "And Stepha, you had better be damn careful. I do not want to have to tell Schram that now all his closest friends and deepest love have been captured as well. That human will have my head if he finds out about any of this."

She hurried over and gave Madeiris a long, deep hug and small kiss on the cheek. "Don't worry, big brother. I will take care of everyone, including myself."

"You better," he said as she disappeared through the door. To the guard he added, "Prepare a small party to make ready for a journey to Draag. If I know my sister, she will have King Krystof giving his blessing before she even arrives, and if they are going to go, I am going to make damn sure they make it there. Assemble a half dozen, putting yourself in charge, and then make trail to Gnausanne. From there, join them and lend any support they require." The guard nodded and quickly disappeared. "May Shriak fly with you, sister," he said to himself as he fell back to sit in front of the fire and became lost in his own thoughts.

⚬↔⚬

53

The sounds of steel crashing against one another echoed from ahead as Stepha raced through the air trying to locate where the fighting was taking place and who was behind it. She rose over a clump of trees to look upon a clearing spotted with a half dozen goblins, two of which fought fiercely against Krirtie, who now was on one knee. Beside her rested the body of one freshly killed blackened goblin corpse, and the three others remaining alive sat and watched from the side, yelling taunts and jeers at the girl in between laughs.

Sweat beaded down Krirtie's face, and it was obvious to Stepha as she let her first arrow fly that the girl was growing weak and tired. The arrow struck true, and without the ability to even gargle a sound, one goblin fell to the ground. The shock of seeing his comrade fall right in the face of victory caused the other to lower his guard, and quickly he joined his friend as Krirtie's sword split his throat. Two of the remaining three were quickly greeted with elven arrows, and with only a slight motion and turn, again Krirtie finished the last in the same fashion. With a sigh of relief and exhaustion, she fell to the ground motionless.

Stepha landed and moved directly to Krirtie's side. Lifting her head in her arms, she softly asked, "Are you injured?"

Krirtie opened her eyes and looked toward the elf. "I don't think so, just a little tired. I seem to have lost some of my endurance, but I will be fine."

"That is common among humans during pregnancy. You will have to act more responsibly and keep that fact in mind."

Krirtie looked astonished. "You know…but how?"

Stepha smiled and helped the girl to her feet. "Elves hold many mysteries about them regarding life. I was not sure until I saw you fighting in the glade. You were fighting more in defense than your usual offensive nature. Furthermore, the fact that you would not wait for my decision, fearing I would refuse to help, only added to the thought. I realize the time you have left that you will be able to act grows short. We will continue on to Draag, but we will first head to Feldschlosschen."

Krirtie showed the deepest relief and gratitude possible to fit onto one face, but also there was a note of surprise in her gaze. "Is that not where I am headed? Also, what are goblins doing in the elven forests? I thought the enchantment would keep them from entering."

Stepha replaced her bow and began walking back toward the east, motioning to Krirtie to follow. "First of all, you left Elvinott boundaries nearly an hour ago, and the path you are following will take you west of Gnausanne. We will have to make good time and be free of further interference if we are to reach the dwarven lands before night becomes too thick, so why don't I lead the way for a while?"

Krirtie skipped forward to catch the elf's pace, both girls smiling at the last statement. "Stepha, thank you for everything. Thank you for the goblins at the glade, for talking with me before, and for just being here now. Every day I learn a little more why Schram fell in love with you so long ago, and why that love never faded for him." This brought a smile to the elf's face, and she thought about the human she loved so. Krirtie saw her reaction and felt the love they carried for each other. She added, "Does he know about the child I carry?"

She shook her head. "I was not even sure until recently, and since he said nothing to me or Madeiris, I suspect that he does not, though he may, because he is also elven, at least in part."

"I think he became elven the first five years of his life," added Krirtie. "The physical changes that occurred over the past years with his training involving the Ring of Ku were only a formality to complete the process."

The elf smiled. "The more I learn about Schram, the more I believe that is an accurate evaluation. He is truly a deep and intricate elf and man."

"As are you…elf that is." Krirtie did not bother to repeat the statement, though she knew it had gone unheard. Stepha was consumed with thoughts of the magician who, although he had only left that morning, had already been gone too long. She hoped

Schram was doing well and his journey would be free of problems, though she knew that was unlikely, as hers had met with goblin attacks only a short ways outside the elven forest.

Krirtie lowered her head. Her thoughts turned from Schram and Stepha to the maneth she had learned to love so and whose child she now carried. She prayed that he was still alive but knew very well that he did not have long in the hell he was now trapped within. Every time she thought about him, all she could see was the pain in his eyes as he was tortured by Slayne in the dragon's attempts to get the magical hammer that had become a part of the maneth's body. Though the tortures were only illusions, the pain was real; and Maldor, no matter how strong he was, could not face them indefinitely. She rubbed her stomach and whispered, "We are coming, Maldor. We are on our way."

"Well, you have decided to stray from the protective walls of Elvinott."

His knuckles gripped his staff tightly while he moved toward the one who now blocked his path. "Yes, I did, Almok. I have business in another land."

"I know of your journey to my homeland, Schram. In fact, I know everything about you."

Schram felt the searching magical hands of the canok as he tried to pry into his mind. However, this time he was prepared, and no such invasion was possible. "You do not know everything, or you would not be searching for what has put fear in your eyes." He felt the strike in the canok that his words had created. He took another step forward, and in a tone hardly his own, he added, "And furthermore, I don't think any canok would consider where I am headed to be *your* homeland."

"I fear nothing, human! You would be wise to remember that."

"Then leave me now, for a battle this night would only tire me and delay my arrival."

"You speak with confidence. Perhaps when you defeated my brother, you lost his wisdom he taught you over the years and replaced it with arrogance. It could be your undoing."

Schram tightened his lips. "Don't try and a put fear in me. Your conversation has grown bothersome." He arched his staff, pointing it directly toward the figure before him. With a short chant, the darkness of the woods exploded as a beam of light erupted from his staff. Shrieks of laughter split the night air as Schram watched his attack pass through the canok's black body.

After his outburst had subsided and its effect had been felt completely through the human's mind, the canok cleared its raspy voice and added, "Do you know that your beloved elven princess has decided to leave Elvinott as well?" Almok created a vision of the beautiful Princess of the Flyer Elves walking through some trees. "Indeed, she is a wondrous creature. Perhaps I will have to pay her a visit."

Schram looked on in horror while the canok turned, sending a bolt of magical power directly into the human. Schram cringed and sat up, beads of cold sweat present on every part of his body. He swung his head surveying the glade, freezing on the point where he had thought Almok had stood. His heartbeat was racing as he pushed himself to his feet, leaving his resting spot unchanged as he again began to walk. He checked the stars to see how long he had slept to find he had only sat down just over an hour ago.

His nights had been filled with dreams, but never as vivid as that one. Could that be what Stepha had talked about her father experiencing? Was it possible to send messages so real between magic sources in the form of dreams; and if so, how was it controlled? Schram was lost in thought, totally consumed by his dream, which had been real enough to cause him to call on the staff's power in his sleep. It was well into morning when he remembered Stepha. He prayed she had not been fool enough to leave Elvinott, but in his heart he knew she had. He could feel she had. Something was different about Krirtie, and although he could not put his finger on it, he knew it to be strong. He only hoped his pleading with Madeiris would be sufficient to persuade them to wait, but as he thought about Stepha and Krirtie, he only shook his head. Even the trees understood.

Schram closed his eyes and searched his mind, trying to locate or speak to Stepha. He concentrated, focusing solely on every fiber of being which made the elf princess what she was, and right when Schram felt contact was about to be made, all was lost and a piercing screech shook the trees.

Schram raised his staff to greet the bent talons of a scavenging minok. Schram's action was too slow, and the human was struck across the chest as the beast soared toward the clearing. It's talon-like feet bit deep into the human's flesh, sending him back over a fallen log, striking the ground with enough force to free his staff to the side. The minok turned in flight and immediately crashed down on the magician's chest. Schram was caught momentarily as the creature's weight forced all his air to be released, but due to his greater strength and agility, it was only a second later when he swung his arm forward, sending the four-foot brown minok's body into a nearby tree with a thud. The creature sat motionless while Schram sucked in deeply and grabbed his staff. He walked toward the fallen minok, but as he pointed the staff toward it, another screech was heard followed by intense pain in his shoulders as two talons bit through his skin hooking under his backbone. The second creature kicked up dust from the ground, beating its huge wings to lift the human above the trees. Schram knew that this second minok was much larger and probably the mother of the first.

Pain shot down his back and spine while the creature bent its talons into fists, tearing at Schram's muscles and bones. Blood was seeping freely from his wounds, but his hands only clutched his staff tightly, not struggling or fighting the attacker at all. Softly he began to chant, causing the pain in his body to subside, and the subsequent altering of the minok's flight pattern. He opened his eyes, when he felt the air being pushed upward across his face depicting the descent of the creature. He looked up toward the minok that held him, seeing its ten-foot wingspan. It was struggling to keep aloft. Suddenly, knowing it could no longer hold its catch, the creature opened its fists, sending Schram plummeting toward the fast-approaching forest ground. With two quick words, his fall gradually slowed until he gently landed, standing above the younger minok.

He raised his staff and shot two beams into the motionless body at the base of the tree. As he left the glade, he heard its wings begin flapping and then saw its shadow pass when it crossed the morning sun.

⚬〰〰〰⚬

"Gone? Where did he go?"

Krystof shook his head and replied, "Well, he and that vile fleabag left the day after the elves made it back to Elvinott. Did he know your visit to be forthcoming?"

There was a slight note of sarcasm carried in his tone that both Stepha and Krirtie noticed but did not know what to make of it. Stepha ignored his question and firmly resaid her own. "Where did he and Fehr go?"

The dwarven king looked annoyed now by the two girls and leaned back in his throne, lifting his long white beard high enough to now fall short of striking the floor. After lighting his pipe, he said, "Well, I suppose you will find out eventually. King Kapmann held a ship for them, and they were to take it down the river. Jermys got the idea and convinced me of the necessity and high probability of success to sail down the Ozaky as far as he could make it and attempt to rescue Maldor. I know of the hammer he possesses, and if legend is correct, in the wrong hands it could be a dangerous weapon. Jermys convinced me that to strike now would be intelligent because they would not be expecting it. Furthermore, their forces would be set to defend an all-out offensive, if anything.

There would be a good chance for a dwarf and rat to sneak in totally unnoticed."

"Why did he not send word to us?" asked Krirtie.

"He felt, and I agreed, that the fewer who knew, the better for everyone." There was a pause, then he added, "They are probably already on the ship and will be in Gnausanne by nightfall."

"Then we will be there in their wake," replied Stepha, her anger at the unexpected turn of events evident in her voice. "Come on, Krirtie, we have a great distance to travel. I hope my wings are up to the challenge."

Suddenly, as the two were walking out of Krystof's chamber, Stepha became dizzy and disoriented, nearly falling to the ground if not for Krirtie's arms pressed around her. "Are you all right?" she whispered.

Stepha shook her head as if she was trying to free some twisted thoughts. With a slight nod, she replied, "I think so. It was the strangest thing. For a moment, just a brief instant, I felt as if Schram were right here in front of me."

Krirtie smiled. "He is always with you, and I imagine he knows we are no longer in Elvinott."

⁂

"Are you well?" asked Stepha as she shook out her wings and relaxed her arms that had become seemingly permanently locked around the girl. "We will have to walk from here. My wings are too tired to carry you any further, and I don't like flying at night without having my hands free to grab my bow."

"I am fine," Krirtie replied, "and you should begin to think of your own health first." She paused while she helped Stepha rinse her wings with water from a nearby spring. "How much farther is it to Gnausanne?"

"About another hour by foot. We shall arrive well into the night, but unless Jermys is in some incredible hurry, he will remain in port until dawn. Knowing how he hates water travel and how dangerous Lake Ozak can be in the dark, I feel confident he will be there."

Krirtie looked over the area as best as her human eyes would allow. "Yes, remembering the experience at the South Sea leaving Icly, I can't believe he would ever get on a ship again, much less develop an entire rescue plan around one."

"I am sure it is a rather large ship that will only travel at a less-than-walking pace, not to mention that it would probably take a tidal wave to rock it and Troyf exploding for it to sink."

Both laughed while Stepha saw Krirtie's questionable gaze. With a quick motion, the elf added, "This way, Krirtie. All I can say is I sure am glad I will never need you to lead me anywhere. You seem like you could get turned around in a tunnel with one exit."

Krirtie smiled and shrugged. "It's just that I haven't spent much time learning the names and identifications of all the different trees. Once I get in a forest, they all start to look the same."

The elf saw the embarrassment in her eyes even in the blackness of the night, and with a smile of her own, she said, "Do not worry about such things now, for in time you will have someone with you who can point out every type of life in the forests for you and your child."

The expected result occurred and the concern across Krirtie's face vanished, being replaced with a grin of pleasure as she thought about the situation Stepha had described. For the rest of the journey, neither girl spoke but let their minds wander to think about the ones they loved.

They arrived in Gnausanne about the time Stepha had said, and quickly they made their way to the docks. The night air coming from the water delivered a chill across the small city, which greeted the two girls as a tigon would greet a rat, with a devouring, unrelenting snap of a jaw. Stepha's elven body prepared her for the drastic change in temperature common in the forest, but Krirtie did not fare as well. Both realized the cold was intense; and although the human woman never complained, Stepha quickly abandoned her search for the ship they believed Jermys to be on and found a room at a nearby inn. Though they both would have preferred to locate the dwarf tonight, they knew he would not leave so early as to escape their detection. They agreed that keeping watch was not a necessity this night, as the gnomes seemed to keep their city well under control, finding a peaceful equilibrium between goblin and troll forces and the free populous. They felt a few solid hours of sleep would outweigh any possible threat they could be facing from attack. They would rise before dawn and begin searching where they had left off.

It was now well past dawn, and although they had come upon three ships that had previously departed from Antaag, none of the dwarves on board knew anything about Jermys or his whereabouts. Furthermore, the ships they had come to had all been in dock over a week in Gnausanne. Jermys, at the earliest, could have only left two days ago, and more than likely it was only one day he had been traveling. The captain of the last ship that they had visited said he believed one large Antaagian ship had come in two days ago at the far dock and by all his knowledge still remained, as their cargo unloading was proving to be quite a chore.

At every ship, the two women had been greeted with jeers and calls from various parts of the dock; but the ship of humans, most probably pirates, seemed to take the calls to a new level. The captain had been overly helpful with his guidance, but as they had been talking, several of the crew had moved in behind the girls. All their lips showed crooked smiles through their unshaven faces usually proudly displaying missing teeth or other such malformations, and both girls quickly realized that they were in serious danger.

Krirtie immediately drew her sword to be joined by Stepha who, although rarely chose to fight with such a weapon, preferring the accuracy and civility of her bow, knew in these close quarters her sword would serve much more efficiently.

The crewmen laughed deeply in unison, each egging the others forward. The first daring attacker who approached carried only a small dagger and was issuing various filths and disgusts, to the approval of his fellow shipmates. The jeers quickly ended when Krirtie's sword bit through his throat, severing his head. The decapitated figure fell limp on the deck, his head rolling to the side still showing the same smirk.

There was a momentary lapse, which took an unknown length of time before the rest of the pirates decided that their original plans were now changed and these two women no longer would be toys for their pleasure but rather become bait to better their fishing. Several men began moving forward, their faces now devoid of the recent humor, and it was apparent that only one idea was fixed in their menial minds—to kill.

The girls surveyed the situation, and although Krirtie's expression showed nothing but the desire to kill these rogues, both knew that they would eventually be overpowered. There were nearly thirty or so crewmen within their sights and probably just as many or more below deck. Stepha reached over without saying a word, and with a single motion of replacing her sword, grabbed her companion and stretched her wings into a magnificent flight. The two girls rose slowly into the air. Krirtie used her shield to protect them from the few arrows or daggers that flew their way, but since it was clear while they were on the boat that most of the crew was waking from a rough night at the hands of dwarven ale, their arrows were rarely near their mark. Krirtie removed the goblin dagger Maldor had given her when they had first begun their journey so long ago, and with a quick flip launched it into the captain's shoulder. Seeing him wince in pain as he fought to remove the knife, she said, "Now maybe he won't be so quick to judge women as pets. I always told Maldor I would only use that dagger for a special occasion. I think he would be satisfied with my choice."

Stepha smiled. "Yes, I suppose he probably would." She paused and became more serious. "I hope that captain was serious about the other boat, for if he was only speaking cheaply to draw us in, we are going to be continuing to Draag alone, a thought I really don't find that appealing. Jermys is only one dwarf, but remember he carries the ring's hatchet at his side. Together, that would make three of four weapons being carried with us. I like those odds much better."

Krirtie only nodded while Stepha landed nearly half a mile from the position of the pirate ship's dock. After a brief relaxing of the elf's muscles and wings, along with a calming of the adrenaline flowing through both their bodies, the two warriors began walking toward where the pirate captain had described the dwarven boat. Krirtie peered ahead and then pointed. "They fly the flags of Antaag, and that is a massive ship. It must be the one Jermys is on. It has got his terrified face written all over it.

⚬⚬⚬

"Come on, dwarf! You got us into this, you green-faced maggot."

Jermys scowled at the rat. "I was told we would have a large ship capable of traversing any waters." He had to cease talking while his eyes rolled to the back of his head, and once again he leaned over the side of the raft. "Don't think I am enjoying this in the least either. At least you are starting to get over the sickness."

Fehr moved to where Jermys had been working the rudder, and throwing the weight of his small body across it, began to slowly guide the raft as it floated with the currents. With a slight smile, he added, "At least your sickness was naturally caused. Not caused by a foul joke that really showed no humor. However, I now am finding extreme pleasure in your, shall I say, discoloration."

"Shut up, rat! Or you will find yourself swimming home."

Fehr frowned, and with a sharp tone added, "Say, Jermys, will it make it any better for you if I did this?" He shifted his weight to the side and slammed the rudder opposite, causing the small raft to rock downward, splashing the dwarf's still overhanging face and nearly tossing him in the water.

Jermys swung his dripping face upward, causing his beard to whip up and spray water across himself once again. The anger within him boiled a mean force beneath his skin, but in his body's current state, he could only sit frozen, not moving for fear of losing more of the little food, which consists mostly of breads, that he had been able to get down. Fehr only greeted his displeasure with a large grin while he moved to steady the boat on its course.

⌒〰〰〰〰〰⌒

A deep moan echoed from the boat. Fehr groggily got up and walked over to where he had tied the boat with the bow resting on the land. He lifted his front legs over the side and peeked down at the dwarf who was starting to wake up. "So you are finally starting to come around?"

"Where are we?" gargled the dwarf, lifting his head. His memory was not fully in place, but as he lifted his head and the green color he had carried the entire trip quickly flowed back to his face, all memories returned in force.

Fehr replied, "I don't know. Somewhere on the southern shores of Lake Ozak. We are fairly near the outskirts of the Gar Swamp. Did I ever tell you about the time I took my family there for a vac—?"

"Yes, damn it, you told me! Why didn't we stop in Gnausanne? We could have gotten a better boat there."

Fehr smiled. "Well, I asked you if you wanted to go there or take the shorter route toward the southern bank. You replied that you only wanted to be free of these currents as soon as possible, so I took that as an order for the southern bank. We made our way down most of the coastline until you started mumbling annoyingly loud, so then I pulled the boat ashore and started a big fire. However, since you looked so comfortable in the boat, I decided that I would leave you there for the night."

Jermys sat up, frowned, and as his head began to spin once again with the environment around him, he crashed back down against the bottom of the raft. Fehr giggled under his breath and added, "Did I do well?"

He was answered with silence.

GNAUSANNE: THE RIVER

Stepha and Krirtie walked the remaining docks quickly, heading directly toward the Antaagian ship resting its sails at a far pier. Though this was the best lead they had followed all morning and their expectations were at their peak, both tried to remain calm and well-composed since they knew that there were a hundred possible ships Jermys could have taken, and this was only appearing to be a normal cargo ship. Krirtie almost cried when she saw Roepkee, one of the first dwarves she ever met, whom Maldor had nearly killed.

His eyes met the two approaching girls, and a broad smile grew across his face. "Ahoy," he yelled, laughing a bit at his attempt at human pirate talk.

The two hurried and greeted the Feldschlosschen dwarf as he moved down the landing plank of the ship to intercept. Stepha was the first to speak, seemingly asserting herself as leader over the two. "Roepkee, pardoning all formalities, but it is truly wonderful to see you, though a surprise. Might I ask what a Feldschlosschen dwarf is doing on an Antaagian cargo ship in Gnausanne?"

The dwarf grinned. "Offering my support for moving cargo, and in return taken along to bring the load here. Where better to go but Gnausanne, the city of the richest food and specialties in all of Troyf."

"Aye," added Krirtie. "I remember when I came here for the first time. I thought my stomach would burst from all the wonderful delicacies we ate. I swore I would never come back here for fear of wanting to stay for good."

Roepkee nodded. "And I wish to never leave myself, and I have only been here for two days. Luckily, as fate would have it, this ship will remain docked here for longer than planned, and thus I have been granted a few extra days of pleasure." His voice changed from the lost revelry of his good fortune to one of serious concern when he turned to address mainly the elf. "Now can I ask, what great evil has occurred that has brought you here? I can tell from your expression that it is not one of pleasure, as is mine."

"We actually came looking for one of your friends and fellow dwarves. We had hoped he would have been on this ship with you, but if this ship is staying in port for several days, I must assume that Jermys and Fehr were not part of the cargo?"

Roepkee nodded. "Well, it is really Jermys's doing that we are in port the extra days." Both the girls became intrigued and excited when it became apparent that the whereabouts of their companions was known. The dwarf continued. "He was supposed to be on this ship as you suspected, but because Gnausanne needed these supplies earlier than it was originally planned, we left before he was able to join us. Kapmann was supposed to supply him with another boat upon his arrival, and it was assumed that he would switch to this ship and take it on to his destination right away. However, as of this morning, he is one day late, and since the captain is not that excited about relieving his command to Jermys, he has said that we will wait one more day before heading back up the river. I, of course, have not spoken to Jermys, but it is believed he either decided on another route and method of travel or simply did not wish to waste the time stopping in Gnausanne and continued across the lake in whatever boat he had acquired. However, either way does not help you."

With Roepkee's speech, both girls seemed to have the final winds blown out of their sails. Krirtie dropped to the ground with a loud sigh, and although Stepha remained standing, it was obvious as she randomly paced about that this additional setback was not well-taken.

Finally, the elf turned back and asked, "Since you have been here, have you seen any merchants who might be selling either boats or passage down the Draag River?"

Roepkee looked concerned. "From what I have heard, Draag is not a safe place to be during these oppressed times. Shouldn't you consider…"

The elf was in no mood to explain her wishes, nor did she want to waste anymore time unnecessarily, and her interruption expressed both feelings clearly. "If we do not make it to our destination within two days, many lives, including Jermys's, could be in jeopardy. Now, do you know where we might find passage?"

The dwarf remained obviously against the notion but told what he knew, seeing that the elf was determined. "I saw a merchant who had small rafts. Maybe even one or two larger ones. They were set along the water just outside the western boundaries of the city. Perhaps one of hers would be sufficient for your needs, though none looked extremely seaworthy. Also, there is one large human ship that, if rumor serves, will be leaving for Icly this day. They would travel halfway down the Draag River, but again, this was a pirate ship, and I'd just as soon see you walk or swim than be trapped on board with that scum. From what I hear, they are some of the worst lot still pirating the river and South Sea."

Krirtie smiled. "Yes, I believe we already met that bunch. I don't think we would be extremely welcome on their ship anyway."

The dwarf caught both the girl's grins, and realizing that he would probably hear the story that night over ales at a local pub, he let the matter drop. However, he also knew the pirate's version of it would probably speak of how two misfit women wandered onboard their ship, and after the crew had their way with them, they discarded the girls overboard. Looking at their faces, Roepkee was certain that was not the case in this situation. He laughed a chuckle in return, and while lighting his pipe, he motioned for them to follow.

"Come on with me. I will walk you two down to where I saw the merchant the other day. She was female and exceptionally beautiful, with long but exquisite bushy hair. Maybe I can bargain with her to get you a good price."

Krirtie and Stepha smiled at each other, each thinking that to see this four-foot, rough-bearded, and nearly 200-year-old dwarf using his debonair abilities to charm a merchant should be quite humorous, to say the least. Without further comment on the subject, Roepkee snagged one hand from each woman, both who stood well above him, and departed at a happy skip, adding a snuff to his pipe before beginning.

A desperate sight we must make, Stepha thought. However, when they passed the band of pirates who stopped and frowned at them, with Roepkee there, the humans only kept their comments to themselves. They would as soon go about their business than risk fighting off a town that was half dwarven and nearly all dwarven allies.

Krirtie realized that the pirates did recognize them and were grimacing in anger under their filthy skin, but also that they were not about to cause a scene or dispute. Therefore, she chose to seize the opportunity and let the cackling behavior she had learned from her closeness with Fehr come to a full blossom. Taunt after taunt shot like daggers into the bellies of the four pirates, and if not for the gesturing hand of the now-terrified dwarf, it was clear that the pirates would attack, regardless of what the repercussions might be. However, when Stepha and Roepkee finally quieted the girl, the four rogues lost interest and continued to their ship, exchanging comments on how their fierceness had scared the group into an utter pale-white silent horror.

Krirtie replaced her scimitar to its scabbard as a proud look of achievement grew across her face. Stepha joined her with a smile, but the angered dwarf only sighed, letting his disapproval shine distinctly through. However, when his eyes caught the beauty he had seen the previous day, all happenings with the pirate band were forgotten, and quickly he began making himself look clean and tidy, finishing by tucking his rough and tangled beard into his belt. Stepha held her smile while she watched the dwarf's preparations, but Krirtie's expression turned long and flat, and she stared blankly toward the female merchant whose eyes were fixed upon her.

Stepha whispered. "Krirtie, what is it?" When the girl did not answer, the elf joined her gaze on the woman they were approaching.

She was of human build; however, her skin was slightly tainted, almost elven in nature. Her hair was light-brown and bushy, with blonde streaks etched through it. Her dress was that of a common peddler, but it was apparent by her exceptional beauty, as Roepkee had rightly described, that she was no ordinary citizen of Gnausanne. The elf tossed different possibilities over in her mind but decided that as long as they could get a boat from her, she could be a dragon and it would not matter.

By now they had left the city and were standing before the woman who still remained locked in a stare with Krirtie. With a sudden tilt of her head, her broad smile soothed everyone and her voice sang like a gentle breeze across the water. To Roepkee, she asked, "What can I do for you, my friends?"

Stepha began to speak but was cut off by the now-much-deeper voice of the dwarf. "It seems my friends here have become stranded and would like to inquire about purchasing a boat, if you might have one that could stand the fast currents of the River Draag?"

The woman's face lost its smile and began to grow with intrigue. "Draag? Not a good time to travel those waters." She was speaking to the two girls, but she clearly focused on Krirtie. Only when Stepha cut her off did the mysterious woman's gaze turn.

"We have business and friends, which take us down that path. If you can help us, we would be much obliged, and we will pay well."

The woman tilted her head again, seemingly sizing up the elf and human before her. With a slight grin, she said, "I have a raft that should suit you. It is not my largest vessel, but it takes the waves well. However, it will cost you. Two hundred sovereigns."

"Two hun..." began Krirtie before being hushed by Stepha's raised hand.

"We can pay you one hundred now, and the other hundred after our business is completed. I am Stephanatilantilis, Princess of the Flyer Elves of Elvinott, and you have my word."

The woman smiled. "I know who you are, Stephanatilantilis"—she began speaking in elven—"and I know your word is good." She turned to the now-blank faces of the small group and in common tongue added, "In my home, I am Enroht-Wah (pronounced "Jenro-Wa"), but you may just call me Lauren, should you ever need to ask for my whereabouts."

There was a brief silence as all were stunned by the speech and the strange content it entailed. Finally, Stepha said, "I will remember your name, Enroht-Wah, for I will return to see you. My companion is Krirtie of the human city of Toopek, and this is Roepkee of the Feldschlosschen dwarves. We are in your gratitude."

Roepkee interjected, speaking primarily to Stepha. "Pardon the interruption, but we have more than enough sovereigns on our ship. I will cover your fare and then you can return it to the dwarves when you are better able. Besides, you are traveling now in aid to Feldschlosschen, it is only fitting we should aid you if we are able."

Stepha smiled and placed her hand on his shoulder. "Thank you, old friend. We appreciate the help and will be sure to repay any we owe."

The dwarf glanced at the woman merchant and shared her smile as he shrugged. "Do not think about it again, Stepha. Now, if you can spare the time, I would like to invite you all to a quick meal before you leave."

Stepha and Krirtie both agreed, as their desires for food had fallen second to their finding passage. Now they remembered their body's needs and were most readily happy to answer them. All eyes fell questionably toward the woman, but none looked closer than Krirtie, who did not know why this mysterious woman bothered her so. With a smile that rivaled the sun's light, Lauren agreed, and all accompanied the dwarf to a nearby inn. Krirtie remained suspicious as they walked all the way to the first few minutes at the table. However, as the good cheer and humor was passed among the small group, all suspicions were seemingly forgotten. It was as if Lauren had gone into their minds and snatched the doubts away.

They all enjoyed their brief time together, but Stepha and Krirtie had a mission that did not have the luxury of time. It was only a short period later, and they were shoving their small raft onto the glass-like surface of Lake Ozak under the late morning sun. They looked back at the two figures of the dwarf and merchant woman standing practically arm in arm. They hoisted their makeshift sail, and the gentle breeze slowly pushed their boat along smoothly, as if they were floating on air. After several minutes, they both became settled, and Stepha turned to bid one more farewell wave to those on the shore. To her surprise, all was still, and all signs of the merchant or the dwarf were absent. Stepha used her elven sight to explore every hidden shadow along the bank, following it all the way back well into the city. Yet still, there appeared to be no trace of those they had just left.

She tapped Krirtie on the shoulder and, without speaking, motioned back toward the land. Krirtie stared blankly at the beach, not seeing anything out of order at first, and then she too saw the emptiness where the past merchant's area had been located. Now, only white sand was shown reflecting the sun's bright light. A worried and somewhat fearful expression grew over Krirtie's face, and suddenly a damper in her mind seemed to be opened and a barrage of knowledge, which had previously been blocked or out of her reach, was thrust upon her.

She stared back up at Stepha. "I know the woman who sold us the raft."

"Know her?" replied the elf. "What do you mean? Who is she?"

Krirtie again stared back to the shore. "I don't know why I couldn't remember before, but she is the one who sold me the sword I now carry and all my armor. Schram bought it last time we were in Gnausanne."

"I was not with you that morning when you two bought the weapon and armor. Schram never spoke about your weapon as being one of the ring until later. What happened when you acquired it?"

Krirtie fell back, totally ignoring the rudder and becoming absorbed by the workings of her mind while she fought to remember the time Stepha had asked about. Gradually, her head lifted, and she began retelling the story. "We had searched for a peddler with armor that would fit me for a good part of the morning. I had disposed of the goblin armor I had worn previously when Maldor told me about what you had seen in the forest that day so long ago." Her voice faded as she remembered the horror of the past. "The day you saw my father leading the attack on Elvinott."

There was a long pause as both girls seemed to become seduced by the harsh memories they were reliving in their minds. Krirtie lifted her head and, gathering her strength, continued where she had left off. "I no longer wished to wear the goblin armor to avenge my father's death. The strange thing was, and I did not notice it at the time, each time we found a merchant with armor that seemed suitable to me, Schram would rule it out immediately for one reason or another. Until…finally we arrived to a merchant just outside of town. She was beautiful, with bushy brown hair just like Lauren's, only shorter. She did, however, have the same smile, which seemed to sing a magical song as you looked upon it."

"Then you felt it too?" interrupted Stepha. "When we first approached, her smile shot a feeling of peace through my elven skin, relaxing my entire body and mind."

"Yes, just like before. Schram spoke to her like they had been friends all their lives. She only had one set of armor, and when I first looked at it, it seemed way too small. However, when I tried it, it fit snugly and wore lighter than any armor I have ever had. She had six swords. I can still see them just like they still were resting in front of me. I liked a sword that had a blue hilt and magnificent double-edged blade, but Schram would have nothing to do with it. He insisted on this sword"—she rubbed the curved scimitar resting at her side—"and now I suppose I know why. The woman did not want to part with it, and thus the price was high. I think she asked 200 sovereigns for it, and he paid them without question. Now that I think about it, the whole situation seemed weird, but at the time I did not take notice, either due to all the troubles already flowing through my mind or some outside force not allowing me to focus on the situation properly." She turned her head to face the elf and took on a much more serious tone. "I don't know what part Enroht-Wah, or Lauren, is playing in this whole ordeal, but I do think it is much more than coincidence we met her here again."

Stepha looked out over the water. In a soft voice she added, "I agree, and I do not know what to think about it. I only hope we can be lucky enough to cross Jermys and Fehr's path and join them on their trek to Draag. Otherwise, we should come to the realization that we are on our own, and this journey has become that much more difficult and that much less likely for success."

Are we going to leave today, dwarf, or spend another entire day moving a couple hundred feet down the shore, stopping every minute so you can heave…?"

"Shut up," yelled Jermys as once again he sat down on the rocks to rest and settle his stomach. "You are lucky you're out there in the boat and not within my reach, or so help me I would…"

"You'd what?" taunted Fehr. "You'd deposit your breakfast on me?"

His laughs and jeers gained in strength as they crossed the water's surface and struck Jermys, causing his green-with-sickness-face to become red with anger. "Fine! Get that boat over here, rat. We head down the river today, for the weather is in our favor."

"Oh, Jermys, take it easy. I was just fooling with you. If you are not ready to leave, then we won't. There is no reason to risk you feeling worse." Although his words seemed sincere, his tone still carried the rat's sarcastic edge, whether it was meant or not.

"I am in charge and I say when we leave. Bring the boat ashore. We have much time to make up for what we lost during my brief illness."

Fehr frowned, knowing that the dwarf was nowhere near travel-ready, but did as he asked just the same. Slowly the raft made its way to the shore, striking the rocky wall making up the lake bottom several feet short of the actual edge only close enough to set the dwarf on fire. Fehr cringed backward while the dwarf laid into him with jeers of his own depicting the rat's inability to do anything correctly. The thought of wading through two feet of water for a short bodied dwarf was not something that was well received.

However, after Jermys was on board and the boat broke free from its secured landing and began to rock with the waves, his jeers stopped and it was clear if Fehr wanted the upper hand, he would have it. Jermys curled up in a little ball on the floor of the small raft allowing his beard to seep up the loose water along the bottom cooling his body after the beads of sweat had covered nearly every inch of him. Fehr only shook his head and then turned their small raft back toward the center of the lake. To the west, a light rumbling could be heard and the river that the lake emptied into shown clearly on the horizon as a light haze rose over where the rapids began.

The small raft rocked forward bringing the bow to point nearly straight downward, and with a thunderous scream broken only by Jermys's moans, nature grabbed hold of the boat and all means of control and guidance were lost. Fehr's little body was tossed wildly about as the fierce temper of the river slammed their raft sideways, and then with a backward thrust, ripped it around so now they sailed in reverse. Even in his worn and sickening state, the much-stronger Jermys had the presence to snatch the rat and secure him under his body, holding the two of them pinned to the base of the raft. They removed the sail to keep the wind from affecting their voyage more, but it was obvious that the current would provide more than enough momentum. The two tightly clutched each other and the boat while they were belted with sprays of water and debris. A loud cracking was heard when the raft struck a rock causing the wood bottom of the boat to splinter and break. Water quickly began flowing throughout the small raft, making it difficult to even be certain where the raft and the river separated. However, with the rapid pace and force of the water, there was little chance the vessel would completely sink.

Jermys carefully moved toward the fracture and tried to cover it with every loose object and debris he could find. However, each time he had a piece of wood in place, the boat would be issued another jolt, and both he and his patch would be tossed aside. He reached his head up and took a quick gaze at the waters which lay ahead. The adrenaline of the situation had given him a brief freedom from the seasickness he had felt earlier, and he wanted now to try to gain control of their raft before it was torn apart completely. But when he looked at nothing but violent hands of white splashing water reaching out to grab them, his fears and dizziness returned in force, sending the pale-faced dwarf down to again fall beside Fehr, the two remaining motionless on the bottom of the beaten raft.

An uncountable amount of time passed before the hardest jolt yet was experienced, causing the raft to nearly explode. Wood went in every direction, but the two terrified individuals remained lodged in a main piece of hull. There were no longer any sides, and it more appeared that the dwarf and rat were traveling down the rapids on no more than a single board. Fehr kept his face covered, trying to concentrate on digging his claws into the wood to ensure his firm position.

The farther they traveled, the angrier the river seemed to get. The two were tossed every direction with the ferocity of a tigon playing with its catch. The green that had accompanied Jermys's face the past days was now totally absent, to be replaced by the pale white of pure horror. His arms were outstretched, wrapping his fingers around both sides of the board they floated on, with Fehr locked beneath his chest. The dwarf's body was rigid, not letting any of the violent attacks win over in their test of wills. It was Fehr's near-silent voice which broke the dwarf from his fierce concentration.

"The rapids have subsided a bit. Perhaps we can make it to a bank?"

Jermys raised his head but refused to unlock his grip from the board. The water around them was still moving rapidly, but its surface was smooth. They were being carried along at a fast pace and rumblings could be heard both in their wake and from those waters in their path ahead. Jermys lifted his hands, and quickly blood began to return to his whitened fingers. Immediately he started paddling, kicking, and doing anything he could to move what was left of their boat to the only shore he could see. The river itself was over a half mile across at this point, and the shore line they could see was at least half that distance away. Their pace with the currents gradually began picking up speed, and the thunder ahead of them grew louder and louder.

Suddenly Fehr quit paddling and moved to stand before his companion. "Our only chance is to swim. We will make better effort against the current even being able to touch bottom in places. If not, we will be sucked down for anther ride to hell, and this 'boat' can't take that."

Jermys frowned. "Out of the question. We are getting closer to the shore every second."

However, it was too late, as the rat had already leaped into the water and was quickly leaving the raft behind, as his steady strokes were indeed more effective against the swift current. Jermys swung his head to the doom, which willingly awaited his arrival, and then back to the rat who was wildly fighting to continue to the side. The dwarf was completely lost in decision-making abilities as he was only weighing the extent of the fears involved with each of his choices. With a loud scream and flailing arms, he launched his body into the water.

Quickly, all his senses vanished as he was freed from the one thing which had given him a slight feeling of safety a moment ago. His body broke the plane of the water and his hollers and flapping arms greeted any within earshot. It immediately became clear to Fehr that Jermys had gained nothing by leaving the board. He was still being carried down the river by the current at the same pace as before, only he now had the additional concern of staying afloat. He stopped wildly swinging his arms when he felt the sharp pain of something biting at his shoulder.

"SHARK!" screamed Jermys in a fear-stricken panic.

The bite released only long enough for the dwarf to hear., "Shut up, you stupid dwarf, and work with me on this."

Jermys swung one hand back to try to free his attacker but froze when he heard Fehr's voice and felt his wet fur against his hand. The rat growled at the dwarf, but his displeasure was only temporary as he tried to concentrate on swimming against the current while pulling more than three times his weight.

Jermys fought and struggled, thinking he was trying to swim and aid the rat's efforts, but in actuality he was only making things that much more difficult. The rat fought and fought, sometimes gaining, sometime losing the battle against the fierce water. The rumblings from ahead were still growing louder with each passing second, and the current was getting noticeably quicker. The rat bit hard into Jermys's arm as he struggled to reach anything they could use to gain an advantage.

Thirty minutes passed of constant fighting, anguish, and pain until suddenly Jermys nearly leaped out of the water. "SHARK!"

The dwarf began flailing his arms wildly, again knocking Fehr free from his grip and actually sending the rat ten to fifteen feet through the air. Jermys continued flopping and flailing, trying to ensure that this underwater attacker did not get another chance to use his body as a midday meal. Fehr's giggles in the background finally broke the dwarf from his stupor.

"Put your feet down, dwarf. Your shark is the river bottom. If I can touch, I know you can too." Fehr's voice was a good attempt at sarcasm once again; however, his exhaustion and panting made his tone get lost in his deep breaths, and Jermys only heard the words as helpful, instead of the rat's usual snideness.

Stretching his feet down, Jermys gripped the river bottom and stood strong against the current. He cleared his eyes and turned to the shore in time to see the rat fall flat on the dry beach, nearly unconscious.

The heat from the fire soothed the dwarf's face, and slowly he began to stir. The pains from the day's activities grew throughout his body, making their staunch presence known. He opened his eyes trying to focus, and he realized that the sun was nearly set, and the shadows of the surrounding forests further swallowed any available light. Gingerly he raised his head to immediately let it return to the ground when the fire began spinning and swirling with a violent passion about him. He issued several grunts, which alerted Fehr that his companion was trying to rejoin the world of the living.

In the background, the thunderous roar of the rolling rapids filled the air, and Fehr moved to sit beside his friend. In a deep and completely out-of-character caring voice, the rat said, "Jermys, are you all right? I have been worried that you would not return."

The dwarf tried to look at his small companion whose little eyes stared blankly back toward him. He coughed slightly, sending a bit more river water from his mouth. Softly, he said, "Thank you, Fehr. You saved me. I shall not forget."

With that he fell back into sleep, and the rat moved closer, placing his head across the dwarf's belly and closing his eyes as well.

⟅⟆

"What do you think we should do?" asked Krirtie, looking down the mouth of what appeared to be vicious and unforgiving rapids.

"It is getting near sundown, and I don't think I would want to be caught in those once it gets dark. We will camp along the north shore and, at first light, do our best to navigate them." Stepha pointed toward the rapids, and it was obvious in her tone and expression that she was not looking forward to their next day's activities. However, knowing Jermys and the extent of his stubbornness, she was sure the dwarf would not hesitate to enter these rapids regardless of his boat and the condition it was in. She believed that if they ever wanted to join with the two ahead of them, they had to continue along their last known course, and that meant the river.

As Krirtie guided their raft toward the nearby shore, both girls got a good look at what lay ahead for them. The first hundred yards or so looked fairly smooth, as far as rapids went, but judging from the noise and the high amount of white foam and spray shooting into the air beyond that point, it was apparent that the first hundred yards was only a test to prepare them for the real rapids. The girls made a small camp in the marshy beach marking the outskirts of the Gar Swamp, and after Stepha checked the area for anything that should not be there, she returned and shared in a meal Krirtie had prepared. The two ate heartily, since it had been late morning since their last meal, and it was now falling well into night. The sounds of the forest were alive with life, which soothed the elf's mind but made Krirtie uncomfortable and nervous.

Stepha saw her discomfort and moved to sit beside her. Softly she said, "That was the mating call of a male cervu. He will bugle like that to mark females that he claims to his herd. It is both a warning to other males and a song to lure other perspective mates."

Krirtie looked toward the elf with a slightly lost and embarrassed expression. "Is it that obvious that I am lost in the forest? In fact it often scares me."

The elf smiled. "Among any but an elf, you would appear like any other? I know the signs when someone is faced with that, which they do not understand. You are not lost in the forest. It is just not known to you. As far as humans go, only Schram was able to find peace among the trees. I believe he is more at home here than in the cities he claims as home."

Krirtie nodded. "Yes, that much is certain. Even when we were growing up, at our closest times he was still distant. There was always something blocking our friendship, a part of him he would never let me near. Often I would go out at night and see him and Kirven, I mean his canok friend, alone talking at the Toopekian forest boundary. Schram would often stare blankly into the trees as if he knew he was missing something—something he could only find out there." Her head jerked slightly in her revelry. "Now I know it was you he was looking to."

Stepha rose and walked toward the fire. "Night after night I would sit and look toward the stars, wishing I could be on one of them looking down at Toopek. My entire life, the only elf I ever loved was Schram, and he was human."

There was a long silence before Krirtie rose and joined the elf's side in front of the fire. "Perhaps some time, when Maldor has taught me more about the trees and animals, all four of us will walk together and share a moment of peace in the forest."

Stepha smiled and placed her hand on Krirtie's stomach. "Don't you mean the five of us?"

CAPTURED: THE BOAT

A roar sounded through the trees, causing Fehr to freeze in the same position he had slept in the night before. Hesitantly, he opened one eye and alerted all his other senses to be aware of any movement in the nearby area. An odd silence crept over the usually active morning air, giving the rat the feeling something was not right. Suddenly, there was another roar, which shook the rat's body at its closeness in proximity. He rolled over and began shouting curses in dwarven as he kicked the snoring dwarf still sleeping next to him. Jermys mumbled a bit but only turned to his side, not coming to complete consciousness but still showing he would be feeling better this day. Thankfully for Fehr, his new position also silenced his echoing snores, so once again there would be some peace for the area.

The rat stretched his cramped muscles and gazed his eyes across their crude excuse for a camp. Quickly, he noticed their fire was all but diminished, and he darted into the nearby woods to gather a few more branches to burn for the morning. Before leaving the area, he took one more brief glance back toward the dwarf to be certain that he was still well and then darted into the trees. Finding the necessary logs proved easy; and knowing that the dwarf would remain asleep for some time yet, he decided to go exploring. It had been a long time since he had been able to go off on his own, and besides, he knew he could not get in any trouble out here, in the middle of nowhere. He would be hard-pressed to even find another form of animal life.

The thick tree cover was providing the utmost excitement for the rat as he leaped over fallen trees and ducked beneath wild brush and shrubs. He climbed and crawled, moving with the silence common among his kind, but not consciously trying to be quiet. As he traveled, any sound which did occur seemed only to be its rightful place in nature. Whether a tree branch snapped or leaves rustled against each other, all seemed to be simply the forest greeting the morning light.

Suddenly, Fehr leaped past an outcropping of trees and landed on a well-marked and seemingly well-traveled path. He stared at the cleared surface, and slowly a completely puzzled and confused look grew across his face. This lost expression froze the rat in his tracks.

"What in the—" His words were cut off in mid-sentence as an arrow thudded in the ground nearly severing his tail.

"Oh, you missed, you clumsy fool!" echoed a rusty voice butchering the dwarven tongue. Fehr knew without looking that this meant dark dwarves, and to dark dwarves, he meant breakfast. "Here, I will show you how to kill tree scum like this."

Fehr did not hesitate a moment longer. He leaped back into the brush from which he had come. He began retracing his steps as fast as he could go while a few more arrows struck his path behind him. However, due to the thick cover and rough traveling, he was certain he could safely put some distance between himself and the bumbling dwarves who had just missed a completely unprotected shot at a meal.

⚬⚬⚬

"Wake up, Feldschlosschen scum!" hollered a voice from above.

Jermys opened his eyes to greet a dagger tip pressed to his throat. He gulped deeply then tried to speak. His words were chalky, and he knew that although most of his sickness seemed to have passed, he was still far from well. "I am Jermys Ironshield. I wish to speak to your leader, for I carry with me the Hatchet of Claude."

He slid his hand to his belt but found only an empty buckle. His face dropped when the dwarves around him started to laugh and shout jeers. The one who had spoken before kicked him in the gut again and removed a small ax, placing it to Jermys's face. In a gnarled voice, much like scraping sandpaper, he said, "Do you mean this hatchet, dwarf?" Again laughter filled the small clearing.

Jermys raised his head and peered around as much as he could, knowing that too much movement may cause the dagger at his throat to become active and begin pressing much closer to his skin than he would be comfortable with. What he saw was a party of about ten DDs around a fire, many eating or talking among themselves, but the ones to be concerned with were the three standing beside him. He looked back up to stare at their leader, who now possessed the hatchet.

He coughed to clear his throat and then in a stern voice, he said, "I trust you will return that to me in time."

The dark dwarf frowned. "I am Eb-Brown, and you would do well to remain silent. It would serve no purpose to return this ax to a dead dwarf."

Jermys stood strong as the jeers and calls once again erupted. "Eb-Brown? Does that mean you are cousin to one Lyl-Brown?"

All noise ceased at the mention of the once-second-in-command over the dark dwarf reign; the one which Bretten, Jermys's twin brother, had brutally killed over a year ago outside Eltak, the old mountain elf city. Eb-Brown grew totally stoic and serious, placing his own knife at Jermys's throat. "You know something about my brother? Speak now, or die!"

His words were harsh, and there was no doubt in Jermys's mind that he was sincere in his threat. Jermys fought to keep the fear from entering his speech, but he knew not what to say. If he said the truth, he would most likely be killed. If he lied, he may not be able to convince them of its merit. His face grew slightly pale before he uttered the words, "Your brother is dead."

He knew he could not speak the entire truth. He knew that if he told the dark dwarf that Bretten killed his brother, vengeance would be his only reward. He ended his statement without comment, waiting for the result, the outcome of which he could not even imagine.

Eb-Brown turned cold, his face dropping without actually showing any physical movement. His eyes turned fire-red as if hot coals were about to explode within him. Jermys knew he was about to be struck dead, but he was helpless to prevent it. Brown's muscle flexed tightly, and he pressed his dagger deep into Jermys's skin, causing blood to begin to ooze from around the blade. "How do you know this, Jermys Ironshield? I give you moments to live save you speak the truth."

He was now being pressed between the sandy soil of the ground and Eb-Brown's sharp dagger. With each passing moment, more blood began to ooze between the blade and flesh and trickle down his neck into his long beard. Jermys stared back deep into the dark dwarf's eyes, and for a moment, he saw only the pain he felt—a pain Jermys knew as well as anyone. For that brief instant, Eb-Brown looked no different from any mining dwarf except for his much darker color. Jermys shook his head, for he knew what he had to do.

His stare carried the same pain when he began to issue forth a response. "Formerly I traveled with a group of companions in search of my brother. It was many, many days ago we found him. His body was cold and still, for he had been passed for many moons. Next to him lay your brother, his life also ended. We found them outside the southernmost entrance to the dwarven mines of Antaag. By the looks of the surroundings, the two appeared to be fighting against a common enemy, although no signs of this enemy remained. The ground was scorched with something equaled only to dragon fire, but it was magical bursts of energy, which opened both our brother's chests. An elf traveled with me. With his help, both Lyl-Brown and my brother, Bretten Ironshield, were granted grace in passing."

The dark dwarf's eyes became transparent, and he slowly removed his dagger. However, when Jermys began to sit up, two hands grabbed his shoulders and held him down. Eb-Brown climbed back to his feet and paced the ground in front of the dwarf before turning back to face him. Raising his dagger to use it as a pointer, he said, "We will take you to our leader. I will leave it in his hands whether to believe you or not, but let it be known that at this point, I do not. If you make any attempts at escape, I will not hesitate to kill you myself."

With a quick motion, the dark dwarf behind him lifted Jermys to his feet. The world began to spin furiously, and Jermys nearly fell straight back to the ground before the dwarf grabbed his arm. "He said not to try anything, scum! Fake a fall again, and I will be the one pushing a blade through your back."

Jermys frowned and concentrated on keeping his eyes forward and walking steadily. He found himself in the middle of the pack as they were leaving the campsite. The DDs paid no mind to the fire, leaving it burning at a full blaze while they disappeared from sight.

Slowly, Fehr crept out from the bushes he had been hiding in and approached the fire. He looked about and then turned to stare over the rapids, which still thundered past. With a long sigh, he gathered anything the dark dwarves had rummaged through and discarded but sighed even deeper when he found nothing that could be considered worth keeping for his collection. Kicking a bit of sand on the fire to lower its stiff flame, the rat disappeared behind the path the group of dwarves had taken.

He remained a good distance back, but following their trail did not prove difficult as they were not trying to hide it. He was out of earshot so the sounds of the forest coming back to rest after a large group had passed, and the now-distant rumbling of the river rapids were all he could hear. It was a much more soothing feeling than he had been experiencing lately, almost giving Fehr the sense that he was back roaming the forests surrounding Toopek and Lawren. The birds were singing and a gentle breeze rustled the leaves, making the dark forest they were in become increasingly friendly.

Fehr bounded along the trail completely carefree. He knew that the only danger he could face in these woods was the large group of dark dwarves traveling ahead of him, and he knew exactly where they were at all times. He thought that this group was probably a scouting party, and now they were heading back to the main camp. Suddenly, Fehr's mind locked. If they were heading back to the main camp, then it was certain there would be more dark dwarves there and thus become less likely that he would be able to attempt a successful rescue. Perhaps his best opportunity would be to act now.

Fehr began to move up the trail more quickly, trying to overtake those ahead and better inspect the situation. However, voices and movement from behind him halted his progress, and the rat leaped into the bushes for cover.

⌒⫘⊙

The girls woke early that morning as the first light of the day greeted their tired faces like that of an unwanted visitor. The two stumbled about, and although they had switched turns at watch, by the time dawn rolled near, Krirtie allowed the stillness of the night to overtake her, and she joined her companion in sleep. Now, however, was a time for serious action. The journey which lay ahead was dangerous and full of many obstacles, the first of which was in the form of a violent storm calling itself the River Draag. Krirtie immediately began preparing a bit of food to hold their bodies for the majority of the day, since there was no telling if they would be able to find a break in their navigations. It was agreed, however, that if a smooth current did interject itself somewhere between rapids, then they would use it as their resting spot. Both only hoped that there were more than one, and that however many there were, they were not short.

The elf moved from the campsite and followed the lakeshore to where it emptied into the river. The beach she was walking along was spongy due to the swamp mud making up its base, and when Krirtie had finished preparing her gear for their trek, her footfalls made gurgling noises as she ran to catch up to her friend. The two circled the edge of the river and began walking its length.

Krirtie stopped and pointed. "Stepha, I cannot be sure, but if you look closely at the water here and then toward the water at the other side, it appears as if this side is much rougher just by comparing the amount of white caps, much rougher at the mouth anyway."

Stepha stared at the river and quickly evaluated the human's observation. With a nod, she replied, "I believe you are correct. It would probably be to our benefit to sail to the other side before beginning our descent."

"Shouldn't we simply begin where it looks the calmest, not necessarily all the way to the other bank, if the situation does not demand it?" added Krirtie.

Stepha nodded again. "That would be true, except because we have such a small raft and neither of us knows much about navigating such a river, I would prefer to stay near one of the banks. At least then if we did capsize, we may still have half a chance to reach safety by swimming. However, looking at these jagged rocks near this shore, and considering the size of our small raft, I think saying half a chance may be stretching our odds."

Krirtie nodded acceptance. "You are right, Stepha. Would it be possible for us to fly? I know it takes much out of you, but it would solve the rapids issue."

Stepha shook her head. "Flight is an option, but only our last option. My wings are tired and it is difficult with the combined weight." She looked back, more serious. "But mostly, I am fearful that we would be easy targets in the sky. These are not friendly forests."

Krirtie shook her head that she understood, and then tilted her head slightly and added, "By the way, you never did finish telling me how you got your brother's blessing to go on this trek. I would have thought he would have insisted you stay in Elvinott, and I know you would not act against his word."

Stepha took Krirtie's arm and began to walk back to the raft. "Well, actually, I have not *yet* gone against his word. I promised I would not continue to Draag without Jermys accompanying us and Krystof's blessing. I didn't give Krystof time to say anything against our plans because I was so infuriated at the situation we were thrust into. I will be accompanying Jermys and Fehr if we could ever catch them. I hope we greet them before we reach Draag because, besides the obvious reason, I would not want to be dishonest to my brother and king.

Stepha threw their last bit of stored food into the raft, which marked the end of their loitering. They could delay the inevitable no longer, which was evident in the total lack of conversation that had ensued. Both girls knew that once they started their small craft toward the moving currents, there would be no turning back. This last chance to back out was issued silently between both their stares, and both answered the same.

Stepha shoved the raft into the water and leaped over the side, never letting water touch her body. And like being pulled toward a magnet, the majestic river sucked them downward. Krirtie worked the rudder and angled the sail while Stepha dug the oars into the water to give the boat the extra surge to push away from the dangerous jagged shore.

Once they had moved about 500 yards out, she turned the rudder, and the small raft began to parallel the river's mouth. Just looking down the massive expanse as they passed gave the girls the feeling that the river was satisfied to simply wait for them, as if it was even daring them to come.

Stepha pushed the raft along using all her strength combined with Krirtie's guidance to keep the river from choosing the time they entered. They studied what they saw before them, with Stepha searching for anything that might give them an advantage. She began thinking about her family and then Schram, wishing any of them were here with her now. Krirtie held the boat turned against the current while she joined the elf in the spectacle rumbling at their doorstep.

The boat fought along its course, slowly finding its way to the southern shore of the river. Stepha dug the oars deep, pushing the small craft backward while swinging its bow around to face the splashing water. Neither girl spoke, but it was obvious both were as uncertain about their next actions as they had ever been in their entire lives. Krirtie had even begun to tremble, doing well to hide her fears from Stepha but not from herself. She was terrified for what they were about to undertake. The horror she was feeling, however, was matched only by that which was experienced by the elf. Stepha's face was pale. Much of her natural green-brown color was lost only to be replaced by an empty hue lacking any definable shade.

Both girls heard the rumble and felt their raft being slowly pulled toward it but were helpless to act. They had been staring at the rapids for the entire morning, but only now, when they were graphically confronted with the idea of traversing them, did the reality of the situation hit.

Stepha broke from her momentary trance to turn and face Krirtie. She wished to speak, but the fear within her made words come difficult. Krirtie noticed her discomfort and, by displaying the same feelings, answered what the elf wished to ask. Only giving a nod, Stepha marked the beginning of the next leg of their journey, the Draag River.

Krirtie lowered the sail while Stepha moved the oars to a closer notch so her use of them would be more quickly answered by the boat. Once the sail was down, Krirtie returned to the back and took her seat by the arm of the rudder. Neither girl had any idea what to expect or how much control they were actually going to have, but both were prepared to give it everything they had, and both knew it was too late to decide otherwise now.

The raft began to increase in speed as it caught the swifter currents, but to Stepha, it did not appear that it was moving as fast as the laws of physics said it should be. It had picked up momentum, but quickly it had seemed to reach an apex; and although the water was moving continually faster, the boat remained at the same pace. However, the elf glanced ahead and tossed her feelings aside, realizing that their current speed was more than sufficient to send them tumbling topside.

A spray of water exploded upward as the bow of the raft took the first wall. They plunged, driving the tip of the boat into the swirling waves before whipping it back to be temporarily level to the surface again. All of Stepha's muscles locked, becoming firmly fastened to the handles of the oars, driving both paddles deep against the current.

Krirtie kept her eyes focused ahead, working the rudder by feel. When the raft was shoved one way, she threw all her weight back trying to counter it in return. She could feel the bruises beginning to form around her shoulders as she leaned with all her might against nature's forces, finding either the rudder arm or her own armor being shoved back just as hard. However, even as bad as it seemed, there was something that was not right, and that something was giving them the advantage they desperately needed.

A large wave crashed sideways into the boat, causing the entire vessel to rock well to its left and then quickly, seemingly unnaturally, roll back flat. Stepha was thrown off her seat; and when she immediately shifted her weight to hold against the new obscured position, she was thrown back to the right as the raft reassumed its old direction. The elf looked up in horror but was not able to spare the time to examine what had happened as now the violent storm surrounded them on all sides.

Stepha rocked back, forcing the oars down to bite into the water, and Krirtie slammed the rudder arm starboard trying to force the boat far enough to pass by the huge, jagged rock face protruding through the white foam in their path. The boat slowly fought against the raging current. Beads of sweat rolled down both their faces but only remained moments until a splash of water washed them away, only to be quickly replaced, starting the cycle over again.

Then, as they looked ahead, at nearly the same time they both saw what was in their path. Their faces remained pale, completely devoid of color, as they realized the raft was not going to turn fast enough to miss the large, jagged boulder breaking the water's surface directly in their line. Krirtie fought as hard as she could, but with every foot they gained, one large rapid would shove them violently back into the original direction. Scratches echoed with the first contact, then a loud crack followed closely by a smash, as the raft was turned broadside against its unforgiving edge. The small craft lunged sideways, becoming perpendicular to the now-incredible pace of the water. Stepha dug her oars in once again, but this time nature won out and the handle of one oar snapped and sliced back toward Krirtie, nearly sending the woman into the water. The elf fell back, but simultaneously the boat struck a second rock, which worked in their favor to straighten their course and throw Stepha back to her seat. She removed her remaining oar and used it as a paddle, switching sides and thrusting it vertically into the water to aid Krirtie in control.

The raft surged forward, but now their ability to guide it was even more hampered. Their speed, however, still puzzled the elf. They remained at the same constant rate. Furthermore, she wondered what had brought the raft back to be flat on the water when everything in nature said they should have capsized. She had not been looking at Krirtie, but nothing the human could have done would have brought the boat back as it had. Stepha's revelry was ended abruptly when a jolt of unimaginable force brought their small boat to a momentary halt in the fast rapids. The elf lay facedown in a pool of water along the baseboards of the hull. Her arms were firmly pressed back, protecting her head from the huge rock protruding through the bottom. Cold river water began flowing over Stepha's hands, and at the rate it was seeping in, the elf knew their boat would stay afloat only minutes longer.

She pushed herself to her knees, hollering to Krirtie that they needed to make a swim for it. When she did not respond, Stepha swung around to see a pool of red water filling the back half of the raft with Krirtie's head submerged in it.

Stepha leaped up and then collapsed again. Her eyes rolled back into her head, and she became disoriented and lost. She shifted her weight completely off her legs, enabling her to regain some conscious control of her thought process. It was at that moment she realized both her legs were broken. The pain previously unnoticed now was unleashed through her body. She looked down to where she had fallen to see the propped-up oar she had landed across. Blood now became visible in her half of the raft as well, and the shock nearly made her fall unconscious again. She struggled to keep her mind clear, knowing that to give in now would be both their undoing. She adjusted her position, and once again pain shot like flesh being torn from the bone. She leaned over the seat while further cracking and breaking wood splintered from the damaged hull. She could tell that the boat was being pushed free from its temporary resting spot.

She reached over and pulled Krirtie toward her, seeing a large gash across the woman's forehead. Yet the blood flowing from it had already ceased. Her eyes remained closed, but her breathing was strong so the elf knew she was well, at least for the moment. Suddenly the boat rocked, and once again it became the play toy for a vicious, unrelenting force of nature. The lunge threw Stepha back against the side, but this time the expected pain from her injuries was absent. However, the shock of this reality was nothing compared to what she felt when she looked to see how the water had changed and witnessed the completely sealed and undamaged surface of the raft.

Then, mumblings of Krirtie's voice broke the air, and Stepha turned to greet the stunned, clean face of the girl whose only sign of injury was a slight scar, which seemed to be fading as she watched. Krirtie immediately came to her senses and was back working the rudder, hollering questions at the bewildered elf pertaining to what had happened. Stepha, having no answers, only stared first back at Krirtie then to the boat. Not only had the hole the rock had ripped through the hull magically vanished, but also the oar which had snapped earlier now rested in its notch, ready to be used in guidance.

Stepha grabbed the handles of both oars and better situated herself to attempt to maneuver the raft toward the shore. Tears began to flow, causing Krirtie to grow instantly concerned for Stepha, not just their situation.

"Stepha, what is it?"

The elf wiped her eyes, the stress clearly showing on her face. She whispered, "My legs are no longer broken."

"What, Stepha?" hollered Krirtie back. "What is broken?"

Stepha turned and dropped her arms down, causing both oars to fall free, splashing off the water's surface. Turning to face the concentrating stare of Krirtie, she hollered, "Let it go! This boat could no longer crash than you could fly. If we get in trouble, I believe my wings have enough strength left in them to lift us out of here."

She spoke firmly, but her voice still carried a clear note of exhaustion. Krirtie looked questionably toward the elf but refused to release the rudder. The raft continued down the river, both oars dangling uselessly to the sides and Stepha simply holding on with both hands, using her feet and legs to secure her position should they greet another rock as before.

Suddenly Krirtie screamed, causing the elf to rip her head back toward the woman as a large jolt from the rear struck their little raft. Stepha saw a large chunk of the wooden rudder being tossed in their wake while Krirtie sat huddled to the side, the broken handle still in her hand. "Now we are lost for sure!" she cried, throwing the rudder handle to the floor of the boat. "We have no way to steer."

The elf motioned with her eyes. "We were never steering before. This raft has a strong will to survive. It is not our doing that we are afloat right now. Some other force guides us."

Krirtie followed Stepha's gaze to see a sight which nearly knocked her from the boat. The previously shattered rudder now appeared brand new as it turned back and forth below the water.

Krirtie's eyes turned back in disbelief. She stared toward the elf and then back toward the rudder. She noticed the sharp, newly carved handle. It appeared as if it had been cut from its birth tree only moments earlier. The water from the river gave the look of sap seeping from its veins. Krirtie flashed her eyes back to where the original broken rudder handle had been tossed. She reached down a grabbed the handle to inspect it more closely. As she lifted the wooden post into the air, it slowly began to fade and become transparent. Within a moment, it had disappeared altogether.

Krirtie's jaw dropped completely. She wanted to speak but all she could utter was, "But how?"

"*How* is not important," replied Stepha. "What is important is to hold on for our lives. As sure as what is now only a faint scar on your head but moments ago spilled all the blood at your feet, it simply appears that we cannot be hurt while we remain inside. I also believe this raft can't be damaged."

Krirtie glanced down and was shocked by the sight of the large amounts of red color mixed with the water at her feet, but even while she looked, it seemed to be lessening in depth, now even showing dryness in several places. Her hand went to her forehead, and although she felt she had been seriously wounded recently, to her touch and sensations in her mind there was no sign of it. She stared blankly at the elf in front of her. "When this is all over, I wish to have a word with Enroht-Wah, or Lauren, or whatever her name really was."

Following that, the girls remained silent, concentrating solely on holding on for their lives while the raft they were in faced bombardment after bombardment of a ruthless and angered river. Several times both girls thought they were about to capsize only to find themselves flopping back down correctly. Twice they struck large rocks, once simply giving the boat a mighty jolt but the second ripped a gaping hole through the bow. Water seeped into the craft, and both Stepha and Krirtie were helpless to stop the roaring water. However, as they could feel the boat begin to waver under the torrid waves, it again began to right the wrong. The torn planks along the base of the raft suddenly began to regenerate. The water slowly vanished, and in only moments, it appeared undamaged.

Stepha looked on in disbelief but thankful just the same. There was no way of knowing how far they had traveled since entering the rapids, but she hoped there would be a break soon. Essentially, having the added pressure of navigating the river lifted. It still was incredible work just to stay inside the raft. It was constantly knocked from every direction, and even holding on and securing a position was a chore. There was a brief channel of smooth current, which gave the elf a chance to survey what lay ahead of them. She pointed to Krirtie when the human woman saw the fork and nudged the rudder to try to guide the boat to stay on their planned course. That small nudge was all it took, and suddenly the raft dove right, taking the rougher water without question.

Krirtie hollered forward, trying to carry her voice over the fierce rumbling of the water. "I only touched it a bit. I can't believe it was enough to throw us this far. Should I try to take us back?"

The elf heard her words but could not risk turning her head to reply. Instead, she nodded and yelled. "No, I think it was only waiting for us to make a decision on our course."

She did not know if she had been heard or not, but at this point not much other than staying inside mattered. Even if Krirtie did try and take control of the rudder, Stepha doubted that it would have any effect. The exiting tributary of the River Ozaky meant they had already traveled over five miles. The boat may be able to make it the entire length of Draag in one shot, but Stepha was certain they would not. They were being desperately shaken about; and although none of their serious injuries seemed to be that serious after the boat's magic took effect, they still were being dealt a tremendous battering. Both girls constantly let out cries when their bodies struck the side or were thrown to the bottom, only to get back up, narrowly avoiding a wave crashing broadside upon the raft's bow.

Suddenly, all motion seemed to stop while a loud creaking and scraping sound spit through the thunder of the water. Both girls rocked forward, with Stepha even cracking her head along the side of the boat. They lifted their eyes to greet nothing but crystal blue sky. The river in front of them had vanished, and both knew exactly what this meant. Their boat was lodged on a rock at the top of a large water fall the depth of which could not be seen. Stepha's eyes drew a deep terror as she absorbed their situation. She lifted her hand to try to signal Krirtie to lean as far back as she could. They had to keep their weight to the rear, or they would fall free of their sensitive hold.

Krirtie understood the signal but she could do little to aid the effort. Water was continually pounding against her back as well as the back of the boat. Slowly, they began to rock back, only to get hit by a strong burst of water, which shifted the raft's resting spot freeing it from its hold to the bottom. With one soft slide, the raft rocked forward, and Krirtie and Stepha could only follow the bow downward.

The total length of the falls was only about ten to fifteen feet, but both girls knew without it being said that a normal raft would have exploded at the force of landing in the liquid storm. However, their boat landed tip downward, and while the rough water kicked and beat the boat at contact, with the aid of their respective forces, it immediately worked back level.

Krirtie crashed into the seat ahead of her, and Stepha was thrown overboard landing several feet ahead of the raft but directly in its path. She burst back up through the water's surface to see the boat being pushed directly toward her body, which was also being carried rapidly downstream with the current. She sucked in a deep breath and dove downward, kicking her feet up in the process and feeling the bottom of the hull strike them as it passed. Krirtie was quickly on her feet, yelling, but had no idea what had happened. The rapids had found a momentary lag following the large falls, and now the boat merely moved with the current smoothly, no longer being tossed by the fierce waves.

Krirtie was still yelling when Stepha answered her call from the far left. "I am over here. See if you can turn the boat and guide it to this shore. It looks as if these waters might be navigatable."

The girl sent an affirmative wave and quickly moved back to grab the rudder arm. At first touch, the raft made a perfect ninety-degree turn and began moving with increasing speed across the current, acting as if it too were ready for a rest. The raft and the elf reached the southern shore at nearly the same time, and after Krirtie had pulled it a safe distance from the edge, both girls collapsed on the ground.

"That was the most unbelievable journey of my life," said Krirtie, gasping for air between broken words.

"Indeed," replied the elf. "I hope the remainder of the river proves less difficult." She shifted her eyes toward the boat. "I do not wish to have to discover any other secrets hidden within this mysterious vessel."

"Nor do I," added the human woman, who had now fallen completely flat along the ground.

Stepha nodded, and then her eyes narrowed. She tilted her head slightly and then she leaped to her feet and drew her bow, placing an arrow in the same motion. Krirtie lifted her head in surprise and whispered at a level that should not be considered a whisper, "What is it?"

As Krirtie moved her hand to the hilt of her sword, the elf continued to focus on her surroundings. In a slightly distressed voice, Stepha said, "There is something wrong. It is well past noon, but I hear no animals or birds. Even at this hour there should be some activity about." She lifted her face to the air. "There, do you smell it? A fire. The scent comes from farther downstream."

"I can't tell," shrugged Krirtie. "Is it from a camp, or do you mean a large fire in the trees?"

The elf smiled. "No, it's not quite that big. Probably a camp."

"Then maybe we have found what we..."

"Do not get your hopes up, Krirtie," interrupted Stepha as she shook her head, giving the impression that she had just identified something about the mysterious scent. "We should investigate, but there is a much higher percentage of dark brothers in these woods. Only a dwarf would start a fire such as this. It burns with a sour odor that is near deadly to many small creatures. I doubt even a human would set fire to a knot-lack tree." She paused as she replaced her bow and then noticed Krirtie's expression and felt a slight guilt grow within her. "I am sorry. I did not mean to…"

Krirtie laughed. "Don't worry about it. Most humans probably would not know, but I don't aim to be one of those for too much longer." She motioned and added, "You lead the way, and while you are at it, why don't you show me what those trees look like?"

Stepha led them toward the source of the fire's scent, stopping momentarily now and again to investigate various sounds she had heard and then continuing ahead. As they drew closer, even Krirtie could sense the harsh odor from the burning wood, and she too began to feel uncomfortable at the unnatural lack of noise in the forest. After nearly half a mile on foot, Stepha rose a hand, and both she and Krirtie peered into a small clearing, which opened onto the face of the river.

"Do you see anyone?" asked the human as she pushed a branch from in front of her face.

"No, but someone had to start that fire, although it does appear to have been burning for some time as it has nearly burned its life away."

"What do you think we should do?" she asked, already stepping through the brush.

Stepha answered, "I'll cover you."

Krirtie hesitantly moved forward, following closely behind the point of her sword. She walked past the glowing fire and scouted through the entire glade, ending near the water's edge. Picking up a piece of torn cloth, she yelled toward the elf.

The elf released her breath and lowered her bow, giving her worn arms a brief break before bounding through the brush. When she arrived at the water, her expression turned to displeasure and she whispered, "Keep your voice down. Whoever's camp this is could be returning, especially if they are within earshot of your hollers."

Krirtie ignored the comment other than showing a distinct frown before continuing in a normal tone. "This material is from the lining of Jermys's armor, and all these prints are dwarven. If what I think is true, nobody will be returning any time soon. Jermys and Fehr have been taken prisoner by the DDs and are either already dead or have been taken somewhere to meet that fate.

The elf displayed great disapproval for the presumption of death but made no comment on the subject. Instead, she inspected the area more closely, and upon finding a trail leading away, she motioned Krirtie over. "Whoever left followed this trail. See here, they tried to cover their tracks near the clearing, and even did a poor job of that. However, if you look a few feet ahead, you can see them plain as day. A blind minok could pick up and follow this band."

"Stepha, look here." Krirtie pointed to the ground near the side of the trail. "That looks like a rat's print, but it can't be Fehr's, it's too big."

The elf looked. "Well, it definitely is a rat's print. No other creature in all of Troyf that I know of has a paw with only four claws. Whether it's Fehr's or not, you would know better than I."

"Can you tell how old they are?"

"A matter of hours, maybe as many as ten, but more than likely about five, if you take into account how the fire has burned down. I suspect they were camped here at night, then sometime this morning they were greeted with company. Fehr might have found a friend or something, and that is who trails them now."

Krirtie thought a moment then replied, "I doubt it. No rat would survive long out here. They do better when they have humans nearby to torment. There must be something else at work here." She paused then added, "Should we follow?"

Stepha was smiling after the first 'human' comment, but now her face grew stoic, and a deep, serious stare seduced her. "First, we will give the birds a break and put that fire completely out. Then, we will follow."

They were making pretty good time along the trail, cutting through the thicket of trees. They seemed somewhat rejuvenated by the knowledge that they now had a definite lead on finding Jermys, although they both carried a certain unsteadiness as to his current situation. However, coupled with the fact that they no longer had to reenter the river, their pace was swift and their faith was high.

Following the dwarves' trail was simply a matter of moving as fast as they could, and every once in a while glancing down to make certain the prints were still there. Both girls had drawn their weapons, and although Krirtie acted better in sword fighting confrontations, Stepha led the way as she was better able to interpret the forest and recognize trouble before it occurred.

The elf had to duck to the side when her sudden stop caught Krirtie by surprise and her momentum carried her sword tip just beyond Stepha's neck. Quickly recovering, Krirtie began to ask what the elf had seen but stopped when she saw Stepha's expression and raised hand.

The Reunion

Fehr crouched in the brush, remaining completely still while the commotion behind him gradually grew louder. His idea that he would be safe while trailing the dark dwarf's party had quickly vanished, and now he sat waiting to see who was following him. A look of anguish crossed his face when he glanced toward the ground to see his footprints clearly showing where he stopped and turned into the brush.

I can't believe I was so stupid to leave a trail that even Krirtie would be bright enough to follow, the rat thought to himself. He knew anyone would be able to find him regardless of whether they were looking or not. After the recent morning's activities and the fact that everyone in this area saw the large rat as breakfast, Fehr knew his options were limited. He cursed under his breath, as he could now see the outline of two figures breaking through the brush down the trail moving at a fairly intense pace.

He toyed with the idea of fleeing but figured he would do better to wait. It could be that whoever it was could only be trailing the dwarven party or, even more likely, simply be following this path back to their camp. If he ran now, he could only be asking to be followed himself, as they would have no idea what actually made the noise. Furthermore, he would have the same chances of a successful escape whether he fled now, or if he waited to be discovered.

Fehr sat motionless while the voices of those who approached were now fairly loud, but he still could not see them clearly due to the depth and thickness of the brush in which he was hiding. As they approached, he could tell the two were arguing, and by the tones of their voices, he also knew of what race they were. The two black bodies reached where the rat was hiding and continued at a pace just shy of a run, without even taking a second notice toward Fehr's tracks, only concerned with blaming the other on why they had been left behind.

Judging from their voices and the fact that both carried bows but were short on several arrows, Fehr assumed these were the two he had met earlier that had been searching for some breakfast. He gathered that their leader, the one called Eb-Brown, either had forgotten about them or wished them dead. Whichever mattered not to Fehr, for all they were to him was a better trail to follow. Not only were they totally unconcerned with their prints, but their chatter could be heard clearly through the thick brush. He only hoped they would catch the main party soon, because if Fehr was to attempt a rescue, he knew it had to be before they reached the main camp, and he knew that had to be soon. However, he still had no idea what he was going to do.

He followed at a heartbeat's distance behind the two, and for the first time in his life, he saw firsthand evidence that the dark dwarves and the mining dwarves were more similar than any would ever had admitted. If the two had been able to keep a steady pace through the trees, Fehr was certain they could have caught the group ahead. However, their constant bickering and fighting frequently delayed them, often causing them to stop and duke it out, once even bringing them to draw weapons. One had drawn a sword and the other a bow. Fehr imagined that if they had both squared off with battle axes, it would have looked identical to Bretten and Jermys the first time he ever saw them in the tunnel leading under the river between Antaag and Feldschlosschen. However, he thought the dark dwarves' disputes could end up being battles to the death, whereas Jermys and Bretten could not have hurt each other regardless of what the argument was about. He took a moment and thought about Bretten and the ordeal at Anbari's Dominion and the staff. He began to wonder if everything was really worth it, and then, hearing another of the disputes end with some harmless shoving, continued behind the dark brothers.

As fate would have it, after nearly a full day of following the two, just when the darkness of late evening began to engulf the forest, they squared off in a fight, which left one dead and the other bearing an arrow through the chest, lying in a bed created from his own blood. Fehr approached the small clearing that had served as their last battleground; and realizing the first dwarf he came to was already a rotting corpse, he moved toward the other. Blood seeped from this one's lips as his hands fought desperately to remove the blood-greased shaft from deep within his beaten body. He issued a deadening groan when Fehr leaped onto his belly just below where the arrow had struck.

The rat showed no remorse for the pain and death he was seeing, nor did he attempt to make the dwarf's suffering any less. If anything, he went out of his way to make certain the pain was as intense as it could be. He found a spot on the dark dwarf's chest above the arrow and pressed his hind claws deep into the DD's chin, tearing at the flesh and hair making up his beard while leaning back against the shaft of the arrow. The dwarf winced in pain, but due to the loss of blood he had already endured, he was helpless to do anything.

Fehr used his laugh to taunt the near-dead figure before saying in perfect dwarven, "I followed you the entire day to find your camp and free my friend, and all you two imbeciles could do is argue the whole time. Well, I suggest that if you wish me to remove this arrow, you will point me in the direction of the camp I speak of, you disgusting river slug." He was using his deepest and most strong voice and drawing on his library of dwarven languages and curses; and although most of what he said was not really true and he knew finding the trail the dark dwarf party had left would be as easy as stealing food from Jermys's locked chest in Feldschlosschen, he was having a good time tormenting this dark dwarf upon his death.

The dwarf spit blood as he replied. "You'll get no such help from me, rodent scum. Go back to your pathetic rock you live under and see if you can torment a snail with your taunts."

Fehr did not reply and, shifting his weight back, pushed the arrow at a new angle, tearing it through the dwarf's insides. He cried in pain, and sheets of blood seeped from the wound and his mouth. Fehr released his weight and his only comment began, "I don't think that was the answer that I was…"

He broke off when the dwarf heaved his body in one last spastic contraction and then fell limp. Fehr stared at him in surprise and then dove to the side, his senses telling him that something was wrong. Just as he leaped from his body, another arrow struck the dwarf exactly where Fehr had been sitting. Looking across the body, he saw the second arrow shaft which had killed the dwarf but had probably been meant for him. Fehr's attention turned to witness three dark dwarves breaking through the far brush, one preparing to release a third arrow at the rat. Fehr hesitated not a moment longer, and as the shot planted itself in the ground behind him, he issued a slight whimper and disappeared into the trees.

He ran hard through the thickest of paths he could find for several hundred yards before turning around and checking for pursuit. Seeing none, he began to try to calm himself and curled up into a small ball to cover the pain of his severed tail. The arrow had pinned his tail to the ground, and even though a bandicoot's tail will separate from its body and almost immediately grow back, that does not stop the intense pain. Fehr cursed a bit under his breath, feeling sorry for the hardships he had faced but gradually brightening when he realized what a fine story this would make. After an unknown length of time, which allowed the pain to subside, the rat leaped to his feet and began backtracking through the underbrush. It was now deep black in the forest, the tree cover even blocking the light reflecting from both moons. However, since a bandicoot did most of its work during the night, the darkness was not a hindrance for Fehr. Within minutes he was back to the edge of the small glade.

He looked across, gathering any light he could from the now-exposed moons but still not seeing with any clarity. He could make out the outlines of the two dead figures, and scanning the rest of the area, he saw no movement or appearance of remaining guards. Knowing dark dwarves, he knew they probably left the corpses to rot and would only steer clear of the area for several days until the bodies were swallowed by the forest. Very rarely did the lighthearted rat feel any fear, and this instance was no exception. With a slight sigh, he bounded forward, landing well inside the boundary of the clearing only feet from the first dwarf. Learning his lesson from earlier, he decided not to remain in the open area for too long; and after rummaging through the dead figure's belongings, only finding a small dagger, which he stuffed in his pouch, the rat departed, taking a quick look for the arrow that had severed his tail but knowing that it and his missing appendage were now trophies on some dwarven wall. He cursed again, and after inspecting the outer ring of the glade, he disappeared down the most recently traveled trail.

It was only about a half hour's walk until he came onto an outbreak of trees overlooking a huge opening spotted with small glows from several campfires. All in all the area looked to be roughly 400 square meters, but he was only judging this by the skeleton created by the positioning of the fires. It was too dark to determine specifics. However, he was aware that the path he currently stood on was probably a main access point to the camp and would be heavily used by leaving and returning scouting parties; possibly even more so with the capture of Jermys sure to send a stir through the entire camp. Knowing this, Fehr had a choice. He could either sneak into the camp tonight and see what he could find out, or wait until morning and survey the conditions from a safe distance, waiting to see what the dark dwarves had planned. His natural-born instinct was telling him not to worry and simply plow forward, locate the dwarf, free him, and escape. However, his common sense told him it would be better to wait. If the dark dwarves had wanted Jermys dead, he would be as such already. Something was amiss here, and Fehr had already had one confrontation that left him without a tail.

With one more glance downward across the camp, he sighed and started to leave to find a comfortable and safe haven to rest for the night. As he left, however, an unseen hand reached down and snagged his tuft of hair between his ears, placing a dagger to his throat. The only thing heard was the rat's deafening dwarven curses.

⚬⚬⚬⚬⚬

Stepha knelt down and began running her fingers over the ground, motioning with her other hand at Krirtie signaling her to remain quiet. She heeded the warning and quickly knelt beside the elf who leaned near her as she moved. "Someone has joined the trail here after the rat passed. It looks to be two dwarves moving at a quick pace." Her voice was only a whisper but it still carried great concern in its tone.

Krirtie squinted at the new prints. "I would never have noticed them. Is there any way to tell about how soon after they passed?"

The elf smiled. "Not with any accuracy. However, I would say they will probably overtake the rat by nightfall at the latest if their pace was to remain at this rate. By the length between their steps they seem to be trying to catch up to someone, or something." She paused, then added, "We will only catch them if they stop." She said no more, but both women understood the danger that may lie ahead for their companions.

Krirtie broke the silence in the strongest, upbeat voice she could muster. "Then we should be on our way."

"Yes," replied Stepha, "but also take note that I do not believe we should be in any hurry. If they walked throughout the day beginning in the early morning, as it appears they did, then we will not have a chance of catching them by sundown. If their final destination is not a full day's walk, then we, starting as far behind as we did, still will probably only reach it after dark. Either way, we will be able to learn nothing until morning. I think we would be better served to save our strength for when we need it. If it is Jermys and Fehr ahead, then any escape will be followed by a sprint

107

back toward our raft. I think the better rested our arms and legs are, the better off we will be."

"I can't argue with that," said Krirtie as she stood and continued, now at a much more leisurely pace, although it was still much greater than a casual walk. "Who do you think those two dwarves following them are?"

Stepha shrugged. "I was just thinking the same thing. All I can say is that I have no idea."

"That isn't very reassuring."

The elf smiled slightly at her tone. "I was wondering if they could have been planted to watch for any pursuit, but I cannot imagine any dark dwarf leader being that adept to prepare that carefully…unless there is another force at work here."

Krirtie's eyes grew dark and she seemed almost scared to say the word. "Dragons?"

Stepha did not answer at first as she lifted her eyes to the sky. Finally she replied, "I do not feel as confident with my previous thoughts as I did when I first spoke them. Perhaps we should keep as quick a pace as possible."

That was all the enticement Krirtie needed to belt ahead at a gallop. Stepha was impressed with the woman because despite being barbarian-like with the way she wielded her sword, she had a more elven-like quality about her when she ran, not to mention being with child. She made very little noise as she ducked below the branches and leaped fallen logs or rocks; and although Stepha could do the same, even a slight bit quieter, there was no reason to fear alerting anyone nearby with their movement. The elf would have preferred to remain in the lead, but Krirtie had a certain passion about her now that would work in their favor should any confrontations commence. Stepha kept her eye on the trail but she was confident the woman ahead of her would not have a problem tracking this bunch. It almost seemed like they wanted to be followed. This idea began to haunt Stepha's mind, falling into one of the old human proverbs Schram used to spit at her: *If something seems too easy, it usually is.* The elf pushed the feelings out of her head but kept all her senses pierced at their surroundings. She wanted to be ready for even the slightest sound or movement that was out of order. They could not afford to be captured as well, even if it meant leaving their friends on their own.

They had moved at a steady pace throughout the day and although Stepha had wanted to make camp several times, Krirtie insisted on pushing ahead. It was now well into the night, and as they approached a small clearing, it was Stepha's elven sight that caused her to grab Krirtie's shoulder and pull her to the ground.

"What is it?"

The elf pointed. "Two dead dwarves. Probably the two we were tracking. Let's remain here a moment. I am not sure everything is as it should be."

The two sat motionless for nearly half an hour, waiting for anything in the night to make a sound. There was a long, ominous silence. It even seemed unnaturally quiet to the elf. They waited for what seemed like the entire night before Stepha slowly motioned to her companion. "Come, let's go." Taking very small and careful steps, they moved into the glade.

They inspected the two corpses carefully, taking notice that the dwarves had died in combat against each other. However, the extra arrows in one of them and the fact that his face was torn and covered in dried, dwarven blood worried Stepha. She could not determine exactly what had happened, but as an elf, she had certain concerns for those passed, which must always be fulfilled given proper time. Reaching into her armor, she removed a small pouch and sprinkled some dust from within it over the motionless bodies. A cold chill streaked down the girl's spine and vanished as quickly as it had been felt.

Krirtie leaned toward the elf. "Don't those passed usually vanish with the chill?"

The elf looked solemn. "Some are taken by the princess and vanish, as you have seen before, while others remain to slowly become part of the forest they lived their lives within. Both are admirable closings for a true life. However, some may be sentenced to be received only by the powers of darkness. This is the case for these souls. It is truly a sad thing to witness, a sad thing for friend or enemy. No creature should ever face such an ending." She paused then added sadly, "We should be going."

Krirtie followed the elf's lead, and after a brief inspection of their choices of trails, Stepha motioned and the two left following a path west. As they were leaving the glade, Krirtie took one more glance back across the opening and even in the dead of night, she could see dark shadows engulfing the bodies where they lay. She squeezed her eyes and turned away, hurrying to fall in behind the elf. Stepha did not look back, yet a tear still slid down the side of her face.

They walked for some time without speaking and remained consumed with their own thoughts. The silence they were experiencing as they walked became quite unnerving for the human. She found herself wanting to hum or whistle but knowing that to do so could mean their death or capture. She broke the monotonous silence by hesitantly asking, "What does the dust you and Schram carry do?"

As if expecting the question, Stepha replied, "It prepares and protects." She paused. "For those who have been forbidden passage, it allows it. It is pure life in death."

The words seemed alien to the human. It was apparent that this was something deep and very elven. The two continued again in silence, but now with a mood of intense emotion about them. They had no guess as to what they would greet next, but without speaking, they both knew they hoped that it did not come too soon.

They followed the trail for a short distance, making no sound with their feet or in speech. Krirtie had begun to relax and calm herself. She had tried to push the emotions she was feeling aside and concentrate on their progress forward. It did not take long for all the previous feelings to return when Stepha raised her hand

and pointed. It was difficult for her to see but when she stared hard enough, the outline could be made out under the moon's light.

Krirtie reached silently down to pull a small dagger from inside her armor, and after handing her sword to Stepha, she leaped forward and grabbed the creature, placing the blade flush against its neck.

Vicious taunts and hollers echoed through the trees, but the language was foreign to the girl. However, the voice was not. She swung the rat around to face her and in a questioning and whispered voice said, "Fehr?"

The rat's grimacing smirk turned into an inverted rainbow, and he began to shout his best friend's name, "KRI—"

The girl pressed her hand over Fehr's mouth to muffle his calls while Stepha quickly moved forward. "Ssshhh! Do you want to get us all captured?"

"Same old Stepha," he chattered happily. "Boy, am I glad to see you two. I have got some story to tell you. First, Jermys has been—"

"Captured," interrupted Stepha. "We know some of your story, and we are anxious to hear the rest, in due time. However, we must first find some cover for the night." She looked across the dwarven camp. "By the look and the spread of those fires, we will have our hands full tomorrow. This looks to be closer to a city than a camp, but why so secretive and well-hidden?"

Krirtie loosened her grip on the rat and was about to answer but then thought better of it. In a tone devoid of pleasure, she said, "Well, whatever story you do tell, please have it start by explaining how the diet I instructed you to follow allowed you to triple in size."

Fehr blushed under his fur but was not allowed to speak, as the elf had darted into the trees and both he and Krirtie had to hurry behind. After a short while, they fell into a tiny break in the trees and here the elf motioned that they would make camp. When Krirtie and Fehr arrived, they were already involved in an argument, and although they were keeping their voices low, Stepha was annoyed just the same.

"You can't tell me dwarven food made you this fat."

"Yes, it did. All they do is eat, drink ale, and smoke. They made me feel bad when I refused to join—"

"Yes," interrupted the elf. "I am sure you just hated having to eat and drink all the time. It goes against your total character."

Her sarcasm struck the rat, and Krirtie fought to hold back a smile, knowing that to further irritate him could only be asking for trouble. Grinning, she added, "Don't tell me you've taken up smoking as well?"

Fehr groaned a bit, leaning back and placing his front paws across his now-rolled-out belly. "Yes, and could I use a puff right now. Some of their tobac is simply amazing. Unfortunately, that damn dwarf has our only pouch."

Krirtie frowned. "I can't let you out of my sights for a minute. After this is all over, you will start eating with me, and while we're at it, no more smoking."

"Who do you think you are?" spat the rat, but he knew it was a battle he would not win this night.

She ignored the question and continued her orders. "And from now on, you will travel by your own resources. I will no longer be responsible for carrying you. Not that I could even do so for long now anyway."

They were glaring at each other when Stepha finished setting up her sleeping area. She stepped over. "Will you two stop this bickering?" Turning to Fehr, she added, "Now I want to know everything that has happened, but keep it short." She smiled deeply then added, "And speaking of short, make sure you include the part about your tail."

Krirtie chuckled, caught off guard by the unexpected shot toward the rat's newfound injury. Fehr's lips tightened into a white pucker, appearing to be a bomb about ready to explode. However, he quickly realized that he was just asked to be the center of attention and to tell a story, his two most favorite things. With his anger soothed, he dove into his tale.

He hurried through all the events leading to the dwarf's capture and his diligent tracking through the forests. However, it was still over an hour before he finished, and Krirtie had already nodded off. Stepha, on the other hand took everything in, and was left with more questions than she had to begin with.

Whatever had caused the dark dwarves to take a prisoner—something they never did unless it absolutely served their gain—probably was very important for both their causes. Whether Jermys's life was in immediate danger could not be determined, but she believed she must assume that it was, or he would not be held against his will. However, if they would truly be able to help the dwarf or not was another more difficult question. She knew they were in unfriendly forests and the longer they remained here, the greater chance they had of being captured. She made a mental note to herself that regardless of the other's objectives, tomorrow they would evaluate the situation as a whole. If she felt that to attempt to help Jermys would be too great of a risk, then they would head back to their raft and continue without him. The thought was not at all pleasing to her, but she knew it was the correct one; and although she knew Krirtie would at first protest, eventually she would see that as well. However, Fehr would be a problem. She glanced over at the sleeping rat nestled closely against his lost friend's curled arms. With a soft sigh, the elf shifted some branches to better cover her two companions in the night and then disappeared into the shadows of nearby trees to keep watch.

∽✲⌀

Jermys's groggy eyes peered around the sides of the tent, which was being used as his cell. In it he sat alone. The only other objects in the room were a small wooden table, on which sat a single candle to give light, with a serving of food and a large mug of ale to the side. The dwarf was in no mood for eating but he also was not one to act unintelligently, especially with the pounding he was currently experiencing in his head.

In what amounted to one swallow and gulp, the plate was clean and the mug empty. With a deep, bellowing belch, he leaned back and pulled out his pouch of tobac and pipe. The green haze depicting his special dwarven blend filled the small room, and gradually the tobac began to work its magic. His body relaxed, allowing every muscle to soften and fall limp against the ground. He noticed no pain in his head as his eyes gently fell closed.

There was no telling how long he had slept when a loud argument ensued outside his door. The dwarf looked up in time to see two dark brothers nose to nose in cursing yells, which ended in two violent swings and then one dwarf being removed by two others that approached. Jermys froze as the remaining figure's shadow moved toward the door. The slit slowly lifted and the dark dwarf pushed through to stand before the still-motionless dwarf.

"Awe, I am pleased to see that your stubbornness did not keep you from eating. The trip was long and I guessed you would be hungry."

Jermys was surprised and somewhat suspicious of the sincerity he heard in Eb-Brown's voice. "I may be stubborn, but so is an empty stomach."

"Yes," replied Brown. "I took the odds that you would eat. I heard your belly shouting the last hour of our trip. I will be pleased to inform them of the outcome."

Jermys raised his eyebrow, and his mood instantly lightened. "You were wagering on my appetite?"

The dark brother laughed. "Yes, but there were no odds on the drink. Everyone knew a Feldschlosschen dwarf could never pass on a mug of ale."

He shrugged. "Aye, the food alone might have been questionable, but with the ale by its side, I had no hesitations."

Now they both chuckled in an uncomfortable tone, and for Jermys, it was the first time he had ever exchanged pleasantries with a dark dwarf, if in fact that is what they were doing. He assumed it was the same situation in reverse. However, he was also aware that this visit was not brought on by the need to determine the outcome of their wagers, but a much deeper problem was at its source. As their smiles slowly faded and an ominous silence seduced the tent, Jermys knew he was about to find out exactly what the true problem was.

Brown paced the small room for a short time, creating a longer period of intense silence. It was a room full of nervousness and emotion. Jermys followed the dark dwarf's motion with his eyes, but looked away when Brown turned to speak. "I have told my leader what you said to me regarding my brother. He says you have no reason to lie about such a thing and therefore should be believed until we learn different." Jermys nodded understanding before the dwarf continued. "However, as for the Hatchet of Claude, my leader has many questions."

Jermys knew he was in no position to bargain, but as far as he was concerned, his life meant nothing if he was to lose the hatchet. "Twice you have referred to him as your leader. Does he not have a name? You may have plans for the hatchet, but let it be known that I will not leave here without it, regardless of the cost."

Brown appeared angered and stung, but he seemed to fight through his natural reactions, keeping a polite atmosphere. "You will learn all you wish to know in good time, but also know that you would do well to improve your attitude. My leader has agreed to meet with you personally, something only three dwarves in this camp have ever done. You will be blindfolded and led for some distance with many different dwarves leading you. Any attempt to escape, and you will be killed immediately. Any knowledge you gain once you meet my leader must be kept with you forever. Any inclination that you will reveal that may jeopardize what we are achieving here will also result in your immediate death. Do you understand and agree?"

Jermys was totally taken by surprise, and although he was not ready to trust those he had hated for so long, he believed that this may be the only way to locate the hatchet. Furthermore, even though Brown had not said anything relating to it, he believed that to disagree now would probably also result in his death seconds after his reply was issued.

Weighing these ideas, Jermys replied, "I agree, Brown, but remember my last words. I will not leave without the hatchet by my side." He paused and lifted himself from where he had been sitting. "Now, when do we leave?"

Shaking his head, the dark dwarf turned his expression into a slight smirk. He walked near Jermys and gave a motion that he was going to blindfold him. However, in one quick movement he removed his ax and, with the blunt end, clubbed the dwarf over the head. Jermys gave a grunt and then fell to the ground, unconscious. In a chuckling voice to himself, Brown said, "We leave right away."

⌒∞〇

"So you finally decided to wake up."

Jermys groggily grabbed his head and tried to sit up and focus on his surroundings. "What happened?" he asked toward the voice that had spoken. Then remembering he had been slugged, he turned with tightened lips toward the dark dwarf guilty of inflicting his pain. "Where are we, Brown?"

The dark dwarf grinned, causing his black cheeks to wrinkle all the way up to his bald head. "Sorry for having to hit you, but it was necessary. As for where we are, that is something you should hope you never discover."

Jermys only nodded, but his agitation was still apparent. He replied, "Can you at least tell me what hour it is?"

"A handful before first light," the dwarf replied. "Are you able to walk?"

"I suppose."

"Good. Put this on and grab hold of the rope, and remember, to let go of the rope will mean your instant death."

He handed a piece of cloth to Jermys, and reluctantly, the dwarf tied it around his face, covering his eyes. Brown handed him the

116

rope, and feeling it pull tight, Jermys began walking behind. He knew he was being led through the forest, and frequently there were stops where he believed those leading him switched positions. Several times he heard soft chuckles to the sides and assumed that he was being paraded in front of some of the other dwarven guards. For all he knew, they simply had made additional wagers that he could actually be made to do all these things. However, for whatever reason, he felt Brown was being honest. He knew that the dark dwarf would never had gone through all these elaborate measures if he was not on the level. Something out of the ordinary was at work here. If not, Jermys knew he would already be dead.

They walked for some time. It was unclear to the dwarf what direction they were or had been heading, but he could tell that it was now well past dawn as light had begun breaking through the loose material of his blindfold. Two hands grabbed his shoulders and their journey seemed to be brought to an abrupt end. Jermys reached up to begin to uncover his eyes, and his hands were slapped away without comment. He heard the faint sounds of two dwarves talking in soft voices some distance ahead of him, but he could not understand or identify the words. The hands holding the dwarf in place were removed, and in their wake was the rustle of several leaving behind him. There was a brief silence before a second movement was detected approaching. Jermys felt a hand reach around his neck and the point of a dagger bite lightly into his scalp. With a snap, the blindfold was cut, and the dwarf squinted as the onrush of light attacked his eyes. Quickly he adjusted and opened up to see the bald face of Eb-Brown staring back at him. He looked briefly around and was quite taken by the scenery. Large trees shot hundreds of feet into the air on all sides except one, which opened into the brightest, most green field Jermys had ever seen. Two bongos were grazing at the far side of the glade, but his eyes were focused on a small black tent erected in a near corner.

Eb-Brown followed his gaze and said, "That is where my leader waits, but there is more I must tell you before you go. What you will learn here will make your immediate inclination to strike out against him. However, hear him out. In the end, if you deem him a traitor and you so desire, I think his honor will allow you to kill him. But, do not underestimate what he is trying to do. If I had been informed of your plans in time, I would have steered clear of your party, never capturing you in the first place. As it worked out, I am only glad I did not kill you during our confrontation. That would only work against what we fight for."

Brown stared for a moment deeply into Jermys's eyes. Then after issuing a motion forward, added, "Remember all that I have said."

The dwarf was now completely confused about the entire situation, but his confusion only grew when he started to walk toward the tent. Eb-Brown hollered one more comment. "We have been searching for your companion, the rat, and he has been spotted several times near our camp. However, he repeatedly eludes us. If we find him, we will bring him along."

Now Jermys was totally at a loss. Why would dark dwarves ever consider doing anything with a bandicoot other than eat it? Furthermore, how did they know of Fehr's existence? The entire time Jermys had assumed that the rat had followed him and now probably was randomly exploring through the camp looking for him. However, now he was several hours' walk away, and the only help he thought he could count on was from those he had called enemies his entire life.

He approached the tent and, with a quick inspection, he could see that it had only been erected within the last hour or so. The flap making the doorway was closed, and as Jermys lifted it, he could see that there was no light within it. Tension the likes of which he had never felt in his life engulfed his body. Part of him said turn and run, find Fehr, and continue on their mission, until a voice from inside, which seemed to be somewhat disguised but still familiar, asked him to enter. When he did so, all light from outside vanished. His eyes could see nothing in the blackness. He could hear the breathing of another to the left, but with the loss of light, he could not even make out his outline.

There was a strike of flint, and suddenly a large flame ignited on a candle, and the room was filled with light. The tent was empty except for a table and two chairs. One of the chairs was empty while in the other sat a figure Jermys could not believe he was looking at. In a soft voice, he said, "King Kapmann."

⟨∞⟩

"I do not see anything," said Stepha as she looked over the camp. "Do either of you?"

"I don't," replied Fehr, but that does not mean anything. We need to get a closer look."

Stepha turned. "Out of the question. Unless we can locate him for sure, we will not even consider any advancement. It is too dangerous and our mission too important."

"Fehr, look," issued Krirtie, ignoring the elf's comments and pointing to a spot at the base of one of the tents.

"Yeah, I see it. Disgusting sight it is as well." He paused and then glanced up to catch the girl's considering grin. "Surely you don't expect me to. No! Absolutely out of the question! No possible way!"

"What?" asked Stepha. "Another bandicoot?"

Fehr swung with hatred painted clearly on his face. "I should kill you now, elf, for even suggesting such a thing. A cotton sig is the lowest form of life there is, not even close to the superior minds of the bandicoots."

She was surprised by the outburst but when Krirtie giggled a little, the elf quickly relaxed. She sent a questioning glance toward the girl who shifted her gaze back toward the camp and then answered Stepha's unspoken question. "You know bandicoots. Most of them have a very choppy language at best. However, cotton sigs have never even developed that. By all appearances and actions, they are bandicoots"—Fehr grumbled and turned away—"but to my knowledge, they cannot communicate even among themselves."

"Is this true, Fehr?" asked the elf.

"No. Their fur is rougher. They are not as large or as fast and by far not as intelligent. Also, if a bandicoot wants to know anything, a cotton sig's menial mind is no match. I could get anything I wanted to know from that scoundrel." Suddenly his eyes fell as he knew he had been tricked.

Krirtie smiled proudly but Stepha drew a frown. "I do not like this a bit."

"It is our only choice, and not a bad one," said Krirtie. "Fehr could get through that camp with his eyes closed."

"Yes, but to lower myself to seek aid from a sig—I just don't know."

Stepha peered down to the camp. "It is your choice, of course, Fehr, but you need to know the risks involved. If you should be captured, we cannot come after you. Furthermore, if you do not return by midday, then we will head back to the river and our raft without you. Finally, if you do not wish to go, then we will all leave now. That is how it must be."

The rat frowned. "I will go, and I understand the situation. However, if I discover that it is possible to help Jermys, then we, or at least I, will do so, regardless of the costs. That is what you should know."

With that, he nodded to Krirtie and then bounded through the trees. The girl looked over to Stepha. "Would you really leave them both here?"

Stepha said nothing.

⚮

They sat in silence for the next few minutes, both peering through the trees surrounding the dark dwarf camp looking for any sign of movement. Krirtie pointed to a clump of trees about fifty feet from where the cotton sig still was gnawing at the meshing of a tent. Stepha followed her hand and then sighed. "Amazing, how could he get there so quickly and how could you locate him?"

"You can learn about how the little guys act if you are around them enough. They are really not that much different from other forest creatures, although Fehr is definitely unique. Most can communicate on some scale, but the different languages he knows is really extraordinary. I think there is some mystery about Fehr we don't yet know, and possibly never will."

Stepha smiled. "I have thought that same thing many times." She paused, and then as she thought about their situation, a worried look grew across her face. "Tell me, Krirtie, are cotton sigs as widely hunted by dark dwarves as bandicoots?"

"I really wouldn't know, but I assume so. I know very little about any race outside humans, but since I understand that they like bandicoots because of the taste, I imagine that sigs can't be that different. Why do you ask?"

Stepha pointed. "Look down at the sig. Do you see anything out of the ordinary?"

"Well, nothing too extreme. He is trying to get into that tent for something, but that would be normal for the rodent."

"Why then, when guards pass, do none of them kill the rat? I am sure they must see or at least hear him gnawing."

Krirtie thought a moment then her face began to grow much more solemn. "You don't suppose it is some sort of trap, do you?"

She shrugged. "We do know that they are aware of Fehr's presence. After all, they did take shots at him back in the field. Also, we cannot see well enough from here to determine if that cotton sig is free or if it could be tied up to something in the tent. If the latter is the case, Fehr may be in over his head.

"I never even thought," exclaimed the girl as she turned back to the camp. "Cotton sigs would no longer make a home here than a bandicoot would. We have to warn Fehr."

"It is too late," said the elf, pointing. "Look!"

Fehr slowly crept forward, keeping to the shadows as best he could. He saw the rodent chewing away now less than ten feet in front of him. He stopped a moment when he noticed the odd chain tied around its neck. The thought had never occurred to him before but now he knew. This sig had been captured and was being saved to be eaten later. Now Fehr was especially glad he had come. He knew he could save the rat from certain death and definitely get any information he needed from him in return.

He inched his way out and made an almost silent chirp to draw the cotton sig's attention. Fehr was nearly twice this animal's size, and when the sig looked over, surprise and fear showed in his eyes. Fehr mumbled a few words but when there was no response, it became clear that this rodent was even a lower intelligence than Fehr was accustomed to. He decided he would free him first and then attempt to dig for information.

He sat next to the rat and examined the lock holding the chain about his neck. With a quick sigh, he dug into his pouch and removed a small bent pin. "Don't worry, it should only be a moment," he said, though he was not sure if the sig could even understand. He started to toy with the lock, and the second before it opened, two black arms tore through the side of the tent and snagged the rat, quickly drawing him inside.

Stepha and Krirtie both bowed their heads as they watched, knowing that they were helpless to act. Without a word, Stepha rose and threw her pack over her shoulder.

Krirtie turned to her. "We can't just leave them. Fehr will be killed."

Again the elf could do nothing but lower her eyes. Both knew Fehr was probably already dead, and if not, would be soon. Any attempted rescue would only get them captured as well. She leaned down, offering her hand to help the girl to her feet. Krirtie refused it, jumping up on her own and moving in the direction of the path leading toward the camp. Stepha grabbed her shoulder and in a stern voice said, "I will not let you go."

She swung to face her. "I will not hesitate to take arms against you now, Stepha. I can move through the trees as well as Fehr, and that tent backs against the forest. In less than a minute I can be in, get Fehr, and be gone."

"And can you outrun the hundreds of dwarves who will follow?" Her voice softened. "I need you, Krirtie. Without your help, there is no way I can hope to save Maldor. Don't let one loss make us lose another. Fehr knew the risks when he went down there. I should not have let him go, but if Jermys lives, he must save Fehr now. Our path must lead elsewhere."

Krirtie broke free from the elf's hold, but she did not continue toward the path. Tears began to fill her eyes and she whispered, "Good luck, you no-good rat. I'll miss you."

⸙

Dwarven curses filled the tent while large black fingers tried to cover the rat's mouth. "Would you be quiet, you no-good rat. I'll kill you now if you don't shut your jabbering trap!"

Fehr bit at anything he could reach, making contact with either a finger or arm; he could not be sure. The dwarf screeched in pain and slapped the rat across the face. "Hit me again, you fat-bellied gar sucker, and I'll bite another piece of your anatomy off."

A deep, bellowing laugh echoed from the dwarf. "A rat that speaks dwarven and carries a temper as well. I never thought I would see the day."

Fehr was caught off guard by the response but was liking the dark dwarf's good humor and quickly forgot any differences he might be feeling. "Well, seeing as I am nothing more than breakfast around here, do you mind if I smoke?"

Again the dwarf laughed. "As you wish," he replied, loosening his grip as he felt the rat begin to calm.

Fehr smiled. "Then, might I borrow a pipe and tobac? Preferably some that burns with a faint green color."

The dark brother shook his head and smiled. "Only a rat would ask for permission to smoke from those who planned on eating him and then not even have any of his own tobac. Then, not only

123

does he ask for tobac, but he asks for the best there is." The dwarf rose, setting the rat down in the process. "Now, Fehr, I trust you will not run off when I go to bring you back your smoke?"

He nodded in reply, completely taken by the fact that the dark dwarf had called him by name and that he was still alive, not to mention about to get a smoke. Whatever was happening, his curiosity would not allow him to leave, though he suspected a dwarf guard remained outside the door anyway.

Moments later, the dwarf returned, carrying a small pipe, a pouch, and leading another dwarf. They both stared at the rat briefly and then the second handed the first a couple of coins. After placing them somewhere inside his armor, he said, "Sorry to keep you waiting Fehr, but we had a bet on whether you would try anything when we entered. As you can see, I won."

He handed the pipe and tobac to a bewildered rat and used the flame from the candle to help him light it. "I am Tal-Gentry and this is Dol-Teo. Believe it or not, we will not hurt you."

Fehr looked suspicious but was becoming more relaxed with each puff. However, as he sized up those before him, one thing seemed to grab his attention. Hanging from the belt of the one called Dol-Teo was a long, curled white-gray tail. Fehr's eyes became fire, and in one leap he was attached to the face of the dwarf digging his claws in for all he was worth. The dwarf winced in pain, and as Tal-Gentry grabbed the rat, pulling him free, Dol-Teo reached to his belt and removed his dagger, preparing to drive it into Fehr's body.

Gentry shoved the dwarf back, putting himself between the two but not being able to stop Fehr's constant taunts and yells. In one motion, he belted the rat across the face, drawing a flow of blood from his nose and successfully shutting his mouth. Then, he turned his scalding voice on Teo. "Stop it now, Teo. We have our orders, and I doubt even you would act against the leader."

Teo's face was oozing blood from Fehr's attack, and his level of anger showed clearly between the deep crevices planted across his stoic stare. However, moments after Gentry's words, his expression softened, and he took his seat without further comment. Gentry looked back at Fehr, and although he could not be certain of predicting the rat's behaviors, by his look he was fairly confident that there would be calm for a short while.

He turned his attention back to Teo who had not moved. In a motion as calm as a gentle spring breeze across a lonely lake, Gentry removed the coins Teo had previously given him and returned them to the dwarf, who accepted without motion. Turning back to Fehr, he said, "I bet him you would not react badly when you saw your tail. By the appearance, I believe I was wrong."

Gentry turned and sat adjacent to the two. Fehr immediately retrieved his pipe and then set it down once more, now completely agitated. "All right, dwarven scum. Tell me why Scrappy Face here first uses me as target practice and now you claim you will not harm me?"

Dol-Teo glared back but made no motion for his dagger. Gentry smiled. "You truly have a way with words, little one. I think it would be in your best interest to hold your tongue for a day. If all goes as planned, you will be with Jermys by nightfall and can continue your journey to Draag tomorrow. However, the only one who can take you there is my counterpart here, and right now, to use your words, you are nothing more than breakfast."

Kapmann Captured

The king grinned slightly. "That's right, Jermys, and let me assure you that I am as surprised to see you as you are to see me."

Jermys frowned and ignored the comment. "Then it is true. You have been a traitor to our people from the start. You tried to stop my companions and I over a year ago, and now you have prevented my advancement as well."

Kapmann was not pleased with the response, and his expression showed it. "We have much to discuss, young Ironshield. I would be pleased if you hold your accusations until the end. However, if the only way for you to hear me out is to give back what you lost, then let it be done." Kapmann still displayed displeasure as he reached down below the table and removed a small item he had locked in his chest. Moving his hands to the table, he placed the Hatchet of Claude across it. "Now will you take your weapon and sit with me a spell?"

The dwarf's face brightened for a moment, then he quickly hid his pleasure with the suspicion he still had harboring within him. He reached over and picked up the hatchet, and immediately it began to glow and then faded. Jermys felt a surge of power flow through his body, to be replaced by a soothing calm. He moved over and took the seat across from the Antaagian king. Lighting his pipe to join Kapmann in a smoke, he said, "I believe you should tell me the entire story."

Kapmann leaned back, letting his beard fall to the floor. After a deep breath from his pipe, he began. "First, let me tell you that from day one, you and your companions have caused me nothing but stress. Nearly two years ago, a dark dwarf leader by the name of Den-Hrube approached me secretively and spoke to me about some changes he saw occurring that he did not like. Of course I thought it was some kind of trick, knowing Den-Hrube and his reputation for acting only in his own best interests. However, when he began to speak of dragons coming to them seeking their aid in exchange for leadership in the 'new world,' I began to see the truth in his words."

The king paused a moment to give Jermys time to absorb what he was saying. His eyes showed confusion. Kapmann waited a moment longer before he continued. "You see, Den-Hrube may have been many things I do not respect, but one thing he was not was unintelligent. He knew that if the dragons did move to take over all of Troyf, dark dwarves would not be near the top of the list to rule under them. He felt a temporary alliance with Antaag would be necessary to help fight against the dragons. However, we both knew that if this alliance was made common knowledge, then he—and I, most probably—would be overthrown in a matter of days. He had nearly 600 or 700 dark brothers who had gained his trust and defected, so to speak, under his leadership. I sent minerals as often as I could, and we kept contact through the secret tunnels of the southern mines." Jermys looked up, about to add something before Kapmann cut him off. "Yes, the ones you and your companions destroyed. However, worse than that was just your simple appearance in Antaag. It was to be the largest shipment of minerals yet. Den-Hrube himself had come to oversee its deliverance. When you showed up, though, all of the scales were moved up for fear that we would be discovered. We sent his ship out a day early before we had the river secured, and as you know, all was lost."

"Why then did you arrest me that night and throw me in that cell?"

Kapmann frowned at the interruption but then continued when he thought about the question, remembering what he had not mentioned. "When I told Den-Hrube about your group's visit, he immediately centered on the fact that I had mentioned dwarven twins. At this time, our camp here in the woods did not exist, so his command was a secretive existence among all the dark dwarves in the Canyon of Icly. You can think of it as a band of rebels not building against their own nation but not willing to follow their leadership either."

Jermys shook his head in understanding but still awaited the king's answer. Kapmann continued in a slightly softer voice. "Well, this situation actually made it better in that they could keep abreast of all the new plans that the ever-growing dragon loyal dwarves had made. Den-Hrube had heard rumors that some Feldschlosschen twin was going to join forces with the dragons and really turn the scales to their favor. When I thought about the two of you, I wrongly assumed it was you who would betray your homeland. In my opinion, you were the most strong-willed, and because of that, I thought you would be more attracted by the dragons' lure. By capturing you, I could solve two problems. First, I might be able to find out for sure where your loyalty fell, and second, if your friends did try and rescue you, it would keep them away from the docks until Den-Hrube could escape."

Jermys eyes fell. "If we had only known!"

"Yes, I know that now. But at the time, I could not be sure. If I brought you into our secret circle and you were to betray us, all that we had worked for would be destroyed."

"What happened following Den-Hrube's ambush on the river?"

The king sucked in another deep breath of smoke and then gave a long, depressing sigh. "Many months went by, and I had not heard a word from any of the dark dwarves. I had instructed our search parties not to attack them unless they had already been attacked. Additionally, if any of the dark brothers wished to speak with me, then they were to be allowed."

"These orders did not cause dissension among your nation?"

Kapmann shrugged. "At this time, I think many already suspected that some sort of alliance had been formed. Furthermore, I feel all believed that if we were to curve the dragons' onslaught across Troyf, all dwarves must bind together. Even with these facts in mind, there are only a few that have openly been brought into this plan. By keeping the number low, if this ever did collapse around me, there would be only a few dead by my side."

Jermys nodded understanding and agreement. "Did any dark dwarves come?"

No, and I feared that the rebel forces had disbanded with the loss of their leader and joined with the dragon forces. Then, more on a thought of desperation rather than true belief, I decided to check the southern mines on my own. That is when I came across Lyl-Brown. He had been wandering them for days, not able to find the entrance because Krystof had changed the magic to block against any unexpected visitors. Lyl-Brown is the dwarf who organized the evacuation from Icly and set up the secret camp here in what he called the Forgotten Forests.

Immediately I began running minerals down the river, and despite a few attacks, nearly all got through. These procedures have gone along steadily since that time, with only a few hitches. Upon Lyl-Brown's disappearance, I moved in and took over the leadership, unknown to all but five of the dark brothers. Most believe that their leader is still Lyl-Brown, though none have seen him in over a year. His brother, Eb-Brown, whom you know intimately, convinced me that this would be the most intelligent way to handle it. They needed an experienced leader, and they feared if word got out of Lyl-Brown's death, then the group might fall apart. That is why when you openly spoke about his death, you created such a stir. Eb, however, passed it off as your foolish whimpers trying to save yourself. Only when he said that he had spoken with Lyl yesterday did he soothe the damage. It was indeed a close call, but we have gotten past it."

"How then did you make it here so quickly? I was only captured less than a day ago."

He shook his head. "If I had ever believed you would end up anywhere near the Forgotten Forests, I would have sent word down ahead of you. Eb and his search parties would have steered well clear, letting you have the run of the forest. As it was, I left a day later telling those in Antaag that I was going to Gnausanne, as I usually did. However, instead, I was traveling here to prepare a small company to act as a sort of cavalry if you needed the support. I was not ready to expose this group of dark dwarves as allies, but if it turned out they could help, we would not hesitate to do so."

Jermys shrugged and restuffed his pipe. "All this is so hard to believe. So much could have been different, but I understand that to trust too many would seal your fate as well. You have done well to hide it."

Kapmann nodded. "Yes, but now that you know, has anything changed?"

Jermys thought a minute, then replied. "How many dwarves do you have here at the camp?"

"There are 500, maybe 600. Our numbers are not growing. If anything, we lose more than we gain. By this, I mean if someone is going to leave our camp to return to Icly, we will do everything in our power to kill them before they get there. Our secret must remain just that—a secret."

Again there was a pause, and both dwarves filled the small tent with their exhale. Jermys leaned forward. "Then we will keep things just as they are. I shall not tell anyone unless the situation deems it necessary and I am sure they can be trusted."

The king replied, "But won't you require some help from the forces here? I assure you they would be loyal to any cause that fights against the dragons, as long as it did not involve fighting their kin." He paused and thought a minute before adding, "Though, if they had to, I believe they would."

"At this time your numbers are not large enough to make a major difference should a massive offensive be planned. However, if we can keep them a secret, they could become extremely important as a strong cavalry. They may just be able to tip the scales if used at the right time. I feel this band could prove very beneficial to our cause, and they should never have to face those they separated from. To do so would split your troops and destroy all you have fought to create and hold."

The king nodded. "I believe your words to be sound and am pleased to hear of your loyalty to us here. I trust what you say, and we will help you if it is ever within our power. However, I also wish you to know that my first loyalty is with Antaag, and I will never allow any evil to infiltrate its boundaries."

He smiled. "I respect all that you have done here and understand your motives. I too agree that Antaag must not pay the price for your actions. If it did, defend you I would not. No matter what happens here or as a result of any dragon army progression, you must never forget your home."

Kapmann shook his head before Jermys continued, his tone and appearance changing as he spoke. "I will be asking for your assistance sooner than you may have wanted."

Kapmann looked surprised. "What is it you would ask?"

"I traveled with Fehr, and due to my capture, we have become separated. I freely admit that wanting that annoying pest back may be considered impossible to understand by most, but he has become a counterpart that each gives strength to the other. If your troops locate him, please point him in my direction. Also, could you give me a direction?"

Kapmann smiled again. "I already have Eb-Brown organizing parties looking for him. There have been several sightings, but he always alludes us." Jermys joined in the smile as the king continued, "And passage for you to Draag has already been prepared. The dwarves here have dug a secret tunnel under the most fierce section of the Draag River. Because the rapids are so trying there, the goblin forces are at a minimum on the other side. You should be able to approach unobserved, but after you pass the river, you will be on your own. I have several dwarves which have been planted in some of the forces around Draag, but they are few and far between. Also, they will not risk exposing themselves to help you. Therefore, even if you could make contact, their help would be small. You will stay here through the day, and then Eb-Brown and two others will lead you to the river. I must return to Gnausanne so I don't bring further suspicion upon myself. Already I fear some of the Antaagian dwarves have begun to doubt my loyalty. In these times of evil, the last thing I need is to have civil war in my own nation. As of today, I am turning over full command to Brown and a dwarf called Dol-Teo, who you will meet when you head toward the river. We all agree that due to your comments during your capture, many are going to begin to talk, and soon the fact that none have seen their leader in over a year will start to make them suspicious. However, Brown has much support and he is certain that with Teo's help, he will be able to keep the band together. I only hope he is right. If word leaks out, it would be a devastating blow to all who have fought to make this possible. After all, we are not many in number; and being so close to Draag, it would be like swatting a fly to wipe our band from existence."

"We will keep it a secret, King Kapmann. That much I promise." Jermys rose to his feet and let out a long breath before adding in a strong, deep tone. "You have returned the Hatchet of Claude, and with it I will free my friend and then move to crush the dragons and the wrath they bring. Above all else I could say, though, I wish to express my deepest appreciation to you and the dark brothers. Your actions will never be forgotten."

The king bowed slightly. "And a thank you goes to you as well, and good luck. You will be faced with much more than can be described or even imagined here, and I pray that even one blessed with such a weapon will be strong enough to face it. May Claudos guard your travels."

The two embraced, and then the king bid him farewell, making a somewhat hasty exit. Eb-Brown returned, throwing down a pack and some blankets. "You would do well to get some sleep. We have a long journey ahead of us, and the forests are not considered friendly, especially for a mining dwarf. We must be alert." He paused, and then sensing Jermys's question, added, "And there is still no word on Fehr, but I also have not spoken with any since I left you. We will not know anything until this evening when the others arrive. Now, get some rest if you can."

Brown left, and being as how Jermys had not slept in over a day's time, he drifted off to a restless sleep. The many worries of the period bit at his mind, but mostly his thoughts centered on the rat who had become his best friend. Questions regarding his whereabouts filled his mind and dreams.

⚬⚬⚬

Two arguing voices woke the dwarf, and judging from the lack of light that penetrated the black fabric of the tent, he guessed it was near sunset. He gathered his belongings, placing his pipe and tobac, which he had left on the table, into his pouch; and after briefly rubbing his hand over the helve of his hatchet, he moved and pushed through the door of the tent. When he looked across the field, the sight which greeted him made his jaw drop, and he drew his weapon while starting a full run for those ahead of him.

"I'll take no more of your lip, rat!"

"Awe, shut up, you fat lump of maggot dump! You are not fit to…"

"Fehr! One more word and I will kill you myself!" Jermys was shouting at the top of his lungs as he approached.

Immediately, the dark dwarf holding the rat dropped him and drew his sword, turning to face the surprise visitor. Seeing it was Jermys, he lowered his weapon and issued an angry stare, which was meant to silence the dwarf.

Jermys caught the look and knew right away he had acted poorly. He drew an apologetic frown when he arrived, but it quickly changed to a hidden smile when Fehr leaped into the dwarf's arms and began licking his face. The embarrassed Jermys pushed the rat down and gave him a stern look of his own. "If you ever do anything like that again, I will cut off your tail." He laughed. "Well, it looks like someone has beat me to it."

Jermys turned to face the dark brother who stood beside him, and seeing the rat's tail still dangling from his belt, held his smile and said, "I am Jermys Ironshield, and you must be one powerful dwarf to cut off my friend's tail and then be able to put up with his annoying chatter about it."

The dwarf shook his head. "If he keeps the chatter up, more than his tail will come off. I am Dol-Teo, and I am pleased to make your acquaintance, though your friend leaves much to be desired."

Fehr grumbled, and when neither acknowledged his displeasure, he stormed off to where a small campfire burned and two more dwarves sat eating. Jermys watched the small critter waddle off but hid his joy at seeing his friend behind the stoic masks all dwarves carried. He removed his pipe and offered some to Dol-Teo as the two turned and made idle conversation on their way toward the fire.

The conversation was cheap and served only to fill Jermys and Fehr in on the plans and what they could expect in the way of resistance. The trip itself was to take the entire night but they would be on a well-traveled path, and the walk should not be difficult. All enjoyed the moments of peace before the journey and the plentiful amounts of food each was served, but most of all, the two reunited companions were pleased with the other's presence.

Despite the brief good cheer, Fehr leaned over and whispered to Jermys, "Stepha and Krirtie were with me in the forest. They are most likely on their way to Draag on their own on the river. They have some magic boat or something."

Jermys jaw dropped. "They're here? Why didn't you say something?"

Fehr frowned. "I was spending time with people who normally eat me. Trust was not high on my list." Fehr then continued to tell all he knew about the two and his time with them in the forest.

Jermys turned to Eb-Brown. "Can we get word to the camp to aid the elf and human?"

"Out of the question. Your presence alone is enough to drive a stake through this band. Now help an elf and human, both women no less? Out of the question."

"Then we are leaving," said Jermys. "Thank you again for your time."

Hesitantly, Eb-Brown raised his hand. "Wait, dwarf, don't be too tough around here. You are still in mixed company, and your friend here does look tasty, with all the meat on those bones. I would hate to kill you and be forced to banquet on him." He paused, then motioned to one of the dwarves. "Go take this message back and send six dwarves to the area described by the rat. Make sure they know not to attack. The elf is with the forest. If they approach without weapons raised, they will not attack first." He turned back to Jermys and Fehr with a stern gaze. "Sit down." He paused with a deep breath. "This is of little use. Based on the rat's words, there will be no way to catch the elf and human before they reach the river."

When they finally left the glade, it looked to be nothing more than an empty field. Eb-Brown, Dol-Teo, Fehr, and Jermys began their long walk through the night toward the heart of the dragon's stronghold, Draag. Jermys had been given dark dwarven armor and then used mud to hide his lighter skin. Fehr was instructed to dive into the trees should they encounter any others in the forest. To an unexpecting observer, they looked like a stray band of dark dwarves heading to Draag to find a new command to serve under. That was to be their story, and Brown or Teo would be the ones to do the talking. They traveled without exchanging words, all hoping that their silence might aid their chances of success, but none knowing what their chances really were.

Stepha stretched her arms and then glanced over to where Krirtie had a fire going and breakfast ready. The roar of the River Draag could be heard thundering down their path, and their raft, which had again taken them down the rapids without any problems, rested well upon the shore. The elf rose and walked over to the fire, bidding a morning greeting to the human who returned it with a large serving of food.

Stepha's expression clearly demonstrated her deep hunger and pleasure as she received the morning meal. As they ate, both looked around the area they had arrived at late the night before. The river had been exceptionally fierce, and if not for a brief period of calm, they probably would still be fighting its violent hold with all their collective forces being drained in the process. They had guided their raft to the northwest shore, but with all the thick tree cover, they had no idea where they were. For all they knew, they had sailed beyond the caverns of Draag long ago.

They seemed to be able to read each other's thoughts when their eyes met, and they both laughed. Stepha spoke first. "I have no idea where we are. What do you think?"

Krirtie grinned. "You are asking me? You obviously don't remember that I got us lost between Elvinott and Feldschlosschen one day after being there. Your question alone demonstrates how truly desperate you have become."

"I am by no means desperate, but I am definitely in unfamiliar territory. By the length of time we were on the river, I would say we traveled most of its length, which would put the Draag Caverns to our west, possibly a bit north as well."

Krirtie tried to look that direction but the tree cover was still too thick. "I really have no idea. All I know is that I do not want to get back on that river if we do not have to. If you think we can walk from here, I say let's head northwest."

The elf finished her food and rose to clean her plate before adding, "I was going to suggest the same thing. However, we should hide the raft in case we need to make some kind of emergency escape down the river. I would sooner sail this river out to sea than be cut off by it and have to either fight, swim, or be an easy target in the air."

Krirtie nodded, and when she finished eating as well, the two set to camouflaging their raft and then departed on foot, the elf marking their trail so they would be able to find their way back if needed. They followed the river a short distance and then set a course by Stepha's lead to the northwest. They moved with utmost caution, and unless they were seen, they would not run into any confrontation, as neither of them made even a twig crack beneath their steps.

Stepha rose her hand to stop their march and peered up the trail questionably. Krirtie slid in next to her but did not speak for fear of giving away their presence. The elf motioned ahead holding up three fingers to alert the girl of their numbers. Krirtie nodded, and then the two separated.

Stepha turned off the trail, as she was more apt to move through the wooded area without disturbance even without a having a path present. Krirtie drew her sword and continued down the trail but at a slow-enough pace to let the elf circle around.

One goblin struck the ground with an arrow squarely through its chest as Krirtie emerged into the clearing, swinging fiercely at another. In only moments, all three goblins were dead, and the two women warriors were replacing their weapons.

Suddenly, the ground beneath them seemed to open up, and both girls were falling downward with a sea of debris and a goblin corpse being carried with them. Stepha reached over and took a firm grip on the human, opening her wings in the same motion. They both glanced down to see the goblin body strike the hard and jagged rock-bottom floor below the trapdoor, but they had already begun to climb. Within seconds, they were back through the opening and safely standing on firm ground.

Stepha turned to motion Krirtie back to the tree cover but screeched as an arrow bit through her wing, tearing through the delicate cell line. Krirtie wheeled around to greet two dozen goblins and a handful of dark dwarves entering the glade from the far side. Already another dwarf was notching an arrow, and if not for the girl's accurate and quick sword work splitting it in flight, Stepha would have been killed. The two looked at each other and quickly realized that to fight would be to die a warrior's death. Without a word exchanged, they turned and fled at the fastest pace they could muster.

Stepha's wing was torn and dangled helplessly down as she ducked beneath branches and shrubs. The pain was intense but she knew that to stop and bandage it would mean to give up the little lead they had gained. They could move through the forest at a much faster pace than the heavier and less coordinated goblins, but that was the end of their advantage. They did not know where they were or what direction they were heading. Furthermore, although they may be able to outrun this band, they both knew these woods were thick with dragon armies. This was only one small group. There were many more scattered throughout the trees, and it would only be a matter of time before they greeted another party. They were both aware of their situation, but all they could do now was run like they had never run before. If they could gain enough of a lead, they would start to hide their trail. Until then, they could only hope they didn't meet any more unwelcome guests.

The two burst through some trees, and Krirtie slammed on the breaks so hard her feet slid out in front of her and she fell hard on her back. Stepha launched an arrow, and its flight passed directly above the fallen woman to strike the dark dwarf through his heart. Krirtie was back to her feet in moments, and an ensuing hand-to-hand combat took place. Both girls fought with terror-driven anger, giving them strength they had never drawn on before.

Stepha used her sword like it was her weapon of choice, dropping a half dozen dwarves before any could even mount a defense. Krirtie was cutting a path through the rest as tears of adrenaline and hate covered her face.

They had begun to dent the camp of two-dozen dwarves when the pursuit from earlier provided the needed support to shut the lid on the two girls. Stepha's sword was knocked free, and before she could retrieve her bow, she found a goblin dagger placed to her throat. Krirtie was backed against the tree line, and once the elf was secured, the brunt of the attack was turned on her. Within moments, she too was disarmed and on the ground.

The goblins threw both women on their backs in the center of the clearing, and the one who seemed to be the leader moved to approach. Both girls were sitting with their heads raised, allowing their long golden and black hair to fall freely behind. The goblin knelt behind them and ran his rough, curved, and nasty fingers through each of their hairlines causing both women to shake them off in disgust. The goblin issued a deep, bellowing laugh, which incited the other goblins around to do the same. He leaned toward Stepha, and in a seductive and forward gesture outstretched his long black tongue and moved it around the tip of her pointed ear. Her face grew dark and tears began to flow, bringing even more laughter and cheers from those around. Krirtie moved her hand over and gripped the elf's, hoping to allow them to share each other's strength.

With this, the goblin removed his attention from the elf and turned it toward Krirtie. He ran his hand upward along the back of her armor and then reached around her neck, moving the backs of his bent fingers across the sides of her cheek. He continued stroking her face to the cheers of support from the surrounding goblins, and she could only tighten her lips in disgust trying to pull away but his grip was too firm.

Without a further gesture, he applied force to the side of her head, turning her face to stare directly into his. Krirtie closed her eyes at the gnarled and disfigured goblin appearance. His face was beaten, like it had been ripped apart by an animal. Large black nostrils sat below deep cuts surrounding his eyes, and his lips looked more like bark than skin. The goblin saw her disgust and became angry at the response. He reached his hand around the back of her neck and pulled her head forward, placing his lips across hers. Gripping her neck and throat tightly, he forced his tongue in her mouth.

Suddenly, the goblin fell back with a scream of pain and an issuance of blood from his mouth. He swung his backhand across the human woman's head, sending her back against the elf. Krirtie fell, nearly unconscious, but spit a piece of the goblin tongue back his direction before she faded completely. As jeers and laughter rose from those around, the goblin leader drew a small dagger and raised it before the two girls. Stepha had helped Krirtie recover, and although she was still groggy from the hit, she knew what was about to happen.

Both girls huddled together as the goblin leader rose and stepped closer. The dwarves in the area were not paying much attention, but the surrounding goblins formed a circle around the three to ensure all could see clearly. The goblin leader pulled Krirtie away from Stepha with another goblin placing a knife to the elf's throat to keep her from moving. The goblin shoved the human woman's legs apart and knelt between them, placing both hands on her waist. Tears filled her eyes while the goblin began moving his hands over her armor. He reached up and separated the breastplate from the back, causing it to fall forward. Again cheers and growls echoed from the clearing.

Stepha swung her hand forward, knocking the knife from her throat, and moved to strike the goblin leader only to be violently thrown and pinned to the ground by several other goblins.

Krirtie's face showed nothing but fear and rage when the goblin leader began running his hands over her body. Blood showed through the meshwork of her clothing as his claw-like fingers tore through her garments, biting into much of her flesh in the process. Krirtie quivered, as the pain in her chest was minimal to that which she felt in her heart. He reached his hand around the top of her leg armor and, in one violent motion, ripped it off, causing much of the metal to scrape and cut her skin.

More cheers rang through the trees, with the dwarves still seeming completely uninterested. Most were sitting, discussing the weapons they had taken from the women, not following the commotion brought on by the goblins. Krirtie's eyes were filled with tears and all her thoughts were centering on the child she carried. She issued a silent prayer for the protection of her baby regardless of what happened to her.

The goblin nodded his head to the cheers, inciting even more applause to fill the glade. Stepha screamed, and one of the goblins holding her belted her across the face, knocking her momentarily unconscious. When she began to come to, she heard a dwarf's voice arguing with the goblin leader. She arched her head up to see Krirtie in the same position. Stepha had no idea how long she had been out, but when she looked into Krirtie's eyes, she knew the woman was all right. Krirtie nodded an awkward smile, although her face was still covered in tears. It was clear she did not know what was going on, but more importantly, it was clear that the attack had been halted by the dwarves for some reason. The elf turned her attention to the goblin leader and the dwarf who seemed very agitated at what he was witnessing.

The dark dwarf raised Krirtie's sword to the goblin and was motioning toward both girls. The arguments could not be understood by the girls, but both Stepha and Krirtie assumed something about the sword had alerted the dwarf, and he was extremely aggressive against the goblin. The dwarf was speaking in some unknown goblin tongue so even Stepha was at a loss to understand. Although the dwarf seemed to think that they should not be injured because of the sword Krirtie carried, the goblin was not in agreement. As the discussion continued, the goblin leader was becoming very agitated, and the argument heated. The other goblins, who were greatly outnumbered by the dwarves, began to move around their leader. The ones who had previously held Stepha freed her completely, and they too surrounded the dark brother and goblin leader. Stepha quickly moved beside Krirtie and both tried to slide over out of the way.

The goblin leader drew his sword and thrashed out against the dwarf, only to find five arrows piercing his chest before his sword made half a swing. The other goblins tried to flee when they saw their leader fall but quickly were greeted with sword tips, drawn on by archers. Those that still fled or fought were immediately killed. Those who dropped guard were ordered to fall into ranks with the dwarves.

Both Stepha and Krirtie looked on in disbelief and horror. They had no idea what was going on, and as the dark dwarf turned his attention to them, they feared they were about to be killed. He approached the girls with a look on his face that gave no answers or support. For some reason, he had saved Krirtie and Stepha from the sexual wrath of the goblin force. However, were they saved to simply be killed now? With the tip of Krirtie's sword pointing toward their throats, both felt the end was near.

"Do you understand dwarven tongue?" asked the dark brother to Stepha.

"Yes, I do," she replied in a cracked and broken voice.

The dwarf showed no change of expression but only made a quick motion to his company then turned back to Stepha. In a flat, commanding tone, he said, "Your weapons look to be some we have been searching for. Replace her armor"—he pointed to Krirtie—"and dress any wounds you may have suffered. We are taking you to our leader and will be leaving as soon as you make ready. However, do not delay. Whether we deliver you dead or alive makes little difference to me."

Stepha relayed the message to Krirtie, and soon the two women were on their feet and ready for travel. Most of Krirtie's wounds were superficial, but Stepha's torn wing was serious enough to possibly mean she would never fly again. She made a silent prayer to Shriak as the dwarven leader approached.

"To speak is to die, you make the choice."

The elf looked at Krirtie and placed her finger across her lips and then across her throat. The girl nodded that she understood, and with a gentle shove in the back, the walking began. The dark dwarf leader was in front, followed by two guards, the girls, and then three guards bringing up the rear. The majority of the company remained back to continue their scouting and guard of the surrounding forests.

The dried tears on both their faces shown clearly and spoke of great despair. However, both also knew where they were headed and the leader they were about to be placed before. They both prayed their death would come quickly. Krirtie placed her hands across her stomach and repeated her prayer from earlier as another tear draped across her face.

HAWTHORNE

Schram broke through a final line of trees to look across a seemingly endless embankment of blowing, grassy fields. Since his run-in with the minoks over a week ago, he had only dealt with two obstacles, both of which consisted of small bands of goblins. However, neither group thought twice about stopping a stray troll, and the confrontations—if you could call them that—were nothing more than passing greetings. Ever since the masquerade that allowed Schram's party to sneak past the troll armies around Elvinott, he had repeatedly used his magic abilities to re-obtain the black body form of the troll; and strangely enough, the more times he did it, the easier it was for him, and the less he relied on the powers of the staff.

As he looked across the large glade, however, he knew it was no longer a necessary disguise. With a quick incantation, his shape became somewhat liquid and flexible until he looked exactly how he should—an elven-human warrior. He sighed slightly and then pulled his staff close, beginning to walk to the only objects, which broke the level plain before him. Two large boulders sat near the center of the field, one the crisp white of new fallen snow and the other darker than the blackest night. They appeared strange against the flat horizon, but none who passed could ever find any value in them. So there they remained, completely undisturbed for eternity.

A strong feeling for the presence of magic grew within Schram as he walked across the field toward the rocks. His mind felt a soothing, which in turn delivered a peaceful sensation throughout his body. When he arrived at the boulders, he hesitated only a moment, running his fingers along the base of the white one before taking his place on his knees between them. He drew a deep breath and then began reciting a poem locked deep within his mind. It was in a total of four languages, but when spoken correctly, the sound formed into a beautiful song. As he spoke, the entire area began to melt as if spurred by the wind that now burst across the grasses. The space between the ground and the horizon became out of focus and uncertain, creating a period where time did not seem to exist. Within that period arose a city. Magnificent buildings or structures shot heavenward, but they were nothing that had ever been built. Moreover, they had been created or reformed from that which was already there. Where originally had rested an open prairie now stood a city. Schram had just entered the homeland of the canoks.

Schram was the only human to have ever laid eyes on the city, and though it held no secret beauty as did Elvinott, he considered it partly his home. The buildings, as they are most easily described, were no more than cavernous mountains whose interiors were home to any who would enter. The city, protected by magic, existed as a vision caught in a rift of time, separate and distinct from Troyf. The only way to enter the city was through the rift. The only way through the rift was to have the key. Schram had the key and stood in time with the city, one black and five white canoks staring back at him.

The human rose and moved from between the rocks. He looked across the familiar faces before him but stopped on the black. "Greetings, Werner. I had hoped that I would find you here."

"Greetings to you, Schram. I was not sure if you would head here or to Icly. I am pleased that I guessed correctly, though I have known so for several days as our scouts located you after you left Elvinott."

Schram turned to the others. "And may I bid my best to all of you as well. It has been a long time, and I bring new hope."

The others nodded appropriately, but it was Werner who continued to speak. "Indeed, there have been great shifts in the forces of evil since we parted last in Icly. With these shifts, I assumed it meant you had been successful. Judging by the staff now by your side and the trollish form you carried as you traveled, I see I was right."

He was about to respond when a soft, human voice interrupted from his side. "Yes, the ability to shape-change truly has dragon origins. Your success is well-displayed."

Schram was startled by the voice, but not just by its presence as much as its familiarity. Furthermore, when he turned to greet who owned the voice, the radiance emanating from her beauty nearly dropped Schram to his knees. She walked as a human, but there was no possible way she could be totally of human origin. Her skin was silky white beneath her long, soft light-brown hair. As she walked nearer, her movement made her appear to be floating rather than stepping. Her legs were long and showed the same delicate tones as her face. She wore no armor, having only two small cream-colored cloths covering her chest and waist. Schram stared at her in disbelief, knowing that he was looking at the only creature on Troyf that had a beauty to rival that of Stepha's.

Werner saw the human's surprise and captured gaze and softly said, "Schram of Toopek, may I present to you Hawthorne. She has come here to help us carry out our plans to return the canok's to the proud race of our ancestors."

Schram made no motion that he had heard or understood the canok, and his stare remained locked on the captivating figure approaching. As she drew near, all the canoks saw that she too looked back at the warrior with the same frozen stare. When she arrived to the group, she ignored the others and placed the back of her fingers on Schram's cheek, running it along his face and over to his ear.

She smiled and in a soft tone, added, "I have learned much about you, Schram Starland. Your story is one which will be told for many years to come. I am very pleased that I will be a part of it, as I have always dreamed I would."

Schram was completely taken with her statement but could muster no words to question their meaning while she touched him. His head swirled while feelings surged and unleashed throughout his body. Great power flowed from this woman, which left the human stumbling over his own thoughts. She suddenly seemed to feel the others' eyes and removed her hand while turning to better face them all. Schram immediately felt his mind clear and stared blankly into open space, trying to understand what was happening. The woman's presence was almost hypnotizing, and the essence of something so familiar still seduced Schram's thoughts. The canoks all displayed questioning expressions but none spoke verbally in regard to them. Instead, Werner made a simple motion with his eyes, and all turned and began to follow. The mysterious woman slipped directly beside Schram.

Werner led the group through one of the cave entrances, which opened into a small enclosed chamber. A small fire burned in a pit in the wall, but as there was no smoke billowing into a chimney, Schram knew it was of magic means. There were no chairs or any other objects in the room save for a long cushion placed across a portion of the floor. The white canoks moved over and immediately took seats along one of the walls while Hawthorne knelt by the fire. Schram began to move nearer the woman, but a nudge from Werner made him halt.

"We have issues we must discuss."

This statement caused a stir among the other canoks, and Schram nodded understanding. The two exited the cave and Werner slowly led them toward a small pile of loose debris and rocks. Schram had always been forbidden to go near this area, though it looked harmless and unimportant, and Kirven had never told him why. As they drew nearer, a growing darkness was felt emanating from its source. Although the sun always shined on their wrinkle in time, this area of the canok's homeland was in permanent darkness. Werner suddenly stopped, and the black's eyes became fixed on the target ahead.

"I can go no further. I know your are not sure of your next actions, but put faith in the staff. It, with the hand of evil behind it, caused this horror. It is only that which you have now harnessed that can undo what has been done."

Schram's uncertainty showed on his face, but he knew he must not let it control his actions. He gripped the staff tightly, and with a quick glance down to the canok, he hesitantly proceeded forward. He felt an odd sensation in his foot, and when he glanced down, he saw it beginning to twist and turn into a gnarled formation. He quickly stepped back in surprise and then realized it was another time barrier protecting, or possibly hiding, whatever was inside. He reached his hand outward. It was as if he was pushing through the surface of a lake as it moved past the barrier separating the two periods. He slowly pushed his whole body forward, holding the staff close to his body as it passed.

A whirlwind of colors flashed before his eyes, and Schram felt his body get ripped into this chasm. He felt as if he was moving faster than humanly possible through a maze of winding and violent turns. His body became contorted and deformed and he could feel his senses beginning to fail. The speed he was traveling was unknown and uncontrollable. He felt himself falling into unconsciousness. Suddenly, the staff began to hum throughout his body and his mind focused on the environment. As the sound began to grow, his travel suddenly came crashing to a halt.

Pain erupted through his head while a barrage of magical hands reached for the staff. Schram fought to keep hold, but the magic driving against him was growing too strong. Too many fists reached, tugged, and stabbed, trying to take control over the staff. Suddenly, branches formed from within the staff and entwined into Schram's arms. The staff had grown into an extension of Schram's own being in an attempt to rid the attackers of their prize. With this, the magical hands turned their fight against the warrior himself. Their fists carried more strength than a hundred maneths. Schram erected no magical defenses, but something was causing the punches to land with force but hinder him little. His eyes were still useless against the environmentless space, but he still could sense a passageway in front of him. He clutched the staff to his body and began to drive forward.

The colors began to streak by him as if his walk was really a pace beyond that capable of any creature on Troyf. He traveled for what seemed like hours, but as adept as his senses were, he actually had no feeling for time. He sensed he was in a place where time did not exist, or at least was not measurable. However, he was certain that time was playing a role on what was happening.

He continued walking, confused at the total inconsistencies with everything he knew to be fact. When he held his legs still and only leaned his head forward, the same rush of colors would nearly blind his eyes as they passed with their lightning speed; and when he would look down at his feet, they appeared as tiny specks nearly a mile behind him as if his body had stretched to unimaginable limits. Then, when he would step forward, it appeared that his body was recoiling like a spring to bring back to its original and proper position. Sounds buzzed by his ears, but even his own words were completely unrecognizable.

Suddenly, he clasped his hands around his head, nearly dropping his staff as a screech of immense intensity shattered his eardrums, dropping the human to his knees. Some power within him calmed his mind while he fought to regain his self. He lifted his head into the air to see a window appear through the explosion of colors and a long, outstretched head peered through. Two large eyes sat atop an oblong disc, with large jagged teeth protruding outward from some type of beak or hard-fleshed mouth. The creature opened wide and emitted a second scream, which this time was high pitched and crystal clear, no longer muffled by the differences in time. Schram still gripped his ears, but there was no protecting from the sound which penetrated his mind, tearing at his nerves like a minok tears at flesh. Schram doubled over, and the creature dove back into its window, causing it to dissolve as it disappeared.

Schram lowered his hands and slowly lifted his head. Again ahead of him was a wall of color, only now it was slightly different. It no longer appeared in the rhythmic motions it had before, possibly due to the intrusion of the creature or some other unknown reason. Whichever did not matter, because Schram now knew what he must do.

The creature had tried to put fear into his mind, crippling him to the point of retreat. However, all it had done was to give him the answer to his quest. Schram had passed into one time shift, and without the staff's protection, he would not have survived. That is why the canoks could not pass. They were strong with magic but this barrier had been erected to directly defend against their attempts. The only way to penetrate this force was with that which created it. If Werner was correct, the staff, under evil guidance, created these traps and barriers. But although Schram experienced their power and force, as long as he possessed staff, they could not be used against him.

Schram rose. With his new understanding he began to speak, attempting with the staff's power to open a window of his own to follow the creature to whatever it was so desperate to protect. However, he stopped after only a few words when he discovered he was deaf.

The monotonous silence bordered on life-threatening to one who had come to rely on his ears as much as any other organ. An overpowering fear and emptiness engulfed him as once again he fell to his knees, only this time he was not certain that he would ever rise. The creature's attack had been precise and well-thought—to destroy that which would be left unprotected but still completely debilitate. Schram had never considered his hearing as a possible choice of attack or he would have protected against it. However, he had underestimated what he faced and now it was too late.

His face grew hard and his mind determined. He did not know how he was to create an incantation such as the one he had planned without speaking, but since he knew every spell originated as just a thought, his belief was that he could. He lifted his body up from where he had collapsed and pointed the staff to where he believed the creature had been, though with every slight moment the environment changed greatly around him. He began reciting his words, but whether any sound emitted was unknown. Suddenly the staff emitted a beam of light, which erupted in the air ahead of him, leaving a tiny black spot where it had appeared to strike the wall of colors. Schram peered at the spot, wondering if what he had tried had actually worked. He took one step forward and the spot more than tripled in size. There was a slight relief planted inside of him when he realized that he had been successful, but it was compounded by the knowledge that he now had the doorway to face what he had come here to face, still having no idea exactly what that might be.

He took two more steps forward, and now that tiny black spot appeared as a large darkened doorway to a place Schram could not fathom. He had worked a spell to follow whatever had previously been there. If he was indeed successful, when he passed through the doorway, he would be at his destination. He circled his staff in front of him, creating a ring of energy around his body, and then he stepped through.

Once again all time shifted and the environment went completely dark. Then suddenly, a bright light filled his eyes. His energy shield acted like a filter to shade his face, and without it, he knew he would now also be blind as well as deaf. He could still hear no sounds, but if the violent swells in the creature's neck and throat were any indication, the walls were shaking with its howls.

He had entered into a small room carved out of solid rock with only two objects in it. Placed on a stone pedestal against the far wall was a black orb with a tiny red light glowing within it, and next to it stood a large brown and heavily scaled body of the same creature as before. It was a creature the likes of which Schram had never seen before. It stood on two legs with taloned feet, but it also had two other limbs, which hung as arms from its body. It had a fat belly, which probably pushed its total weight into the thousands of pounds. Its neck was equal to its tail in length, both incredibly long and well-stocked with heavy armored projections. Schram knew one of its main attacks would be with the violent use of its tail like a sword. One touch with one of its spikes could create a hemorrhage so deep and true that death would be instantaneous.

For a brief moment, the creature calmed and seemed to better inspect the man before him. However, a moment was all Schram was granted before the first attack struck. Magical shells of fire, heat, and wind bombarded Schram, accompanied with the same blinding light as before. The creature moved quickly and followed its magical barrage with a forceful physical attack. Schram held his staff high and let his mind control it faster than his conscious thought would be able to do. The two struck each other with a stubbornness that would rival that of the meanest dwarves. Schram was hit with a blast of energy, which somehow passed unhindered through his defensive barrier. The jolt knocked him back to the ground, sending a piercing pain through his chest. The shield around him still remained, but if the creature had discovered a way though it, Schram knew his time would be limited. He rolled to the side as a second bolt struck the ground behind him. He wheeled to his feet and came up returning the attack with the staff. The creature opened its arms and let the bolt penetrate its chest. Its large eyes turned a beet red while it slowly absorbed the power unleashed upon it. Schram fell back in disbelief. For a moment, he could not even fathom what he was facing until a distant memory curled to the surface of his mind.

His eyes narrowed and he thought deeply to himself. *A bantis? It couldn't be.* Elven for "magic-grabber," a bantis was a mythical creature that was supposedly originally created to be pets of the gods. They eventually turned on their masters and created the first Death of the Ages, a time when all gods ceased to exist as mortals. Never had one ever been seen, and always they were believed to be only a fictitious legend created by some elven storytellers.

Schram now knew different. Who better to guard against that which only magic could free than a creature that would capture any magic used. Slayne had been thorough in his work, more thorough than Schram could have ever dreamed.

The bantis arched back with its newfound strength and put forth another display of incredible power. Once again Schram was beaten down, having to force all of his magical abilities into mounting a defense that might help him survive long enough to escape, whether his mission was successful or not. Moreover, he still was not sure what he was there to do, yet he assumed it must be related to the black, faintly glowing orb that the bantis would not let him near. In fact, this last attack did not seem to be meant to injure, but rather it seemed to be designed to push back and better position the human away from the orb. Now Schram could not even see the orb, much less reach it. Schram held his elven shield, the gift from Stepha before he left Elvinott, up to block those bolts able to pass through his protective barrier. He was at a loss to explain how the creature's magic was penetrating his defenses, but with all his prayers, the elven shield seemed to be efficient where his magic was not.

The creature, no longer satisfied with simply wearing him down, momentarily halted its attack while it fought to develop a way to finish its prey once and for all. Schram saw the porthole he had just passed through to enter the room only a few feet away. During this pause, he knew he must capitalize on the opportunity. He leaped to his feet and made a sudden lunge to the door but then abruptly stopped and turned on the creature. Seconds later an explosion occurred where the door had been, and Schram knew that had he been inside, he would be trapped or dead, or eventually both. Without hesitation, he charged at the creature slapping his shield with as much force as he could muster into the bantis' head. It rocked backward, being caught by surprise, and quickly lost its balance. Schram leaped onto its back, placing the arm holding his shield around its neck, and gripped with all his might. The creature flailed wildly, and just as it appeared it might falter, Schram felt a sharp pain shooting through his back. However, even when his grip fell loose, the creature did not break free. They fell down in a heap, neither making any effort of attack or withdrawal from the other.

Schram reached his hand to his back and could feel a jagged projection from the creature's tail lodged deep within him. Blood was flowing at an alarming rate down the back of his leg, and he was certain that if he could not remove the tail, he would soon pass out from the loss of blood, but to remove it would cause immediate massive loss of blood. The pain was too much for the human magician to bear and he accepted that death was the only option. He thought about Stepha and Kirven, his mom and even his father. He also thought of Hoangis. A tear began to form in his eye as much from the stress he was experiencing, the feelings of failure, and the friends he had lost and those he would not see again. He closed his eyes tight.

In one motion, he gathered up all his remaining strength and pushed at the huge creature, but the tail was wet and slick and would not budge. He studied it as best he could and realized that most of the blood was not his own but was the thick brown blood from the bantis. Schram followed the tail up and saw where another spike had pierced the creature's own throat.

Though the bantis was still alive, it probably would not be for long. Using his staff for leverage, he pried upward at the tail, giving the additional torque needed to break the spines free. The armor projections released from both of them, causing each to give a soft screech of pain as the tail struck the floor. Schram rolled away from the bantis just to be certain the creature would not have one last feat of strength, but when he looked back at its glassy, rolled-back eyes, he became aware that this creature's attacks were over. He felt weak from the loss of blood and collapsed back down on all fours. He slowly reached his hand back to feel the depth of his wound. Blood now flowed freely from his back, but the pain had subsided.

He grabbed some cloth from the lining of his armor and tied it tight across his wound. His only hope was to stop the blood flow long enough to recognize a spell he could draw on to save him.

He gripped his staff between both hands and closed his eyes while his mind began shuffling through various enchantments. Gradually, the remaining pain in his back subsided, and his blood stopped falling onto the ground. In time, no scar would even remain.

Schram leaned back with a long sigh and drew a deep breath of relief. He glanced toward the motionless creature, which looked back at him with mixed terror and mercy as it fought to stay alive. Then, his eyes moved toward the orb. It was a shadow of an object, and Schram could sense the evil magic that created the darkness around it. Still, there was a faint, red light which softly showed through the opaque exterior, which seemed to draw Schram toward it. He gathered his strength and pushed himself forward, a slight fear filling him as he slowly approached the object. As he drew to an area within his reach, great powers struck him back, nearly sending him into the bantis' idle body. He closed his eyes and lifted his staff to face the dark object.

The air around them became ignited when the first bolt struck the orb. A brilliant display of colors and light filled the small room as the faint light from within seemed to burst through the shadowy exterior. Swirls of light encircled every inch of the area as the beams danced about, giving an extensive peace the like of which Schram had never felt before. Several streams of the red-and-blue illuminations began to wrap the human in their brilliance, slowly and gently lifting him into the air. He was amazed at the power and the strength he could feel flowing from their contact. He became aware of nothing else in the room other than his own comfort.

A second group of lights and sensations began to encase the bantis, causing its eyes to return to their natural shade, but its ferocity and hatred was no longer present. It turned its head toward the origin of the lights with an ease as if it had never been injured.

Nodding its head twice and then bowing slightly, it moved to stand beside the now-immense brightness of the light.

Already Schram had his eyes locked closed and was unaware of the bantis' movement due to the bright light and intense power filling the room. However, when the explosion hit, although he could not hear or see it, he still was confident in its existence. The flash penetrated his closed eyes with a painful brightness. The air shook the human as if he was standing on ground that had just ripped open and was trying desperately to swallow him. He was near unconsciousness with his only physical thought being focused on holding onto his staff. Suddenly he felt his body being thrown through the air, and all the fingers of brilliant light which had engulfed him were suddenly stripped away to be replaced with a solemn darkness the level of which he had never before believed could exist.

His body continued through various displacements until he began to realize the sensation of ground beneath his feet. The clutches of magic upon him slowly dissipated, and while the light once again could be sensed through his eyelids, he was released. Schram's body did not react to the freedom well. His muscles gave way to the need to hold his body, and he doubled over onto his knees.

Slowly, he lifted his head and opened his eyes to gaze into the wondering eyes of Werner. He followed the canok's black nose down to his black fur and in a distressing voice said, "I failed."

Then, shock struck him again as he realized he still could not hear. His eyes remained on the canok and he could see that he was speaking, and concern showed on his face. However, there was something else different about him and the entire area, but Schram could not focus well enough to digest it. Now he had to inform his friend all that had happened, including his loss of hearing. He concentrated a bit and tried to put forth a telepathic message. *Werner, my friend. I am sorry I failed you and your nation. I will again try to bring back the canoks' pride and unity, but you must also know that I have been struck with a loss of hearing. The battle I fought was intense, and save for luck, my hearing would not have been all I would have lost.*

Werner smiled softly. *Schram Starland of Toopekian humans, the elves of Elvinott, and the canoks of a home out of time, you did not fail anyone. Look to the sky, my friend, and see what wonder you have returned.*

Schram was startled by the clarity of the canok's telepathy but more so by the words he spoke. The human turned his head to the sky to see what he had not noticed was different about the area. The only sun he had ever gazed upon in the canok homeland was the same in appearance as the one which shined over Toopek. However, now their sun was a magical red color, glowing much more softly, and illuminating the entire area with its reddish brilliance. Schram's amazed gaze was interrupted with another passage from the canok beside him.

You see, you have given us back what was stolen so long ago. Our colors will return in time as each accepts the nation back as a whole. Already blacks and whites from all around Troyf have felt the change, and many have since begun their return. I feel deeply saddened at your losses, but if my suspicion is correct, there is one here who may be able to help you. I wish now to say something you will hear again and again for the rest of your days. Thank you, my friend. What you have given this nation can never be returned.

Again Schram was taken by surprise by the statement and by the embrace from Werner which followed. It was an awkward encounter, as a four-legged creature is not properly designed to fit into a human's arms, but Schram could feel that it was important to Werner. Furthermore, if what he said was true, there would be many more such embraces to come.

Their arms fell limp, and without another word, the two turned and started back toward the cave. Several times whites and blacks alike approached him, bidding thanks and appreciation, which gave the weary human a newfound strength. His mind was essentially bombarded with messages from those around, and only after a message from Werner in return did he find a break. The entire situation was one of the proudest of Schram's life, but nothing could match what he felt when Werner led him to a small cave near the one they originally had gone to. In it he saw a large white female canok who had just given birth to a litter of five pups. The young canoks were being cleaned by their mother when they entered, but it was still obvious beneath their wet fur to see the brilliant color they carried. Each small pup was the color of the light in the black orb, which now rested above their nation. Their eyes, nose, coats and tongue were all a bright, peaceful red.

Schram could not muster a comment, but the white female looked up to him; and although she did not speak, her love and happiness was well communicated. Werner added, *All newborns from this day forward will only feel the peace you have given them. From now on, we will know nothing but one nation beneath our red sun.*

With a slight bow from the mother, Schram and Werner continued on to where they had left the others to what Schram felt was days ago. When they entered the cave, Schram saw the same scene he had left before. The beautiful Hawthorne sat to one side while the small group of white canoks remained huddled together across from her. Werner went over and began speaking to the woman softly in an unrecognizable language while Schram remained staring at the others. They all seemed at peace, and several began to show faint signs of pink and red hues appearing in their fur.

One rose and approached to greet Schram in the same embrace as before. His voice sounded like music in Schram's mind. *We have been instructed not to speak at length, but I wished to extend one notion Werner may not have expressed. The one who first brought you to us, that same one whom you have always felt was your greatest friend, would be very proud of you this day.*

Schram's mind locked on his old friend Kirven, and although canoks did not hold to the beliefs of elves in speaking the names of those who had passed, they still respected all other being's beliefs. Schram nodded in return and closed his eyes as he thought about his old friend. *Yes, he would be proud,* he thought to himself. He reached out and stroked the white canok in return.

A hand on his shoulder broke him from his trance, and he swung up in surprise. The soft eyes of Hawthorne greeted him and quickly calmed his racing mind. She reached her delicate hand to the sides of his face and telepathically said, *I understand you cannot hear. I wish you to relax your mind to me. You have only lost your human hearing, but you have a much deeper sense within you, which only needs to be brought out.*

Schram felt a presence within him, which had a captivating sensation about it. While it was part of him, he knew he was as safe as he would ever be. Somehow he had felt it before but was like from a dream. Suddenly, faint whistles and scratches could be heard until her touch and mind released, and he was again alone.

He watched her mouth move, and although the sound struck his senses fiercely at first, he unconsciously adjusted to where it was correct. "Your hearing range will now surpass anything you have experienced before. Do not be shocked or afraid of it. It is a part of you. I have just pulled from deep within your mind."

He nodded, but it was only due to feeling the need to give some response. He was totally consumed with what he was now experiencing, and although he had heard her words clearly, most of their meaning had been lost in his mind. He experimented with what he was now sensing until Werner added, "Please join us now, my friend. We have much to discuss, beginning with our trip to Cindif."

Slayne's Plan

Schram dug into the meal that had been put before him. It was much more food than he needed, but he knew the conversation could grow long and he was famished. He held his staff close to his side, and frequently he even cradled it across his lap, drawing more strength from it at all times. He kept his eyes on those around him but found he focused on the woman more than any other others. To his surprise and often discomfort, she usually returned his gaze with one of her own.

After the meal, which had been filled with only polite conversation, Werner rose and began speaking. "My friends, we have all felt and witnessed the evil growing across the land for the past 200 years. Each in their own way has fought to defeat that evil. However, it is still among us and becoming more powerful with each passing day. We have now been granted our lives back through the incredible strength of our friend, and with our lives comes our powers to again play a major part in finally bringing to an end the raging terror of one mad dragon."

There was a brief pause while everyone adjusted from the shallow conversations of dinner to the deep and intense words the canok now spoke. Schram was quite taken by Werner's abruptness into the discussion, but he was more surprised with Hawthorne's apparent sadness when he mentioned the dragons. The human rose. "I hear your words now and understand the need for action. However, I am at a loss for what choices we now have. The great Anbari, the master of this staff I now hold, spoke of Slayne's new plan. Now you speak of a trip to Cindif, a place I have never heard of even in ancient elven folklore. I have the feeling that you too

160

know what Slayne and his dragon forces are now planning, and if this is the case, what is it we should do to act against it?"

Werner seemed a slight bit surprised by the interjection and its content, but smiled in response nonetheless. "I was not aware that you did not know of Cindif. This lack of knowledge will also explain why you have not anticipated Slayne's next move to acquire the Rift Amulet."

The human stared on blankly. Hawthorne stood and added, almost in defense of Schram, "Really, Werner, there is no way the boy would have known. He is only just shy of twenty-seven years. Nobody has spoken of the amulet in ten times as many years. Most who even know of it believe it to be nothing more than legend. The times of rift travel have long since died."

"I supposed you are right. Even I did not believe in its existence until you convinced me."

"That may be true," replied her soft, musical voice. "But you were also seeking to find answers to your other suspicions. To those, let me only say that in time you, as well as Schram"—she turned to the human who was totally lost in the conversation's meaning—"will come to understand all."

Werner nodded. "Yes, I suppose we shall." Smiling and joining the beautiful woman in her gaze upon Schram, he added, "I am sorry that I spoke ahead of myself."

"You never have to be sorry to me, my friend, but please do explain further. I need to learn about this amulet and what powers it holds for Slayne."

The canok sat back, stretching to get comfortable, giving the impression that a long speech was forthcoming. His eyes were carrying a soft red tint, but for the most part, his body remained engulfed in shadow. However, it did seem that a giant weight had been removed from his back the moment the sun was returned to the land. Werner was one of the only blacks he had ever spoken to, and most definitely the only one which was a friend. Schram did not know for sure what happened to the minds of those canoks who turned to the dark reign, but he had always assumed some great evil twisted their thoughts to strive for those things that canoks normally would hold unimportant. Schram believed that Werner must have faced a constant battle to be able to hold to his old ideals in the midst of this powerful evil. He was truly a strong canok and one to be trusted.

However, now he looked troubled once again and almost seemed to be struggling for the right words. Hawthorne saw his inability to know exactly where to start, and she broke in, saying, "In actuality, the entire situation revolves around the capture of your friend, the maneth who holds the Anbarian hammer."

"You mean Maldor?" asked Schram, now growing worried as his thoughts trailed to his friend.

Werner now leaned forward. "Yes, the maneth is the key. We have had what essentially were spies planted throughout critical areas in Troyf since the day the evil first struck. We knew that the canoks would not be able to fight as any great force, but we would be able to follow all that was occurring in the hope that someday we might return to strike against those who struck us. With each of Slayne's acts, it seemed fairly clear what he was planning. However, when we received word that he had gone to such lengths to recover the hammer, we became worried. There was no reason the weapon would be of any use to him other than stealing something that could potentially be used against him. However, of all the weapons of the ring, the hammer is the weakest, and his own power could defend against it with ease. There is no logic to it." Werner's voice trailed off slightly as he contemplated the words he had said.

Schram stood and with an inquisitive tone, added, "Yes, I many times have questioned the risks he has gone to for it as well. His motives were not clear to me but very deliberate. He wants the hammer. Why is another question."

The canok nodded. "So you see, we became extremely worried that we had misjudged Slayne and began to believe his plan may be more complicated than we originally had anticipated. We could not construct any theory on why he wanted the hammer's power, not until Hawthorne visited us that is." He motioned to the beautiful woman who was locked in a stare with Schram, measuring his response. "She reminded us about one thing our minds had long since forgotten—the Rift Amulet. We had only been concerned with the idea that Slayne wanted the hammer to use its power, never thinking it to be a possible bargaining tool. However, as the legend holds, those who guard the amulet will only allow its use in return for the only thing that was ever stolen from their keep—the Anbarian hammer. How the hammer came into their belongings or how it was stolen has long since been lost in memories longer than mine, but if all else which remains with the tale is true, then it can be the only answer for Slayne's actions. He seeks to gain the Rift Amulet."

Schram's eyes fell slightly as gaps in his knowledge was something he was not accustomed to dealing with any longer. Somehow, in his training, he had learned more than he ever thought a mind could hold; where it came from and where it was stored was unknown to him, but it was always there. However, he had no knowledge of the Rift Amulet or the legend Werner spun. Further, how could Hawthorne know so much? Who was she? His pause was too long, and as he raised his eyes to address the comments, he saw Werner's crooked glance and could feel Hawthorne's stare still locked upon him. In a softer voice, very distant from that which was his norm, he asked, "What power does this amulet hold? In all my training, I have not experienced it in any fashion."

Werner frowned slightly, expecting Schram to be able to shed additional knowledge to the group. Hawthorne used it as a cue to interject. "All space has counter space. By this same meaning, all universes have counter universes. In these, anything that is naturally occurring—meaning the trees, the creatures, the land—each has its parallel somewhere else. Comparatively, those things created by the different creatures of each world—the buildings, tools, armor—find their existence only in that world for which they were created. Therefore, no magic weapon has an opposite somewhere else that can be used against it because all weapons are created, with one exception."

Schram gripped the ordinary-looking tree branch he held by his side. "The staff, there is another staff like this one on another world, and the Rift Amulet can be used to find it."

"That is what we believe," added Hawthorne softly.

Schram's face now showed deep concern. "Does the other staff have greater power?"

Werner motioned toward Hawthorne, and she returned a smile as the canok stepped forward to reenter the discussion. "All questions regarding the possible strengths of those on other worlds are unknown. We are not sure if a second staff truly exists or if all creatures even have counters somewhere else. All we have are legends and theories and a large group of minds searching constantly for answers. However, with the latest information we received, we cannot wait for those answers. We must seek to reach those who guard the amulet without delay."

Schram's concern had not faded when he hesitantly asked, "Who guards the amulet?"

Werner nodded. "We must go to Cindif."

Schram knew there was more because although the canok had not answered the question, only renaming a place Schram had never heard of, he also felt something within his new friend—something he had not felt for a long time. He turned and softly added, "Werner, what is this new information that you feel so strongly about? Why does it mean we must move with such expedience?"

His voice was caring and held much pain. "We believe that Slayne has acquired the hammer. We received word that he has left Draag on a course directly northward."

The human rose with a look of terror now plain on his face. "What word do you have of Maldor?"

Werner did not answer but only bowed his head. Hawthorne rose and moved beside the human, placing her soft hand on his shoulder. Her touch was as soothing as before and her voice could have calmed a storm. "The friend you knew in the maneth has most likely passed. He will be well-accepted by his princess."

Schram felt his knees begin to weaken, then a surging strength flowed through him from the woman's touch. He moved back to retake his seat, allowing Hawthorne to move to rest beside him. He did not speak for several minutes but he was aware that the group was waiting for a response. His voice was tainted with his emotions pushing him down, but he pushed through knowing there were no other options. "When do we leave for"—he paused then added—"I do not know of Cindif."

Hawthorne replied, "It is the land across the North Sea. It does not have the size to compare with Troyf, but life flourishes there like none you have ever seen. It is truly a beautiful place with many mysteries and hidden powers. The Rift Amulet is but one of them."

He looked completely bewildered. "Across the North Sea? I never even considered. How will we cross? I have an excellent ship and a somewhat trustworthy but definitely fearless captain who would be more than willing to attempt the journey, but he and the ship are in the Toopekian harbor, if they are not out stealing from some innocent merchant somewhere."

The canok smiled. "Our method of travel has already been arranged."

"Then do we leave immediately?"

Hawthorne looked briefly at Werner then turned to face Schram. With a care much like that of a mother, she said, "We will leave when you are ready. However, we do know that your human half requires more sleep, and after this night, sleep may become a luxury you will not find. Search your inner self to determine what you need. Only you have the answer."

Schram was surprised by the "human-half" reference but quickly looked past it. He looked toward the group and replied, "I am ready as we speak. Sleep is something I have learned to do without, and with the aid of the staff and all the powers around me, it is now easier for me to do so."

"Then we will be off at once," replied Werner, who seemed pleased with the response. He turned and telepathically said something to the other canoks, which sent them hurriedly out the door.

Hawthorne and Schram began to move toward the door when Schram stopped. "I do have one small problem which remains."

"What is it?" asked the woman.

"I have a group of friends at Elvinott who are waiting for my return to begin a journey to attempt to rescue our friend, the maneth. They must be informed about what has happened and where I am now preparing to go. Further, I fear they have already began a journey to Draag in my absence, as I have felt certain things about them. Are there any canoks who can carry the message to them?"

Both Werner and Hawthorne appeared surprised, but it was the canok who replied. "Our teams are already following two groups, a dwarf and rat and an elf and human woman. Both trails disappeared in the Forgotten Forests where even canoks rarely go. There was a rumor that the two females were seen days after their disappearance on the River Draag again, but their trail could not be confirmed. Most canoks have been clearing all the dragon-army-held forests for several weeks due to your approach here. I assumed you knew of your friends' attempts, or I would have spoken to you sooner."

Schram did fall to his knees this time before Hawthorne could reach him, the pain in his eyes evident to all those around. Schram had felt this already, but now it became real. Hawthorne knelt beside him, but the human did not even recognize her presence. All his thoughts were on his friends, especially the elf he loved like no other. He turned toward the canok. His pain had be replaced with an emotion more closely related to anger. "I cannot go with you now. If it is true that my maneth friend has been overcome by the evil he has been facing, then my companions currently trying to save him are walking into a trap. I had a dream during my approach here that this had occurred, and if everything in that vision is true, then those forces at Draag know of my friend's approach. I must see to the needs of those who rely on me."

A concern struck both their faces. Hawthorne's soft voice carried a deepened tone. "You cannot jeopardize all they fight for because of love. You have given them the weapons they need to survive. Furthermore, their presence at Draag will benefit our cause if we can recover the amulet. Slayne will have no choice but to return, and although they are not strong enough to fight him alone, they can defend against and possibly defeat the dragon lords. Without the dragon lords, the magic controlling the unity of the goblin, troll, and dark dwarf forces will be broken. Slayne will see his power collapsing around him. Then together, we can overtake him. The best help you could be to them now is to prevent Slayne from recovering the amulet. If he does find the other staff, they will all be killed upon his return. We must act now."

Schram seemed to be fighting through the logic of her words, but the tense level of the situation made rationality out of his reach. He shook his head. "No, I leave at once for Draag."

Werner moved to speak as Schram walked out the doorway, but Hawthorne's hand silenced him. "I believe another can make the boy see what he knows to be true."

Schram was moving at a quick pace, almost as if he wanted to escape this place before he changed his mind. Suddenly he stopped when heard a voice he had not heard for some time. *Schram, my son, be strong for me now.*

Schram looked around, but the voice had not been physical. "Mother?"

If you believe that to be the case, then let it be said, though I was never a mother to you. However, I love you like no mother could. I offer you now my advice as I helped you when I could in the past. Trust in the strength of your friends as they trust in you. If you go to them now, help them you could but risk all life in the process. You must be free to follow your own will, but please search your mind to make the choices you know to be correct.

Schram remained motionless for several moments before replying telepathically, *The first time I met Slayne, you told me the necessary words for my friends and I to escape to the Dry Sea of Nakton. I remember your voice, but, who are you?*

There was no reply and Schram knew he was now once again alone. He turned and slowly walked back to the cave where Hawthorne and Werner still stood at the entrance. "Come on, we have a long journey ahead of us, and we must not delay our leave any longer."

Schram walked off without any further explanation or word. Werner and Hawthorne fell in behind him with the canok telepathically speaking to the woman. *I do not understand all that is occurring, but I suspect, as you have said, that in time all will be told.*

Hawthorne showed no expression but replied, *I hope it will, my friend. I hope it will.*

⚬〜〜〜⚬

Stepha fell to her knees, exhausted from the days' occurrences. The dark dwarf leader approached the two girls but spoke only to the elf. "I have just received word that my leader has long since departed on a mission and will not return for some time."

A worried look grew over her face while she relayed the message to Krirtie, who also had dropped to use the break in the most restful way she could. The dwarf waited for her to finish and then continued, his voice still hard and totally devoid of emotion. "This brings me to the problem of what to do with you. Upon further examination, I am sure your weapons are the ones we seek, so killing you is out of the question, at least not until you are put before my leader." Stepha let out a sigh and quickly recapped again for Krirtie, who also breathed slightly deeper; however, both knew a "but" was probably coming next. "I sent word to the lords and expect they should arrive shortly. We will remain here until then." He paused,

168

and then added in a voice which bordered on sympathetic, "Make yourselves as comfortable as you can, but you will be bound to ensure that you do not get any heroic ideas."

Stepha nodded once again and filled the human woman in on the update. The two girls were tied to each other and to nearby trees, but each binding was not overly tight. Stepha believed these dark dwarves to be high in the dragon army ranks and quite civilized because of it. Furthermore, she knew any escape attempt would be a useless gesture at this stage due to the unknown forests they were in and the high amounts of guards throughout it. She even saw towers in the breaks armed with dwarves ruling out flight as a possible answer even if her damaged wing could handle it. She twisted her hands within the ropes and believed the bindings served more as a symbol to behave rather than to tie down.

The girls sat quietly. Though they were now free to speak, they really had nothing to say. Each went over in her mind what she could have done differently, and both only could come to the realization that their plan had been foolish and not well-thought all the way from the beginning. They had gravely underestimated the now-much-stronger dragon armies than when they had been to Draag previously. Since that time, the armies had become much more organized largely due to the fact that the dragons and dragon lords had effectively taken command. Moreover, besides just the goblins, now both trolls and dark dwarves acted unified with the dragon cause. Stepha wondered if all hope was quickly fading for the old life on Troyf. She let her head fall, and Krirtie heard her saddened plea but could do nothing but sit and experience the same burdens.

Time moved slowly as they waited in the forest somewhere near Draag. It was pushing on sunset when two figures approached, causing a stir through the glade. Both girls had been falling in and out of sleep, but now they were awake and anxious about what was occurring. The two newcomers remained a good distance away from where the girls were being held, but Stepha, still with her acute elven sight, was able to see them clearly. Her expression told all as she waited for their approach.

"Well, Stephanatilantilis and Krirtie Wayward, we meet one more time. You know, your reoccurring persistence at causing me problems is becoming quite an annoyance."

"Greetings, King Starland," began Stepha, "but trust that I use the title loosely."

The dragon lord smiled. "Ah, yes, Stepha, charming to the end. Tell me, do you recognize my counterpart?" He raised Krirtie's sword, which he now held and pointed at the second figure, the same human appearance save for a long coiled reptilian tail appearing from his lower back.

They looked, and though the face appeared strikingly familiar, with all the subtle changes that had occurred with his transformation, she could not be sure. Krirtie, however, recognized the individual immediately. "He is William Meyer, once highly respected council member of Toopek and friend to my father."

William smiled. "Yes, Krirtie, I am pleased you remember. Also, let me extend my disgust at your brutal murder of Derik. Your father was always my friend."

The statement was directed to strike Krirtie a blow, but when she killed her father in the mountain elf village, she knew she was giving him what he most wanted. She had freed him from the dragons, and nothing said today would change that. "He is not your friend now. In fact, I suspect he sits with your son overlooking every horrible act you perform and feels nothing but hatred and, to use your word, disgust for what he sees."

"My son?" William's eyes took on an immediate look of surprise and then became fierce once again. "What lies do you now speak?"

Both girls were caught off guard by the response, but not as much as Keith Starland, the other dragon lord. The once King of Toopek frowned and firmly interjected, "There will be no more talk of the past. The future is what we hold. We have the weapons and the two prizes for our emperor. When he returns, we will crush the rebel forces in one stroke."

The strength and hatred in his words sent shivers down Stepha's spine. She glanced at Krirtie and knew the girl would no longer speak what she knew of William Meyer's son. The elf was not familiar with the situation surrounding him, but at her first opportunity, she aimed to find out. They had little to bargain with, but whatever Krirtie had struck on had cut the dragon lord deeply. It was not much, but it was something. Stepha did not feel this was the proper time to pursue the idea, but she was not one to be led into things she did not understand. She tried to pry into the dragon lord's plans. "You talk with large words and threats, but I can see your fear. You know Schram is still out there becoming stronger every day. You will never crush him."

Starland had begun to walk away but quickly turned and faced the elf. Liquid beads of water and lava-like drool fell between his lips, striking the ground with sizzling heat. Both girls watched the display in horror before the dragon lord opened into a deep laugh. "You are but a child in a world of men. Do you not see what your foolish endeavor has done? You have given Schram to us. How can he resist not to come rescue the two women he loves more than any others? You are nothing more than bait for another fool."

Stepha's head dropped while both dragon men continued their taunting laughter as they walked back in the direction they had come. Stepha took notice, however, when Starland stopped laughing abruptly and peered into the trees. He turned back to the girls and added, "Yes, Schram indeed will come." He then started another bellowing laugh before both dragon lords disappeared.

Stepha did not want to believe what he had said, but she knew it was the truth. This whole journey had been a mistake, and now it may have not only cost them their weapons and lives but ended the one chance they had at victory. They had sentenced Schram to be trapped as well.

Her large green eyes were red from the recent tears when the dark dwarf leader returned and untied them without a word spoken. His mood was pleasant, and the elf assumed he was to be well-rewarded for his work. To the elf he said, "We are to lead you through the caverns. When we arrive, you must swallow these." He handed two strange herbs to each woman. "They will cause you to sleep. There are many secrets to Draag you cannot be allowed to see. If you refuse, you will be forcibly dealt with until they are swallowed. Do you understand?"

Stepha nodded, and as they walked at sword tip behind the leader, she replayed the information to the stoic ears of Krirtie. The two dragon lords were no longer in sight, and since nothing had been said to them about remaining quiet, probably due to the leader's good cheer about his forthcoming wealth, the elf decided to seize the opportunity. She whispered, "Who is William Meyer and what is the situation surrounding his son?"

Krirtie glanced at the guards at her back and, seeing no notion from them at the start of conversation, she returned, also in a soft tone, "He is who I said he was, a high council member of Toopek. His son was someone I knew as a child. He was athletic, strong, and well-liked throughout the city. However, when the war started, he watched his father get taken by the globe, just as I did. I then escaped with Schram the following day whereas he stayed behind. When we returned to Toopek, I learned that his son, Billy, had been killed in the town square by a large black dragon. Following that, all the citizens who remained were stuffed into a deep storm shelter until the maneths and elves who fought to regain Toopek freed them. I believe the black dragon was Slayne, and by William's reaction, I do not think he knew his son was dead."

Stepha drew a brief aura of disappointment in the mention of his name, which Krirtie immediately nodded apologetically for. The elf then drew a soft smile and leaned closer to the human woman. "I think you are right, but what use this could be to us, I do not know."

⟨≋⟩

The roaring rapids of the River Draag could be heard thundering above them. Eb-Brown led the way through the long tunnel, followed by Jermys and Fehr and then Dol-Teo bringing up the rear. Brown had instructed the others to remain silent because they never could be sure if any goblin armies would be near the tunnel exit. It was well-hidden, and due to the ferocious nature of the river at this area, the surrounding forest was not heavily patrolled. However, they had in the past run into a few isolated goblin parties, so caution was always observed.

Eb-Brown poked his head through some brush and motioned back for the others to do the same. After a brief moment of inspecting the area, all pulled back into the tunnel to talk.

Brown spoke first, to both of them but mainly facing Jermys. "You two are on your own now. You should not run into too much, if any, resistance approaching from this side, but you never know. Since you are but two individuals, you should hope that you do not. You are well south of the caverns and need to head only northward to come upon a rear entrance. Several trails are well marked, but I would stay off the paths if I were you. There will be a large force waiting at the other entrance of this tunnel if you require a retreat, but we would prefer that you do not give away this route unless your life depends on it. We will also have forces scattered throughout the Forgotten Forests, so if you can make it back across the river, there you will find allies. Last of all, good luck, and may Claudos travel with you.

The two shook hands, and the thought came to Jermys that it was probably the first time a dark dwarf and a mining dwarf had acted as such to each other. Besides the handshake and the leadership through the forest and tunnel, the reference to the dwarven god of travel showed the mining dwarf how similar the two really were. Jermys used the clasped hand to pull Brown forward and engulfed the dark brother in a tight hug. "Thank you for everything, cousin. I will not forget it."

After a similar exchange with Dol-Teo, Jermys motioned to Fehr that they should be off. The rat looked to the two dark dwarves and said, "I don't suppose you want to lay one of those hugs on me, do ya?"

They shook their heads but all could see a small smile curl under their beards. Dol-Teo looked back at both the rat and dwarf. "One thing at a time, rat. One thing at a time."

Fehr nodded, leaned forward, and whispered something to Teo and then, with a quick shuffle, skirted out through the brush.

Jermys smiled at the two and replied, "May Claudos travel with you, my friends." With that, he was off following Fehr's path.

Eb-Brown smiled, and after slapping Teo on the back with a chuckle, the two headed back to their camp.

Jermys caught the rat in moments. "What did you say to him?

"I told that no-good dark dwarf that if I make it out of this alive, I'll bet him two pouches of tobac he can never get my tail again."

Jermys laughed. "*Never* is an awfully long time to a dwarf."

The rat frowned. "It is an understood word."

"Yes, I know, my friend. But your understanding of time may be different." The rat shrugged as Jermys changed his tone. He looked around a bit and then added, "It will be morning soon. Let's get some sleep while we're in this relatively safe part of the forest."

Fehr nodded, and after they searched to find a thick patch of overgrown shrubs and trees to act as additional cover, the two sat down to rest. Fehr was to take first watch, but when he had relaxed for a short spell, he found himself fighting to keep his eyes open. Soon, his breaths became long and deep, displaying the rhythmic sounds of a bandicoot deep into an adventurous dream.

A distant voice broke across the wind, causing Jermys to rise and draw his hatchet in the same motion. He head was groggy, and since it was still before dawn, little could be seen. He surveyed every direction but could not see anything out of the ordinary.

Then, he heard and eyed the sleeping rat. With a look of disgust and a few choice words, he turned his head away, frowning ear to ear, and took his position on watch.

The pre-morning air was soothing to the dwarf, and he let the feeling seduce his small frame. The tumbling waves of the rapids could still be heard through the gentle breeze, but from the distance they had taken from it, the sounds gave only a peaceful notion to the area. He stretched his arms out and replaced his ax before retaking his seat.

"Jermys," echoed a soft, faint voice through the air.

The dwarf leaped back to his feet, his face showing a ghostly white fear. He looked back to Fehr, who still remained motionless. The dwarf spun around, searching through the blackness for that which called his name.

"Jermys, are you there?" came the voice again, this time louder and clearer.

The dwarf was reaching a new level of anxiety. Twice now he had heard the voice, a soft female tone carried like music, but there was nobody around to issue it. Sweat began to bead down his face, and then he saw something. It was not anything clear or solid, but simply a discrepancy in the forest. It appeared as if a tiny cloud had fallen from the sky to rest among the trees. The dwarf stared at the space but was helpless even to approach it.

The haze around it began to swirl and change, and suddenly it took the shape of an elf. Then, with another breath from the wind, it swirled to form a beautiful human female. Long light-brown hair danced across soft delicately white skin. However, the shape was only present a moment and even then was partially transparent. "Jermys, I bring a gift from a friend." Then she vanished.

"You stupid ale-bellied river slug, it is your turn to take watch."

Jermys opened his eyes to greet the agitated stare of his counterpart. Sweat still beaded down his cheeks, and he quickly wiped it away as he swung his head over to where he had seen the cloud, or at least had thought he had seen the cloud. However, now only trees stood in their place. He turned back to the grimacing smirk of the rat. "You were asleep as well, troll bait."

Fehr looked stung. "I resent that. I may have dozed for a moment, but no one can sleep long with all your tossing, snoring, and rustling. You make more noise asleep than when you are awake."

His face went flat, and the tips of his ears started to turn red from anger. "Fine, I will take watch now. I doubt I could sleep more anyway."

"Fine," replied Fehr. "Try to stay awake this time."

Quickly he was back to his makeshift bed and in only moments was once again fast asleep. Jermys rose to his feet and paced around their camp area. He was not one to dream, especially a dream such as that. He did not like what had occurred, nor did he find any comfort in this forest that he originally had thought to be relatively safe. The sooner they would be on their way, the better. He looked toward the trees again and, feeling concern, grabbed for his hatchet. However, he nearly dropped it when he felt the lump now present in the helve. He lifted it up to reveal a small, diamond-shaped stone now cast into the wooden handle. The rock appeared to be nothing more than an ordinary piece of granite cut to form a three-dimensional diamond, but it had been placed in the wood as if done by the greatest elven carver. He stared at it, completely lost in what it meant, but certain it was not dark forces at work. His hatchet had many hidden qualities, one of which was to protect itself from evil. This stone, however, only caused the ax to take on a new level of peace. Seemingly soothed by the occurrence, Jermys relaxed and even laid his head down a moment to sleep.

CINDIF

S chram stood beside Hawthorne as they looked across the vast expanse of the North Sea. Werner had moved ahead and entered a discussion with the five white canoks, who had moved to sit along the coast, wearing odd expressions. Schram stared questionably at the group, but then his eyes widened with amazement when he saw the surface begin to ripple and break.

At first it appeared that a huge sunken ship had lost its hold to the sea floor and was fighting to regain life above the surface. However, when the object dove, kicking up the huge tail as it descended, it was obvious that this was no manmade edifice but moreover some forgotten creature from the deep. A tremendous spray erupted from what appeared to be a crack in its head as it surfaced a second time. Schram turned to Hawthorne to see the woman was completely captivated by the sight. However, her face was lacking in the surprise and disbelief that was present on his. Hawthorne was focused on the creature like she was witnessing the return of a long lost friend. She began to take a step forward, and without turning her gaze, softly said, "Is it not truly amazing?"

She had moved several steps before Schram even began to form an answer for her question. He quickly realized no response was expected and took several quick paces to catch the woman's stride. Hawthorne did not even acknowledge his presence and only continued her path to join the canoks. The two met the group, and although Schram had many questions, when he saw the woman's calm demeanor and expression, he relaxed a bit and decided to hold his thoughts for now.

Once again, the smooth, almost glasslike surface of the water began to churn and bubble before the enormous deep-blue back of the sea creature emerged for a second time. Another spray fired upward, like the strongest of geysers, allowing the water to catch the breeze and shower those on shore. All smiled and relished in the cool water except Schram, who was too stunned to take notice. He stared blankly back into the huge, brown eyes of the magnificent beast before him.

Hawthorne noticed his gaze and smiled slightly. She placed her hand on the center of his back and softly whispered, "*Physeter catodon.*"

His jaw dropped and he turned down to her. "A physeter?"

A thundering voice burst through his head, cutting him off. The language was common tongue, but its intensity was unmeasured. He was not sure if he would be able to understand all the words, as his natural instincts worked to protect him against the incredible volume. "Who dares call me in this way?"

Werner moved forward. "I do, my old friend."

"You speak with language and mind of a race I have always known to be good. However, when I look upon you now, I only see shades of the creatures I once knew."

"I am Werner, canok and friend to all on Troyf and beyond. The nation you knew so long ago has faced the most powerful and dark evil, and only now has our divided family been able to counter and attack this evil that inflicted us."

"I recognize your heart, canok known as Werner, and I will welcome any relations you would have forthcoming. I am Khaled, leader of the lost colony of physeters"

Werner bowed. "I am pleased to meet you, and I too share your enthusiasm for our long lost relations."

Khaled's eyes narrowed. "Do not misinterpret my statements, one called Werner. My nation has dealt awful blows by those who live on land. Millions of my family were brutally stripped from these waters." Schram's face grew saddened as he listened, but he did not dare interrupt. "I would welcome the canok again as friends because they have never acted, nor do I believe ever would act, against us. We lost contact many years past by your measure. Only now, as I look upon your hardships, do I begin to understand why."

Again Werner nodded. "I too know of the evil and wrongdoings you have faced. Though we were acted on by different forces, perhaps now when we join, all could be made right."

Khaled dove briefly under the water and then resurfaced, wearing an expression that was completely devoid of pleasure. "I do not know to what you are referring, but if it would carry the chance of returning the physeters to the open sea, I will listen. Those with me for many years have been slowly dying. We have many times wished to strike against those who sentenced us to the life we now lead, but our nature would not allow it. However, as I continually watch those around me suffer, my peacefulness is slowly withered away."

"I feel your pain and have for many years." Werner said sadly and then slightly lifted his tone. "The best description I can give is to introduce those with me."

He began to name the whites who had controlled the calling but was cut off by the creature's powerful speech. "I feel the knowledge of those of your nation with you. Their hearts carry the same harmony as yours, the feelings of a family reunited." Khaled turned to look upon Hawthorne. "And you, fair one. I too know of your race and feel your heart. My trust is with you, as it has been since the beginning. I am pleased to once again feel your presence."

"And I yours," she replied softly. "I believed your race lost forever. Whatever magic has kept you alive beneath the sea is truly an act of good. Hopefully that good is about to envelop the world."

Khaled's eyes showed a brief moment of pleasure before he turned to Schram. His voice became hostile and cold, as if it were reaching out to draw the human into the water for one final war of vengeance. "You cannot hide behind the elven mask, human, I feel all that is in you"—he stopped and looked questionably toward

Hawthorne before continuing—"and it is your people who have nearly destroyed us. For over 200 years you were totally unprovoked when time and time again you slaughtered everything we were. I saw hundreds of those around me brutally murdered, filling our waters with our own blood. Any contact we attempted was greeted with spear tip. Had I the strength and ability to be free of the water for even a moment, I would spit on thee with my last breath."

Again the whale glanced toward Hawthorne, but now the woman only stared at Schram. His head had fallen into an adolescent bow but his eyes remained locked to carry his hidden strength. As Werner started to speak on Schram's behalf, the human rose his hand and cut him off. "One known as Khaled, I am not about to insult you with a bland apology for the horrendous hell humans dealt you. Nothing I say in words could ever make up for what has happened. However, I want you to be sure, as I am now king of the human city of Toopek, no further harm will ever come to you and those with you by human hands. As of this day, by my word as Schram, man and elf, the physeters are free to return to the seas. Upon my return all shall be made law and strictly enforced. I realize this is little payment for all that has happened, but hopefully it is a new beginning. Perhaps in time we shall learn to act with one another as friends. I only hope that today you look into my elven half and find the trust you value so dearly. Feel my heart, oh great one, for I feel yours."

Hawthorne smiled while all the canoks turned from the human to Khaled, Werner giving a pleading nod as he did so. The creature spent several minutes doing nothing but staring at the young man and then Hawthorne. Schram was intrigued by the attention the woman was getting, especially since he believed she too had to be at least part human herself, though her beauty exceeded that of any human woman. Khaled turned back to Schram and replied, "It is not your elven half which has earned it, but know that you do have my trust."

Schram bowed his head. "And know that your nation will soon be home again".

"I pray you are right, one known as Schram." He turned back to Werner. "Now tell me, friend. What is it of which you speak?"

The canok was surprised by the address but showed little sign of it in his voice. "A great evil has engulfed our land over the past 200 years. Its fingers have touched every creature on Troyf, whether in recent direct attacks or repercussions of those from the past. However, we have reached an apex where destruction of that evil is within our grasp. One black dragon, who is called Slayne, is at the heart of the progressive darkness. Schram has put fear in his eyes, and the dragon has fled to Cindif to recover the Rift Amulet. If Slayne is successful and the legend about the amulet is true, then the fate of every creature on Troyf could be in jeopardy. However, we can stop him if we can prevent his acquisition of the amulet, but to do that, we must have passage to Cindif at a pace that only the legendary *Physeter catodon* could achieve."

Khaled turned to survey the group, and then his eyes fell back to Werner. "The canoks have throughout time been our friends, and that action in itself will never be forgotten. If there is a chance that we may aid those who live free of the water's boundaries, then we will not hesitate to do so, for we recognize the symbiotic relationship we have. Should those on land not survive, then we shall eventually reach the same fate. There is no other creature in the sea that can move at the pace at which I will carry you, but if that should be faster than the wings of a dragon, I do not know."

Schram stepped forward. "Whatever we have is yours in return. I, and all who face that which we do, thank you, Khaled."

The creature's tone lightened. "If we are successful in our endeavor and the physeters can return to the sea, as you have implied, then all will be considered whole once again."

"It shall be as I have said. You have my word."

"I believe that to be of worth, one called Schram." Khaled moved to rest parallel to the nearest pier. "Now quickly, climb upon my back, for Cindif is a long journey. And if it is true that the dragon called Slayne has already begun his trek, then to waste further time would be foolish."

Werner bid the other canoks farewell and turned to Schram. "They will send word of our plans to those they judge the information pertinent. Those at Toopek, Elvinott, and most likely Feldschlosschen will be made aware of your journey. However, there have been strange reports coming from Antaag, and the situation must be evaluated there before the dwarves are fully trusted."

"Schram and Hawthorne joined the canok climbing onto Khaled's back, and after finding a safe position near the center and a quick enchantment to secure their seats, Schram looked questionably toward the canok. "What reports from Antaag?"

Werner shook his head. "The information is not authentic. King Kapmann has had frequent disappearances, which have suspicious circumstances surrounding them. There has been much talk of civil war throughout the Antaagian dwarves' mines. Whether it will occur or not and what is at its core are both unknown. However, if Kapmann has indeed turned to aid the dragon armies, specifically the dark dwarves, then it is certain that Antaag is in for some violent times. This would put Feldschlosschen in the no-win position of dividing its forces between defending its mines and trying to settle the disputes at Antaag. A divided nation is one which I understand fully, and to say it simply, they would be exposed."

"In any situation, the door would be wide open for a dragon attack," added Schram. "Perhaps Slayne is in a better position than I had thought."

"Yes," replied Hawthorne sadly. "It seems the times continue to get worse even as we make great strides forward." She stroked Werner's coat, which now showed many red streaks piercing through its blackness. The canok only nodded.

⁂

They broke through the water at an unbelievable pace, traveling what would take a ship three days in the first five hours. Frequently

Khaled would spray through his blowhole, dousing the group, and after repeated soakings, Schram erected a small magical barrier around the group. They seemed pleased with its effects and now found themselves relishing the amazing new environment they had never witnessed the likes of before. Schram used the first few hours drawing maps of the area, including any small island or rock outbreaking he saw. However, as they moved further into what was becoming an expanse many times the size of all the land he had ever traveled, the landmarks were very few and the usefulness of a map was lost in importance when compared to the stars.

Schram became consumed in thought as he stretched out on the back of the huge creature they were using as transport. His eyes stared across the vast expanse in the sky, and for the first time he began to realize how small and insignificant he really was. He folded the charts he had created and placed them into a pouch, resting his head back to fall across the tip of his staff. His long hair acted as a cushion, and while he lay motionless, his mind focused on his friends. Where were they and were they all right? He thought about Fehr and how pleased the rat would be with the maps he had begun to make. Then he thought of the dwarf, what troubles had infected the mines, and how Jermys would be involved. Next he remembered Krirtie. What had been different about her at Elvinott before he left? And Maldor, his fears were immeasurable. However, most of all he thought about the elf he loved. Was she all right? Suddenly, he leaped to his feet and hollered. "Werner!"

The canok, who was only a couple of paces away, nearly jumped from Khaled's back. With a worried gazed fixed on the human, he asked, "What is it, Schram?"

He saw the fear in his eyes and tried to relax to calm them both. Hawthorne had heard also and moved over beside the canok. "I am sorry to alarm you as such, but I have a question only you can answer."

Both Werner and Hawthorne appeared concerned but remained silent as Schram continued. "I have frequently perceived visions or dreams that were too vivid to be natural. Stepha told me that her father used to have similar visions, and she believed them to be messages sent between magic sources. Is this possible?"

The canok's face was long. "I believe it is, but I speak only from theory. Canoks naturally can use telepathy, but the receiver has to be within what would match a normal voice. Great distances are out of our abilities. However, I believe there is someone who might more be able to aid you." Without speaking further, the canok simply turned to the women next to him.

Her beautiful eyes and hair showed clearly even through the darkness of the night. Her concerned expression had changed slightly but still remained somber. She took a step closer to Schram and reached out her hand to place it on his shoulder. He felt power in her touch but still thought of her as some distant relation to human. He felt something strange within her but did not understand it. It was as if he knew something was there, but it was just out of his reach. However, he did sense something out of place with her, and he believed Werner too must feel it. When she spoke, her voice seemed to cause all suspicions to be cast aside, and a soothing song seduced the human magician. "Tell me, Schram, what brings this question now?"

He stared back toward her, taking her hand in his. "I was thinking about my friends, and I know something that will help them with what they have planned."

"What is this you know?" she asked softly.

"It came to me in a dream, or a vision, or something. It was when I was in Anbari's Dominion. I did not, at the time, know what it meant, but as I was lying here searching the stars, I saw it. I know where at Draag the dragons hide." He reached into one of his pouches and pulled out a long-forgotten artifact. "This diamond stone was given to me by Stepha's father in his life pouch. It is the key to Draag and the mirror room. I must send word to them if it is possible."

Hawthorne did not move or change expressions as she eyed the stone. It was almost as if she had been expecting it to be placed before her. Werner, on the other hand, stepped forward, inspecting the seemingly ordinary diamond rock with utmost scrutiny. Khaled went unnoticed through the conversation but rolled his eyes back to also look upon what Schram held so important.

Hawthorne replied, "It is well within your powers to send the message you wish. However, the forests surrounding Draag—if that is truly where they are—are also very powerful, and whether your message will reach its intended destination is another question. You may believe it does, when it really is received by a source with which you do not wish it to be."

"I must try. Tell me what do I do?"

"You already know, for you have attempted it before."

Schram's jaw dropped. "Who are you, Hawthorne?"

The question was completely out of place, but too many unusual inconsistencies had been occurring to allow it to go on unasked any longer. However, Hawthorne continued from her previous statement, leaving it unanswered just the same. "Take your staff, concentrate every fiber of your knowledge about the person through its power, and when you appear before them, say what you will."

He appeared displeased with her avoidance, but he would have time later to pursue the point, and the immediacy of the problem at hand had to take to precedence. He lifted his staff between both his hands, and as he began to concentrate, he could feel a sudden burst of power surging though him but centered on his fingertips. He felt like a child set free with no restrictions or limitations. He set his consciousness on every conception of Stepha he held within his mind. He saw and felt his environment begin to change, although he was certain his eyes were closed. The cool air blowing across the North Sea changed to the warmth of the southern boundaries of Troyf. He began to see shapes and forms giving him the impression of being in a forest. The trees he envisioned were not definite or crisp but held enough form to place himself somewhere near Draag. They were a darker variety, with twisted and contorted branches, which often appeared to be reaching out to grab those who passed.

Then the picture became blurry, and he began to move, though on Khaled's back he remained motionless to those watching. He was gripping his staff so tight that his knuckles began to crack and bleed. As he floated through the trees, a path began to show beneath him. He concentrated on the path, and almost magically various sounds and shapes began to appear.

Schram looked in horror as two dragon lords, one being his father, sat above Krirtie and Stepha, who appeared well but were bound together to a tree. They were speaking angrily to each other and a slew of dark dwarves looked on, possibly expecting the argument to end in the girl's immediate death. However, as the two lords turned away laughing, it was apparent both girls would be left unharmed, at least for the moment. Schram could use the current commotion to relay his message.

He remembered what Hawthorne had instructed him to do and he drew slightly closer to the girls and began to speak. As the first sound began to form, he felt a sharp pain in his sides and looked down to see the ghostly, almost transparent talons of a large dragon gripped tightly around him. The creature shrieked loud enough to shake the ground, but nobody in the area reacted except Keith Starland, Schram's father and dragon lord. He turned and looked straight toward them and then entered a deep laugh. The next thing Schram knew, he was being pulled through what appeared to be a vast red tube. The dragon was no longer present but its grip was, and Schram was helpless to break free.

He felt himself falling prey to the power which now held him. Pain shot through his wrists as new talons reached and fought to crush his hands and arms. However, he gripped his staff even tighter, knowing that to let go would leave him defenseless against what was trying to capture him. Suddenly there was a dragon screech louder than before, and Schram felt the grip around him loosen.

He pulled his staff close and concentrated on the only thought he believed could help him—Hawthorne.

There was a strange blurring sensation, and when he opened his eyes, he was greeted with nothing but darkness. As his elven sight quickly returned, he saw the outline of Werner standing over the motionless body of the woman. He was on his feet and next to them in only a moment more.

"She is fine," answered the canok to Schram's question his eyes must have asked. "Only exhaustion makes her sleep this moment. I am not exactly sure what took place, but near as I can tell, you owe her your life."

"I believe you are correct, but as with you, I do not understand why or how."

"Two problems," broke in Hawthorne's soft and seemingly tired voice, catching both Schram and Werner by surprise. "First, you must try to make contact when she is asleep or awaiting a message. You can alert her in the same way so she will be prepared for it, but if you only begin to speak, it could cause her to collapse from your presence suddenly entering her mind. This would be detrimental to you both. Second, the forest is enchanted to capture any magic sent into it. Probably after they were captured, it was made stronger in that area. Under normal circumstances, you should be able to break free on your own. You did well to hold true to your staff. It was the only thing which brought you back."

"What happened? All of a sudden the dragon released me?"

Hawthorne tried to show a small smile. "I was with you when you went through space. However, the magic that captured you did not know of my presence. I simply, as you would say, attacked from behind undetected with a simple spell. I had no desire to take on the entire force of the magic with you, only enable you an opportunity to break free. I am pleased to see it worked. Had you not attempted to return that instant, you would have been pulled into that environment as your reality"—she paused then added—"and the grip of the dragon could have been fatal to your mind, and thus to you."

"Do you mean he would have been transported to Draag?" asked Werner.

"Though it has never been achieved before, that is exactly what I mean. I cannot say whether you would have survived it or not."

Schram's face displayed grave worry and concern. "Did any of my messages get through?"

"No, the trap was designed to prevent exactly what you were trying to do. It seems that Slayne's plans are thorough."

There was a long pause while all speculated on their various choices. Each knew that their mission to Cindif to prevent Slayne's acquisition of the Rift Amulet must take precedence, but Schram also knew that without the knowledge he had learned from the diamond stone, his friends would never find their way through the Draag Caverns. Even Jermys, whose dwarven heritage should naturally lead him through any maze of twisting tunnels, in his first experience with Draag, had become confused and lost, only to end up where he had begun. The secret is with the diamond stone and the mirror room. "They must be informed," Schram continued his thought at loud.

Again there was a moment of silence until suddenly the human's expression changed. "If it is possible to capture me and transport me through, as the trap was designed to do, is it also therefore possible to transport the stone through?"

Hawthorne's eyes narrowed. "If the power controlling it and that person to receive it were both strong enough, perhaps then it could be done." She paused briefly then added, "Under normal circumstances, maybe, but Draag is not normal. Its magic would have to be accepting of it. You were going to be pulled through because it was designed to pull you through. It would not be designed to pull the stone through. Furthermore, neither Stepha, Krirtie, or Jermys would be blessed by enough magic to receive such a powerful spell."

Again his eyes fell, but only momentarily until he said, "The Hatchet of Claude. It could receive the stone."

An intrigued look grew across the woman's face. "I don't know. It might work, but it might not. Khaled, have you any knowledge regarding such a procedure?"

The whale-like creature twisted his head slightly, letting his large grey eyes fall back toward the group. His deep voice seemed powerful enough to further disrupt the sea but still landed gently upon their ears. "If the legend regarding the lost hatchet holds truth at its base, then it should prove adequate for such a transfer. However, it will take your combined power to perform it, and possibly that of mine and Werner's, to help guide you back. Further, I would test the area before attempting speech. The elaborate traps could prove too much for all of us if they expect another attempt. They know you were there once, and they now know you had help. It is my guess that Slayne did not anticipate one thing, the one called Hawthorne, to be present. Now that anticipation is present for him."

Hawthorne turned back to Schram. "His words are wise and should be considered as those of one who would know."

Schram nodded. "But then we will try—together."

"Yes, we shall," she replied. Her voice raised slightly. "Khaled, will you require any aid or special contact to join in our endeavor?"

"No," he replied gravely. "Simply instruct the one called Schram to keep his staff against my back. That should be enough to keep us together."

Schram nodded that he understood. Hawthorne added, "We too must stay joined. Your mind and power must get us to them while I remain in both places. However, if there is to be any word spoken, I will be the one to speak them only after I evaluate the enchantment we have entered. If there is any attack upon us, then center your thoughts toward Khaled and Werner and your staff, and they will guide you back. Keep hold on me only if it does not jeopardize your own secured return. Do you understand?"

Again Schram nodded.

"Good," continued Hawthorne as she moved behind him to place both hands in a tight grip around his waist. "Then concentrate every fiber you have on Jermys. If he is asleep when we appear before him, then we will act immediately, as I have discussed. If not, simply follow him watching over his trail. When he sleeps, we will fulfill our plans."

Werner bowed his head in a motion of praise, and Schram closed his eyes while pulling his staff against his body, resting its tip on the immense back of the whale. Each of their eyes became filled with a blank, entranced loneliness before closing tightly.

Schram's environment became cloudy and lost, as it had previously. Rarely could he make out any definite shapes, only seeing strange figures that made no sense, as his mind traveled through space. Gradually, faint light was seen among the clouds. It danced and spun as if it was being tossed like water over hot oil. With one final burst, he appeared to be floating over a roaring river. He surveyed the land on the north side of the rapids but could see no movement. He wanted to ask for what he should do, but as he felt for Hawthorne's hand, he realized he was alone.

With his mind, he moved from over the water to land at the much more conscious-pleasing position of standing on solid ground. As he stood on the embankment, he began to hear the sounds common to a forest under the controls of darkness. With each moment, the sensations were becoming stronger, almost as if he were being pulled into a deeper reality. Suddenly, he heard some stirring from nearby brush, and he about collapsed when his friends, the rat and dwarf, bounded out from a hidden tunnel to leap essentially right through his body. They were joking lightly and seemed to have no idea regarding Schram's presence.

Without delay, the two made their way into some thick brush and began to prepare a makeshift camp to catch some brief rest. It was when Jermys fell asleep that Schram realized he really had no idea what he was supposed to do. *How do you communicate with a hatchet?* he thought as he began to grow nervous and uncomfortable.

Gently, he felt two hands pushing against his sides. He did not need to look back to know Hawthorne was there with him.

Her touch gave him a power and confidence like he had never felt before. Slowly, he approached the sleeping dwarf. Like an angel singing, he heard the wind call out the dwarf's name. "Jermys, Jermys, are you there?"

When the dwarf rose, drawing his hatchet, Schram was struck by the appearance of two dwarves; one who lay sleeping peacefully in the same place as at his first sight, and another who stood hard, staring violently in every direction. However, he was drawn to the more striking oddity adjacent to him—a magnificent dragon with a green body and two large silver wings about twice human size peering back toward the human. It made no motion of attack, only stared with grandeur and excellence. Long moments seemed to pass where nothing was taking place. Schram searched his mind over and over again, and without hesitating further, he removed the diamond-shaped stone he carried and with one motion launched it at the beast before him.

There was a loud scream, and Schram felt two talon-like hands bite into his sides. He tried to turn and face what had grabbed him but did not have the strength to fight the unexpected attack. As his eyes move back toward Hawthorne, they dropped when he saw she was facing the same fate. He cursed himself for letting his guard down but knew their only chance for escape would be the staff and Khaled. He only hoped Hawthorne would be safe with him.

He cleared his mind and focused his power through the staff and Khaled. Immediately, the environment began to melt and reform. Darkness engulfed his mind, and he could feel strong hands trying told hold onto him. He began to be pulled back when with one mighty swipe, like a hand ripping down a sail before a storm, he was back on the North Sea.

He immediately swung his eyes. "Hawthorne!"

"Easy, son, I have her," echoed Khaled's slightly strained voice.

There was a burst of light, as if the air itself had just become charged, and then darkness again engulfed them. Where the energy had been now rested the still body of a woman. Schram ran to her side and placed his arm and staff against her. In moments, her eyes opened to reveal the softness and peace he had always seen carried within them. Her long hair fell against her back and onto that of the whale's as she threw her arms around the young man next to her. "You did well, even better than I would have believed. Your power was so strong." She rubbed one hand along Khaled's back. "Thank you for the guidance, my friend. You were truly my light to see by. I shall not forget."

Khaled's deep voice was filled with pleasure. "No thanks are necessary, for I have longed to be free to use my powers again. If I should die before this morn, what you have given me this night would justify my life. For too long the physeters have lived prisoners in a pocket beneath the sea. From this day on, that will change."

Schram pushed a short bit away from the tight embrace he was sharing but was not ready to completely lose contact either. He kept his hand tightly gripped around hers, letting her magical beauty flow through his body. "Were we successful?" he asked when their eyes fell to each other.

"Were we?" she replied back.

Schram shook his head, not knowing how to reply to her riddle. "Who was the dragon?"

She smiled as if a memory of one deeply loved was just recalled. "When you gave the diamond stone to the young, silver-winged green dragon, it was as if two children, almost brothers, had just realized their identities and began working together. That dragon is known as Cameron, and he is that who is the hatchet."

"The Hatchet of Claude is a dragon?"

Again she smiled. "No, the spirit and magic, which was a dragon, now resides within the hatchet."

Schram still showed disbelief, which was only matched by that of Werner. Both peered blankly back toward Hawthorne, who turned and took Schram's other hand in a tight grip. Rubbing her soft fingers across Schram's Ring of Joining (the ring he and Stepha shares) and the adjacent finger that once wore the Ring of Anbari, she answered, "Just as you are able to call on the powers of Ku carried within the ring, Jermys can call on the powers of Cameron."

Schram's face lightened with a notion of understanding. "Then who is Cameron, and what magic placed his spirit with the hatchet?"

Hawthorne appeared slightly worried but then calmed. "He is one of the sons of Anbari."

Werner's thick red eyebrows lifted while Schram sat frozen. There was pause of unknown but significant length before Schram forced his reply. "Then Anbari has four sons, each who have given their beings to the four weapons of the ring?"

"That is essentially accurate, though more simplistic that I have ever heard it defined."

Schram was somewhat displeased with her answer, wanting to not simply be provided ideas but truly understand the essence of what everything meant. "Please, Hawthorne, explain it to me. I must know more. I must understand."

Hawthorne placed her hand on his cheek and then moved it to his shoulder. "You are so young…" Her words were soft and fell off as she spoke. Then, seeing his expression, she gave a gentle sigh and fell back to rest in a more comfortable position. She began in a gentle voice, "Anbari is a great dragon. Often he has been called by enemy and friend the most powerful creature ever to walk Troyf. However, even with all his abilities, he never wished to rule or control any other creature. It was those around him who had the desires to use him to improve their stature. Ku, Claudos, Slayne, and uncountable others all used Anbari for their own benefits. He was trusting—too trusting—and by the time he realized what was happening, the damage was done. However, he is still wise and very powerful. He used his insight to undo what had been done. The weapons, his sons, even your birth and our trip to Cindif, all were given their initial push from Anbari."

The sun was beginning to break across the horizon and all could see the surprise on the young magician's face. Werner smiled a brief grin as he knew Schram's mind had focused on one statement—

your birth. Hawthorne paused a moment, giving all a chance to digest what they had heard. Schram only sat, staring blankly into space, with his wide green elven/human eyes seemingly locked on nothing but air. The woman was about to continue when Schram broke in. "How do you know all this?"

Her eyes softened. "At a time a long while in the past, a great, powerful, and also much younger silver dragon saved a small girl from a deadly encounter at a time where death was all around. She has remained with him since that day, and with every passing century, has felt nothing but a deeper and deeper love for the one known as Anbari."

There again was a long silence broken unexpectedly by the thundering voice from Khaled. "Anbari is the greatest creature to have ever walked upon Troyf. The physeter carry a heart equal to his own, and if there is ever a time when those in the sea may lend aid to him or those joined with him, then we will be at his call. If not, then I bid thee leave until our paths should cross again, for Cindif is upon us."

His comment snapped Schram and Werner from their trance, but Hawthorne had already risen and moved toward the huge creature's head. She knelt down, and after a moment Khaled closed his eyes and smiled. In a voice so soft it did not appear to be his own, he said, "And I thank you as well, great and most powerful one." He opened his eyes, and after a strange recitation that was foreign even to Schram, a magical bridge formed across the water to reach the shore. It was as Schram's eyes followed its reach that his eyes first caught site of the land before them.

He nearly fell over from the shock of the sight. A huge continent stretched as far as the eyes could see. Thick forests greeted the white sand beaches, and in the distance across the tree line, large purple mountains with white peaks spotted the skies. Schram's face showed only amazement when Werner said, "Il nok fal thalton."

"Aye, friend," replied Schram. "The lost country indeed."

Fehr and Maldor

"Get up, Fehr, you've been asleep all morning. If you had your way, you would enter another hibernation, and I would have to haul your sorry butt all around."

The rat's eyes grew with an appearance of a brain at work. Jermys frowned and added, "Don't even think it, or you will be a doormat in minutes."

Fehr smiled. "Oh, Jermys, you know I don't hibernate anymore. Lately we have had enough excitement to keep even a mining dwarf on his toes"—he paused then added—"but he probably still wouldn't get through his watch without falling asleep."

His laughter grew as he spoke, but when Jermys lifted his hatchet to reveal the diamond-shaped stone lodged in its helve, all noise ceased. "It came to me last night in a dream. I don't think it is evil, or my hatchet would act against it."

"It's not evil," replied the rat as he stared in disbelief. "It's from Schram. I saw it when I was going through his pouches"—he choked then finished—"I mean, when he dropped one of his pouches and I was helping him retrieve it."

"Are you sure it is from Schram?" asked the dwarf, ignoring the follow-up comment.

"Sure I'm sure. If I consider taking something, I always inspect it closely to be certain of its value. In this case, very little value I would guess," he added more to himself as Jermys was totally consumed by the new information.

"That blasted magician, he is always here when we need him." He turned to Fehr, who had begun to lose interest. "Come on. I don't know what it means, but the voice said it was a gift from a friend. Schram must have had a reason to attempt such a feat. I only hope when the time comes, I will know what to do."

Fehr trotted behind the dwarf with an intrigued look growing on his face. "What voice?"

"The voice that gave me the stone," replied Jermys angrily.

"I thought we just determined that Schram gave—" Fehr was silenced with a dwarven hand clasped over his mouth. Jermys lay on the ground next to him trying not to even breathe. The expression on the dwarf's face alone told the rat not to utter a sound. When Fehr blinked that he understood, Jermys removed his hand while both could already hear the voices.

"Run the brush for a raft," hollered a command in the butchered dwarven tongue common to dark brothers. "Lord Starland said there were intruders in the protective barriers. We are to find those responsible and bring them before the lords."

There was an onslaught of acknowledgements, and then the trees erupted with creatures. Most stayed on the paths, but a few more dedicated pushed through the thickest of cover. Jermys and Fehr remained motionless as a troll and dwarf stepped so near as to bend the grass under their feet and have that same grass strike the rat across the face. Fehr took the brunt of the strike without a sound, but when the troll's foot shifted and drove a thorn into his eye, the rat let out a shriek to rival a wounded swine. The troll and dwarf nearly fell over from the shock, which gave Fehr the chance he now deemed necessary. Without a word, he shoved off Jermys, pushing the dwarf deeper into their small brush cavern. Fehr let out another screech as he bounded in front of the troll heading directly toward the thickest cover he could find.

Within moments, the air was laden with arrows all striking in the wake of the rat's little feet. Trolls bounded with their misshapen bodies and swords hacking a furious path through the brush. Hollers were heard from nearly every direction behind Fehr, but their intent was lost in the air. All he was certain of was that he had to get as far from Jermys as he could and hope that the dwarf would not be fool enough to attempt to rescue him. Fehr knew from the beginning he would not be any tremendous help in their plight to free Maldor, but he never dreamed he would cause their capture. *Jermys had to remain free,* he thought, as a arrow struck a tree, grazing his forebrow as it passed.

With that, he veered left and headed for the river. There were fewer voices, and he was certain he could find a place to hide if he could lose the pursuit for even a moment. However, this luxury was one he quickly learned he would not be blessed with when four trolls crashed through some trees immediately at his heels. Fehr ducked through the last thicket quicker than they could manage, but this advantage only left him at the water's edge, trapped between the roughest rapids the river had to offer and perhaps twenty of the dragon army's finest.

Just as the first troll broke through the trees and the first dark dwarf arrow was lifted into flight, Fehr made a silent prayer to the only thing he believed to be god-like—Anbari—and then leaped into the water. He immediately disappeared beneath the surface only to burst through spitting up water several seconds and about a hundred feet later. Again arrows filled the air, including one troll who leaped in after the rat, but as the violent storm of the river roared, both disappeared, presumably never to resurface again.

⌒∞⌒

"That damn rat! If I had half a brain I would have killed him the day we met," Jermys said to himself as he was tearing a path through the thick overgrowth, mumbling as he ran in the opposite direction Fehr had gone. His heart was telling him to turn back and help his friend, but his mind knew better. The only hope Fehr had would be his own natural skills alone. Jermys could do nothing against those numbers and Fehr had given him a chance to escape, though even his chances were low. The entire troll and dwarf force had followed the rat's noisy path toward the river. This left Jermys an opening that he would not have again. However, he was certain they would

197

regroup soon and come to the realization that Fehr was not alone, and soon after, the dwarf's trail would be their focus.

The adrenaline pushed his concerns for his friend from his mind and drove the dwarf forward through some of the most dense ground cover he had ever seen. His priority at hand was to leave as many confusing counter trails as possible to do whatever he could to increase the distance between him and all those trying to locate him. He repeatedly retraced steps and broke branches along different trails to at least make any pursuit stop and question what direction to take. He was no elf, and he longed for Stepha's abilities, but he also took much of what she and Schram had taught him over their past journeys and knew that save him now it could. He knew he was only going to delay the inevitable unless he could construct a different plan. When he heard several shouts and hollers a good distance behind, he instantly slid into a panic state, knowing he was running out of time.

He held up his magical hatchet and stared longingly into the delicate diamond stone now set into its helve. "What would you have me do?" he asked, though there was no one around to answer. Yet, after he said it, the hatchet began to glow, and Jermys's mind calmed and relaxed. It was the most soothing feeling he had ever experienced. Issuing a long sigh, he almost fell to his knees.

Suddenly, his eyes grew wide and a large smile appeared across his lips. Without another moment lost, Jermys turned and ran at a full sprint back toward the pursuit. Their voices were growing louder at a constant rate, and he estimated that they were about 200 feet short of overtaking him. He quickly made several false trails and then examined the nearby trees. Replacing his hatchet and without making the slightest mark on the bark, he jumped up to a low-hanging branch and swung himself up. Within seconds, he was thirty feet off the ground watching the trail below him.

There was too much tree cover to locate the group by sight, but he could hear their shouts. It was then at this brief moment of safety that he realized the appearance of pursuit meant Fehr was dead. A deepened anger grew in his eyes and body, and his muscles became rigid. The appearance of the first troll beneath him caused the dwarf to wipe his eyes and set those emotions aside, for the time. He had to protect himself, or everything he and Fehr had worked for would be for nothing. Right now he was sitting on a large branch above a group of creatures that would as soon slit his throat than drink a pint of ale. The thought made the dwarf thirsty.

A group of ten goblins broke through the brush and joined the dark dwarves and trolls. Immediately the goblins seemed to place themselves as leaders over the entire group, causing the dwarves to draw weapons. After an ensuing exchange of jibes and a brief scuffle, leaving one of each group dead, all seemed to accept a substantiated equality. Jermys rolled his eyes and wondered how this scum even posed a threat, but as he remembered their numbers, he answered his own question.

"You bloody fools," hollered what appeared to be the lead goblin. "Here is his real trail. You have been searching down all his tricks. By the time you get your act together, this dwarf will be to the South Sea."

The thought of the South Sea did not appeal to Jermys, who remained amused at what was taking place below him. Luckily, however, the big goblin had actually found the right trail, so hopefully soon the entire group would be moving on. Assuming all goes as planned, they will trail him to where Jermys turned around and then backtrack a ways before giving up and blaming the others. Most likely that would end in another dispute and more duals to the death. "Maybe if I did this enough, I could make a real dent in their population," he said quietly to himself, smiling at the thought.

With a quiet thump, he landed on the ground and proceeded at a swift pace back to where they had first met the group. However, due to his quick exit, Jermys had lost some of his natural sense of direction. He knew that Fehr had darted out on a path heading upstream to give Jermys the clear shot to the rest of Draag, as they had planned, but now he knew Draag would be heavily guarded and alerted to his presence. Although Dol-Teo had advised avoiding the front face of the caverns because he knew them to be nearly impenetrable, it now appeared to Jermys that surprise at the front would be better than prepared to the rear. Furthermore, he believed Stepha and Krirtie were somewhere in this part of the forest, a comforting thought for the dwarf. He also knew they would not use the rear entrance because they did not know it existed.

Jermys pulled to a violent stop when he heard something out of the ordinary ahead of him—a faint rustling, as if someone was moving with the distinct effort of trying to hide their presence. Jermys drew his hatchet, though in his heart he knew who it was. He stared ahead and watched a large bush begin to slowly sway as if a gentle wind was lightly pushing its branches. However, the air was still, and no breeze was upon him. Slowly, two eyes appeared out of the bush, accompanied by some chanting, which even Jermys did not recognize. Suddenly, out leaped a small goblin, though it was somehow different from the goblins he had seen in the past. This one was unarmed, as far as he could tell, and his language, which he continued after his appearance, was as foreign as any he had heard. Jermys rose his hatchet to throw and realized he could barely move his arm. Just then a fierce pain shot up his leg as an arrow bit through tissue and bone.

Jermys doubled over, striking the ground hard as he was helpless to break his fall. He now recognized the goblin to be a magic user, but what good that knowledge would do him now was unknown. His muscles seemed locked. He was lying, as good as dead, powerless to move or even defend himself against the dark dwarf's laughter pouring across him. Blood was seeping from his wound, but for some reason, the pain was not as intense as he believed it should be. However, by the look in the dark brother's eyes, in a short while there would be little reason to worry about pain. The Hatchet of Claude was humming intensely, but Jermys realized he no longer held it. He cursed in his mind from dropping it. *What would Fehr think now?* he thought, remembering his friend as if he were still with him.

The dark dwarf walked over to where Jermys sat motionless while the goblin became intrigued with the hatchet which rested at his feet. His laughter had subsided slightly as he bent down and forcibly removed the arrow, not concerned in the least with the amount of blood and flesh he brought with it. Jermys winced in pain, but again it was not what it should be. He looked back to his Hatchet and then to the dark brother.

The dark dwarf appeared pleased with his distant cousin's anguish. "I am not the fool the others are, miner. I knew you would double back. You are as predictable as all stupid Feldschlosschen dwarves."

Jermys had begun to retain some mobility, and his disgust showed through his tone. "I can see by looking at the worn spots on the knees of your armor that the pathetic goblin"—the magic user glanced up, supporting a hideous grin—"is the brains behind your actions. You spend all your time kneeling to his authority." He paused then added smugly, "No Feldschlosschen dwarf would ever be servant to a goblin." Jermys filled his dry mouth with saliva and spit across the darkening face of his captor. "Imagine, a dwarf, a servant to a goblin. Yes, you can truly not be called a fool, for that would give you too much intelligence."

The dark dwarf's face was devoid of any emotion except hatred. His eyes formed balls of fire piercing beneath Jermys's skin. After wiping the spit from across his face, he removed his dagger from his side and, drawing a large smile across his face, plunged it into the dwarf's other leg.

This time the pain was profound and concentrated. Jermys tried to consciously calm his mind, but the agony was too intense. He felt his reality begin to melt and blur and knew that in moments, he would be unconscious. The last thing he remembered was a final bellowing laugh from the dark dwarf as he removed the knife and struck the butt across Jermys's face.

"Where are we?" asked Krirtie as she tried to sit up but quickly realized she was firmly tied to the ground.

"I'm not sure," Stepha replied. "Somewhere inside Draag Caverns. The last thing I remember is standing in the rain outside the entrance after taking those awful-tasting herbs."

She shook her head, now also remembering. "Did they carry us or wh—"

"SILENCE!" echoed a dwarven voice through an open doorway. Krirtie did not understand the language, but the message was clear in the tone. "Utter another word and it will be answered with a sword tip!"

The statement was followed by a series of chattering hollers depicting up to a dozen dark dwarves in the room. Both girls remained silent. Stepha signaled with her hand to not speak, knowing Krirtie had not understood the comments, but both girls continued to investigate their surroundings, pointing out various items to each other. The room they were being held in looked identical on the surface to the caverns Stepha had seen before, but there was something different, almost out of place. The walls were of the same jagged rock; however, they were too clean-cut and perfectly shaped. It was as if they were not natural.

Stepha turned her eyes to Krirtie and tried to relay what she was thinking. The look in her face told the elf that she too saw something she did not understand or could not define. Neither Stepha nor Krirtie really knew what had happened to them or even where they were for sure. As near as Stepha could tell, they were not in Draag Caverns, but they were being led to believe they were. Her thoughts were interrupted by footfalls approaching from a separate hallway far on the other side of the room. A dark arched doorway marked the passage, which appeared to be the only entrance or exit other than the adjacent room with the dwarf party inside.

"Greetings, Stephanatilantilis and Krirtie Wayward. I am pleased to see that you made the journey safely."

"You don't know how happy its makes us to please you, Starland, though there is little of that family name left within you now." Krirtie's words were exaggerated and sarcastic, catching both dragon lords and Stepha by surprise.

Dragon Lord Meyer replied, "Those are strong words from a dead girl. Would you not rather plead for your life while you can?" He did not give her time to answer and directed a deep and cold tone at her. "You should not have lied about my son. When you said he was dead, I had a brief period of loss. However, I have been led to understand that his death would have only occurred if he had directly attacked one of those trying to bring a unified peace to the land." He turned to Starland with a smile, then back to the girls, he added, "Further, he is not dead. With magic, I was allowed to see him through Starland's eyes." The once King of Toopek and now most powerful dragon lord smiled a cold, loathsome grin. "He argues even at this moment for the submission of Toopek to the dragon rule. He, much different from you, Krirtie, makes his father proud."

Krirtie's face reddened as each word from Meyer bit through her, but none more than the reference to her father. "You have been brainwashed by your own, Meyer." Her tone was hard and direct. She left no question about it. She paused and remembered what she knew. She had not actually seen his death because she had already fled with Schram and Kirven. However, many had spoken of the brutal unprovoked attack where one boy approached the great, black dragon who had landed in the city. A heartbeat later, the dragon had reduced him to ashes. Krirtie had visited the grave. She knew he was truly dead. The dragon lords had been reduced to using magic against their own. She was outraged and about ready to proclaim fraud when a pain like none she had ever felt before struck her side.

Beams of intense energy were projected from Lord Starland's outstretched hand, striking the helpless girl with an unmeasured brutal force. Stepha screamed as she watched Krirtie's completely secured body wildly convulse against the intense force. Sweat rolled with tears down her cheeks as every vein in her body began to appear through her skin. Blood oozed from several areas where her repeated jolts had allowed the rock floor beneath her to tear at her flesh. With one final burst of energy, all was silent.

Blood slid from her lips, ears, and even her eyes teared with red. Her body lie motionless and to Stepha, it appeared the woman was already dead. She prayed for Krirtie and her baby. Her motionless body coughed slightly, spilling more blood from her lips but giving Stepha a relief she had not felt in a long, long time. Her breathing was inconsistent and broken, but she was alive, at least for now.

Lord Starland stepped toward the girl, striking Stepha with his tail as he moved. The elf flinched a little, but the worry for her friend made the action go nearly unnoticed. He reached where Krirtie lay and leaned over her. "If you speak these lies again, your baby will not be the only thing you lose."

Krirtie was too far beyond consciousness to understand, but Stepha was not as her scream showed. "You knew, you bastard! If it is the last thing I do, I will end your reign of power being the hand at your death."

Starland turned, still wearing his smirk, his eyes depicting his total absence of emotion. "Now, is that how you should speak to your father-in-law?" He ran his finger along her face. "Maybe I should see what Schram has been enjoying all these years."

"Schram spat on you long ago, when he removed you from his family and Toopek, as did I. To him, you are already dead."

"The dragon lord frowned. "Then he will be given a rude awakening when I ride to Toopek to reclaim my city. It is he who is already dead, and I do not speak figuratively. There was a tremor in the barrier around Draag. Only he could have created it, but he was as foolish as always. He painted a trail for me to him. As we speak, that source is being annihilated. Your faith in him is as far-reached as your attempt to save the maneth. Now all of you are mine." He paused, "You will serve me, Stepha. In time you will."

His laughter, combined with that of Meyer's and the party of dark dwarves' who had come to watch, bit Stepha deeper than anything she had experienced before. With one final word before the two lords vanished into the hallway, the ropes binding them magically disappeared. "Take them to the dungeon, Whi-Tead."

The dark dwarf who had captured them in the forest moved out from the group. To Stepha, he said, "Carry the girl. If you cannot, she will be given to the goblins and trolls. My patience has grown thin with you, and I will tolerate nothing more than strict obedience."

She had crawled to her feet but her anger still was clouding her judgment. "What, are you certain enough of your status that you no longer require us? Or is it that you think you can go against the dragon lords without answering to them?"

Whi-Tead wiped the elven blood from the back of his hand before placing a dagger to the fallen elf's throat. "Another word, and your friend is given to the trolls while you watch." With a quick slash of his blade, a large clump of Stepha's hair fell to the ground. He reached down and scooped it up, tying it in a knot around his belt. "I need something to remember you by since never before has anyone ever left the dungeon, alive anyway."

He gave a motion which indicated that if she did not do as he said, his previous threats would hold true. Stepha struggled to her feet and, as gently as she could, lifted the battered woman into her arms. Krirtie's body was completely limp, and she was losing blood at an alarming rate. If she could not stop the bleeding, Stepha knew there would be little chance she would survive; not saying anything for her baby, a subject she found odd that Starland was aware of.

The guards led them through the small adjacent room where a large wooden wheel and a series of pulleys sat at the far side. With a gesture from Whi-Tead, Stepha moved onto a plank, which swayed as she stepped across it. The dark dwarf smiled, allowing a ball of drool to fall between his lips. "Only way in. Only way out."

Stepha said nothing as the other dwarves began to turn the huge wheel. It creaked loudly at first and, as it broke free from its rest, began to turn with surprising ease. The plank rocked back hard, bringing the elf to her knees, nearly dropping Krirtie as she fell. Small jeers and laughter filled their wake as they began to descend.

As they were lowered for what seemed to be an unimaginable distance, Stepha began to hear screams of an intensity beyond any pain and agony thought possible. The voice issuing them was male but sounded as if his vocal cords had been stretched to their limit. It was muffled and rough, but the torture was evident. Three successions took place before they suddenly silenced.

The lift struck ground in a room that had little to no light. Stepha's elven sight helped her but only to locate a doorway, which appeared to have a torch burning in the room beyond it. She glanced back up the rope and knew that the minute she was off it, the lift would immediately be pulled back. Her wings had been injured several times; and although she thought she may be able to fly herself out at some level, she could not do it holding Krirtie's full weight, at least not yet. Despite the issue with stepping off, she knew Krirtie's needs must take precedence and with that, she pushed herself up on her weakened legs and, with the girl still in her arms, began to move away from the lift. As she suspected, it jolted upward, nearly knocking her back over with her first step. She moved to the doorway cautiously, for she could still hear some odd movement occurring inside, the likes of which she could not place. As she slowly peered into the dimly lit room, she nearly dropped the woman at what crossed her eyes.

A small circular room made entirely of rock. Blue blood was scattered across nearly every corner stretching halfway up the wall as if violently sprayed there from some massive explosion. Lying in the center, violently tearing at what essentially was exposed leg bone, was a maneth. When he rolled over in one of the spastic fits Stepha had been hearing on her approach, she saw the outline of one she used to know to be a friend and companion. His free arm swung over, revealing the hand that had transformed around the Hammer of Anbari. The hammer appeared ordinary in every aspect and struck the ground hard as the maneth fought against the illusion.

"MALDOR!" screamed the elf as she laid Krirtie on the rock surface near the entry to the room. The maneth barely appeared to hear, but he did notice enough to look her way. When his eyes met hers, he screamed, his hoarse hollers sounded as if a dead creature had returned to life. He leaped to his feet. How he was standing, Stepha had no idea, but it was apparent that he was only living on pain now. It was also apparent that he had no recollection of her. His hammer swung back and forth in violent slashes, throwing what was left of his body into random stumbles.

Suddenly, he made an unpredictable lunge, which sent him crashing into the elf, sending them both to the ground. Stepha hit and slid on the rock floor, causing a surge of pain through her back. It was then she remembered her wing. With all the occurrences of late, she had forgotten to replace her makeshift bandages on her arrow-damaged wing. When she struck this time, she knew the wing was severely injured.

Maldor swung his hammer as if trying to kill his most hated enemy. However, due to his injuries, confusion, and weakened and panicked state of mind, his strike landed on the rock wall above Stepha's head. She shifted her weight and sent the maneth, who was over twice her size, to the side.

Both jumped back to their feet, their adrenaline allowing them to stand. "Maldor, it is me, Stepha, your old friend. Please hear me." She pleaded as she stared deep into his eyes, and for a moment, she saw the spark she knew from the past. But quickly, it was extinguished, and the terror and hatred once again took precedence. He swung his arm, bringing the attached hammer across as if he was chopping a tree. Slowly he stepped forward, Stepha matching his steps in reverse.

Nothing but fear was etched into his face. His jaw was torn and scratched with enough dried blood left unattended to make his flesh appear to be a sickly blue. Each step exuded enough pain to bring a normal creature to its knees. Yet Maldor pushed onward. What he saw attacking him was not clear. What he had seen over the period of his torture had changed his mind. Now all he saw was pain. Be it strength from the hammer or his own will to live, that power that drove him made Stepha realize that she had no hope of defeating him without killing him, if she could even do that.

She let out a soft scream and sigh as the wind was knocked from her chest as she tripped over a stone. Maldor seemed to thrive on the opportunity, pouncing down to straddle the elf with a speed common to their times together years before. He raised the Anbarian hammer above his head while holding the terrified and exhausted Stepha beneath him. His arm locked upward and Stepha saw cuts and raw flesh across nearly every exposed area of skin. She closed her eyes, knowing the pain he had experienced now controlled his actions. There was nothing she could do.

"Maldor, I forgive you." The elf began to cry through her words. "It is me, Stepha. We came to help you. Krirtie is with me, but she is not well."

The elf opened her eyes as the maneth's broken and cracked and bleeding lips began to tighten, and she knew he was about to strike his final strike. A tear fell from her large eyes and she thought about Schram. The maneth's arm flexed hard, but he simply stared at the woman, frozen, within a moment of taking the elf's life. Sweat appeared on his forebrow beneath his blood-matted mane. His free hand lifted from the elf's throat and moved to touch her face. He fought for several moments but then Stepha saw his mind release, and she knew he was about to give into the pain and strike.

"Stepha, are you here?"

The voice was soft and the words not well spoken, but instantly Maldor turned. The previously unobserved girl was moving slightly, but as he looked at her, Stepha saw a different expression on the big maneth. His eyes held compassion. His love for Krirtie was there, at least for the moment. The fear and terror carried throughout his muscles seemed to have vanished or at least lessened. She thought that if the hammer had not been attached, it would have fallen from his hand. *He recognized Krirtie's voice,* she said to herself.

"Yes, Krirtie, I am here."

"Krirtie?" whispered Maldor's rough voice.

There was a long silence before Stepha added, "Maldor is here, Krirtie. He is with us now."

The girl tried to look up but could not move. "Maldor? Are you truly here?"

The maneth let his arm with the hammer fall to his side and slowly rose, moving over to her. Stepha pushed herself up and went to kneel beside the girl. To Maldor, she said, "Krirtie is not well, and for that matter, neither are you. Do you understand?"

Maldor stared longingly at the elf. "Stepha?"

"Yes, Maldor, we are here," she replied, softly placing her hand on his shoulder. "Now, please lie down, and I will take care of both you and Krirtie."

TREES OF DEATH SAN-DEENE

The group descended onto the magical bridge, Hawthorne and Werner leading the way, followed by Schram. He was the only one who had not had any parting words with Khaled, for what he wished to say he preferred to say for Khaled's ears only to hear.

"Khaled, my new friend. As you know, my companions and I are traveling in unfriendly lands, which put us on a timetable out of our control. I wish you and those like you to be free in the waters, but I fear if you begin making your presence known before I return, greedy sea dogs with distant memories may see your race as a quick profit, as it was in the past. It is my will that you return to the seas peacefully, and although I am more than positive that the ability to crush an attacking human ship is well within your abilities, I sense you would as soon perish rather than bring about death as such, even in defense. Regardless, I cannot allow either situation to occur."

"I understand, one known as Schram. I will wait for your word before I, as you say, make my presence known."

Schram smiled. "No, there is another way. Go alone to the Toopekian waters. If you run into obstacles, do your best to get by them, harming few. Seek out the one called Geoff, a maneth. He has taken over ruling Toopek. He feels as I do and his word is law. As I say it now, soon you will be free again."

"Thank you, young Schram. I will do as you ask, and if all goes well, perhaps my assistance here you will desire."

"That would be very much appreciated, Khaled, though how much help you would be, being confined to the water, is unclear. However, safe passage back sounds appealing."

Khaled laughed, his deep voice carrying over the water. "No, a ride back is not what you may require from me, though I would be pleased if that were all." With a large flap of his tail, the whale turned and disappeared beneath the surface.

Schram glanced down to see that he was hovering above the tossing waves on a bridge that seemed fastened to the air. As he took a step toward the shore, the bridge behind gradually faded. He shook his head, with a smile, and then proceeded to join the others on the white sand beach of Cindif.

"Where to now?" he asked when he greeted the others.

Hawthorne replied, "Did you see the mountains as we approached?" He nodded as she continued. "If we follow the legend, we need to travel between the two largest peeks that rise up from the center of the chain. Beyond them, there should be a crystal pool known as Ice Lake where we will find a path that leads directly to the Realm of Darkness."

"Between the peaks, across the Ice Lake, and down the path to the Realm of Darkness—seems like something from Dora."

"What's Dora?"

"Nothing."

Schram then added, "The Realm of Darkness? Are you saying the guardians of the passage to the afterlife are who control the Rift Amulet?"

"Would it have made a difference if I told you that at the start?"

He shrugged knowing he did not actually answer the question but also knowing it would not have made a difference.

There was a pause before Werner asked, "Do you know how long of a journey it will be?"

She turned to the canok. "Like you, friend, I have never been here before, and we are following only a legend. I would guess two days by foot. I was hoping we might find another answer."

Schram wanted to ask what other answer she might be referring to, but after thinking about it a moment, he decided he would keep quiet. The fact that an enormous *Physeter catodon* from a wrinkle in the past took them an unknown distance overnight was enough to keep his mind occupied for a while. Without another word, Hawthorne gave a motion, and behind Werner's lead, she and Schram followed.

The air flowing off the water was cool and as fresh as any Schram had ever breathed. All too quickly they seemed to run out of clear land, and a thick forest opened its arms to invite them in. He took one look back across the water before descending into the trees, hoping that maybe the peace he felt at that moment may be carried on throughout their journey. However, in what seemed to be only moments, they were trudging through marshy wetlands that sucked their feet to the ground, making each step require added strength. The sun, which had shown brilliantly on the beach, was now absent, totally eclipsed by the tall tree cover. Schram even believed it to be raining due to the constant dew drips that fell from the leaves. The humidity drove beads of sweat down their faces, making Werner's thick red coat turn almost maroon and matted. Hawthorne seemed least affected by the marshy ground, but even she was showing the wear of the hot, heavy air.

They continued for the better part of a day before they decided to rest. Schram knelt down between the other two and spoke the first words since the beach. "It occurred to me a ways back, we have no provisions for food."

Hawthorne leaned forward. "I will not require anything for some time. I can gain enough nourishment from the vegetation until we are in a better area to gain food."

"Catl lac nuf," said Werner. Suddenly a strange haze formed on his back, which twisted the space into an array of colors before ending as a small pack. "I brought some food along to keep us going as well. Once we clear the marsh forest, there will be food available to us."

Schram was shocked by the appearance of the hidden pack but was more glad to have a bite of food. He was intrigued by the magic and wanted to inquire about it but knew this was not the time for such discussions. He also was caught by Werner's knowledge that they would be leaving the marsh area and further, that he knew that where they arrived to would be better and contain an abundance of food. Both thoughts held his mind while he reveled in his first few bites.

The three ate with relatively light conversation, speaking mainly about the legend of the Rift Amulet and how much of it they believed to be true. Basically, Schram learned nothing that he did not already know except about what they would encounter. The marsh forest would gradually become dryer and, at some point, the trees would thin, and they would reach the first mountains. After that, it was basic mountain traveling. They only hoped they would be able to determine the location of the two peeks without going too far into the mountains. Yet, they would cross that bridge when they came to it.

"Come on," said Werner. "We should be on our way."

"Sounds good, my friend," replied the human. I think we will make better time now as the marsh is not as thick and the tree line appears to have better pathways through it."

"I agree," added Hawthorne. "We should travel as best we can and gain any time possible."

The three proceeded forward, and as Hawthorne and Werner entered a conversation in the front, Schram held the rear and simply let his mind concentrate on his journey. He gripped his staff, and it provided some level of comfort that he still did not always understand. As he thought, strange and obscure visions came to his mind. He saw large dragons of every color and size roaming freely across open prairies and mountains, creatures from dwarves to minoks all sharing the same lands to live on, and human villages completely saturated with all forms of life. Then, as quickly as it had started, the vision changed. The land became desolate, almost desert-like. Every race of creatures lived as vagabonds, robbing and vandalizing other races and themselves. Several dragons could be seen soaring above the barren wastelands, but their disunion with the rest of the creatures made them appear foreigners to this world. Then Schram saw one dragon, large, green, and immaculate. She was female and alone. A moment later, she held a young blue in her arms. Suddenly his mind cleared, and all he saw was brilliant white light, which slowly faded into a dense forest.

"Schram, did you hear me?" repeated Werner.

He looked over toward the canok. "No, I am sorry. My mind had wandered."

Werner replied, "I said, 'Hawthorne says that someone is tracking us. She has moved ahead to check for a possible ambush.'"

Schram was instantly alert and ready. "I will slow my pace and see if I can get a glimpse of who is in our wake."

"No, Hawthorne wishes us to stay together. These forests are unknown to all of us, and we should not become too widespread. We will wait here for her return."

Schram was not pleased with the decision but saw the wisdom in it. He moved to stand beside Werner and asked, "Do you ever have visions of the past, or possibly the future? Visions in your mind as clear as if you were standing there as part of them."

"What brings this question, my friend?"

Schram looked down at the canok, surprised again by his response, but quickly realized how out of place his question was. "I am sorry. It is just that lately I have seen things in my mind, things which do not make sense and even contradict themselves at times."

Werner shook his head. "From the little I understand of your life, you have a gift which will take a lifetime to learn. I have always believed that a mind takes things in as soon as it is capable. In your case, I believe it is the opposite. Your mind lets knowledge out as soon as you are capable. Do you understand?"

"Yes, but there is so much in my mind I do not understand."

"Good, because there is very little I understand." He smiled and paused before continuing. "If you have questions about the magic you possess, Hawthorne is the one you should turn to for answers."

"Who is she, Werner?"

He shook his head. "You know as much as I do. To answer that question, it is up to Hawthorne to say." He paused then offered, "She arrived at my homeland only days before you. Her magic, much like yours, is totally protected, or maybe a better word is "hidden," from my understanding. When I look at her, I sense things I have never felt before in a human. My heart tells me two things: First, she is someone to be trusted, and second, her presence will have a tremendous bearing on the outcome of our war against Slayne."

Schram nodded, but all questions left unanswered in his mind showed in a strained expression across his face. Werner rose to his feet. "Do not worry yourself about such matters now, my friend. One thing I am certain of is that in time, you will understand all."

Schram stroked his thick red coat. "Thank you, Werner. Your words remind me of a friend from the past."

The canok smiled and walked to the path Hawthorne had followed. "She is returning."

A moment later, she burst through the trees, carrying a small hooded figure in her arms. She dropped the creature on the ground in the center of the clearing, causing its hood to be knocked off as it landed.

Once again Schram was speechless. As well traveled as he was, he had always believed that there were few things he had not seen. However, from gar to whale, this journey had never ceased to amaze him. Now, once again, a creature the likes of which developed in a nightmare sat motionless in front of him. It had what appeared to be only one eye, but its two long tentacles could have some optical activity. Set deep in its black, hair-covered face were two flat holes, most probably for scent. Its mouth was made up of hundreds of short hair-like projections functioning as tiny arms to pull food in. However, it was the rest of the body which Schram was more captivated by. Its structure was hidden under a robe, but little was left to the imagination. It appeared to be a large ball with approximately twelve thin, sticklike legs protruding from it. There were six on each side, which extended up above its head and then down to the rest on the ground. It also appeared to have incredible rejuvenating abilities, as one of its legs was severed as Hawthorne dropped it, only to be replaced almost immediately. Schram's eyes froze on the creature, making him not able to speak or move as he stared.

Hawthorne asked, "What interest have you in us?"

The creature's tentacles swung to the woman, its one eye pivoting around like it was on a swivel. When Schram took a closer look, he saw it could move its head completely around its body, enabling the creature to see all directions without moving. It stared at Hawthorne, not issuing any verbal words but acting as if it had understood hers.

She tilted her head in return. "I assure you we are not here as enemies. I am Hawthorne, and these are my friends, Werner and Schram. We are traveling to Ice Lake and would like to know the quickest route."

The creature cringed, cowering back. Schram glanced at Werner to see if he knew what was happening, but by his look, he appeared as lost as the human. Further time passed while no words were spoken except for some unspoken ones that seemed to be carried through the creature's actions. Hawthorne was the only one who understood and the only one who provided answers to the creature's questions.

After a short time, there seemed to be a break in the conversation, or whatever it was that Hawthorne and the creature were involved in. She smiled pleasantly and then entered in what appeared to be a strange greeting ritual. She stepped forward, and one by one took the creature's hands—or legs—in hers. Schram and Werner were both quite taken by the intensely passionate exchange but more surprised when Hawthorne parted and motioned to them to do the same.

Werner stepped forward as best as his four legs would allow, and the look across his face and in his eyes left Schram speechless and amazed. When the canok finished, all eyes fell toward the human.

Schram moved forward with as much confidence as he could muster; his arms nearly shaking, however, in anticipation and wonder. As his fingers made contact, his mind was bombarded with a flood of knowledge. However, it was not knowledge of any world of lifetime. It was simply a language. One moment he had no idea what it was, and the next, all was perfectly clear.

"I wish you luck on your journey, Schram of Toopek. I am Kuen, and I am pleased to make your acquaintance."

Schram replied a proper return, though he had no idea how he had done it. The words came as easily as his common tongue. The creature laughed slightly and then scurried off with a truly remarkable quickness. Schram turned to the others. "I do not have a clue what just took place, but I am truly amazed."

Werner added, "Aye, the same can be said for me. Never have I encountered one so adept at opening their mind but transferring only certain information. I felt a new great knowledge nearly within my grasp but just held out of reach; enough for me to know they are greater than I, but not allowing me to see exactly how much."

Hawthorne smiled. "You are correct, Werner. The spydigs do carry a great knowledge, but that is their only saving grace. They trust nobody who does not speak their language, and to know their language, one must be taught it. The only way to be taught is how we just were, through direct contact. However, to touch one who does not wish to be touched or to hold evil intensions to a spydig within your mind means death to most creatures. We were fortunate."

"How were you able to capture it?" Schram asked.

She smiled. "Dragons are impervious to their deadly touch. Anbari prepared me for what to expect should we encounter a colony. If he had not, in less than a mile, we would have entered a thick outcropping of trees, which we never would have exited from."

Both Werner and Schram glanced at each other, with the canok stepping forward. "Did you learn anything else about our quest?

She nodded. "Yes, and it is not all pleasant, beginning with the fact that we must continue as we talk." She turned and headed out of the glade on a course perpendicular to their previous direction. Schram and Werner fell in close behind, still listening to what she was saying. "It seems we are well south of Ice Lake, and traveling through the mountains would add several days to our journey. If we move parallel to the mountain chain for only a short while, then we can follow good trails that will cut between the mountains, leading right to the lake. I did not inform Kuen that our true destination was the Realm of Darkness, and if we should encounter any more creatures as such, I think we should continue on those lines. The realm is not a place the inhabitants here wish disturbed. I believe it would be detrimental to our cause to inform them of this."

Both nodded that they agreed and would oblige, but Werner still appeared concerned. "From what you have said, this is a much easier and shorter passage to take. What then is not pleasant, to use your words from earlier?"

"That is something I cannot answer for certain. Kuen was vague about it, but it was obvious that the topic was extremely sensitive to him. It seems that the area of the forest we are about to enter stretching all the way into the mountains has recently become what Kuen called the Trees of Death. Any creature that enters, never is heard from again. Over one-third of the spydigs have mysteriously vanished somewhere within its boundaries. They believe that a displeased god has brought an evil hand down from the Realm of Darkness and poisoned the land. They no longer even approach the forest, preferring to travel around its borders."

Schram's voice cracked a bit. "How wide is it?"

"According to Kuen, his only word describing its length was vast. The trail of bodies has yet to definitely establish firm borders."

He replied more strongly now. "Am I then to believe we are going to pass through some of it?"

Hawthorne stopped and faced the two. "No, we are going to dissect its heart."

There was a short pause, which everyone felt, until Werner issued, "How long until we enter?"

Hawthorne turned back and continued on her pace as before. "At this rate, I believe we should reach it by nightfall."

Nobody added anything further, but all their minds were thinking the same thing—*what better time to reach something known as Trees of Death than at nightfall?*

∞

The sky thundered, sending sheets of water across all of Draag. The water splashing off his face woke Jermys to greet the barrage of pain he now felt. He did not move as his memory of the past events slowly filtered back into his mind. As near as he could tell, he was somewhere outside the caverns. Rain was falling profusely and, by the looks of the accumulation around him, had been doing so for some time. It was dark so he assumed whoever held him had stopped for the night. His legs were both well dressed, but it did little to hinder the pain he was feeling in them and in his head. He was certain he must have a lump the size of Fehr growing out of his forebrow, but as his hands were tightly bound to a tree, he was helpless to inspect it directly. Finally, he realized all his weapons, but most importantly the Hatchet of Claude, were gone.

A helpless feeling began to grow inside him, reaching its apex as his mind turned to the memory of his friend. *Surely Fehr was captured or killed*, he thought, and to himself he said, "For what? So I could be outsmarted by a fool dark dwarf and spell-weaving goblin. If it is the last thing I do, I will make that damn rat rue the day he ever got captured." He struggled with his bindings but became quickly aware that they were not of natural origin. Most likely some magical restraints, which only Schram might be able to crack. He let out a soft sigh, which drew the attention of a previously unseen dwarven guard.

"Ah, awake at last, miner. I have been waiting for you to stir."

Jermys frowned, "You can take your—" With a punishing thump again from the butt of his dagger, the dark dwarf knocked Jermys unconscious.

An unknown amount of time passed before he woke again. All he was certain of was that it was morning and his head throbbed. He felt worst than if he had drank two barrels of the strongest dwarven ale the night before. As he sat up, more pain shot through his body. Looking around, he saw he was now in a camp of about ten dwarves. The one who slugged him twice was on the far side of a large clearing, discussing something with a dwarf decked out in well-polished black armor bearing a dragon's head on the breastplate. As he gazed across the camp, he realized that all the dwarves, with the exception of the one who captured him, wore the same dragon head insignia on their armor. It was a new symbol, which made Jermys believe the dragon armies were becoming more unified.

He fought against his bindings, which this time did feel to be of real rope as the twine bit into his flesh as he struggled. Despite his grumbling and displeasure, none of the dwarves seemed to give him a second look. Perhaps they were certain he could not escape, or perhaps they knew even if he did, there would be no place for him to go, a fact he was beginning to realize firsthand. Whichever the case, he decided that he would let the dwarves make the next move. He would have to escape sometime regardless. If they took him under guard into Draag, one of his problems would already be solved. Then it would simply be a matter of breaking free. However, if he escaped now, he would still have to find his way into Draag.

Jermys leaned back, proud of his evaluation of the situation. He made a few more grunts and sighs to get the dwarves' attention, but once again they seemed not to care. His eyes fell back on the dwarf who had captured him. The goblin had joined his side and together they were both receiving two large sacks from the dark dwarf leader. With that, they turned to leave. The dwarf took one glance back toward Jermys and, seeing him awake, laughed and made a quick jester with his free hand, which any dwarf, whether miner or dark brother, knew meant only one thing. Jermys cringed and spit in the air, bringing further taunts from the dark dwarf before he disappeared in the trees behind the goblin.

The dark dwarf leader, who had handed the two the sacks, walked over toward Jermys when he noticed him awake. "I am San-Deene. I will have food brought over, as well as new dressings for your injuries. If you are well enough, I would prefer to leave by midday, but we will put your needs first for now."

Jermys gave a suspicious grin, cracking some of his dried blood from his cheek. "You must be a truly sad case to banter me so. If I could spit my last breath on thee, I would."

"Relax, dwarf. Though we are not friends, I hold to the belief that we are kin, no matter how distant. There will be no more beating, at least from this party."

He held his stare. "If you speak the truth, then I thank you. I am Jermys Ironshield of Feldschlosschen."

"Do not misinterpret my words, Jermys Ironshield. If you attempt any escape, you will be dealt with severely. Mark my words well, for you are still a prisoner to Draag, and whether you ever will see Feldschlosschen again is no longer your choice to make."

Jermys nodded that he understood, and San-Deene turned, issuing several orders to nearby dwarves. Moments later, guards returned with food and new cloth for bandages. They cut his bindings and when he reached his arms forward, shifting the weight under his legs, Jermys really experienced pain in its most primal form. Immediately the movement caused a new outburst of bleeding from both legs. He removed the blood-soaked rags that had been in place for an unknown amount of time to reveal two wounds, both pus-filled and green, secreting both blood and moisture. One of the guards turned away, either from the sight or the smell. Regardless, Jermys knew that without a healer's aid, his legs would have to be severed to keep the infection from spreading.

The commotion within the guards brought San-Deene back to the group. He glanced at the wounds only briefly and then back to Jermys, the mining dwarf's eyes showing fear for perhaps the first time in his life.

"I am sorry. I had no idea the wounds were as such. If I had, I would have changed the dressing myself as soon as I arrived."

Jermys said nothing and only looked on in horror. The pain he was feeling no longer occurred in his legs as much as his heart. A dwarf without legs was like a flyer without wings, a part of their life was gone. A dwarf's heritage took him to explore, mine, and live their extended life for every minute. The thought of ending it unable to do so and as a prisoner of the dragons turned his stomach.

San-Deene ordered the guards away and knelt down next to the dwarf who, for over 200 years, had cried only once—in the wake of his brother's death. But now he found himself fighting back the tears. The dark dwarf leaned forward. "I am truly sorry, Jermys, but we have no healers. If you wish to live, we must remove your legs."

Jermys felt his head beginning to spin and let his body fall back to lie flat on the ground. His thoughts went to his friends and his feelings of failure to them. He cringed when he heard the order from Deene. There was some shuffling of dwarves and then he heard two approach.

Deene's voice carried a sympathy he knew he would not have duplicated if the situation was reversed. For all his life, he had hated the DDs, and now in the last week he had seen a whole new side of the race, which his heritage was actually closest to. A deepened shame filled his mind. The dark dwarf said, "If you wish, I will strike your heart rather than your legs?"

Jermys looked up and replied sternly. "No, by approving as such I would be accepting suicide disguised in another's hand. Be that no different to me, and not an option."

"I understand," Deene replied. He handed him a bottle. "This is mathol taken straight off the surface of the ale barrels. It will help the pain."

Jermys took the bottle, but his mind had become focused on his last comment. He began to say something then refrained. Deene saw his discomfort and asked, "What, a mining dwarf that refuses a bit of spirits?"

A light laughter ensued from the surrounding guards but was quickly extinguished with the situation. Jermys, however, could not let the comment go unanswered. He opened the bottle and downed half of it in one gulp, a feat which would make most heave within moments. Jermys bit hard, concentrating on the pain in his legs to help ignore his trembling belly. With a large smile in its wake, he issued a deep and proud belch, bringing a certain nod of approval from the dwarven guard.

He cleared his throat and replied, "I would never insult such a kind host by refusing his drink." Again there was laughter, which even Jermys offered a smile toward.

It was probably the most ironic situation imaginable. A mining dwarf facing death needing to impress a group of dark dwarves holding him prisoner by drinking unsurpassable amounts of pure mathol. However, if serving no other purpose, it gave Jermys the confidence to ask for something he knew would be a futile suggestion. Not even dark dwarves would do it.

"Before removing my legs, will you please return the Hatchet of Claude to me? I will not attempt escape but it has guarded my well-being in the past. I believe it has healing within it."

The laughter stopped abruptly, and the two guards nearby even drew their weapons. San-Deene regarded Jermys with speculation but did not show it as much in his speech. "We have heard rumors of the hatchet's return but know nothing about its location, or being part of your possessions. Do not try to trick us, Jermys Ironshield, for we will only leave you here to die if that is the case."

Jermys was taken by the response, but as the mathol began to take effect, his rose-colored cheeks were all that this expression spoke of. His words, however becoming choppy, did get their point across. "That fool magic goblin kept it from you, aye. Stole it from me and hid it from you. He…"

Jermys continued into a rambling stupor, but San-Deene had heard all he needed to. He relayed orders, sending three of the dwarves out to bring back the dark dwarf who had captured Jermys and kill the goblin spell weaver on sight. He turned back to Jermys, who was still mumbling. "If I find out you do not speak the truth, my honor means I must kill you, but I don't suppose you find that altogether displeasing."

Jermys still comprehended enough to shed his disapproval of the idea. Dwarves, like all creatures who live through centuries, value life above all else. Although losing his legs may end the life his mind wants to live, he would choose that over losing his life in every situation. San-Deene nodded that he understood and left the dwarf to be alone.

The day seemed to crawl by. Jermys sat and could almost watch the condition of his legs deteriorate. It was clear that blood was no longer circulating to his feet, as their normal color had faded to a pale blue and their size had noticeably changed. There was mild talk from the remaining dark dwarves but none mentioned Jermys except by gestures with their eyes. Jermys was no longer bound, though no escape could take place anyway. The lack of binding was simply to allow him to sit as comfortably as possible.

Blood no longer flowed from the wounds. It had been replaced by massive amounts of a green slimy substance with an almost jelly-like consistency. He also felt no pain. In fact, all feelings in his legs had vanished. Jermys made no sounds of agony or pleads for help. He only lay motionless, having nothing left but to try to remain sane.

It was late in the afternoon when San-Deene rose and walked over to the nearly unconscious dwarf. "There has been no word from my guards. If we do not act now, it will be too late."

Jermys made no comment that showing understanding, and only took what was left of the bottle of mathol in one additional swallow.

San-Deene waved two guards over, and as one held the dwarf down at the shoulders, the other removed his ax. Its blade glistened in the evening light; and when he lifted it into the air, Jermys thought he saw a star bounce off its razored edge. That was his last memory before falling unconscious to the most intense pain of his life.

⌒〰〰〰⌒

He was unsure how long he had been out, but when he woke, he saw nearly a half dozen empty mathol bottles and enough blood-soaked rags to change the color of a river. The sun had fallen, and torches provided the only light. He could not feel any pain in his legs but his upper thighs surged in an almost convulsive torture. His eyes teared under the anguish to join the sweat which beaded down his face. Jermys looked up from his demise to greet the stare of San-Deene sitting next to him.

The dark dwarf tried to force a smile. "I am pleased to see you are awake, or even alive for that matter. I have been worried."

Jermys attempted to sit up, but the pain was too intense, and his movement only caused the bleeding to begin again. "Have you been here the entire night?"

I have. We could not stop the bleeding. The cut was clean, but I never realized how much it would still bleed. You lost more blood in the first half of the night than I knew was in your body."

Jermys showed despair, and his voice was weak. "How long?"

"Just through nightfall. It will be dawn shortly."

"Did your scouts return?" He began to ask more, but a fit of coughing bringing blood up from his belly cut his words short.

"No, there has been no word yet. You rest now. We will not leave until I learn if what you claim is true, regardless of what the high command demand of me."

His final statement fell on deaf ears as Jermys had already fallen back unconscious. The dark brother shook his head and to himself added, "you are the toughest miner I have ever seen."

He awoke a second time to a mass of commotion occurring nearby. He was groggy and his vision blurred, but he was certain he saw the goblin spell weaver's body and its dark dwarf accomplice held at sword tip by San-Deene. There was some angry words being shouted back and forth, which were not understood by Jermys, but ended in two dwarves tearing cloaks from the dead goblin. A hush ensued as one of the dwarves removed and lifted the Hatchet of Claude into the air. San-Deene turned his attention from his new prisoner to behold the legendary hatchet. Taking the prize from his guard, a cheer echoed throughout the glade. He issued a final statement to one of the guards who quickly moved over and, with one swing, beheaded the dark dwarf who had originally captured Jermys. He nodded in some deep-held pleasure when he saw the body go limp.

San-Deene held the hatchet high, further enticing those around him to cheer greater than if they had just won a war. He then turned and approached Jermys, his camp falling in a semicircle behind him. "It seems you have spoken the truth, Jermys Ironshield, but to let such a treasure fall back into your possession is not for me to decide. Furthermore, it is too late for your reason for wanting it. I shall let the emperor decide your fate." His voice no longer carried concern for Jermys. Now only the pleasure of his find controlled his thoughts and tones. "We leave at first light tomorrow for Draag."

A slew of cheers followed as the group returned to their camp. By the looks of the sun, it was already past midday. The care for Jermys, which had been present the previous day, now fell victim to an ego-filled leader who saw himself sitting well in the emperor's eyes. One plate of food was tossed to Jermys, but it was mostly scraps, which he had to crawl about the distance of three paces to reach, causing extreme pain and further bleeding. The day moved slowly, which set the stage for a nighttime of eternity. To make matters worse, at nightfall, the dark dwarves bound him back to a tree, although they knew he was not in any condition to escape. However, as the first moon began to shine on the glade, Jermys felt a strange sensation in his wrists.

There was a tearing sound, and then his hands were free. Instantly he wanted to turn around, but the pain was too extensive and a blindfold was placed over his eyes to prevent it anyway. He felt a hand grab his and place an object in it.

Immediately, a warm peace began to seduce and comfort him. The pains throughout his body were replaced with a harmony sung by a magic beyond comparison. Though his eyes were covered, he was certain that his entire aura glowed. The individual who had helped him fell back, completely taken by what was occurring.

A bright light encompassed Jermys's body, becoming brighter as it reached his legs. The light stretched out, forming an outline around the limbs, which were no longer present. The humming grew louder, and the one watching glanced toward the main camp, worried that the dark dwarves may wake. Yet, they slept deeply, slowly allowing their bodies to wear off the ale from the past night's celebration.

Jermys said nothing, only displayed in his face the most intense inner peace that one could extend. Time seemed to completely stop over the next hour until with one strong motion, he leaped to his feet. Softly he whispered, "For whatever reason you have for requiring the blindfold, I will respect your desire to go nameless. Just know that my appreciation is something I will spend the rest of my life trying to repay."

There was no answer to his statement, but he did hear movement. Then, in his free hand, he felt a dagger being placed. The individual grabbed his arm up to where his elbow bent, taking a firm grip, not allowing any movement that he did not want. With a violent thrust, he forced Jermys's arm forward, forcing the dagger into his own belly. Jermys forced his arm back, but he could already feel the warm blood spilling across his hand.

A raspy, contorted voice said, "Now go. When I am found, they will hunt you down, and this time not to capture you but to kill you. I have just witnessed something amazing, and I therefore know I acted correctly."

With that, he heard the individual double over. Jermys's first inclination was to run, but he knew that he could not leave the one who had helped him so greatly alone to face the brutality of San-Deene and his guards when they woke. The dark dwarf leader had become seduced with his own self-interests, and whoever had risked everything to save him would certainly be faced with the most morbid death imaginable.

Jermys reached up and removed his blindfold. Looking down, terror grew in his eyes as he watched the blood spill onto the ground, but he did understand. With a silent thank you and nod, which went unnoticed, he turned to make his escape. Stopping abruptly, he spotted a small pack lying on the ground. He glanced back in disbelief and then scooped up the provisions and disappeared into the trees.

The Next Attack

"This is the darkest forest I have ever set foot in," said Schram after he had bumped into Werner.

Hawthorne added, "It only appears that way. The cloud cover is blocking out the moon, and the trees do not allow any free light to pass."

"Regardless of the reasons, it is dark, and with that, tense. To say it differently, I do not like it."

All found the description unsettling, but as they thought more about what he had said, they realized how accurate it really was. They were now well within the somewhat-obscured borders of the region known as the Trees of Death. Though they had come across nothing threatening since they entered, that fact in itself was a little disturbing. Not finding any animal life of any kind left the forest absent of a degree of nature. Furthermore, Schram had had the distinct feeling that someone or something was watching them, although his senses could not pinpoint how many, or in what direction. He frequently stopped and peered through the trees, but even with his elven sight as an aid, he could see nothing but dense forest cover. Each time issuing a long sigh, he would turn and walk at a quick pace to catch the others who had not bothered to stop.

Hawthorne looked back as he approached. "Do you feel it too, Schram?

"If you are referring to a presence somewhere among the trees, then yes, I feel it too."

"Can you identify it?"

He looked annoyed. "Not only can I not identify it, I cannot be certain of its existence."

"Werner, do you have any idea what..."

"I also feel nothing definite," he replied. "Never have I experienced a sensation such as this."

Schram added, "What do you think, Hawthorne? Is there some foreign dark magic at work here?"

She shook her head, tossing her hair over her shoulders. "I think there is magic at work here, but I am not sure it is foreign or evil. I have felt this before, but I cannot place it."

Schram looked up. "Now that you say that, I have felt it before also. It was..."

"There is a party of five moving to cut us off," interrupted Werner.

"Yes," Hawthorne said. "I feel them too."

"There are at least that many, maybe more. They are moving in behind us." Schram turned and began incanting a spell."

Suddenly his hands became heavy and fell to his side. Just as quickly, magical bindings appeared and quickly fastened his arms behind him. He tried to call out, but a gag appeared and took its place about his head. Telepathically he sent the single word, *Ambush!* As quickly as everything set in, his mind became clouded, and he fell unconscious.

He woke in a small room to the gentle shaking of Hawthorne. She asked his condition, and he answered her with a simple affirmative nod. Slowly pushing himself up, he saw Werner standing to the side, and the two moved over to join him. They kept their voices low but felt more confident speaking outright rather than using telepathy.

Schram had an aching head, the origin of which he was not sure, but he was certain that it was related to where they were. "What happened?" he asked.

"We were made fools of," replied Hawthorne.

Werner then added, "They had been working a spell for some time to capture us. They covered it up but every once in a while making their presence felt so we would concentrate on locating them. By the time we realized what was occurring, it was too late.

Their spell was in place, and any magic we used against it was immediately reverted upon us. If you tried telepathy, which both Hawthorne and I did, you were instantly overtaken, sending your mind into darkness."

"I too tried telepathy," he added despairingly. All I accomplished was acquiring a beating headache." He paused and took a quick look around the small room, which appeared to have no exits. "Now my only questions are, Who are the *they* you were referring to, and what need do they have with us and my staff?"

Hawthorne had not noticed the missing staff but now appeared even more concerned. "We have no idea. The last thing I remember is seeing a robed figure, armed with a bow, drawing down on me, and approaching at a quick pace."

The canok nodded. "I don't even remember that much."

She continued, "I felt for sure we would be killed without question. If the rumors about this forest are correct, we should have been, but for some reason we were spared, possibly something to do with the staff. I should have realized its absence immediately. I will have to rethink our situation."

Each of their faces showed a different level of distress but none quite as much as Schram's. The pain in his head was growing more intense, and as every moment passed, it became more of a chore for him to just remain conscious. Hawthorne noticed his discomfort and moved toward him. Is the pain still there?"

"Yes, don't you feel it?" Sweat had begun beading down his face, and his large green eyes had become dull and faded.

Hawthorne glanced toward Werner. The canok shook his head. She smiled, trying to ease his pain. "Schram, I am going to enter your mind. It should not harm you, but if you feel any added pain, say something, and I will stop."

He nodded that he understood, and Hawthorne placed one hand on the side of his head, taking one of his hands in her other. There was a brief period of silence while she seemed to be fighting against something, causing both her and Schram to jerk in rapid and violent motions. Werner looked on with great concern, but he knew that he was helpless to offer aid. Any interference of two such joined could be detrimental for all involved.

Schram felt two hands caressing his mind, but the pain remained consistent. If anything, it returned stronger. Suddenly, the hands he had felt vanished, and an ear-piercing scream broke him from his trance. For a moment, he saw a huge dragon bearing down on him, then there was nothing, and the pain was gone.

He opened his eyes to see Werner standing over Hawthorne, her body resting motionless on the floor. "What happened? Is she all right?"

Werner looked up. "I do not know. One moment she was in contact with you, and the next she was screaming in agony." There was an odd look in the canok's eyes that made Schram believe he was not hearing the entire story. He began to move toward the two, but suddenly the space between them became obscured. He froze as the air began to take shape forming what Hawthorne had previously described perfectly—a dark, hooded figure.

The only noticeable characteristic on the figure was its two large round eyes, which reflected the slight light in the room like two green moons. The figure glanced at the woman on the floor and then approached Schram. Without a word, it reached an arm out toward the human, and upon first touch, both disappeared.

⁂

Jermys had run throughout the remainder of the night and been greeted with only a light rain as morning broke through the darkness. The woods had been surprisingly and suspiciously free of goblin and dark dwarf forces. He satisfied this absence by assuming that the threat to Draag had become minimal with his capture, and therefore the dragon army forces had been pulled back.

Although his theory may have worked to settle part of his anxieties, he still found little comfort in the fact that he was near the heart of the evil-occupied land and had little idea where he should head. He had spent the last three hours running blindly through the forest on his legs, the existence of which he did not understand. Now, well past dawn, he found himself wandering through dense trees, which gave little aid to determining his whereabouts.

He gripped his hatchet tightly as he walked, making his knuckles turn a bare white. Frequently he found himself swinging outward at low-hanging limbs and branches that blocked the path he was trying to follow, though calling it a path was a bit of a reach.

With one fierce chop just past midday, he found himself entering a small glade that he immediately knew he had been in before, though he was also certain that he had not left by way of the path he entered from now. He looked around the clearing and a chill slid down his spine as he saw burn marks. They most probably were left from his previous visit to this area with his companions during their first confrontation with Slayne, Kirven, and Almok, in which their escape had only occurred by Schram's recitation of words, which had magically been spoken to him. His incantation had called on the ancient powers left in the Ring of Ku, which he had received from the dragon Sabast only hours before. A moment later, they found themselves on the Dry Sea of Nakton to begin a trek back to Toopek, minus Schram who would leave on his own to follow a destiny understood best by only him.

Jermys issued a long sigh as he remembered the desperate situation from nearly two years ago. He wondered if the times had gotten better or worse. The one striking difference for him was constantly present every time he wanted to speak. Then, he had his companions to speak to. Now, he spoke only to himself for he was alone. All his friends, the rat included, had gotten mixed up in situations, which, for all he knew, had already brought their death. The dwarf pushed his lips together tightly, fighting to keep what composure he had left. He was determined to hold to the idea that all his friends were well and more than likely worried about him more than themselves. He was about to move further into the glade when suddenly the sun disappeared.

Jermys dove into the nearest brush, not hesitating to look at the sight he had grown to recognize so well. As quickly as it had vanished, the sun reappeared, and the dragon's shadow moved out across the trees. He stared to the sky to catch the sight of the creature just before his vision was blocked by the edge of the forest. It was a large blue, probably one of the oldest of the young dragons. It was traveling on a direct course toward what Jermys now knew to be the center of Draag Mountains. On its back was a large goblin, dressed in black armor, with some sort of insignia in place across its breastplate. At the speed they were heading away, Jermys was certain they had not noticed him. However, their velocity was obviously depictive of something important, and whether he was able to save Maldor or not, Jermys now had a second reason that he must infiltrate Draag. He had to discover what emergency would send a high-ranking dragon and goblin into such a frenzied flight. He gave a brief glance to be sure the rest of the sky was clear before starting at a soft jog up a path, which he had traveled in the other direction two years before. Despite the dangers involved with traveling through the evil forests around Draag, Jermys found comfort in knowing where he was and the idea that he might have accidentally stumbled on the safest place to enter the caverns, though perhaps also the most difficult.

It took him several hours of hard trudging, but by late afternoon, Jermys broke beyond the tree line and could see several hundred paces further ahead to the strange cutaway depicting the sky window to the mirror room of Draag Caverns. There seemed to be no activity in the area, but due to its openness, he thought it better to approach after sundown. Furthermore, he would need some items from the forest to make what he had planned possible.

He slid back into the tree cover and spent a short time rummaging through the pack, which had been prepared for his escape. He found a dagger, a normal dwarven battle ax, and most importantly, several days' provisions of food. He placed the dagger and ax opposite his hatchet and then broke off some bread and dried meat to eat. After finishing his short meal, he leaped to his feet to fulfill his other requirements.

Well past sundown, Jermys slowly crept up toward the sky window. Behind him he pulled a long vine, but whether it would be long enough to reach the cavern floor, he did not know.

What I would give to have Stepha here to fly me down, he thought to himself. "What I would give to have all my friends here," he now whispered softly. He shook off his emotions, trying to keep focused on what he had ahead of him. He had already made it further than he had expected to and now found himself roughly the distance of one hundred paces from being in the heart of Draag Caverns. However, these one hundred paces were not actual steps but the approximate distance he was above the cavern floor. He cringed as he peered into the dimly lit room below him. As he leaned his small frame further over the opening, a soft hum began to emit from his hatchet, sending a cold chill down the dwarf's back.

Jermys pulled back, immediately startled and confused. However, as soon as he was clear of the opening's face, the hum ceased and the night once again became ominously still. He grabbed his Hatchet and stared at it, taking notice of the peculiar diamond stone lodged into its helve. The hum this time had sounded slightly different, and his curiosity had become intrigued. He climbed back to his feet and peered over the edge, this time holding the hatchet behind him. There was no sound. Slowly he moved it forward until once again it crossed the plane of the opening. As if lighting a fire, it began to hum. Jermys stared at the magical weapon and saw what had previously gone unnoticed. The diamond stone was glowing with an unimaginable shine each time it drew over the sky window. He shook his head, totally clueless to what it meant but hoping that it was not a warning of upcoming evil. However, for where he was about to go, he was not about to believe he would be free of hindrance. He slapped his Hatchet back to his side and, after securing the vine to the support, began to lower himself downward.

The stone sang a constant song as he descended closer to the floor. It seemed to grow louder the lower he went. He was still about thirty to forty feet from the ground and felt that to leave the hanging vine would be a mistake. With a quick word to Claudos, he removed his battle ax and flung it spinning up toward the sky window. It impacted the framework with the blade, cutting through the vine as it struck. Jermys and the remaining piece of vine were sent at a free fall downward, striking the ground with enough force for dust and small rocks to break free from the wall and the giant mirror to vibrate abnormally.

He groggily raised his head to catch his reflection staring back at him. Once again, he was completely taken by the absolute perfection contained in the cut of the glass in the mirror. There was not a mark or scratch across it. If not for the constant hum from his hatchet, he possibly would have stared into it for days. However, when the intensity of the song bit his ears, his attention was quickly drawn to it if for no other reason than to attempt to silence it. Yet, all his efforts were useless. The sound continued, and its glow seemed to give light to the entire room. He knew if this continued, a blind troll would be able to find him.

He began scurrying around trying to carefully roll up the vine but not wasting too much time worrying about it. He had decided he would head down the same passageway he had his first time here, with the idea that he must have simply gotten turned around before. However, as he began to leave, he took one more gaze into the mirror. That was when he saw it.

Jermys's eyes widened, and he slowly stepped closer to the mirror, raising his magical hatchet as he moved. He stared a long time blankly into the reflection but nothing changed. The diamond stone, which was placed in the helve and glowed so brilliantly when he looked directly at it, was totally absent in the reflection. He gingerly reached forward, attempting to touch the absent diamond stone as it was seen in the mirror. However, as he did so, his finger felt only the smooth glass. Immediately upon the touch, however, the song and the glow stopped, and the stone now appeared in the reflection just as it did in the hatchet.

Jermys almost fell over. He spun around the room, but nothing else had changed. Turning back to the mirror, he again studied what he saw. Reaching his hand out as before, Jermys tried to touch the stone as it now appeared in the mirror. Again, immediately upon his touch, the humming began, and its reflection seemed to dissolve from existence.

He stepped back and confidently slapped his hatchet to his side. He threw the coiled vine over one shoulder and, bearing a large grin, moved toward the mirror. He believed he had just found the key that had opened Draag to him, and put his mind to rest as to how he could have gotten lost his last time here—the only time in his life he had ever been wrong in direction. Reaching out, he touched the mirror a third time, and once again the noise from the diamond stone ceased, and it returned to its original dull self. He only paused a moment before turning and heading down the cavern, which every icon of his rationality was telling him led back to the cave entrance. However, he knew it did not, and within a few hundred meters, he had found the proof he needed.

The tunnel he was in no longer appeared to be one carved through the existing rock. Its sides were smooth and made not of rock but some artificially molded stone-like material. He was certain only a powerful magic could have created such a hidden world. With this in mind, he also knew that he was definitely nearing Slayne's base. However, locating the black dragon was not part of his plans. He wanted to first discover what the dragon and goblin had been in such a hurry to report, and then second, locate his friend and escape. His idea to come here alone had steadily become clear to him to have been the most foolish thing he had ever attempted. It had almost cost him his life and had caused Fehr, who had become his closest friend, though he would never tell the rat as much, possibly the same. He let out a slight grumble but sucked it back in when several voices from ahead broke the silence of the halls.

Jermys crept down the corridor, and as he turned around a narrow bend, he saw from where the sounds originated. Two large doors left ajar filled this part of the hall with light. Due to the echoing acoustics, the room appeared to be very expansive. However, Jermys was not ready for what greeted him when he peered inside.

A chamber stretching as far as the eye could see with enough spots to seat several armies filled his eyes. At the front of the hall was probably the largest throne ever constructed. It reached twenty or more meters in length and possibly at least half as many in depth. Its cushions were not of some fine embroidered material. Moreover, they were dull and flat black, giving a truly ominous impression to whoever should look upon it. Between it and the first seats were three figures, two of which Jermys recognized for sure. The goblin he had seen riding the dragon only hours before was speaking with Lord Starland. The lord's hood was pulled down, but his scaly tail shown behind him. Next to Starland stood another dragon lord, whose identity was left well hidden. The only factor that revealed anything about him was the same dragon tail appearing through the back of his cloak.

Jermys could tell they were talking, but he could not be certain of their words. He knew he must move closer, but to do so would be extremely risky. Slowly he began to enter, crawling down the aisle until he could reach the safety of the back row of seats. He continued moving underneath until he was nearly halfway through the room and he could hear Starland's voice clearly.

"Then if the troops are in place, as you have said, it will only be a matter of time."

"They are as I have said, master," the goblin replied.

Starland turned to the other dragon lord and whispered something, which sent him with a nod out of the room. Returning to the goblin, he said, "Prepare those who shall ride the dragon forces. I will assemble all the young dragons, and we will leave at once to join the front. Then, at first light, we will crush Toopek."

The goblin issued some sort of salute before hurrying down the aisle through the back doors, never even pausing as he passed the crouched dwarf. Starland seemed to be drooling in pleasure as a starved tigon would when a thick slice of flesh was placed before it. He turned and knelt beneath the throne. After a short recitation, he stood, formed into a small ball of light, and then vanished.

Jermys sat frozen for several minutes, trembling from the knowledge he had just gained. Then he sat forward, using his strong will to regain his composure. He knew what he must do and that he must act swiftly if he was to be successful. It was too late to help Toopek, and he could only pray that the human city was prepared; but with the dragon forces concentrated in the attack, there would not be any better time to help Maldor.

Jermys took one more look toward the throne and then turned to slip out the back. However, as he moved, one object caught his attention. He stopped and looked back, trying to inspect it further. It was a large, delicately carved wooden box, but its presence itself was what ignited his curiosity. It was out of place with the rest of the room. The longer he stared at it, the more he realized that it had only recently been brought there.

He turned back to the throne and silently crept toward where the box rested. As he drew closer, he began to feel a strange warmth in his leg. He glanced down to see his hatchet beginning to faintly glow. The chest was not even locked, and as he lifted the lid, his eyes grew to wondrous balls. Krirtie's scimitar and Stepha's bow both rested peacefully inside its fitted case. They too seemed to begin to glow as he reached out to take them. Without hesitating, he placed the sword, which was nearly as long as he was tall, through a notch he had in his back armor. He tossed the bow over his shoulder and then, closing the chest, swiftly and silently darted from the room. Two things immediately struck him: First, he had no idea where to go, and second, what happened to Krirtie and Stepha that they no longer carried their weapons? Both thoughts seduced his mind only moments as he realized that as he stood loaded down with weapons in the cavern hall, he stuck out like a rat at a dark dwarf dinner.

"And that's a dinner I don't want to attend for a variety of reasons," he said to himself as he began to move forward in the only direction his gut told him to go.

Characters

Schram: King of the Human city of Toopek.

Stepha: Princess of the Flyer Elves

Krirtie: Human warrior. Friend to Schram.

Kirven: White Canok with black diamond spot. Friend to Schram.

Jermys: Twin Dwarf leader

Slayne: Black Dragon behind the evil attacks.

Fehr: Bandicoot rat. Friend of all the companions.

Madeiris: King of the Elves of Elvinott

Geoff: Leader of the Maneth.

Maldor: Head of the Batt Line of the Maneth. Was captured by Slayne.

Alan Grove: Human officer overseeing leadership of Toopek.

Anbari: Greatest dragon ever to live. Resides in the black pool of the South Sea.

Almok: Black Canok with white patch on forehead. Travels with Slayne.

The

DRAGON
UNKNOWN
PART II

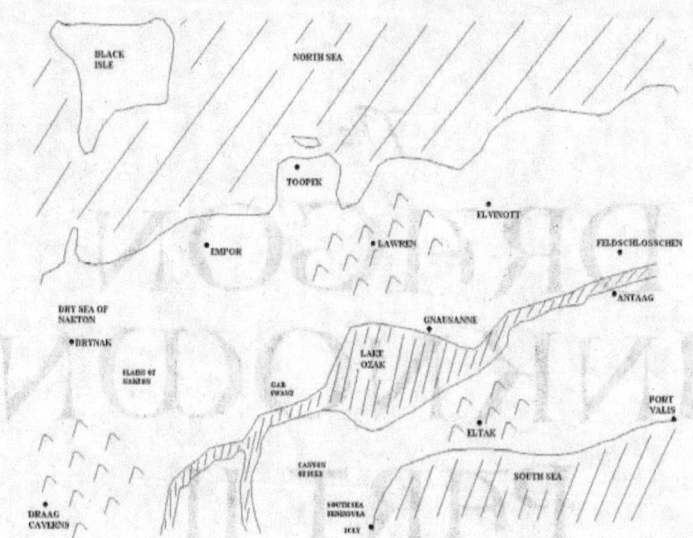

Map of Troyf

Prologue

The companions' trek had continued through many hardships. More importantly however, they had become divided in their efforts, and with that division, their chances of success seemed to be fading. Schram's goal to reunite the canoks appeared to have been successful, but its impact to the onslaught of the dragon oppression was still not known. Slayne's actions had shown no changes since the canok's reunion and with that, perhaps Schram had misjudged its importance in the process.

Schram had clearly instructed his friends to wait for his return before heading to try to save their friend, Maldor. However, he was not aware that Krirtie carried Maldor's baby. He did not realize that her draw to save the one she loved would overrule any direction he set forth. Furthermore, Stepha, whose stubborn but confident nature drove so many of her actions, did not take much convincing to join Krirtie on her journey to save Maldor. Madeiris' only direction to his sister was a requirement to join with Jermys in Feldschlosschen before heading to Draag. Only together did he believe they had an opportunity for success.

However, when Stepha and Krirtie reached the dwarf's village, they learned Jermys and Fehr had already opted to head to Draag on their own. The human and elf's only option was to try to meet with the two before they got to close to the Draag forests which all knew were very dangerous to pass. Through a variety of complications, they did not meet, and with that, each party continued on their rescue mission on their own.

During these treks, Jermys learned that King Kapmann of Antaag had built a rebel force of dark dwarves that were loyal to protecting Troyf against the dragon rule. This union was secret because to reveal it, could mean the total destruction of the dwarven city of Antaag.

Stepha and Krirtie met with many hardships. At the hands of goblins and dark dwarves they faced nearly every attack imaginable. They did reach Maldor, but as prisoners awaiting their fate at the hands of the Dragon Lords and Slayne in the caverns of Draag.

Schram joined with his friend Werner, the black canok who had helped him so long ago in Icly. The only black canok he ever trusted. With them was a new mysterious woman. She had no past and appeared as if planned, but her knowledge of the time was great. Her power with magic was great, and her union with Anbari was revealed. Although many mysteries surrounded Hawthorne, the trust she seemed to gain with very little support left both Schram and Werner with many questions. This trio set on a new trek to try to prevent Slayne from obtaining the legendary Rift Amulet. This amulet was said to provide passage to a world where each living thing had its opposite. The goal they believed Slayne held was to go to this world and recover the Staff of Anbari's twin. This staff would carry the same power as Schram's staff and with it, defeating the human magician would be well within Slayne's power. On this trek, Schram was introduced to a new creature on Troyf, the physeter. Khaled proved, much like Hawthorne, to have many mysteries about him as well as many powers. His potential impact later is believed to be great.

Although Krirtie and Stepha met with obvious very serious consequences in their attempt to save Maldor, their fate was not as desolate as that of Jermys and Fehr. The bandicoot is lost and believed to be dead or captured. Jermys lost his legs only to be saved by the powers of the Hatchet of Claude provided to him by an unknown individual who in turn, allowed him to escape. Jermys received a magical gift from Schram and only recently believed he understood the reason for its presence. With the two warrior women trying to save Maldor and bring him back to their reality, and Jermys now roaming alone the magical caverns of Draag, each of their next actions can lead to their escape and the saving of their friend or a serious strike against their attempts to stop Slayne and the Dragon Oppression with their capture and death.

Schram too has been captured. He was taken by some entity in their trek in Cindif to recover the Rift Amulet. Krirtie is seriously injured. Stepha has lost her flight and is imprisoned in Draag. Maldor is near mad with the torture he has faced, and Jermys, though well, has lost his closest friend and now wanders Draag searching by feel and gut rather than knowing where his steps should take him.

Most importantly however and known to only Jermys is the impending all-out offensive being organized by Slayne and the dragon armies against Toopek. Jermys overheard that the forces are in place and in very short order, all dragon forces will be descending on Toopek in an attempt to destroy the largest human city and with it, Schram's base for any offensive of his own.

Can Maldor, Krirtie, and Stepha be saved by one single dwarf carrying a magic hatchet? Can Schram, Hawthorne, and Werner get free from their captures and obtain the Rift Amulet? Has Geoff built a defense for Toopek that will withstand a full dragon army assault, something two hundred years earlier he did not do in his mancth homeland? These questions and others must be answered as the story unfolds with the Hidden Magic.

LOST CITY REVISITED
MALDOR

"Who are you?" Schram demanded.

"Silence unless spoken to!" The hooded figure responded in common tongue, though the tone and inflection clearly showed it was not its native language.

Schram stared at the figure, but due to the tone in its voice, he decided to remain quiet. It simply paced back and forth, never taking its eyes—the only part of the face Schram could make out—off the stout magician. Schram could not fathom what was taking place, but for some reason he and his friends had not yet been killed. All he could be sure of was that he was now in a small room with apparently one exit other than the doorway that brought him there, and that he no longer was in possession of the one thing he knew would be at the heart of defeating Slayne—the Staff of Anbari.

His thoughts were interrupted when the hooded figure moved to greet two more hooded figures who entered through the door. After a brief talk, they all moved over to do what could be called "inspecting." They stared completely over every inch of Schram, spending extra time on all those qualities which made him appear elven.

Finally, one of the newcomers asked flatly, "Who are you?"

He turned to the figure who stood slightly below his own height. "I am Schram Starland of Toopek, a city in a land a great distance from here that has fallen to face the evil of the time. Who are—"

He was cut off by the angry stomping of the same figure. "Don't compound your situation with lies, fool boy. I know of Toopek and Prince Schram, and you are neither. It is a human city two days' travel from here. Now, speak the truth or die."

Schram was intrigued by the comment, and his one raised eyebrow told as much. He moved to sit down, hoping the others would do the same. The three looked suspiciously at each other and then two of them sat down as well, while the third remained at the door with a strange bow, the likes of which Schram had never seen, at the ready. Schram smiled and then began. "You obviously do not believe what I speak, though it is the truth. However, let it be known that what you say is also completely impossible. I will do my best to tell you how I, born a human, came to appear as I do now because I believe you to be free of the evil trying to envelop the land. I hope that you will see the same feelings within me and show me the same courtesy." Swapped looks, but they said nothing. Schram let out a sigh and then continued, "Toopek was attacked by forces unknown at the time. I escaped, and with the help of friends, I acquired the Ring of Ku." The group became restless and the one standing knocked an arrow in place. Schram paused and felt he better finish his story in a hurry or he may not finish it at all. He went through the entire sequence of events leaving out specifics but hitting the key points. He continued all the way to where they entered Eltak, the abandoned mountain elf city where they found Anbari's diary, which told of the ring's true origin. At this point, he saw the fingers on the bow tighten, and he thought his life was about to end.

"Stop!" said the one who had spoken previously. "Leave us, for I must be sure."

Schram was surprised by the outburst but no more surprised than by what happened next, after the other two cloaked figures had left. The remaining one turned toward Schram and continued speaking. However, his voice was no longer in disguised common tongue but now came distinct and clear in perfect elven. "If you speak the truth, Schram Starland, then I ask you to tell me my name." The figure raised his arms and removed his hood, revealing deep, green-tinted elven skin and two large elven ears.

Schram was completely at a loss. He could not even begin to understand what was taking place nor could he muster a sound to describe his confusion. He stared motionless at the elf, his jaw resting closer to the ground than to his face. He issued a deep breath to calm himself, and in a soft, distant voice, he said, "King Cowhanis, you live."

The elf also showed surprise, not actually expecting Schram to answer. There was a long silence as they both stared in disbelief. Then, Cowhanis said, "Come, Schram, I will hear the rest of your story. You have earned as much."

⁂

Hawthorne pushed herself up. "Where is Schram?"

Werner stepped back. "I do not know, but you should worry more about your own condition."

She stretched her arms and neck, causing her hair to be tossed from side to side. She looked back at the canok, ignoring his comment. "How long have I been out?"

"I would say two or three hours, but it is difficult to know for sure since time seems to have little value when trapped in a box."

"What happened after I lost contact with him?" There was a definite concern in her voice, which Werner did not hold as important as what he wished to question.

"The canok moved closer and in a soft voice said, "I am more interested in what occurred while you were in contact with him."

His thick red coat seemed to stand on end as he stared at the woman. Hawthorne returned his gaze, but when she looked in his eyes, she knew her secret was out. "I can see by your expression, Werner, that you have seen the proof to settle those suspicions you have been feeling for some time. However, I cannot say anything else to you at this time. Did Schram witness the same sight which you evidently saw?"

The canok nodded to the negative.

"Then I must ask that we keep him ignorant to that which could mean his or our death. He is not yet strong enough to hold such knowledge."

The canok did not react directly to the comment, but his agreement to keep all secret was clear. However, in actuality, he also did not hold any understanding of all that was occurring. Yet, instead of pursuing it at this time, he simply answered her previous question. "Upon your separation, a hooded figure appeared, and with the touch of his hand, both he and Schram disappeared."

"Have there been any changes since then?"

He shook his head. There was a long silence, then the canok added, "With your obvious ability as—"

The canok was interrupted by a strange occurrence on the wall. There were several bright flashes before a large door appeared in their place. With one push, Schram broke through, staff in hand, to greet his friends. "Come quickly. I have much to explain and little time to do it."

The group hurried through a series of corridors before coming to a large dining hall. Schram motioned each to sit and quickly several elves, much to the surprise of Werner and Hawthorne, brought them huge plates of food. Schram, who had already eaten while he had spoken with Cowhanis, began relaying the story to his companions. "For starters, it seems we were spared because they had not seen another elf since what they called the cataclysm occurred. It seems that many years ago, a black dragon appeared in their city of Eltak..."

"Eltak?" broke in Werner. "These are the mountain elves from Troyf?"

"Yes," replied Schram, "and they had no idea they were still not on Troyf. It seems that the dragon, presumably Slayne, demanded their obedience to his rule, or he would graphically change the face of their city, making all other creatures their enemy. He, of course, had no such power, and the elves therefore refused, even going so far as to attack the dragon where he stood. As it turned out, Slayne's power is even more immense than I have thought possible. Accompanying a series of ground rumblings, the elves of Eltak found themselves in a totally changed world. They sent out scouts only to find them later dead, with several foreign creatures also dead around them in what appeared to be fierce battle. Since then, the elves have not allowed anyone to approach what they still believed to be Eltak. Hence, we have the trees of death."

"Two questions," broke in the canok again. "Why did Slayne even bother with Eltak, and second, why did he not just wipe the city out, the elves with it? What was the reason behind all the elaborate schemes?"

Schram turned to the canok. "It seems that Slayne needed something from the city. That is why the dragon lords were there waiting for my companions and I when we arrived—because he had not found it. I believe he wanted the Diary of Anbari, but since it was not labeled or signed, the fool goblins could not locate it. As for why the elves were sent here, I think it was an ingenious move. It got the elves out of his way, and if the situation did grow to where he anticipated it could, the elves were now here to do exactly what they did—attempt to kill us or, at worst, slow us down."

Hawthorne looked saddened. "Slayne is still one step ahead of us," she whispered.

"Yes, and by this we must assume he is already at the Realm of Darkness and bargaining for the Rift Amulet."

"If he does not already have it," added Werner.

"Therefore, I believe we should possibly consider rethinking our plans and try to outguess his next move. King Cowhanis has guaranteed us safe and well-protected passage in whichever direction we choose to go, though even his elves have never dared to enter the mountains too far."

"No," said Hawthorne. "We will continue as planned to the Realm of Darkness. The Guardians of Passage do much more than simply guard the Rift Amulet. If we are to have a chance against Slayne, we must seek their knowledge."

Werner stared at the woman. "Are you certain?"

There was a pause as he stared at the woman, whose eyes or mouth did not move. The canok added, "Then I am in agreement."

Schram was taken in that there was no discussion. He was not sure that the realm was the right direction, but he also knew he did not have enough knowledge to say it was not—too many unknowns in this new land. "Very well, I trust both of your judgments. I will inform Cowhanis of our decision, and we will leave at once."

"There is no need to inform me," said a voice near the entrance. "I had to be sure of your intensions. I did not mean to distrust, but you must understand that what you have said comes to us as a complete surprise. I hope you will not hold feelings against such a deceptive act."

Schram rose as the form of Cowhanis began to take shape out of open space. "I could never hold such feelings for one I call friend, nor could those with me. You have a kingdom to protect and therefore you have acted in that fashion. The once King of Elvinott"—Schram avoided using Hoangis' name as elven lore dictates—"and I as Prince of Toopek would have acted accordingly."

Hawthorn rose. "Might I add that I am equally impressed with your magic as with your behavior. It is much stronger than I have been led to believe the Eltakian elves were capable of. To be able to completely block your presence from me—and Schram and Werner, of course—is truly impressive."

The king smiled. "Yes, it amazes us also. Ever since the cataclysm or our transformation, however you prefer to call it, our powers have seemed to become steadily stronger, plateauing at the level they are now. We always assumed it was some sort of fallout, so to speak, from the magic that was used against us. But now we have learned we are no longer in Eltak, meaning it could be something related to this place we now live."

"Either way, I would like to learn more about it," she replied.

The king nodded and motioned that they should leave. As they began to make their way down the hall, he added, "Packs have been prepared if you require them, and any weapons you desire also can be made available."

Each of their expressions told that they had all they would require, and Cowhanis clearly understood. His only other comment on the subject was directed toward Hawthorne. "Would you require any other armor or blanket packs? It will become quite cold in the mountains, much too cold for two small cloths to keep your body protected from its bitter bite."

She smiled but again shook her head. "No, my body does not feel the cold, but thank you for your concern."

"Go now, and may all our gods be with you."

⟨∞⟩

"Blasted maze of confounding uselessness," said Jermys as he removed his dagger from another dead goblin, bringing his total to five goblins and two trolls killed since leaving the throne room. "It is obvious dwarves did not build these tunnels, the craftsmanship is beyond reprisal." He was muttering constantly just to keep his mind working. There was nobody around to hear, but he knew the trail he was leaving in his wake would eventually catch up to him.

He had been randomly wandering through the extensive system of corridors, having little luck finding anything that led him to believe his friends had been there or were near. Furthermore, as he moved through the halls, he was making more noise bumping into things and dropping parts of his now-overloaded packs than if he was traveling with an army rather than solo. Even with this awkward method of travel, he had stayed relatively free of confrontation. Frequently he had dove into nearby rooms or turned back as needed to avoid those in the halls. He had only seen trolls, goblins, and dark dwarves, and no further signs of the dragon lords. Regardless, he knew he was going to have to find his friends soon and make an escape, for each hour he spent in Draag made it that much more improbable that he would ever leave.

The one thing in his favor at this point was that nobody knew he was there. The element of surprise was still on his side, although even that was evaporating. He no longer was only searching for Maldor, but with the acquisition of Krirtie's and Stepha's weapons, he also believed they were here as well.

He continued his pace through the winding passageways, with the intent of doing exactly what he had been considering for some time. He would find a troll, goblin, or if it must be, a dark dwarf, and literally beat the information out of them. Time was too precious to wait to find them on his own. He entered a small room, which was made of the same unnatural configurations as the rest of the tunnels. This room was empty but with all the scattered dust cleaned from the main path, it appeared that it got a lot of action. Also, there was light emanating from the only other apparent exit—a small doorway on the side of the room. Within the adjacent room, several voices could be heard speaking the broken dwarven tongue common to dark brothers.

Jermys shook his head and then began to creep forward, peeking his head around the doorway. Inside he saw a half dozen dark dwarves all sitting around a table with large ales. His immediate response was to charge the room if for no other reason than to retrieve the ales. The odor bit his nose like music. Upon further thought, however, he realized that in the process, the table would probably be knocked over, and therefore all the ales would be lost. He peered back, clearing his mind of the delicious scent. The room had no other exits, only a large system of pulleys which appeared to have some lifting function. *Probably a well or something*, he thought. This room probably acted as a base office for the guards. He pulled his head back around and began to make his way out of the area, assuming he had only run into another dead end.

◯〰〰◯

"Maldor, can you hear me?" Krirtie turned back toward Stepha with the exhaustion and pain of her injuries clear on her face. "There is still no response. I am afraid he will not pull out of it."

Stepha moved over to stand beside the two, placing her hand on Krirtie's shoulder. "I know the situation seems bad, but it has only been two days since we found him. He had nearly four months to acquire these injuries. Be thankful we, including your child, are well. Your wounds have been cleaned and are healing as best as the conditions will allow, and although I may never fly again, the pain in my wing has at least subsided. For Maldor, it will take more time."

Krirtie dropped her head. "But what are we saving him for? To be killed a violent and careless death? We can't even get out of here."

"Don't plan a death too early, for life is too precious. Never forget, we have many friends."

Suddenly a strong, deep voice appeared behind them, in a side of the room opposite the entrance, which led to the lift that brought them down and gave them their daily ration of food. "Yes, but your friends are now all acting completely as the emperor has foreseen. The dwarf is dead, and Schram has walked into a trap, which was set over two years ago. It is truly ironic that it will be elves who bring about his death."

"Don't try to frighten us with your lies, Meyer. You are a puppet for a mad creature bent on domination no matter who is killed in the process." Stepha stared hard at him as she spoke. She then stepped toward the dragon lord, being joined by the still slightly shaking body of the human as she did so.

"No!" He pointed toward Krirtie. "You are the one who has lied, and even as I speak, we are acting to prove your statements to be false."

"I did not lie, you bastard lizard-man. Your son acted admirably in his defiance of dragon rule. He acted as such in your name, and Slayne did not hesitate to wipe him from existence because of it."

"You lie!" A beam of energy shot from his finger, sending Krirtie sailing through the air to land next to Maldor's still-motionless body. She struck hard against the rock and immediately knew that all the careful bandaging had been for nothing as her injuries again began to seep blood around them.

Stepha made a move to strike but was quickly halted as the lord's finger turned to her. She returned to her position but was not ready to let the subject drop. "Tell me then, Meyer, how does Slayne plan to bring your son back from the dead to prove this to you?"

Lord Meyer's face became narrow and deep, and it was clear he was running on hatred and emotion. Stepha hoped that this condition would be favorable to extract information, which he normally would hold too deep in this state of mind. He took a deep, slow breath, and a charcoal tone bit through the silence. "Lord Starland has already made ready for the attack. He is leading the largest force ever assembled into Toopek. Nearly 2,000 land troops consisting of goblins, trolls, and dark dwarves will attack from three fronts. Then, from over the North Sea, he will lead one hundred dragons. There will be only one survivor—my son. If he will not join us, then he too will be among those killed. There will be no more defiance. There will be no more Toopek. The dragon rule has found its place and for the rest of time will remain in outright control—the way it should have been 200 years ago when we were denied what was rightfully ours."

Stepha had no reply. She was only able to stumble backward as she thought about Toopek, Geoff, Schram, and her home, which she knew would be next in line. The terror she was feeling for the situation that was just described totally clouded any rational thought she could fashion. Krirtie still battled her condition, but she had been able to understand the words. She sat with eyes of fire locked on the dragon lord. It was her home he had just described—a home which she may never see again and where her mother was headed when she left.

Meyer laughed deeply and spoke to Krirtie. "Yes, child, only now do you begin to understand. Your little band of rebels is nothing to us." He paused then took a few steps toward her and whispered, "You should be glad you are not there, or you would be dead too, just like your sister."

Krirtie looked down as she remembered her sister. For Krirtie, the day this whole journey started was when her sister was killed in the alley, and Schram and Kirven had saved her to flee to Elvinott. She gripped her fist tight and pushed herself to her feet. "No, it is you who remains ignorant. When the battle is over, you will not have your son beside you, nor will you ever see him alive again. The ones you call comrades or master will return from Toopek with a sad story about how he was killed, possibly by mistake, but more probably how he fled and somehow eluded their capture. This situation would keep you in their trust for a short while longer, until they deem you more of a nuisance than an aid."

"You lie! I am as…"

She would not let him continue. "If you are so high in their ranks, then why do they not trust you enough to accompany them on this mission? Did not Dragon Lord Starland insist that you stay behind? I ask you, for what reason? To ensure that we do not escape? My god, a blind gully dwarf could ensure that we do not escape from this fortress. Is that your equal? Are you a proud gully dwarf?"

Her words struck deeply, and she knew he could react one of two ways: strike her down in moments or realize she spoke the truth. Meyer sat in a cold stare. Although Krirtie had only guessed at the situation surrounding his presence there instead of Toopek, it quickly was apparent she had hit the mark on the head. Without warning, he turned with a shutter to Stepha, who remained in the same frozen position. He formed into a small white orb and then vanished.

Stepha swung her gaze toward Krirtie, smiling. "You never cease to amaze me. You were excellent, and your words really nailed him. I would be surprised if he was not already on his way to Toopek. I only hope he finds out the truth. It might be our only legitimate chance for an escape. Without some help from the inside, I think our odds are less than good.

"I think you are wrong," said Krirtie, smiling as well. "We have just been shown our way out."

The elf's smile vanished and a serious look crossed her face. "What do you mean? I have been all around this dungeon. There is only one way in and one way out, and it is controlled by dark dwarves in a room well above us."

"Wrong. Meyer did not use the lift contraption."

Stepha's face immediately dropped. "I thought you were serious. I am gifted with a different magic of the forest common to all elves, but that is not by any measure enough to perform a feat such as we just saw."

"Yes," she replied, "but Maldor has the hammer. In it is a great magic, I am sure of it. I feel the power every time I hold my sword. I don't understand it and I can't identify it, but I know it is there. If he could harness its power, perhaps we use it in the same fashion that we just witnessed."

Stepha moved over and sat on an outbreak of rock as a small smile of intrigue began to curl on her lips. "I don't know if it's possible, but I too have felt the power in our weapons. I only hope Maldor can pull out of his condition soon. There would be no better time to attempt an escape with almost the entire dragon force spread out across Troyf. It may be our only chance."

Even as she spoke, Krirtie's eyes had widened while she witnessed the large maneth's first movements since he had fallen unconscious. She could not speak, only making absurd noises and pointing to draw the elf's attention.

She followed her gaze. "Maldor, can you hear me?" She ran to kneel by his side. "It is me, Stepha, your friend." There was a short pause before she added softly, "Krirtie is with me."

The big maneth went through several spastic convulsions before his eyes opened wider than could be imagined. His muscles were rigid, and his expression showed nothing but intense terror. Stepha placed both her hands on his shoulders and hollered to the still-frozen stare of Krirtie. "He is still not free of the illusions. Talk to him, Krirtie. You are the only one who can pull him out of it."

Krirtie did not move. She sat staring at the one she loved more than any other, though her eyes now showed more fear than love. Stepha glared back toward her, but it was not Stepha that brought the woman back to her senses. It was Maldor's fit of seizures and violent moves against the elf who brought Krirtie to her knees. She clasped her arms around him, shouting his name and hers, trying to bring reality to his consciousness. Stepha had fallen back and now only sat as a spectator knowing that all was riding on the love the two felt.

Maldor was fighting like a caged animal, but Krirtie refused to break her hold. She had begun whispering in his ears, and by his reaction, it was slowly having an effect. His arms began to relax and lose their rigid resistance. His cheeks dropped, and his eyes returned to a more normal appearance giving way to the hard, glassy look he had awoken with. However, the most important change was in his voice when he said, "A son?"

Stepha moved over beside him. "It is all right, Maldor, we are here now."

"Stepha?" There was a pause, taking all of his strength to focus and turn his head. "And Krirtie? It is not a dream? You are not dead like I was told?"

She fell across his chest, pressing her soft lips gently against his dry and blistered ones in return. "No, my love, we are truly here. I am so sorry I did not come sooner. As I speak it now, we shall never be separated again."

"I love you, Krirtie."

"And I you."

Stepha gave them some time, but she also knew that time was the one thing they did not have. "I don't want to interrupt, but, Maldor, I can only tell you how thankful I am that you are back with us. We truly missed you." The two embraced softly, with Maldor not letting go of Krirtie in the process. "Are you able to talk, old friend? What is your condition?"

"I am in pain," he said, with his voice carrying the words to reality. "However, I feel it will not last. Even as we speak, I can feel a peace within me."

Krirtie glanced toward the elf, and it was clear she had an idea. She placed one hand on the maneth's cheek. "Maldor, before we were separated, Schram told me to trust in myself and the weapon I carried. Both were powerful and save me it could if I used them as such—"

Maldor interrupted. "Schram is gone. Where? When?"

"Relax, my friend," said Stepha softly. "We ourselves are in great trouble right now. Listen to Krirtie. Her words come from powers we do not understand, but they are real. Let's save ourselves too, then help Schram."

It was clear he was not pleased not understanding the entire situation, but when he tried to protest, he was greeted with Krirtie's raised hand. "The hammer, which is part of you, is strong with magic. I have felt it just as I have the power within my sword. Open your heart to the hammer, Maldor."

Maldor felt the words were strange to hear from Krirtie's mouth, but as he let his body fall to the magic of the hammer, he immediately felt a soothing from within. The more he accepted the hammer's power, the stronger his sensations became. The girls looked on in amazement. Krirtie even fell back beside the elf when Maldor began to emanate a strange aura. A red glow formed around him, but he did not seem to notice. His face had become laden with a deepening peace, which could not have been broken even if all of Troyf at that moment exploded into oblivion.

The exposed bones on his legs slowly vanished beneath a thick layer of skin that was natural to him. His thick maneth coat, from his mane to his feet, seemed to go through a metamorphosis. The cracked and dried blue blood, which was matted in nearly every crevice it could find, was replaced with the brilliant shimmer of a well-cared-for hide covered by the polished shine of new maneth battle armor.

His eyes blinked several times while the soft red haze gently faded. He raised his head up to meet the two ghostly white faces of his companions. Neither girl could utter a sound, but Maldor was not so affected. "I think I might want to hold onto this hammer." He raised it in the air and realized that his hand was still embedded around the helve. "And I am pleased to see the hammer feels the same."

Stepha's large elven eyes had not blinked. "That was truly one of the most amazing things I have ever witnessed."

"And I too," added Krirtie.

Maldor leaped to his feet. "Well, I feel as if I have been absent for much too long and now I am home." He looked around the area and his smile quickly faded. "Where in all of Troyf are we?"

Krirtie did not answer but simply fell into Maldor's arms. The maneth could not have been more pleased to receive her. The elf smiled and took a step forward. "I believe we are somewhere within Draag, but the caverns we were in before being sent into this dungeon were different than the ones we saw two years ago."

"Two years ago?" he said, slightly pushing Krirtie aside. "Perhaps you should start from the last thing I remember, traveling through some hidden tunnel along the base of the Canyon of Icly. Your no-good boyfriend had just caused a rockslide, which revealed the hidden passage, and that is when we came across this hammer."

Stepha smiled at his description of Schram and motioned the others to sit. "Fehr is going to be upset that I get to tell the story, but prepare yourself; it is going to be a long one, though about half as long as the rat would tell it."

There were high points and low points as the girls rummaged through the tale of the past couple of years. Maldor pulled Krirtie close and even blushed under his furry cheeks at the talk of their child. However, he nearly brought the ceiling down on top of them when he learned what Geoff would be facing in Toopek. "We must escape," he said. "No matter what the cost."

Stepha stood. "There might be a way, but I don't know exactly how, or even if it is really possible."

"That does not sound encouraging, but we must try."

"With the exception of the lift, I could not find any other way in or out of this place. That is, until the dragon lord appeared. Then it dawned on us—magic. If he could do it, why can't we?"

Maldor shook his head. "For starters, your boyfriend is not here. Dragon lords have been tainted with evil magic, Schram has some hidden gifts, but we have nothing like that. We are but—"

He was cut off by Stepha's hand. "I doubt Meyer could have done what we just witnessed with your hammer. We just don't understand it. However, even if we cannot get ourselves out, if Schram is trying to contact me, like I believe he did before, then I think we could at least get a message to him."

Maldor's eyes widened. "It might work. At least then he can prepare Toopek for what is about to hit. It might be their only chance. You are correct. Even if we escape, we could never make it to Toopek in time. We should begin at once."

"I only hope Schram is listening," Stepha added quietly.

Maldor leaned over and whispered. "If I could hear Krirtie through all my pain, Schram will hear you. He always has."

REALM OF DARKNESS

"A re the mountain forests always this peaceful?" Schram asked as they trudged along.

Cowhanis turned back to him. "To be honest, I don't know. After our first parties were believed to have been slaughtered by whatever lived out here, we simply quit investigating it. We cut a small region out of the foothills that we claimed as ours. Anyone or anything entering was subject to our society. In time, the other races began to respect that, and we respected them, never leaving our region. My elves have never set foot in these mountains, nor have we ever approached the Realm of Darkness, partially because we did not know we were near it."

Hawthorne added, "There is peace here because no creature would ever enter these mountains with the intention of doing harm. They fear the realm and the Guardians of Passage."

"What about Slayne then?"

"Slayne is the exception." Her voice became open, as if she was speaking into the air rather than to anyone specifically. "Slayne fears nothing, and although Schram is a concern, he is not, in Slayne's eyes, a threat. Those facts alone make him doubly dangerous."

There was a long silence while each thought about what they were up against. It had begun to seem to Schram that with each new bit of information they learned, Slayne took one more step closer to bringing his plan full circle. It was terribly frustrating for the human to always be one step behind him, but he did not know how he could change it. He had been consumed with visions of his friends in trouble, but he knew he was powerless to help them. With each day that passed, he began to feel more and more like a game piece in a game someone else was playing. He no longer was in control of his actions but was going where he had to go, or at least where he was led to believe he had to go.

His head began to sag low, and for the first time since the entire trek had begun, Schram felt that he was not going to be victorious. Somehow he had gone from fleeing his homeland two years ago not knowing why to being the key to saving the land he knew. There were many things he did not understand, but those things he did understand were not in his favor. His drop in attitude was apparent only to Hawthorne, but she did not have time to speak with him about it.

Cowhanis broke in, "Werner and the elves are returning."

Schram glanced up to see the red canok leading a small party of elves back through the trees ahead of them. Werner appeared calm, but the group of elves looked sick. Each of them had lost most of their natural color, replacing it with a ghostly white of the dead. Their eyes were all propped open wide, almost as if they could no longer even blink to hide what they saw. Hawthorne appeared indifferent at the sight but Cowhanis's feelings were clear.

"What happened?" he said.

None of the elves were able to reply, but Werner felt no hesitation. "We have scouted to the Great Ice Lake. Your elves did well to help see us safely there, but it will not be necessary for you to continue with us."

The elf king appeared displeased. "On the contrary, we will accompany you until you reach your destination."

Werner glanced back to face the path ahead of them and then turned with eyes of stone back toward the elf leader. "King Cowhanis, take your elves back to the New Eltak. Do not question this decision," the canok said, now much more direct leaving no area for further questions.

Hawthorne moved to stand next to the canok, looking back at Schram, giving him a silent message to do the same. He began to join them but first turned to Cowhanis. "I will tell of the tragedy that struck Eltak. Of course, if you wish, when this is all over, we will help you return to your old home. You will always be welcome. But now, this journey has met with our time to separate. You have acted honorably and your actions will always be remembered."

"I thank you, Schramilis, for helping us learn how foolish we have been. Perhaps, once we open our arms and greet those forest creatures around us, as our forefathers did so long ago, then we will truly have found a new home. Maybe this is simply part of our natural evolution, but it is nice to know we still have a home among the mountains."

The two parted with a quick embrace, allowing Werner and Hawthorne the time to move ahead a short distance. After catching the two, Schram took one look back in time to see Cowhanis leading the small party of elves back toward their camp. Schram issued a sigh before asking, "Tell me, Werner, what happened to them? What did they see?"

The canok did not turn his head as he spoke. "They saw the coldest, loneliest place in all the worlds of worlds. They saw pure, unbridled death—a sight which would strike an elf even harder than any other mortal."

"You must keep your head, Schram," said Hawthorne. "It will attack you in much the same way."

Nothing else was said for some time, and Schram became further consumed in his own thoughts. With each step they took, the temperature would drop another degree; and although it was still a few hours before noon, the sky was growing darker and darker. He really had little idea what to expect. All he was certain of was that they were heading to a lake known as the Great Ice Lake. From there they would travel to the far side and locate a path to take to their destination. However, when they finally broke through the last clump of trees between the two largest peaks of the mountains, Schram was brought to the realization why he had not been told anything more. No words could describe it.

He had been caught up in the name thinking it had meant a frozen environment. Probably a glacier mountain with a runoff pool, which remained icy cold throughout eternity. Instead he was greeted with a pool of shadow. Icy, cold, and lonely were the only things he could feel. It was an area totally devoid of life. Yet, as they drew nearer, he could see that beneath the surface there were many mysteries.

Creatures of all races furiously fought to break through the liquid face while others rested at the bottom, staring sadly and palely back to those who passed. Their skin no longer held any color and their bodies seemed to have little density. They were the condemned dead, who would never be granted passage, wanting throughout eternity to be released from their immortal swim of death.

Schram looked away in horror as a cold chill crept up his spine. He jumped in a fit of dismay when Hawthorne's long, soft fingers reached out and touched his shoulder. "Come on, young Schram. To wallow about in such a place can only bring sadness. You must accept that this is a sacred place for death. To grip its evil hands and its existence only balances that which is not here."

He looked at the woman and once again was completely taken by her beauty. The softness in her eyes and in her touch created a deep love in Schram he had never truly felt before, but not like his love for Stepha—different—but present nonetheless. He wanted to reach out and embrace her, but she gripped him first. The two held each other tightly for several minutes before she pushed him away. "There is much you still need to learn, when the time is right."

He was not prepared for the comment, but when she took his hand and began to lead him toward the other side of the pool, his mind became calm.

They joined Werner, who was speaking as they approached. "This is the path which will take us to the guardians. From this point on, if not already, they will be aware of our presence. Do not use any magic, not even to speak. We are entering totally in peace. Any attack upon us will have to be defended without magic."

They both nodded that they understood, but there was a different concern carried in Hawthorne's expression than Schram had seen before. Werner looked back at the woman, "No, I think it will be all right, but if the situation calls for it, you know what you will have to do."

"Yes, I do, my friend," she replied. "Thank you."

Once again Schram was completely confused, but Hawthorne's gentle touch relaxed his anxiety. The three pushed forward with Werner leading the way. It was impossible for any of them to determine where they were headed or where they had been as the environment around them kept going through graphic changes. Trees, storms, wind, or anything possible in nature would appear in their faces and as quickly vanish. They traveled through sun and rain for what seemed to be uncountable hours. However, when they arrived in an environment that was constant and secure, it appeared that time had not moved. The black clouds were in the same positions as they were when they had first approached the lake. The three looked around aimlessly, none of them knowing what they were expected to do next.

They were on a plateau. It was a large, flat, circular plane which appeared to be something a large bird would use to land safely on. Tall rocks formed a semicircle around the plateau, making the only entrance or exit being the path they had taken to arrive here. The group disbanded across the clearing but again had nothing to look for. Each was staring blankly at the others, their frustrations evident.

Suddenly, there was a strange sound. It was a high-pitched ringing, which sent Werner into a wild frenzy. Schram moved to try to settle him, leaving Hawthorne alone on the far side. As he was seeing to the canok, the space between Schram and Hawthorne became obscured. He looked up in time to see the huge figure of an unknown creature appear in front of the woman. The ringing had subsided, but Werner had fallen near unconscious due to its previous intensity. Schram jumped to his feet, arching his staff to mount an attack when he remembered the canok's warning—*no magic*. He ran at the creature but some invisible barrier struck him as he moved. Strange digits, much like huge fingers, gripped his shoulders and pinned him to the ground.

The creature turned toward the human, and when it was certain Schram was no longer a threat, it swung its head back to the woman. The sight alone nearly made Schram lose consciousness. Its head was oval, with a large snout stretching outward revealing a foot-long length of jagged teeth. Saliva and various-colored fluids oozed from its mouth and several pores about its globular body. It had no defined limbs, moving more as a ball of slime than a conventional creature. However, the most vile parts were the impressions on the sides of its main body. Outlines of human faces and hands seemed to be pushing from the inside, trying, with no success, to escape. They rolled around in convulsive manners but could not break through the thick lining.

Schram wanted to turn away, but he could not. He had to try to help Hawthorne, whom the creature seemed to be most interested in for some reason. Yet, Hawthorne did not move or appear the least concerned with the creature. She looked more concerned for Schram's welfare, staring more often toward him than at what was before her. However, when the creature spoke, both were drawn to its attention. "Why do you hide behind a false exterior? Do you bring your evil into the realm?"

She wore the most serious expression Schram, who had no idea what the question meant, had ever seen. Calmly she replied, "I am not hiding as much as I am protecting the interests of those I travel with, and no, I could never seek to harm or bring evil to the realm."

The creature stared at her then back at Schram and Werner. "Open your mind to me, Hawthorne. I must be brought to understand."

The woman nodded, and a bright light encompassed her head. After several relatively quiet moments, the light diminished, and Hawthorne fell to her knees as if from total exhaustion. The creature lowered its head to her level. "I understand and believe your presence may be of importance to us as well. However, if you remain in this state, you will never be granted entry. I leave the choice in your hands."

With a flash of light to rival the most viscous storm, the creature vanished. Werner, who had since made it back to his feet, stared toward Hawthorne. "The choice is yours, but know the boy will find out soon enough regardless. I do not see how this fact would harm him, but I do still sense your misgivings."

"Yes, I know," she said as she approached the two. "But we must continue."

Schram's deep concern was carried in his voice. "Hawthorne, I have sensed you have always kept something from me, something I did not or could not understand. I have grown much since this journey began. I have lost many close to me. I have lost my family. There is very little you could say that I do not feel I would be able to understand and accept."

She smiled at him and softly reached her hand up to pass by his cracked and worn cheek. "Schram, it is difficult, but simply said, I am not as I appear."

Schram did not know how to react to the statement, so he only tilted his head slightly and nodded.

Hawthorne took a step back and began to concentrate on something known only to her. Several moments later, a green haze appeared around her, nearly engulfing her entire body. When the fog finally cleared, in its place was the largest, most magnificent dragon Schram had ever seen. Its skin was green, but not the pale green he had seen before. This green was bright and exciting. Her wings were the same brilliant golden brown that was carried in her hair. She stepped forward to again take a position before the two.

Schram was speechless. His eyes did not even feel comfortable looking at a sight so magnificent. He fought over his emotions to form the statement, "You need not hide from me. I truly believe it to be the most incredible thing I have ever seen. I have heard of shape-changers, including stories I have learned regarding Slayne, and I have even handled some spells of my own to help us in run-ins with trolls and such, but never have I believed someone could hold one indefinitely. I never really believed they could be so real as to be unnoticed by me."

"Do not let what you did with the trolls fall short. That was truly amazing for someone so new to this type of magic." Her soft voice was identical to that he had heard before. "If you did it then, why do you not wish to believe it now?"

He shook his head. "That was a simple incantation. Had you passed me by, you would have known it was magic. For you it is, well, natural."

She smiled but did not pursue it further. Instead she turned to the rock wall surrounding them. "We have been accepted to stand before the realm. Come with me."

Schram turned and was quite taken when he saw the dark cave, which appeared where solid rock had been moments before. Usually his magic allowed him to see through such things, but for some reason, here everything seemed different. Hawthorne entered the cave first, followed by Schram and Werner, both of whom carried a restless and uncomfortable feeling with them.

One would expect light from outside the cave to give some aid to seeing once inside. This was not the case. The cave entrance acted as a mirror and no light from outside was able to penetrate its face. Moreover, Schram's elven sight gained him nothing. To him, he felt as if he had just entered a place where the laws, as he knew them, did not exist. It was when he considered taking another step that he realized all his senses were absent. It was the most total emptiness he had ever felt. He believed he may actually be dead—no sight, no hearing, no touch.

Hawthorne and Werner had moved slightly ahead when a sudden explosion of light, which struck Schram with the force of a mighty storm, appeared all around him. The woman spoke softly. "Come now, Schram, the guardians did not anticipate your discomfort. Sensory perceptions mean nothing to them and it is rare that a human should pass their gate. I or Werner should have prepared you. We are sorry."

They were in a large room with apparently no exits. The walls were of rock, and there was nothing to make the room appealing or at all a place of comfort. Werner and Hawthorne stood beside each other well ahead of him, pulling him forward with their eyes. Beside them stood two human figures, both young-looking and strong. They wore simple armor, which sat in Schram's mind as being strikingly similar to the peasant armor of some small, isolated human villages he had crossed when he was a boy. This only further confused the human.

Issuing a sigh, which had become a familiar sound from his mouth, he began to move forward. He reached the small group, and Hawthorne stepped aside to allow room for proper introductions. "Schram, these are the representatives of the Guardians of Passage, whom we will be speaking with regarding the amulet."

He was still quite taken, hearing her soft voice coming from such a huge creature, but he was even more captivated by the sight of the two men. They were exactly that—two human peasants. Schram bowed his head. "I am pleased to make your acquaintance, though I am a bit surprised by your appearance. I was not expecting to see humans."

The two men did not change expression. They simply bowed in return and telepathically replied, *We too are pleased to greet you.* There was a short pause while the two seemed to be discussing something, then with a nod, one turned back to Schram. "You must realize that a physical body means nothing to those who reside here. We have taken this form to give your conscious a level of comfort to speak. It would be as simple for us to appear as a bantis." The human speaking suddenly took the shape of a huge brown-scaled bantis, even larger and more threatening than the one Schram had faced in the canoks' homeland only a short time ago. The creature brought back vivid memories of the ordeal he faced, which sent a cold chill down the warrior magician's spine.

Schram stepped back and worked to calm himself. "I understand your abilities and am grateful for your presence as a human. It would indeed please me to speak with you as such."

The raving bantis was instantly returned to human form with a somewhat unnerving lack of change in expression or tone. "We have much to discuss, and I fear time is growing short. In my first contact with you, Hawthorne"—he motioned to the large dragon who had moved to stand beside Schram—"I was able to learn a small bit of the reason you and your group have come to this dominion. However, I wish you to explain your presence here fully, so all can be made aware of the evil at hand."

Hawthorne spread her golden brown wings and then brought them to rest against the smooth, soft green plating making up her armor-like skin. With a light bow, she began. "The story I would tell is not that which has brought my friends and I into your graces. I feel that Schram, the one who has truly been at the head of helping this world, would be better fit to relay our tale to you. He holds the key to both our dilemmas."

The two human figures turned toward Schram, but the same one remained speaking. "Please, young Schram, free your mind to us. If Hawthorne is correct, you must leave no word unspoken, for both your world of the living and ours of beyond are facing perhaps the most serious threat since their origin."

Schram appeared nervous as he fought to find the correct words to explain all that had occurred over the last two years, but as Hawthorne moved next to him, allowing her wing to touch his side, a newfound strength filled his body. After a near immeasurable length of time, the room fell silent as he completed his story, ending by learning about the true existence of Hawthorne, the most magnificent green dragon he had ever seen.

There was a long period of ominous silence, making all mortals in the room extremely uncomfortable. The two human figures stared blankly forward, their bodies totally devoid of any movement including those commonly associated with life. Their eyes did not blink nor did any muscles move due to the presence of breath. It was then Schram realized that the two human figures were even less real than he had been led to believe. They were not forms that guardians had taken to please him. They were images, illusions they had created to allow his mind to accept them. Now, during a time Schram assumed was being used for intense discussion, they had left their illusions unattended so even they appeared dead. As unreal as each seemed, Schram was still somewhat comforted in obtaining a better understanding about what he was witnessing. However, he found little comfort when the human figures before him once again sprang to life.

"That is truly an amazing tale, Schram. As Guardians of Passage, we have little knowledge of that which is occurring outside our Realm. The understanding you have brought leads us to discover exactly what fools we have been."

The Guardian's voice became solemn and soft. Hawthorne pulled her wing away from Schram and stepped forward. Also in a gentle tone, she asked, "I fear for what I hear in your tone. Please, tell us why you deem yourself foolish. Possibly, all can still be made right."

The human figure rose its head. "In our existence here throughout eternity, any who came to us free of evil wishing for our aid, we would most graciously oblige as best we could. Since our origin, we have had four such visitors. The first was a magnificent dragon, strong and honest. With him he carried enough power to be considered a threat to any other power, including our own. However, he did not desire any additional power, nor did he desire to bring harm upon any race. He had the gift of foresight, and all he wished was to prevent that which he saw occurring across the land he called home. However, he could not do it alone. In exchange for our help, he gave us the only possession we have ever known—the Anbarian hammer. How he came to possess it is unknown to us, but it was also unimportant. Never before had we been given anything, so its importance to us was immense."

"However, many years later, this dragon would return to our realm under the idea of seeking out aid once again. Yet this time he used his power to deceive us, and his only purpose was to steal that which he had given to us previously."

"Why would this dragon have given it to you in the first place if his only intention was to steal it back?" asked Schram, in his characteristic voice, to gain understanding.

"That is a very good question, young Schram, and one in which only that dragon can answer."

There was a brief pause before Werner spoke. "You said you had four visits from those from the outside world. Who were the other two?"

The guardian turned toward the canok. "Following the theft of the hammer, all remained quiet among the realm. Then, besides your party today, it was two days ago when another dragon approached us bearing the return of that which had been stolen from us. He was a strong black dragon whose intentions we could only feel were to return the Hammer to us. Nothing else could be felt from him, but we had no reason to believe there was more. However, for the possibility of retrieving the hammer, we had to hear his words. He told the same tale you have just said. In exchange for the Rift Amulet, he would return the Anbarian hammer to our possession."

Schram immediately interrupted. "Did he truly have the hammer in his possession?"

A saddened look crossed the guardian's face. "No, he did not. He showed us a magical replica of its location, which we could feel was accurate. It was at his home."

Hawthorne then softly added. "Do you still possess the Rift Amulet?

"No, we do not."

"Then Slayne has obtained the one thing he could use."

The guardian looked intrigued. "No, he does not. Not by our doing, that is."

"But you said you no longer possess the Amulet. If you don't, who does?" Schram's voice carried a message of urgency, but the guardians seemed to be hurried only by their own need.

The second guardian now stepped forward and spoke. "For one who is repeating our statements, should you hear only those you feel are important, or should you listen to all we have spoken?"

"I am sorry, but I do not understand your riddles." Schram glanced at Hawthorne and Werner, but it was clear they too did not follow the direction of the guardian's statement.

The first guardian continued. "There is no riddle. We said that we had only one possession, the Anbarian hammer. We have never possessed a Rift Amulet nor do we know of its existence. Our first knowledge of it dates back two days, when the one you call Slayne asked for the exchange."

All appeared stunned by the knowledge but none more than Hawthorne. The beautiful dragon arched her neck back, displaying a certain ferocity not natural on her face. Her voice was strong but still carried a certain plea hidden beneath its surface. "There must be a mistake. Anbari himself told me the legend."

"We here at the Realm of Darkness know of Anbari and respect him well. However, for whatever reason, he has told you a legend not based on facts. I am sorry, for I wish we could help."

"Then are you saying that our entire purpose for coming here was only a waste of time," said Schram, not necessarily asking a question.

"We are not in a position to judge the purpose of your actions. If you feel your only purpose here was to recover the Rift Amulet, then yes, you have gained nothing in your trek. However, only you can determine that."

Werner, Hawthorne, and Schram all looked to each other for answers, but each came up empty. A silence ensued, which further lowered the current mood. For the first time since the takeover of Toopek, Schram had a definite enemy and knew the means by which to bring about his defeat. Now that enemy was growing stronger, and his one chance at victory was based on a lie. Schram really believed that time was running out, and now he did not even have a direction or a plan.

"Wait," said Werner. "We have lost nothing. Let us assume that we were led here to recover the amulet, then Slayne too has wasted the same time. We are no worse off than before."

Hawthorne remained soft-spoken. "But then where do we go from here? I was led to believe that this was the answer, the key move to defeat Slayne."

Again nobody spoke for several moments before Schram replied, "We have another purpose here."

"What do you mean?" asked Hawthorne.

"I mean I just felt Maldor's presence. He is alive and trying to contact me."

Hawthorne lifted her wings slightly. "Maldor does not have that ability nor would he know how to use it. Further, I feel nothing. How can you be sure?"

He looked toward the large dragon eyes staring down upon him. "I can be sure because I feel it." He turned to the two human figures. "Guardians, I told you about sending the diamond stone to the Hatchet of Claude. During that transition, I was nearly pulled into that world with it. Is it therefore possible to bring the hammer back to this world, should it be trying to contact me?"

Again the human figures took on the ghostly appearance of death as discussions among the guardians commenced. Then, they turned to the group. "We believe that such a feat would be possible, but it would require immense strength. The magic, which nearly captured you, was across all of Draag. Its power was drawn from every aspect within its boundaries. We here are but a small region."

"But you do have great power. We have all felt it."

Again there was silence. Suddenly, both human forms vanished, as did all the light which had accompanied their presence. An immediate and uncontrolled fear struck Schram, but his mind quickly brought a calming presence. He remembered what Hawthorne had said regarding his senses and tried to draw on that to aid him now. He could not use magic here without the guardians' permission, but he could use his senses. Slowly, he began to see outlines and hear the breathing of his companions. With each breath, his body relaxed more and more.

Suddenly there was a voice which seemed loud enough to shatter the walls. "We will help you, Schram, but it will take all our strength, and success is by no means a guarantee."

Escape from Draag

"**B** lasted maze," said Jermys as he struck another dead end. "If these damn dragons are so great, why don't they have a map of these confounded systems of tunnels somewhere to help someone trying to locate prisoners?" Jermys smiled to himself as he had begun talking out loud, almost daring to make himself known to at least bring about some change to the relentless walking he had been doing since leaving the base room where the dark dwarves were playing cards.

He continued talking to himself as if he had Fehr right next to him. "I have killed at least ten dark brothers but gained nothing. If Krirtie, Stepha, and Maldor are here, then I must be missing something. Further, why have there been so few patrols? Where is everyone? In truth, this can't be good. I need to find them now. Damn rat, where are you? If I see your sorry fat butt again, I am going to rip you a new…" He landed with a thump, with his weapons clanging enough to wake the dead.

His temper was now flaring from deep within him as he knew that somehow his thinking about Fehr had caused him to trip over his own beard. "I hate that damn rat. I am over 200 years—make that 175 years old—and that bastard rat still gets me." He gathered up his load of vine and arsenal of weapons and then just shook his head in disbelief.

"This is a waste of time. I need someone to tell me where they are, which means I need to go to the one place I know I can find someone—the card room."

Although Jermys would have appeared to anyone to be bordering on insanity, he actually was more focused and prepared than he had been in sometime. He felt as if he knew what he was facing, he had a goal, and he knew where he was going, at least for now.

He arrived back to the card room in very short order. *This will be easier than I thought,* the dwarf mused to himself as he stared across the room of guards. The six dark dwarves still remained, and by the looks of their eyes and bodies, the last hour of heavy ale drinking was not treating them kindly. Three had moved from the table to find quiet corners in which they could snore to their heart's content. And the others were playing some sort of card game, the likes of which seemed to be growing in stakes as one dwarf had thrown all of his weapons into the pot.

Jermys looked over the situation and then decided on the only plan he could think of that would solve all his problems—keep one dark brother alive to gain information. He needed to remain alive, and finally, he needed to be close enough to keep the table from being knocked over, spilling all the ales. The moment before Jermys acted, he made a silent prayer for all the dark dwarves who had recently become his friends. If there were any other way, he would not act against the dark brothers, though he was certain this band was definitely loyal to the dragons. He had come to the belief that it was time for dwarven blood to become thick again. However, now was the time to locate his companions, and that meant acting now.

"You ale-bellied rat lover. That dwarf is a cheater. Stole five hundred sovereigns from me with marked cards." Jermys was shouting in the most deep, drunken, and dwarven tones he could muster.

The guards sleeping did not move, but those at the table drew weapons immediately. Jermys threw his arms up. "Wait, don't attack me. I might be of Feldschlosschen, but I am loyal to the dragons, and besides, I am the one looking for you." He pointed at the dwarf who appeared to have the most winnings. "Thought you had left me for dead in the forest after cheating me out of my gold. Well, I am back, and I have come for my gold—and your head."

"You lie, Feldschlosschen scum, and the only thing I want from you is your head."

He started to move toward Jermys but another of the dwarves grabbed his shoulder. "Marked cards, eh, Ed-Penel?"

"This Feldschlosschen dwarf lies, but if you wish to argue as well, I will not hesitate to kill the both of you."

Jermys could hear the ale driving the dwarf's words, bringing his plan into motion even better than he had intended. The third dwarf rose from the table and placed himself between the other two. "Listen, we have cards to play. If the Feldschlosschen dwarf has a problem with Penel, then let them settle it."

The one called Ed-Penel grabbed the third dwarf by the throat and, with his other hand, jabbed his dagger into his gut. The body fell limp, with black blood spilling to the floor beneath him. Turning back to Jermys, "Now it's your turn. I killed him nicely. After all, he was my friend. You I am going to make feel pain slowly, the way your kind should die."

Before Ed-Penel could even make a move, Jermys had lodged his battle ax between his eyes. The other dwarf leaped over the fallen bodies to attack, swinging a similar battle ax as he moved. Jermys was unprepared for the charge but was able to throw up the Hatchet of Claude in defense. The two weapons struck, and the attacking dark dwarf's ax shattered on contact. Jermys wheeled around, and with a quick jerk, the dark dwarf's head separated from its body.

Jermys moved over to inspect the sleeping dwarves. To his surprise, one was already dead—a slit throat, probably at the hands of Ed-Penel. "He did seem to have a temper," Jermys thought half out loud and half in his mind. He moved to one of the remaining two sleeping dark brothers, and although he tried violently to wake him, there seemed to be no hope.

Jermys sighed and then approached the last of the sleeping beauties. He reached down and gently tickled his nose. Slowly, one of its blurred eyes opened, and after a few seconds to acknowledge the circumstances, jolted up to greet the blade of Jermys's Hatchet at his throat. The dark dwarf grumbled in answer to Jermys's laughter.

"What do you want, Feldschlosschen Gar-Bait?"

He was stung by the reference. "Listen, you black-bearded goblin puppet, I ask the questions. Your buddies thought they were clever with words as well, so I inspected their voice boxes."

The dark dwarf glanced around the room and saw the beheaded and slit-throat remains of his former comrades. His face cringed in anger. "Speak your will, dwarf, but know that you shall never leave these caverns."

I want to know the location of my companions—a maneth, an elf, a human woman, and possibly a rat. I will only ask once."

"I don't know what you are talking about. We have no prisoners, and…a rat is your companion? You are not a dwarf. You are a…"

The dark brother screamed in pain as one of his arms left his body. Black blood filled the area and the dark dwarf hit the ground hard. He fought in a convulsive pain huddled on the ground below the dwarf. After a moment, his body slowed and his blood-streaked eyes locked on Jermys. "As my name is Dar-Knipp, I spit my last ounce of black blood at you."

"Well, Dar-Knipp, I will expedite your last breath if you do not answer my question. Where are my…"

His statement was interrupted by a loud, echoing screech coming from what Jermys originally thought was a well, but as he swung his head toward the noise, he saw it was really some sort of lift for transport to a lower floor. However, as his attention was drawn to the noise, Dar-Knipp swung his remaining hand upward, sending the dwarf sailing to the side and knocking his hatchet free of his hand.

Jermys quickly recovered but found that the one-armed body of the dark dwarf was already bearing down upon him. A crossarm crushing blow again put Jermys on his back, leaving him still weaponless. Knipp laughed a deep, bellowing laugh, seemingly able to ignore the constant flow of blood from his missing arm. He reached down to the fallen dwarf and lifted him above his head, grabbing nothing but a handful of Jermys's hair to hold him. "You are a typical Feldschlosschen dwarf, all yap and no bite. Remove your ax, and you are weaker than an elven peasant girl."

Jermys's face turned red with anger. "By my word now, I shall kill you this day with no weapon but my two fists."

The dark dwarf laughed and launched Jermys crashing into the wooden box used on the lift. Wood fragments exploded everywhere while Jermys struggled to hold onto the edge of the floor of the room with his legs hanging wildly downward. Below him he heard pieces of wood strike the ground, a great distance he could only describe in his mind as a very long way down that he did not want to see in person. Then came another ear-piercing screech. Jermys tried to look down but could not see anything through the blackness. Then, accompanying another laugh from above, came intense pain originating in his fingertips.

"What's the matter, scum? Do I weigh a bit much for you?"

"You are a fat one, but you probably only outweigh three of four goblins added together. That is not too bad for someone of your limited intelligence and abilities."

Dar-Knipp lifted his foot and placed it on top of his other, bringing his entire weight upon the fingers of one of Jermys's hands holding onto the floor of the lift opening, pinching them into the hard rock base framework. Jermys felt each of the bones in his fingers breaking one after the other. His other hand fell free, and if the dark dwarf had not held him practically fastened to the ground, Jermys would have fallen to his death. As it was, he sucked in all his strength, and during Knipp's final fit of taunting laughter, he swung his arm up and grabbed the top of the dark dwarf's boot. With a quick jerk, Knipp's laughter ceased and was replaced with a scream of terror as he free fell through the hole before being silenced with the impact to the ground.

Jermys scratched and clawed with his one good hand, trying desperately to get a firm grip on anything. His strength was fading, but he knew he could not give up yet. He pushed his hand forward one more time and locked his fingers around the edge of one of the stones in the floor. After swinging one leg up, he rolled his body over and was free of the hole.

He turned over on his side and let out a long sigh. "What a bastard," a feeling he assumed was mutual. Reaching over, he grabbed his hatchet and held it close to his body. Immediately there was a soothing, and Jermys entered into a state of pure peace.

∽∾

"Do you think you are strong enough, Maldor?" asked Stepha, her voice showing both concern and urgency.

"I am not sure, but we have to try again. I know we can get through. Each time I feel we are about to make contact, something here prevents us. There is magic here surrounding Draag that is protecting it from our attempts."

Krirtie walked back into the small room. "We must try. There is no food again, and I feel that the guards have decided that we no longer require any. We must get a message through regarding Toopek even if it means our death."

Stepha cringed at the comment. "Do not talk as such, Krirtie. We are not beyond escape yet. Much can happen in a short while."

"I do not mean to offend, Stepha, but if there is a chance I can give my life to save all of Toopek, I will, without question."

"As would I," the elf replied. "I hope you have never doubted that. I would just ask that we accept that each would give anything to help others, not necessarily speaking only of death."

Krirtie dropped her head. "I am sorry, Stepha. Schram has always taught me proper behaviors, and sometimes I just follow my emotion."

Stepha smiled. "You do not need to apologize to me. We are sisters, and both learning of the other's belief's and knowledge. Forgiveness is carried within our relationship, as is every other emotion and response. We have been through too much together to be anything less."

"Your words are always so perfectly spoken. When I first met you, I believed you to be some foreign creature that stole our prince from our land. Now I know that Schram is the one who is lucky. He was tied to you for his entire life."

The girls embraced and then looked at each other. Indeed they had been through a lot thus far, and as each stared into the other's eyes, they were certain their trek was far from over.

There was a grunt from the side, causing both girls to swing to its origin. "Maldor, are you all right?"

"Yes, fine, Krirtie. That was only my stomach. I think I am ready to attempt the message again, but I will need your help as before, and this time we must make sure we get through the barrier."

"We will do our best," replied Stepha. "Our only chance of success is if we all concentrate fully."

Maldor reached his hand, which still was attached to the helve of the hammer, between the girls. "I will provide the strength, but you are the key, Stepha. You must take us to Schram. He will feel your presence before he will feel mine."

The two girls placed their hands across the hammer and closed their eyes as all began to focus their minds toward their old companion. At first there seemed to be little effect, but slowly they began to sense their environment beginning to change. Stepha felt as if she were flying again, high above the clouds, but able to see everything below her clearly. However, what she saw below her disturbed her greatly. She wanted to ask the others if they saw it also but knew to do so would be detrimental to their cause. Instead, she remained concentrating on Schram. Why she was traveling over a huge expanse of water would be a question to determine the answer for later.

However, when she began to move across land again, she became even more disturbed and distracted. Then, she entered a place which brought tears to her yes. Never before had she felt so much misery and death. Never before did she believe that so much death could be held in one place. Beads of sweat and tears covered her face, and her speed through the darkness seemed to slow. The area was beginning to suck her in, almost capturing her in her lost mind.

"He is dead," she screamed. "Schram has been taken to a world beyond."

As she spoke, she lost all contact with the hammer and their journey was broken. Stepha fell to her knees and buried her face in her hands. Krirtie knelt down to comfort her while Maldor turned to see what was moving in the adjacent room. It was his deep gasp that caused Krirtie to glance around, and once she too saw what was approaching, she let out a high-pitched scream.

However, her scream went unheard as a screech of unbelievable magnitude echoed off the rock walls. Stepha was immediately brought out of her disillusionment to witness some sort of huge dragon-like creature slowly bearing down on them. Maldor leaped in front of the girls as he was the only one with any sort of weapon. Yet, even with something as powerful as the Anbarian hammer, it did not appear there would be any chance of a successful outcome. Maldor would have to get in close to do any damage, and the creature's long talons would then be free to tear him apart. Therefore, he did the only thing he thought might give them a chance. With two swings, he brought the doorway crashing down, sealing them in the small circular rooms like it was their tomb. However, it also separated them from the creature. Another loud screech was heard as it screamed its displeasure.

Maldor turned to the others. "It was our only choice." Maldor frowned as several pounding noises were heard through the wall.

"We must contact Schram quickly for this wall will not protect us for long."

Stepha looked up. "He is no longer in this world with us. I was able to see and feel it if you were not."

"I felt as much," the large maneth added, "but I also felt he was waiting for us to make contact. It is as if he wants contact to be made." Maldor paused and then added, "Do you not wear a Ring of Joining with him?"

"Yes, I do," she replied, rubbing the ring gently.

"Then can you not feel his life within it?"

The elf's eyes were closed in a peaceful meditation. Softly she said, "Yes, I feel his spirit within me."

"Then we will make contact this time."

They joined as before, and soon the monotonous pounding of the creature trying to break through was a distant hum and then silent altogether. Stepha realized that the creature was simply part of Draag's protective barrier. When they first attempted to break through, the creature was alerted and came to stop them. However, once they are beyond the barrier, the creature can no longer harm them. It is when they return that they are at its mercy. She wished there was a way to remain outside the barrier. All of this was her theory, however, but to think about it now would only reduce their chances of success. She had to focus.

They had just crossed the vast expanse of water when she felt Maldor turn to pull away. Stepha held tight to the hammer, refusing to let him break. She was certain his action meant that the creature had gotten through, but as long as they remained in contact with Stepha through the hammer, it was beyond the creature's ability to reach them. If they broke contact, then they would be back with the creature. Either way, Stepha knew this would be their final chance to get their warning through.

Again she became saddened as she passed the area of darkness and death. The tortured souls seemed to reach out to her and try to pull her in, or more likely grab onto her, to get them out.

She concentrated all her mind on Schram, doing anything in her power not to be seduced and overtaken by those trapped eternally below her. Soon she felt herself climbing up a narrow path only to arrive at a strange platform.

There was only one direction to continue—through a dark cave where even light did not seem to penetrate—but for some reason her mind would not allow her to go. It was as if she was going somewhere she was not supposed to, at least not yet. She tried and tried, but she could travel no farther. She became frustrated and tired. Once again her anxiety caused beads of sweat to roll across her delicate green skin.

Suddenly, the darkness of the cave began to change, and leaping from its boundaries was Schram. He had one arm raised in a gesture to join him, and immediately Stepha relaxed. She came and stood beside him, and together they slowly moved forward. They came into a small room where Stepha saw a beautiful green-and-brown dragon, a red canok, and a half dozen humans. The group sat around a circle with their hands intertwined, except at a place where Schram had once sat. Schram led the elf over and motioned to her to enter the circle. Once inside, he took his seat to seal the ring around her.

There was not a sound made, and Stepha was unsure what she was supposed to do next. Then, she felt the presence of Maldor and Krirtie beside her. Maldor stepped forward. "Schram, I have to warn you about…No!"

All around began to change. The darkness of the cave became more clear and distinct. Maldor swung back to rejoin Krirtie and Stepha, but his hand passed right through them. The last thing he saw was the terror in their eyes, and he knew they were back in the room with the creature, and they were totally without protection.

"What happened?" shouted Schram. "I thought you said we would be able to bring them all here."

The guardians shook their heads. One moved forward to speak. "The powers holding them at Draag were too strong. Had they all been well with magic, then perhaps. As it is, we could only bring that who possessed the hammer, and even that was uncertain until the very end."

"They will be killed," echoed Maldor's first words to Schram in nearly half a year, and they were words he would never forget.

☙❧

"Krirtie, are you all right?" screamed Stepha as she ran to help the human woman up from where she had fallen.

"Yes, the landing hurt worse than the creature's strike." She paused and stared at the wet grimace of the creature as it simply looked over its prey. "Why does it toy with us so?" It could take us outright. Why does it wait?"

"I do not know. Do you think you can get around it?"

"No, even when it turned on you, its tail acted like a whip to keep me at bay."

Stepha looked even more discouraged, and for the first time in her life, she felt her death was imminent. She glanced back to the hardened glare of her counterpart and thought of the child she carried. She sighed deeply then said, "Krirtie, listen to me and listen well. Regardless of what happens, I want you to run and not look back. Do not try to go around the creature, climb over it. That will keep you clear of the tail."

"What are you going to do?"

"I am going to keep its head and talons busy."

"No, I will not leave without you." Krirtie was staring as strong and powerfully as her terror-driven face would allow.

"We have been through much together Krirtie, but that does not mean we will die together. You are two lives now. The needs of two out-weigh the needs of one. If one of us is to escape, it must be you."

Tears filled the human's eyes as the two gave a quick embrace. "I shall never forget you, Stepha."

The elf turned in time to greet a shrill shriek from a creature growing impatient. "I believe it is going to attack. Be prepared to act."

Krirtie nodded and then Stepha leaped. Her quickness was amazing and caught the creature by surprise. She had grasped out and locked her arms around its neck. She was protected from its jagged, razor-like teeth, and it was using both free talons to pry the elf off, but Stepha held strong. Just as Krirtie began to move, the creature let out a scream of pain and began to convulse wildly. Stepha was thrown into Krirtie and both girls struck the far wall. Another screech blew through the caverns and then all was silent.

Stepha looked disbelievingly toward the now-motionless creature.

"Jermys!" she screamed.

Standing on top of the slain beast was their companion from so long ago. "What are you girls doing with this nasty bastard? Don't you know they fancy humans and elves? You should really be more careful."

Both girls leaped up and ran to him. "Oh, Jermys, I could not be happier to see an old friend." Krirtie grabbed the dwarf, who stood only just above half her size. "But how?"

"Well, you are both finally learning the proper greeting for a dwarf bearing gifts." He pushed them back to reveal the sword and bow he had been carrying since the throne room.

"Our weapons," exclaimed Stepha. "But how?"

As the elf touched the magical bow, an instant soothing caressed her body and even seemed to settle in her wings. "With each breath, I can feel my wings growing stronger. I pray someday I will be able to repay you for this gift, Jermys Ironshield."

"You can do that now by helping me find that blasted maneth and then getting us out of here."

Krirtie looked over at the dwarf who had begun to clean his ax. "Maldor is with Schram. They are both a great distance from here."

Jermys nearly toppled over. "Schram! What the hell was he doing here, and how did he get Maldor free? Krirtie began to talk, but the dwarf interrupted. "And how about letting us know so we did not risk our lives coming to this place? That damn human. When I see him, I am going to…"

Stepha placed her hand across his lips. "It is a long story, my friend, and one which should be told as we move. I feel it is never wise to remain in a dungeon." Stepha removed a pouch from her belt and sprinkled some of the contents across the fallen creature as Krirtie recovered her weapon. However, as the woman looked back, she saw the strange stare of the others as they looked upon the beast before them.

Krirtie asked, "I thought whatever life was lost was aided in some passage. Why does this creature remain?"

Stepha lifted her large eyes and softly replied, "This creature was created by magic. It has no spirit. The only thing which could have stopped it was stronger magic. At some point, this place will take it back, and new magic will be born from it." She turned her stare back to Jermys. "Guard your hatchet well, my friend, for it is truly powerful."

He smiled in return. "Trust in the knowledge that I know, and my legs know, your words to be true."

She joined his smile. "Your legs? I imagine you have a story of your own to tell, or more probably, Fehr has a story to tell. Where is the not-so-little rat?"

Krirtie became instantly attentive to the discussion, but when she saw Jermys's smile quickly fade, her concern struck with force. The dwarf motioned forward. "Come. Stepha is correct. We must hurry. I will explain all as we move, but I have overheard talk regarding an attack on Toopek possibly already commencing. We must get word to some outside forces or it could be too late."

Stepha nodded. "We too have heard such talk. We will have time to mourn those lost in time. For now, we must help those still with us."

Krirtie reached to the dwarf's shoulder to stop his pace. "Jermys, I must know. Is Fehr…" she paused as she could not say the word.

Jermys cupped his hand over hers. "I do not know." He paused then softly added again, "I do not know."

There was nothing else said for some time as all thoughts went to the lost rat. Although Jermys said he did not know, he was fairly certain that Fehr could not have escaped; and being different than the other companions, he would have had no key weapons or other intrinsic value to the dragon forces, and with that would have been killed immediately. As the dwarf looked upon the faces of Stepha and Krirtie, he knew they thought the same, and with that, further discussion was not necessary. He needed to know what happened to Maldor and, for that matter, what had happened to them, but he also knew it would wait. Their first goal had to be to get out of the caverns safely.

They had been moving at a swift pace behind Jermys's lead, carried by their newfound strength from their weapons. Their only trouble occurred when trying to climb back up the vine Jermys had thrown down to get in the dungeon. Once all had successfully made it back into the guards' room and Stepha had aided those passed, they were able to move without difficulty. During that time, they had begun to talk about their activities and actions, which brought them to Draag.

Now they stood in the reverse side of the mirror room, and Jermys showed them the reflection of the diamond stone in the helve of his hatchet. "It is just like I said. All we have to do is touch the mirror and you switch." The dwarf slowly raised his hand, and upon first touch, the diamond began to glow and hum. He looked around, and he was alone.

He stepped back from the mirror and in only moments, both Stepha and Krirtie appeared. Stepha stepped forward. "Truly amazing, Jermys. I would never have known, but now it is my turn to act. Please finish your story as we move." She turned to Krirtie. "Will you be all right alone for a moment?"

"Of course I will."

"Yes, I knew you would. I would take you both at once, but as of yet, I do not trust my wings fully. It has been a long time since I have flown."

The dwarf grimaced. "There is no way I am letting a woman stay down here alone while I get pulled to safety! I will not hear of it. If word of this got back to Felds—"

Stepha cut him off. "Jermys, we are alone here right now. The danger is up there. I need you up there ensuring that it is safe for Krirtie and me to return. Further, you are smaller, and although I feel confident, if I should fail, I want you with me to assist."

Jermys grumbled but accepted the answer, and with that, Stepha grabbed the dwarf, spread her wings which had gained in strength from the moment she held her bow again, and lightly lifted off the ground. Her exhilaration was evident as she did turn after turn and flip after flip. By the time she had completed her second trip, both Jermys and Krirtie shared the elven-green skin of the elf. Yet, that did not affect their speed as they sprinted toward the familiar path into the trees.

By the time they came to their first large glade, all had been caught up with the others' stories completely. However, Stepha motioned that they should stop. She was breathing hard and quite hungry. "We should break to eat, if you carry any food in your pack. It will be dark within the next half hour, and I would prefer to face what is ahead with some energy."

"I have enough food for each of us to have one meal. After this, we will have to fend for ourselves."

"Krirtie stepped forward. "I also think we should discuss our next move. Where are we headed? Toopek? Simply out of Draag? We must still try to aid Toopek. Should we try to contact Schram again?

Stepha bit into some bread Jermys had handed her before she replied. "You are correct, Krirtie. We do need to get out of Draag and try to help Toopek. We cannot try to contact Schram until we get out of here, and even then, I sensed he needed those with him to connect with Maldor at that level. We must assume Maldor was able to get through and word of Toopek was passed. With that, we must also assume Schram is no longer with those who could aid in that communication. Therefore, I believe the best help we can be for Toopek is to get aid from Elvinott and Feldschlosschen. We need those forces to compete with the dragon numbers we have been led to believe are there."

"Then are we bound for Feldschlosschen as a group?" Krirtie asked, looking for a mutual response.

Jermys stood. "Yes, we will not split up again. We will head to Feldschlosschen and then to Elvinott. If we move without sleep, we can reach Feldschlosschen in two to three days and one day more to Elvinott. Agreed?"

"Agreed," added Stepha and Krirtie in unison.

"I disagree," said a rough voice from the side of the clearing.

The three spun around, but it was Stepha who spoke. "Whi-Tead, I am pleased I will still have a chance to repay you for your kindness when we met before." Her eyes focused on the golden lock of hair he wore around his belt. She knocked an arrow in her bow.

Both Jermys and Krirtie drew weapons on the single dark dwarf as well, but all he answered with was laughter and a raised hand. "Before you charge and repay me for my kindness, I think there is something you should see, but this is especially for your eyes." He motioned toward Jermys. Suddenly two other dark brothers broke through the trees and dumped the bloodied remains of another dark brother before them—a dark dwarf Jermys recognized immediately.

His eyes hardened and his knuckles turned white around the helve of his hatchet. Stepha whispered. "Jermys, who is it?"

There was nothing but silence. Whi-Tead stepped forward. "What's the matter, dwarf? Tigon got your tongue? No matter, I will tell her. This is—or was—San-Deene, a highly ranked dark dwarf leader. However, when he returned the Hatchet of Claude to your friend here and allowed him to escape, the troops were a little upset." The other dark dwarves laughed. "It was a lucky thing his self-inflicted dagger did not kill him. His guards would have missed out on several days of fun learning all about you three. Poor soul, he died only hours ago."

"You shall join him soon, Whi-Tead, let that be certain to you." Jermys was locked in a cold stare with the dwarf leader who, for some reason, did not appear at all concerned with his current situation. Jermys was not thinking clearly, but both Stepha and Krirtie were extremely worried, and Krirtie had no real idea what was taking place. They had been speaking only ancient dwarven, and Stepha had no opportunity to translate. However, she understood enough, and it all came completely clear when the trees seemed to come alive with dark brothers. Where originally had stood three now stood nearly twenty, all with axes or daggers at the ready. The only sound as the three companions spun around, each taking a direction, was Whi-Tead's bellowing laugh.

Krirtie said flatly. "We fight them here or we end up back in the dungeon."

Both Stepha and Jermys nodded. Whi-Tead stepped forward. "Drop your weapons, scum. We have you surrounded. There is no escape, and let me remind you, there are many ways to die." As his raspy voice died off, he crushed his foot into the head of San-Deene, splitting what was left of the cut, beaten, and exposed skull. "You make the choice."

The three stood stoic and frozen, their weapons drawn and at the ready. "Jermys spoke in the old dwarven tongue forgotten by most. "We made our choice two years ago."

"As you wish," the dwarf replied so all could understand. He moved behind his guard and raised his hand. Before his hand dropped to begin what could only be a slaughter, seven dark dwarves on both sides fell dead bearing arrows in their chests. The remaining dwarves, including Whi-Tead, stared back in disbelief. The dark dwarf leader shot a glance toward the three in front of him, but their expression clearly showed they were not responsible.

In another moment another seven fell, followed by five more, leaving only Whi-Tead. The dark leader turned, but as he moved, he was greeted by a knocked arrow tip of two elves. Slowly he backed up until he stood eye to eye with Jermys. The dwarf removed the dark leader's weapons and, without a word, stepped over to the fallen San-Deene, retrieving his dagger, which still hung at his side. The dwarf moved back over to Whi-Tead and softly whispered in his ear, "There are many ways to die, and it is a pity you will only experience one of them." He plunged San-Deene's dagger into the dark dwarf's leg, causing him to fall to his knees in pain.

Jermys raised his own hatchet above him, causing Stepha to move between him and the bleeding body of the dark dwarf. "I promised you your death would be by my hand, but I will take that promise back by removing that which you took from me from your pathetic and weak body." She grabbed her lock of hair and proceeded to the side.

Jermys again raised his hatchet, causing Whi-Tead's eyes to grow wide with fear. Moments later, his head rolled free from his body by the blade of Krirtie's sword. "Go back to the hell you put us through" was all she said.

There was a short period of silence while each tried to regain their composure and bring their emotion back into check. It was Jermys who nudged Stepha and motioned to the seven elves, who had appeared at the edge of the clearing. Stepha moved over to them and embraced the one who appeared to be the leader of the small band. "Travasis, I don't have to ask why you are here, and I sure thank you."

"As do we," added Jermys, motioning to Krirtie as he spoke.

"No thanks is necessary, Princess Stepha. The king was worried for your safety and sent us to meet you in Gnausanne. When we could not locate you, we continued here, thinking it better to face whatever we came to here rather than to face your brother with the news we could not find you. We have been trailing this band of dark dwarves for days, assuming they would either give us a clue to your presence or, at some point, cross your path. Today seemed to be that time."

"My brother, I shall have words with him."

Jermys smiled. "With all due respect, Princess, because of your brother and Travasis's small force, you will have a chance to have words with him."

Stepha frowned as she understood his meaning. "Madeiris has to learn that I can take care of myself."

Travasis added, "He told us you would say that. I was to give you this message." He paused and pulled a small parchment out of his armor. Unrolling it, he read, "My sister, I am king."

"I guess he likes to keep things short and to the point," added Jermys. "Is that his way of saying if he wants to send a group out to help you, he can, and there is nothing you can do about it?"

Stepha tried to appear angry but could not. She smiled and said, "Yes, Jermys, that is exactly what he is saying.

They all smiled, and a few more hugs and pats were exchanged as Stepha gave the short version of what was occurring to the elven team. Following the formalities, the elven guard darted ahead to scout the forest for other trouble. If they could avoid any further entanglements, they believed they would be outside the boundaries of Draag by dawn. They all hoped this would be the case.

The Time Is Set

"**W**as there any way they could escape?"

Maldor shook his head. "If there was, we had not seen it yet. As far as we could tell, there was one way in and one way out, with the exception of magic doorways like the one which brought me here."

Schram turned to the guardians. "I must ask another favor. Please, you must discover a way to either send me back to Draag or bring my friends here. There has got to be a way."

There was a period of discussion before one of the human figures answered his plea. "I am sorry, Schram of Toopek, but without a definite source to lock on to, there is nothing we can do. We are quite limited when it comes to things with life."

"Things with life?" repeated Maldor. "Where on all of Troyf are we?"

"I am sorry, old friend," Schram began in a somewhat bewildered voice. "I neglected the fact that you are completely in the dark about all that is occurring. Be sure in the fact that all will become clear in time, but right now I must come up with what we can do to help Stepha and Krirtie."

"And my child," added Maldor proudly. "Krirtie carries our baby and is only a short time from its birth."

"A child? I knew that I sensed something in Elvinott, but I could not put my finger on it." He patted the big maneth on the shoulder. "It is good to have you with us again, my friend. And don't worry, we shall figure out some way to help them."

Hawthorne interrupted. "I am not sure it is within our reach to attempt such a move, but I do believe I could reach Draag by flight in two to three days. Even then, however, it may be too late if what Maldor says is true."

Maldor, stunned by the gentle unexpected softness of such a magnificent dragon's voice, stumbled over his words as he added, "She is correct. The creature they were up against would already have them if they could not devise an escape. To travel there at even our fastest pace would serve little to help them." His words seemed to trail off into nothingness as he spoke to them.

Schram too bowed his head, but his sorrow was once again interrupted by Hawthorne. "We also need to think about Slayne. He left here two days ago. His plans had failed. What will he do next? He has been a step ahead of us every move. We must think as he does and beat him to his next step."

Schram shrugged. "I don't kn…"

"He is going to put everything he has into one fatal swoop on Toopek." Maldor's face told of nothing but the most intense emotion as he interjected that which he learned at Draag.

'Toopek, how can you be sure?" Schram stared with deeply concerned eyes back at the maneth as he spoke.

Maldor paced. "One of the dragon lords, I think his name was Meyer, was disturbed with something Krirtie had said regarding his son's death.

All eyes fell quickly to Schram for embellishment. "Yes, William Meyer's son was publically killed by a black dragon in the main square of Toopek."

Maldor continued, "Well, it seems that the dragon lord was not aware of his son's death, and while the main force was away from the caverns, he came down to further question Krirtie regarding what she had said. During that time, he became infuriated and quite loose with his speech. According to him, the largest dragon force ever assembled is bearing down on Toopek, and possibly even as we speak blood is being shed."

"Good lord," cried Schram. "What have I done?"

"You have done nothing that should bring you shame, young Schram," broke in Werner. "Toopek is in very capable hands and supported with a fortress-like strength. She will hold against a mighty blow."

"But to hold against dragon strength, I don't think so." His head fell, and his voice fell softer. "I placed a weak barrier over the city, which will protect against a mild dragon offensive, but they would get through within a day. I was supposed to see if the canoks would be able to offer aid and possibly strengthen the barrier, but with all the complications, Toopek lost importance to me, and for that they will now suffer."

"You did nothing of the sort. You asked me to send word of our plans to those groups who could be trusted, and only Antaag and Feldschlosschen have been left ignorant. The day of your arrival at my homeland messages were sent. There has been plenty of time for the canoks to have reached Toopek. They will not let your homeland fall without defending it to their own destruction. You gave the canoks that much in return already."

His eyes softened on the now-completely red-coated canok. "Thank you, my friend. I will not forget."

Werner nodded but spoke no more. It was Maldor who broke in firmly. "If we are not able to help Krirtie and Stepha, then we must help Toopek. I would not begin to estimate the powers both this dragon and canok carry with them"—he motioned toward Hawthorne and Werner respectively—"but Schram, I have witnessed your abilities firsthand, and I now wield a weapon I have only recently begun to understand. At Toopek, we can make a difference."

Hawthorne was about to speak but was cut off by Schram's raised hand. "Maldor is correct, as far as I am concerned. I cannot speak for either of you, nor would I ask you to join us, as it could be a mission destined to fail. It must be your decision and your decision alone. Maldor and I must go, that is simply how it is."

300

Werner nodded. "I will not leave your side, Schram. I have been fighting this battle for over 200 years. For most of my life I have been fighting the dark evil that turned my coat black and split those I called kin. Whenever this war ends for me, let it be known that I did not back down before it."

"It will be known, my friend." He turned to Hawthorne.

The golden-brown-winged dragon took a step toward Schram until their eyes were only inches apart. Her soft voice sounded like music soothing all the emotions soaring in the room. However, her words were spoken only to one of them. "Until my death, I shall never leave your side again. For my entire life, I have longed to stand beside you and let you know the whole truth. Perhaps in time, that will happen."

A tear crossed her soft cheek as she backed to face the others. Schram was caught in a daze staring into open space. It was not until the maneth's deep voice struck his ears that he broke from it. "Our only problem now is, how do we get there? Since I am not certain of where we are now, it might not be a problem, but judging from your expressions, it might be."

"Well said, Maldor," replied Schram, now turning and walking as if nothing had just occurred but inside still puzzled by the large dragon's words. "I do not have an answer for sure, but do have a few questions. Werner, could we call on Khaled once again?"

The canok shook his head. "No, I feel he is a great way from here. I think our best choice would be by flight."

Hawthorne added, "I agree, but although I could make it carrying the entire group, it would stretch my physical strength, and by doing so, I would limit my abilities upon arrival. If there are dragon forces there, I believe I will need everything I have within me. We must find another answer."

"Guardians," began Schram, "is there—"

He was abruptly cut off. "Your transportation has been previously arranged. We are able to place you back at the Cindif Coast, and there you will find your passage."

301

"Previously arranged?" he replied. "By whom?"

But even as he spoke, the environment was altering, and all at once they were standing on the sand with rolling waves crashing to their side. Each looked around completely stunned, but it was Maldor who spoke first. "All right, the magic travel is one thing, then I can learn to accept the fact that there are good dragons, but there is no way you will convince me that those humans you called guardians were anywhere close to human. Their words came to my ears before their lips would speak them. Besides that, there were other things that I just couldn't place. There were feelings of loneliness and sadness surrounding the entire area. You said you would catch me up with all that has happened. Well, I will travel no further until it is so. Stepha said you left Elvinott on a path for the canok homeland. Why don't you begin there?"

Schram smiled slightly as he looked around. Both Hawthorne and Werner shrugged when their eyes met his, meaning neither had any idea or knowledge of the method of travel that had been "arranged" or who had "arranged" it. When he turned back to the maneth, he was greeted with a stern ultimatum given not in words, but in a stare of fire defined as, "Either fill in all the details regarding their whereabouts, or deal with a powerful warrior who does not like not understanding a possibly unfriendly situation."

Schram motioned to the others. "For starters, we need a rest. Night is beginning to fall, and until this transportation becomes known, we should eat and conserve our strength."

Werner interrupted. "There is a small amount of food left in my pack. Maldor looks famished. You two share this while Hawthorne and I will search out some more provisions."

Schram nodded his approval, much to Maldor's pleasure, and then the other two departed across the beach. After grabbing a bite of bread, he turned to the maneth. "To begin, you were correct. The 'humans' we just left were not human. They took that form so we would be able to comprehend their presence. They are the guardians over the Realm of Darkness. The limits of their powers and existence are beyond our ability to understand. As for how we arrived here from Troyf is a much more complicated story, so clear your mind because some of it—I should say most of it—will be difficult to believe."

He raised his hand. "Are you saying that we are no longer on Troyf?"

"Yes, that is precisely what I am saying."

Schram proceeded to explain his entire journey, leaving no detail absent as he replayed the series of events. Maldor sat in amazement, with his eyes and ears almost locked and ready to explode with the information being relayed. The one thing Schram was certain of was that Maldor was upset by the fact that he had missed everything.

Schram looked around and began to become a little worried over the delayed return of his friends. His storytelling had taken over an hour, and night had greeted them fully. Maldor saw his look and asked, "Should we look for them?"

"No, I am sure they are all right. After all, think about who they are. My mind is troubled by the absence of another."

Maldor nodded. "Aye, I too feel the loneliness."

They sat in silence for a few moments before Maldor jumped up. Schram was instantly alerted by his quick movement but relaxed when he saw his face. The maneth seemed excited and then even a bit scared as he spoke. "I almost forgot, but it could tell us at least one answer."

"What is it? I don't understand."

"When we were trapped in the dungeon, Stepha had a vision of death and misery, but now I know it was just this place you were in. However, she thought it meant that you had died. It nearly destroyed her. It was not until she concentrated through her Ring of Joining that she felt your life. Even at that distance, she knows you were alive."

Maldor looked down to Schram, but before he could say anything else, it was clear the magician was deeply concentrating on the ring. He rubbed his hand across and even brought his staff in contact with its band. Gradually, a warmth began to fill him, and a smile crossed his face.

He opened his eyes as if he were awaking from a beautiful dream. "They are alive, my friend. I can feel them."

Maldor too drew a deep grin. His thoughts trailed to Krirtie and their unborn child. He made a silent pledge to never leave her side again. It was a whisper to their side, which brought both he and Schram back to the present. Schram swung his staff toward the sound, to be joined by Maldor's hammer still attached almost naturally to his arm. Their faces looked blankly across the open beach.

"What was that?" whispered the big maneth.

"I am not certain, but I still feel a presence among us."

"Do not fear us, Schram and Maldor. Away from the realm we can come to you only as what we are—in spirit."

Schram's arm softened as he recognized the feelings. "Guardians, why have you returned? Does it relate to our passage across the sea?"

"No, the plan for your passage was set long ago. You will know in time."

"I do not understand, but I will respect your word." He paused then asked, "Why then have you come again to us?"

"Part of the arrangement is left unsealed."

"What arrangement?" broke in Maldor, a question Schram was about to ask as well.

The Anbarian hammer was a gift to us a long time ago. We respect your need for it, and only ask that when the time is right, will you return it to us, knowing that should you ever desire its use again, you would be free to retrieve it from the realm?"

Schram replied. "I cannot speak for Maldor, but I am not certain it is within his power to release it."

Maldor nodded agreement.

The guardian continued. "If it were within your power, would you do so?"

The maneth stared at the hammer he had only begun to experience and understand. The power within it was great, and to lose such a weapon was a difficult choice. Maldor glanced toward Schram and tried to read his thoughts but gained nothing from his expression. After only a moment more, however, he knew his answer. Lifting the hammer in the air, he said, "The Anbarian hammer was yours long before it found me. I feel blessed to have ever been able to wield its power at all. If you can teach me to free it from my body or if you can do it yourself, then I will surrender it back to you, for you are those whom it was created for."

There was no reply, but a strange feeling crept over both of them. Schram felt a surging in his staff and Maldor in his arm. The presence of the guardians suddenly vanished, and with it went Schram and Maldor's consciousness. The two huge men fell to the ground motionless.

∽∾

"Schram, Maldor, it is time," spoke Hawthorne softly so as not to cause a start to their resting minds.

Maldor slowly opened one eye while Schram leaped to his feet, his staff drawing on what caused the shadow across him. His eyes grew wide with amazement, and in only moments, Maldor's mind too alerted him to the oddity.

Together the two stood staring in disbelief. Hawthorne had returned to her human woman form, but if that was not enough for the big maneth to handle, beside her stood an enormous red dragon. Schram stepped forward and placed his hand against the lower neck of the beast, causing the dragon to bounce its head in return. "It is good to see you again, Draketon, although I am completely taken by your presence." He motioned to the side. "This is my friend and companion, Maldor. He is still not used to the presence of dragons, so please do not misread his stare."

The dragon bowed, and Maldor did his best to greet him politely in return. Draketon smiled at the maneth's discomfort but acknowledged that Maldor was also totally captivated by something else as well. Feeling he might not know, Draketon added in his deep, pure voice, "I was saved by your friends after an attack on their ship outside the Black Pool surrounding Anbari's Dominion. Are you familiar with the story?"

Maldor shook his head that he had heard about the magnificent red dragon that Jermys had first ridden through the black storm and then saved with the powers stored within his hatchet, but even the memory of this tale could not break the maneth from his gaze. Schram followed his eyes to find them locked on the beautiful human woman. With a smile, he said, "And you already know, Hawthorne." Maldor's jaw dropped while Schram continued, "She is able to shape change and will take this form when her presence as a dragon is not required."

Maldor said nothing. He only stared on in disbelief. Hawthorne remained smiling, but her tone carried a more serious message. "Draketon, by your presence here, I assume that you are to aid us in our passage across the sea?"

Draketon was still intrigued with the maneth's behavior but turned to face the woman for his reply. "Yes, although I am not certain it was suppose to be as such. It is simply how things came to pass."

"Will you be able to carry us all for that distance?" Werner asked.

"Yes, it should not be a problem. I owe Schram and his companions much. This will be little in return." The dragon's eyes scanned the area briefly and then fell back to the magician who was smiling appreciatively, but the smile faded when Schram saw Draketon's eyes. His tone changed and his wings became stiffened. "Where is Jermys?" he asked abruptly, his voice not hiding his displeasure with not having him still traveling with his group of companions.

Schram's face dropped and showed the signs of sadness. "We do not know. There has been no contact with him or Fehr for some time. Both were involved in a rescue attempt at Draag and they became separated. Stepha and Krirtie also have found themselves alone. We are all worried."

Draketon shared the feelings. "When your party has reached its destination, I shall proceed to Draag to search for them."

"That is very admirable, Draketon," added Schram, "but you will be recognized and hunted. You would be putting yourself in extreme danger, and we are not even certain they are there."

"Those facts are unimportant. Jermys gave me a new life when he saved me. It was an act I would not have returned had the situation been reversed. I was humbled by the dwarf. Because of it, I live today, and I will use that life to help those who gave it to me."

Maldor stepped forward and slapped his hand against the dragon's side. "Very admirable words, Draketon. I would like to accompany you should the situation at Toopek allow it."

"As you wish."

Maldor nodded. "Then let us be off." He raised the silver hammer above his head. "To Toopek."

Werner's eyes froze on the helve. "Maldor, your arm. It is freeing itself from the hammer."

All looked on, amazed at what was ever so slowly taking place. Schram inspected the joining. "Perhaps the hammer knows it is safe again."

"Or perhaps the guardians know a secret which we are ignorant of," added the maneth, turning with a suspicious tone to Schram. "I am unsure of when, or even how, we let ourselves fall asleep last night. Are you?"

He shook his head. "No, friend. I was wondering about that myself."

The group began to mount Draketon's back, but a worried look growing across the canok's face halted their actions. "What is it, Werner?" asked Hawthorne.

"I do not want to sound negative, but I am not sure this is correct."

"What do you mean?" Schram asked as he dismounted to stand next to the red canok.

"I do not believe we should travel to Toopek as one group. Would it not make more sense to bring more help?"

Hawthorne too leaped down. "He may be wise in his question. To fly directly to Toopek could prove foolish."

Schram frowned. "It would not be foolish if the attack has not commenced as of yet. We could warn them and help prepare Toopek for what to expect."

Maldor added, "Schram is also correct. I know Geoff and he will be aware if troops are approaching to attack, but he would have little certainty regarding their numbers, nor would he have any idea that a full dragon force stands behind the troops. They have to be prepared for the dragons, for they are the most dangerous to Toopek."

Schram remained speaking totally on fear and concern for his homeland. "If Toopek falls, so will our rebellion against the dragons. We have several isolated groups who would remain, but Toopek is our largest stronghold. In dragon hands, we would be only a heartbeat from defeat."

Hawthorn said nothing but closed her eyes as she heard his words. With a sudden shifting of space, her body changed until she once again took the magnificent form of the green dragon. Her eyes opened and she focused on Schram. "What I am about to say is something I swore I would never again do." She paused as a soft tear slid down the side of her face. "You and Maldor must fly with Shriak's grace to Toopek."

Schram smiled at the reference to the elven god of flight, but his smile was short-lived when he realized that it meant that he and Hawthorne would be separating.

He had feelings growing within him that he did not understand. His voice cracked slightly as he asked, "Does this mean you will be going to Elvinott with Werner?"

"That it does." Her response showed the same feelings carried in Schram's.

The two simply stared at each other, neither knowing what to say or what to do. Suddenly Schram broke the motionless stare and moved toward her with a deep embrace. Instantly she was back to human form, and the two held each other very tight. Schram felt love, but not the love he shared with Stepha. It was different. He wished he had any idea regarding its meaning, or why it was even there, but he did not. He did not understand how someone he met only a short while ago had a place so deep within him. However, all he could do now was let it flourish.

Pushing her back, he wiped a tear from her eye. "I…"

"And I you, Schram." She paused and added, "Do not worry. In time you will understand."

With that, she motioned to Werner. Moments later, she was back in dragon form, and the two were sailing across the sea. Schram reached out his hand and caught a final bead of water, which fell behind their path. He rubbed the water between his hands and softly whispered, "Someday I will understand. I only pray it is not too late."

He turned to greet the suspicious stare of Maldor and the confident nod of Draketon. Without a word, he leaped on the dragon's back, clutching his staff to gain both mental and physical support.

Maldor quickly fell in behind, but he would not remain silent. "You have not forgotten your ring, have you, Schram?"

The magician turned with a flat stare on the maneth. "This does not involve Stepha. It is something more, something different—I don't know—something from the past."

"Aye, Schram," added Draketon. "I too believe that it is."

The huge red dragon spread its wings and then gently lifted into the air. No other words were said except Draketon's answer to the unasked question. "About two days. Make yourself comfortable."

"Travasis, what is it?" Stepha could see the concern blanketed across his face.

"I can see no way we can make it through the forest and past the boundaries of Draag without conflict. The groups of dark dwarves and goblins are not large, but they are well spread. It would only take one to alert those nearby. Twice I almost walked into stationary camps. It is as if they are planted throughout the trees just waiting for anyone to enter their traps."

"I am afraid it is the same to the north," began another elf as he entered the glade as Travasis finished explaining what he had found. "The passage to Drynak is crawling with small bands. They are barely an army, but as scattered as they are, we cannot pass, and I could not guarantee success should we engage them."

"Damn," said Stepha. "Slayne has taken his total force to strike Toopek but left just enough to keep us at bay and prevent any warning we could give."

Krirtie moved closer. "But remember, Maldor is free. He can also spread the word."

"That is true," replied the elf. "But as well as I know Schram, he will feel obligated to head directly to Toopek. He will rely on us to bring the aid from the outside."

There was a moment of silence while each turned over their choices. Jermys broke the silence. "How about the forest to the south?"

"Toward the river?" asked Travasis. "I don't know, but even if they were clear, we would have to travel the length of the river all the way back north because the rapids are too intense. There is no place to even cross."

Stepha shrugged. "I would have to agree, Jermys. Krirtie and I got a brief taste of the southern river when we traveled part of it on our way to Draag. It nearly proved to be too much even in a magical raft. We could never cross it."

Krirtie nodded in agreement, but Jermys would not let it go. "Listen, I cannot explain fully due to a promise I made to a friend. However, let it be known that I can make it across the river. Once there, we might find some help."

"Are you sure, Jermys?" Stepha asked.

"As sure as I can be in this place." He paused, then said as he turned to the south, "Besides, we just learned we have no other choice."

Travasis leaped forward and grabbed the dwarf's shoulder. "If we must go this way, let my elven guard find the safest path. I mean no disrespect, but remember, we are part of the trees."

Jermys grumbled under his breath but still moved over and plopped down on a stump. Stepha slid to stand beside him, placing her hand across the top of his bald head. Jermys smiled and pulled his pipe and tobac out of one of his pouches. "Blasted elves."

Stepha smiled. "I know. We are almost as prideful as miner dwarves."

The old dwarf smiled briefly. "At least Fehr trusted my lead."

Stepha continued rubbing his head and back. "I know. It is difficult when you have lost your closest friend. It is easy to feel very alone."

Jermys swung his head up. "Closest friend? That thieving, no-good rodent. Have you seen how fat he has gotten? He ate all our safety stock of food one night after I was asleep. He only cares about himself. He is not my closest friend, and I tell you that most assured.

Stepha smiled out of the corner of her mouth, and then the dwarf added as a swirl of deep smoke encircled his head. "Fine, maybe I miss him."

Krirtie walked over and knelt down beside both of them. "I wonder if we shall ever all be together again."

The elf tried to hold her smile. "That is something I am sure will occur." However, it was clear in her voice that she was not as confident as her words would imply. In fact, inside she felt fairly sure it would not.

A short while after, the disgusted expression of Travasis burst through the trees. Jermys glanced up and sarcastically asked, "What happened? Did you get lost? I thought I was going to have to come find you and bring you back myself."

Stepha smiled slightly, but she was the only elf to do so. Travasis glared at the dwarf who still puffed heartily away, seemingly pleased with his comment of superiority. "No, it was impossible to get lost with the two-foot chimney smoking our trail back for us. We could as well have followed the entire dragon army forces along the same trail."

Jermys looked stung, though he only heard and understood the meaning behind part of the elf's comment. "Two foot!" He removed all his small weapons, leaving only the Hatchet of Claude hanging on his belt. Taking an extra moment, he fastened it securely in place so it was apparent it could not be drawn. He moved several steps into the clearing and removed his chest and shoulder armor. "All right, elf, it seems I need to use all 200 years and four feet plus to teach you a lesson."

Travasis firmly threw down his bow, sword, and a pair of daggers. His large green eyes become locked on the much-smaller dwarf before him. "As you wish, dwarf, but I think it is your stubborn pride that needs to be schooled."

"Stop it, both of you!" demanded Stepha. "If either of you makes another move, I shall fight you myself, and I will win."

Jermys ignored Stepha's plea, but Travasis could not forget that it was his princess who was speaking. The elf dropped his arms and stared at his leader. Stepha only frowned. Jermys took two more steps forward and then stopped abruptly as an arrow landed directly between his legs, slightly cutting him right at the tip where his two legs touched. "One more step, Jermys, and I aim one arrow tip higher!" Stepha already had another arrow knocked, and the line of flight seemed to match her words to the spot.

Jermys slowly reached down and removed the arrow that had become fixed in the ground, pointed upward, still touching his inner leg. Carefully he raised it up and handed it to the elf. "Travasis, I assume you understand that there are certain parts of a dwarf's body that deserve the utmost protection. Stepha seems to have located one of them. With that, I will stand down and respectfully withdraw my previous comment."

"And I as well, Jermys. I should not have reacted as such." He then added with a slight smile, "And elves do share the same area of protection, and I am confident had I continued, the result would have been the same."

Stepha and Krirtie were the ones carrying the largest smiles, but it was Krirtie who first asked, "Travasis, what did you find? It did take much longer than we expected."

The lead elf and his team stepped closer to the others. "We wanted to be certain, so we expanded our search. It appears that all the dragon army guards are scattered to the north and east. We saw only a few signs of guards over the entire area. In this sense, it appears that Jermys was correct." It was clear the last statement came somewhat reluctantly to his lips. "However, it is still a full day's walk to the river, and once there, we are trapped. It must be your decision, my princess."

Stepha glanced down at the dwarf who was already preparing to leave. Shaking her head, she whispered, "You better be right, you crazy dwarf." Then louder she added, "We will head south to the river. From there we will follow Jermys's lead."

Travasis frowned at the last comment but did not argue. With a shrug, he motioned the elven guard forward and then stepped down the path himself with Jermys, Krirtie, and Stepha right at his heels.

They traveled throughout the night, never stopping even to eat. The elven guards twice steered them clear of dark dwarf camps and one traveling goblin party, but by dawn, they had begun to put some distance between themselves and the caverns, and their confidence level was proportionately growing. Just as the sun crested above the trees, Stepha told Travasis that they should rest and use the time to pass around some food. Krirtie was altogether ready to collapse, and although she had learned never to complain, Stepha could see it in her stride. Furthermore, the elf knew that traveling with child could be twice as difficult as normal, especially if nourishments were not kept up.

With the signal to stop, Krirtie found the nearest clear spot and dropped to the ground. Jermys sat down beside her, and Stepha quickly brought over some bread and water. Krirtie happily accepted the bite of food, but her expression spoke of a longing for something more filling. Stepha smiled. "Don't worry, for there is much vegetation here. Let this only satisfy you for a moment."

Krirtie returned the smile and, in between breaths, replied, "Thank you, Stepha. This trek is taking a bit more out of me than I expected."

The elf nodded to both and then turned to relay further messages to the elven guard. Soon there was much to eat, all which would quickly replace all the necessities to give them added strength for what they had ahead of them. The elves were taking turns rotating on watch, and Jermys insisted on filling his place. By some odd twist of fate, Jermys and Travasis ended up sharing duties together.

The two traced through the trees, the elf glaring at Jermys each time a twig snapped beneath his boots. Jermys in turn became openly agitated with the elf for not listening to his warning that a rock formation was not correct.

"Listen to me, you green-skinned humanoid. That cliff should not be cut like that unless it was done for a purpose. I am telling you that more than likely there is some sort of camp below it."

"That is ridiculous, dwarf. We have searched this area completely. There are no hidden troops behind the ridge. That formation was created by water before you were born, and that was a really long time ago."

"By water?" He paused again, as he did not like being questioned about formations in the ground. "I have lived in mines for 200—I mean 175 years. Nothing but a massive excavating plan would clear rock like that. If you checked it out, it was only by sight from a great distance away. A setup like that is made to conceal who is using it. We have to get closer and check it out."

The elf swung around until he was standing directly in front of the dwarf. "Now you listen to me, half pint. Stepha is not here to protect you, so let me tell you how this is going to be. Elves do not waste time inspecting areas that are free from concern. My elven sight is much more acute than yours, and I am telling you that your hidden camp does not exist."

Bellowing laughs interrupted Jermys's next strike. The two swung and drew weapons to greet the smiling faces of six dark dwarf guards. Travasis's jaw dropped but he said nothing. Jermys recited several choice dwarven swear words, which sent the guards, three of which had arrows drawn on the two, into deeper laughter.

"Yes, you Feldschlosschen mud slinger, you are caught." The guards continued to lock their arrows on Jermys and Travasis while the leader continued jabbering in the broken dark dwarf tongue.

Travasis whispered, "What is he saying? I am not as fluent in the dialect."

After the leader finished, Jermys answered him with a response that sent laughter through all the guards and brought a large grin to Jermys as well.

"What?" asked the elf again. "What is being said?"

Jermys looked up to the elf who was staring questionably around. "He said I was right. There is a camp beneath the cliff. Furthermore, he has been watching your guards move around all morning. Then he asked if elves were as stupid as they appear."

Travasis was becoming red with anger. "And what did you answer?"

"I asked him if he had seen any swamp slugs lately because you were lonely and needed something of your own intelligence to talk to."

The elf was infuriated and moved to strike the dwarf but halted as the dwarven dagger greeted his throat. The dark dwarf leader shoved against the elf's chest, sending him to the ground. Turning to Jermys, he said, "I wish I did not have to kill you, Feldschlosschen scum. You are my kind of dwarf. It must be hell traveling with the likes of that."

"You are telling me. I am the one who has had to deal with his and the other's stupidity. He actually got tough with me once and wanted to fight."

The dark leader smiled. "What happened?"

"The fool elf backed down and went running to his sister for protection. He thought I would not hit a girl. After I slapped her around a while, I discovered he had run off. By the time I had caught up with him, all his pathetic whimpering disgusted me so much I decided to give him a break. Now that his foolishness has led us into this mess, I would give anything to have that chance back."

The dark dwarf slapped him on the back and said in his raspy voice, "How bout if I give you the chance?" The other dwarves turned and began to chant for a fight.

Travasis made it back to his feet and, in a snide voice targeted toward Jermys, asked, "What have you and your buddy decided?"

The dwarf turned and stood before the elf with his back to the guards. Beginning with a wink of his eye, the dwarf leveled the elf with a blow across the face. Cheers rang out from the onlookers as Jermys knelt before the fallen elf. "He suggested that since I had to put up with you for so long, he will let me teach you a lesson before he kills us both." His voice softened to a whisper.

"I'll take the three with bows drawn. You are responsible to keep the others at bay."

"Fine!" exclaimed the elf as he kicked Jermys in the face, sending the small dwarf tumbling to the side and causing blood to flow from his wrinkled nose.

"So that is the way you want to play it, huh, elf? Well, this morning is turning out…"

Jermys was interrupted when the dark leader's hand drew out a dagger and had it rest on his shoulder. "Why don't you remove all your weapons first?" There was some mumbling among the guards and then he added, "On second thought, why don't you each keep a dagger."

A slew of cheers followed as both individuals tossed all their weapons to the side; just by chance it happened to be the side away from the guards. Jermys and Travasis refused to take their eyes off each other as they circled, each satisfied with using just their fists for the time being, keeping their daggers attached to their belts.

The elf made the first move, charging at the well-prepared dwarf. Jermys ducked to the side and kicked upward, sending the elf to the ground. Travasis quickly recovered, but not before Jermys was sending another punch, this one landing cleanly across the elf's nose. Blood seeped across his cheeks, but it only served to infuriate the elf more. A violent exchange of blows ensued where both participants took as many as they received. The small group of onlookers cheered and chanted some rooting for their closer kin, and some even hoping that the Feldschlosschen miner got torn to bits.

Both Jermys and Travasis had completely forgotten about being captives, and now their only concern seemed to be beating the other. The elf was on his knees, bringing him about eye level to the shorter Jermys. Yet, neither would completely go down. Punch after punch each would throw and then receive. It became a slow, grudging fight where the dwarf would gather all his remaining strength and land a shot, sending the elf nearly to his back, and then after a sizable length of time, Travasis would be strong enough to counter.

The dark dwarves were near ecstatic with excitement as both the companions had bruises and blood which were swelling by the second. Wagering among the guards was going wild with each throw, seeing a change of sovereigns. Finally, with one cutting hook, Jermys took the elf to the ground. Seeing his competitor face down, the dwarf stumbled slightly away, saying, "And let that be a lesson to you," before he too struck face down in the dirt.

The dark leader moved forward, still bellowing deep laughs. "It is truly a shame I have to kill you. I would love to watch that every—"

His statement was cut off as an arrow landed in his throat. Jermys was to his feet before those around could regather their bows. Even in his exhaustion, he dropped three within moments, which matched what fell from elven arrows. The two stood staring around the mass of bodies and then met on each other.

The elf smiled through cracked and bleeding lips. "You are an admirable foe. I was waiting for you to take a dive, but I had to, for I was not sure I would be able to last if I didn't."

"To be honest, I was going to fall with your next punch. Damn things were beginning to hurt like you wouldn't believe."

Travasis remained smiling as he gathered the rest of his weapons. "Oh, I can believe it, most definitely."

They were about to leave the glade when the elf stopped and removed a pouch from his pack. "It is our way."

"I know. I have traveled nearly all of Troyf with Schram and Stepha. I have learned much from the elves, and all of it is very worthy."

Travasis nodded appreciatively. "And over the last two years, I have come to understand that Elvinott is not the only place on Troyf with merit and honor. When we fled our home and sought refuge in Feldschlosschen, I learned much about the dwarves. You too are very worthy."

Jermys smiled profoundly. "There is much we can learn from all races, even those we do not call friends."

Travasis found truth in the statement as he spread the elven dust across the dark dwarf bodies to aid those passed. It was a solemn moment that transpired in that small glade, both for the passing and everything the dwarf and elf had shared. Then, with a shout from a nearby dark dwarf alerted by the previous noise, their moment was done and they began to run.

"What are our choices?" hollered Travasis.

"Can you land an arrow from here?"

"Not through the trees. He will have the full guard unit on us in moments."

Jermys thought about the others. "How far is it to the river?"

"Not far. An hour, maybe two." The elf paused then asked, "Why? Won't that just trap us? We can fight them here or we can fight them there, and I would prefer within the trees."

"No," replied the dwarf. "We must make it to the river. With false trails and occasional bowfire, I know we can do it. But we must hurry."

Travasis shrugged. "I guess we have nothing to lose. I should have listened to you regarding the cliff. I will trust you now. Come, let's get the others."

The two continued running through the trees with a speed unsuited to their exhaustion. As they drew near their friends, their warning shouts alerted the camp, and when they arrived all stared in disbelief.

Stepha was first to speak. Travasis, what happened? You both have been beaten."

The elf guard seemed surprised. "Oh, the bruises. Jermys and I got in a scuffle with each other but we did it to escape."

"Then why isn't Jermys bruised?"

Travasis swung around and stared at the dwarf, who greeted him with an ear-to-ear smile and a face completely devoid of any signs of a fight. The dwarf's tone carried nothing but pride. "The hatchet does wonders for a complexion."

The elf frowned, but before he could speak, Stepha broke in again. "What? Escape from who?"

"A dark dwarf camp," replied Jermys. "Come on, we have to make it to the river."

The group set out at a run. Travasis, Jermys, Krirtie, and Stepha remained at a direct pace toward the river while the other elves darted through the trees covering all trails and creating false ones, then, if there was time and a clear shot, slowing the pursuit down with a barrage of bowfire.

Those trailing them numbered about forty. Jermys believed it was probably the majority of the dark dwarves in this area of the forest, as they did not need to be scattered as approaching the river would not have been a typical direction. If not for the elves buying them time and due to Krirtie's slower-than-normal pace, Jermys was certain the dark dwarves would have caught them before they reached the river. As it was, he thought they might have a chance.

Stepha took Krirtie's sword and was swiping branches out of the way with one hand while helping her along with the other. The work was tedious, but she seemed to be having success. Krirtie was doing her best to keep a strong pace, but her exhaustion seemed to come quick, and her strength was fading fast.

It was just over an hour later when Travasis raised his hand for silence. The group halted, and all in the forest became very still. They looked around briefly, and it was Stepha who first said, "I hear it. The river is not far."

Jermys listened, and his eyes widened as he too heard the rolling rapids of the River Draag. Travasis waved them on. "You three go ahead at the swiftest pace you can manage. I will signal the others together, and we will cover our trails."

The three wasted no time, but Travasis grabbed the dwarf by the shoulder before he could leave. "It is up to you now, my friend. Find us a way, for if not, we are greatly outnumbered."

Jermys gave only a nod and quickly disappeared behind the others. They reached the river's embankment, and all were panting from the intense final sprint. The dwarf pushed in front, but it was clear in his eyes that nothing was looking familiar. He scanned the water's edge, but the only thing that signaled a direct memory was the thunderous rampage of the rapids, and they looked the same for as far as his eyes could see.

Stepha stood next to him. "What you are looking for is no longer here, is it, Jermys?"

Her voice showed nothing but care and sympathy, but it did little to aid the worried dwarf. "No, it is still here. I am just not able to find it. The passage is well hidden. It did not occur to me that it might be too well hidden."

Stepha looked down. "So there is a passage here? Across the river?"

The dwarf smiled slightly. "Well, more precisely, under the river."

She nodded. "Then perhaps if we follow its edge, we will stumble across it." As she spoke, the other elves broke through the trees. "We seem to have no other choice." She smiled as she repeated his line from when they made the decision to head to the river.

Travasis said, "We have covered our trail but have only gained maybe a quarter of an hour at best. We must move quickly. Jermys, lead the way."

The dwarf glanced at Stepha and saw nothing but courage in her large green eyes. With a confident grin of his own, he darted down the embankment. They were running for only moments when Jermys put on the breaks so hard that one of the elves tumbled over him.

"What is it?" asked Travasis.

"Look, Stepha," Jermys replied, pointing at the dirt-and-sand mixture at their feet. "Tracks."

"Rat tracks," Krirtie added. "And they head toward the water."

Jermys followed the tracks to the edge with the rest of the group at his heels. "You don't think he tried to swim this, do you?"

Stepha shook her head but was cut off by Travasis. "I am not sure what the concern is here, but we are extremely pressed for time. The tracks do not circle back so you must assume…" He stopped in midsentence when he saw the dark dwarf appear ahead of him. Knocking an arrow, he drew on the inquisitive figure.

Jermys glanced over, unaware of either the dark dwarf or Travasis's intentions. Seeing the dwarf, he immediately drew his hatchet as well. Taking a step closer, however, he quickly relaxed and turned back to the others. "We have found…Travasis, no!"

The elf let his arrow fly. Jermys wheeled and fired his hatchet in its wake. The dark dwarf it was intended for froze as he saw the long wooden shaft going straight toward his heart. Only inches before the rigid tip of the elven arrow met the center of the dark brother's chest, Jermys's hatchet bit into the shaft in flight, and the impact split it cleanly in two. The dark dwarf swore distinctly under his breath but quickly replaced it with a praise to be alive.

All looked on in amazement, but Jermys was out to waste no more time. Leading the group at a full run, he was in front of the dwarf in no time. With a smile he said, "Dol-Teo, I never thought I would be so happy to see a dark brother."

The dark dwarf replied, "Quickly. Our scouts have said a large group trails you at a fast pace. We must keep our passage hidden. Elves, your expertise at covering trails greatly exceeds my own. Will you assist in this process, for it is of dire importance?"

Travasis nodded, though he did not understand nor trust this situation. He turned to his princess, who also showed a concern in her eyes and held her bow close, but pushed the warrior elf forward with her stare. The group quickly fell in behind Teo's lead, and soon they arrived at the outcropping of trees marking the passage. With a wave to the others, all descended into the tunnel and Teo replaced the cover.

A blank stare crossed all the elves' faces, including the gazes of Stepha and Krirtie when they saw what was before them. Jermys followed their stoic pose down the tunnel to find himself staring into the heavily armored and war-ready faces of over 500 dark dwarves, an amount Jermys imagined to be the entire camp. All were standing broad with weapons drawn, wearing hard expressions depicting troops preparing for battle.

Jermys swung back to Dol-Teo. "What is all this?"

The dark dwarf's face was devoid of any pleasantries. He rechecked the tunnel exit and, seeing no pursuit in the area, turned back to the others. "Much has happened since you left, Jermys. Kapmann has been overthrown at Antaag and is feared dead. Antaagian dwarves have been scouring the Forgotten Forests looking for whoever he has been in contact with. There have only been a few confrontations, but that was enough. We could not bring arms against our kin in a civil war."

Jermys nodded that he understood and then relayed what had been said to those with him who showed they did not follow the dark dwarf language.

Dol-Teo broke a brief smile and then continued in common tongue. "I am sorry. I sometimes do not recognize all that I should. As I was saying, with our tie to Antaag broken and the nation in war, which in turn is being felt all the way to Feldschlosschen, we are caught without many choices. Should we help King Kapmann, it would probably make things worse at Antaag. Although he said he was certain some dwarves were ready to accept peace talks, most were not. Furthermore, should we remain in the forests or even head back to the Canyon of Icly, we would be thrown into war against those we do not wish to fight."

"So you have moved your entire camp to hide in this tunnel beneath the river?"

There was an uncomfortable shuffling and several whispers from the dwarves within earshot at the comment. "No," replied Dol-Teo sternly. "We hide from no one. Tal-Gentry and Eb-Brown have led a small party through Draag to find us the safest passage. When they return, we will all move in and attack the only true enemy we have—the dragons. Our scouts have said we will never find the caverns less defended. We are going to go in, destroy everything we can, and get out. Only then, after word has spread regarding our actions, can we expect any sympathy from the dwarves at Antaag and Feldschlosschen for that matter."

Jermys dropped his eyes. For the first time in his lifetime, they were close to having peace between rivaling dwarven nations; and because of some ignorant dwarves at Antaag, all was about to be lost. Jermys raised his hatchet and said, "I will return to Antaag and bring order to the chaos with the powers and values carried within the Hatchet of Claude—the one thing in this world that all dwarven races recognize as true. After you do what your must at Draag, seek me out at Antaag, for peace there will be."

His words were powerful and even brought cheers from some of those behind. Dol-Teo stepped forward and took the dwarf's hand in his. "We shall do just that, Jermys Ironshield."

His comment was interrupted by a sound from outside the tunnel. Teo spun around, immediately holding his sword at the ready. Should they be discovered, although he was certain he outnumbered any opposition, his current position was defenseless. All his troops were behind him and in tight corners. He did not want an invasion now. He motioned for silence, and immediately that command was carried throughout the entire forces. The small group of companions was caught by the ominous silence that seduced the entire tunnel. Then again, the same odd sound was heard, this time repeating in a set rhythm.

Teo raised his sword with a smile. "Dwarves, ready yourselves. That is the signal, and the time has come to attack."

Stepha leaned closer to the dark dwarf. "Teo, if you are truly going to attack the caverns of Draag, there is one thing within its walls which must not be left intact. Once in the caverns, you will see a large, round room with a beautiful mirror. It is a magical port to the rest of the caverns. Do not touch it; do not spend time gazing into it. Simply destroy it. Whatever it is separating has some powers we do not fully understand, but its destruction has to be damaging to the dragon forces."

"We will destroy this mirror, young elf." He turned to the others. "Good luck in your travels, for I am certain there is no path free of danger this day." He paused then turned to his Feldschlosschen counterpart. "And Jermys, until we meet again."

There was another signal from outside, and Teo turned to lead his dwarven army forward, but before he could move, Jermys grabbed him. "There is something else you should know before you begin. Most of the resistance we found was from dark brothers."

Teo drew a sad breath. "Understood."

"Until we meet again, Teo. I shall be waiting."

The dwarf nodded, and with what equaled a near roar, the dwarves filed through the tunnel. It was an army like Troyf had never seen before. Dark dwarves fighting together perhaps for the first time not interested in filling their pockets with wealth. Their goal was only to try to grow their nation. As the last dark brother exited, Stepha whispered to herself, "Slayne could not have foreseen this." She smiled under her breath and turned to their small party that now stood alone in the tunnel, seeing all their eyes drawn back toward her.

Jermys motioned forward. "Come on, we still have over a day's travel to Feldschlosschen, and even that is dependent on if we can find a boat on the other side of the lake."

Krirtie glanced at Stepha and whispered, "I can't get over Jermys suggesting a boat ride."

The elf just shrugged. "I shall believe it when I see it."

TOOPEK

"Lower the gate! Lower the gate now!" shouted Geoff. "Alan, lead the main group into the large community center and begin explaining what we have done here and what has happened over the last seven days. Then, find out what has happened that brought them to flee their city to come here."

"Aye, Geoff, I will do what I can." Alan Grove, the once third lieutenant in the Toopekian army now placed in charge over all the human forces, began shoving through the crowd of people who had just fled Empor to seek safety behind the walls of Toopek. With shouts, waving arms, and aid from others under his command, he began filtering the majority of the people through the streets.

Geoff hollered back, "And if you see Prince Reynolds or any of the other leaders of Empor, send them to the conference room at once and then join us there yourself at your earliest convenience."

The large maneth was not sure if his words had been heard or not, or whether they were understood. Alan tried to issue some sort of signal, but its meaning was lost as he was pushed along by the crowd. "Yeah sure, lion man, I will be right there. Right after I get these thousand people settled, maybe early next week."

Geoff sat atop the outside wall he had erected around Toopek and peered with a concerned stare into the nearby forest.

"What do ya see out der, Geoff?"

The surprise voice from behind nearly made the maneth fall from the wall. He turned to greet the dirty, unshaven face of Captain Max Pete, his torn eye patch pushed up to his forehead, allowing his missing eye to be the first sight one would see.

Geoff's face showed little emotion though even the maneth, who had seen tremendous tragedy in his lifetime, could not stare directly at the old sea captain. "I see many questions and not too many answers for them."

"Aye," the captain replied. "I'll not be one to ever shy from a fight, but what the bloody hell these dragons are planning is beyond me."

"We have seen the goblin, troll, and dark dwarf forces out there for days, but they do not attack. What are they waiting for?"

"Perhaps they be waitin' for us."

"I have thought that myself. Do they want us to grow weary of their presence and be unprepared? Do they want us to attack them? I keep having a feeling that I am missing something, something I should not be missing."

Pete smiled his characteristic toothless smile that he seemed to proudly show stared toward the maneth. "A good leader will always second guess himself if he be truly good. It'd be their way of makin' sure all is how it should be. Like I said before, don't you be too worried 'bout them goblins and the like. It's them winged beasties we have to watch out for."

Geoff nodded. "Yes, I have the smiths forging lances and spears and steel arrows to try to create something that will have an effect on the dragons, but I don't know."

Pete only shook his head, agreeing that he had little faith in the weapons but not willing to voice it as such. "Them dragons 'ol be a tough lot, all right, but we'll figure 'em out."

"I only wish I had heard back from Schram. He said he would send help to prepare should a dragon attack occur, and as yet, no word. I doubt whatever magical barrier, if one even still exists, will have any affect for long. We need to be prepared for the worst."

Geoff walked along the wall until he reached one of the ladders, and then with Pete right behind him, the two descended to the ground. Quickly they moved through what he called the wall forces until he found Meris, a maneth who wasn't high on the Dimat line but whom Geoff had put in charge of the outer wall activity.

"Greetings, Geoff, Pete," Meris began. "Any word on the evacuation of Empor?"

Geoff shook his head. "No, and I am worried. I want the guards doubled on the walls every twenty feet and ten feet around all access roads. I also want all the elves divided among the maneths and humans. It is no secret they are more precise with a bow, and this is not the time for pride to get in the way."

Meris became concerned. "Geoff, I am spread thin as it is. With that many more on the outer wall at a time, I will not have any left to trade off, and then all the troops will grow tired and less effective. The elves especially grow weary. They are too few, and I do try to keep them on the wall longer, which they all seem to understand, but I can't ask them for any more for they don't have it to give."

Pete broke in laughing. "If me men did not give what I asked, I'd be sendin''em to the sea for a bit to dance with them sharks. I say throw an elf or two to the goblins. The rest be fallin' in line."

He was cut off by Geoff. "I'll send you another hundred or so men. Use them as I have asked but above all, keep the guards fresh. We can't have lazy or tired eyes on the wall."

"Where will you get more men? You are as thinned out inside the walls as I am out here."

"We just got a full army from Empor. If they seek refuge, then they will need to help defend it. Distribute them throughout the defenses."

"Aye, warlocks and wizards with no real powers. They originally left Toopek because they refused to follow the king's rule, which meant to be prepared to fight if called upon. I have heard stories from other humans, and you know Prince Reynolds. They will not defend this city."

"Put a bow and a sword in their hands and make them targets on a wall and see what they do. Humans have a will to survive.

Let's use it"—he paused then turned to Pete—"and if not, consider Pete's idea."

Pete laughed deeply again. "That's the way to think, ol boy. Kill or be killed, eh?"

Geoff nodded. "I'll have them meet with you. Spread the Emporians thin and never pair two together. Have someone answer any of their questions regarding their weapons. I am sorry, but we have no choice."

Meris accepted the notion though his displeasure was not hidden. As Geoff turned, he was greeted by hollers from the top of the inside wall. "Geoff, Grove says he has located an Emporian you wanted to see and awaits word from you, also signal from the east gate guard regarding some movement in the nearby forests."

The second statement grabbed his attention. "Movement? What kind of movement?" he hollered back.

"I don't know, sir. They just relayed it to me as I was looking for you. All they said was one of the elves saw something."

Geoff glanced at Pete and Meris, and both showed the same concerns. "Meris, send as many extra guards as you can spare to the front gate as I want support there in case this is a diversion, and then accompany more to the east gate where I will be. Pete, begin getting your company together and prepare your ships to sail." He hollered back as the other two quickly moved to carry out the requests. "Tell Alan to hold whoever he has and I will meet with them shortly. Also, tell him I am at the east gate and that we will need several of the Emporian men to help on the outer wall." He paused before adding, "And hurry." He turned and began running toward the far side of the city between the two walls that created a hallway around it. "Blast it! Is it all about to begin?" Whether his words were heard was unknown.

⁂

"See, there is it again."

Geoff had just reached the top of the ladder at the east gate. The big maneth was breathing heavy but did not let it show. "There what is again?"

Meris glanced up, surprised at the comment, but relaxed when he saw the speaker. "Ah, Geoff, I am glad you are here. Perhaps you can see it." He motioned to the elf who had just spoken beside him. "This is Fritzonismalonis Stac..."

The elf stepped forward. "I am Fritz, sir, and might I say it has been a while."

"Yes it has," replied Geoff. "About sixty years or so I would imagine."

"At least that. I wished circumstances here were different, but it is still good to stand beside you again."

"Yes, I remember, and it is good to see you again as well"—he motioned forward—"now, with the matters at hand?"

Meris broke in. "Fritz has repeatedly seen movement at the first outcropping of trees, but as yet, no one has appeared."

"That's too far for me to see clearly," replied Geoff, staring toward the point. "Have you been able to make out who or what is creating the movement?"

"No, they appear to be staying in the shadows but also wanting to make their presence known."

"They?" he asked. "You mean there are more than one?"

"I cannot be sure, but there seems to be four, maybe five. The movement is too widespread to be any less. And those are just the ones moving. There is no telling if there are hundreds more deep in the tree cover."

Geoff looked on but still could see nothing. His frustration was now carried in his tone. "How many flyers are there?"

Meris motioned to Fritz for the answer. "That I know, about, six. But more could have come in from Elvinott over the last few days, I would not have known."

"Ask the strongest flyer to accompany me. I need elven sight and flyer capability."

Fritz nodded and hurried off. Meris appeared concerned. "You are not considering going out there, are you, Geoff?"

Geoff turned to the smaller maneth. "Considering it, no. I am going to do it." He paused then added in a tone much like a teacher speaking to a pupil. "For some reason, something is hiding outside boundaries but not hiding to hide, hiding to be seen. I need to understand why."

"Let me go. You are too important here to justify putting yourself in that position. The highest probably says it is a trap. They are bait to bring you out."

"No, this is something that my duty requires me to investigate. My feelings hold that a group wishes to approach, but they are not certain they will be accepted. If that is the case, only I can determine if we should allow them in."

"And if you are wrong and it is simply a dragon trick?"

"Then hopefully"—he glanced over and saw Fritz returning, being carried by a large flyer elf—"Tantis will be able to get us out of there quickly."

"Greetings, Geoff. It has been too long," the large, older flyer elf said as he landed.

"Tantisolandis Arnolin," replied the maneth leader. "I never thought I would see you again." He looked toward Fritz, smiling. "I thought I told you the strongest flyer, not the oldest."

Both elves smiled, but it was Tantis who spoke. "I am younger than you, you old war maneth." The two locked hands and then hugged. "So we are doing it again, eh?"

"It looks that way," Geoff replied. "Do you fly as well as you did 200 years ago?"

"I will give you more than you need, my friend." He paused, turned toward the woods, and added, "Fritzonismalonis Stacis filled me in on the situation. I am ready when you are."

"Very well," the maneth replied. "Meris, you and Alan are in charge should anything happen. Do not open the gate for anybody. If for some reason I come back without grandpa here, I will use a ladder, but wait for me to ask for it in elven tongue. I sense strange magic at work, and I am not afraid to take every precaution."

"As you command," he replied. "And Geoff, be careful."

"Always," the large maneth answered. He motioned to Tantis, and the elf moved over behind him, grabbing Geoff about the shoulders. Geoff stood nearly a foot and a half above that of the elf but Tantis did not show any sign of fear at the maneth's weight. With a second nod, the maneth said, "Whenever you are ready."

Tantis added, "I'll be ready as soon as you remove this medieval club from your back. I am going to ask you the same question I asked you 200 years ago. What kind of weapon is a club?"

Geoff held up his maneth club proudly. "I am going to answer the same way I did then." He turned about and faced the elf. "Reach for your bow, elf, and find out!"

Tantis smiled, but it was cut short as he stared at his old friend's weapon. "Oh my, please do not tell me so?"

"What?"

"That is the same club you used 200 years ago."

"You bet your elven ass it is. Carved from the finest of red oaks."

"That was carved?"

Geoff was about to detail the meticulous craftsmanship that went into his club when Meris interrupted. "Are you two going to leave?"

The large maneth glared at his counterpart with a smile under his stare. He reluctantly turned back to stand where the flyer elf could best lift him. He whispered to Tantis, "You still using that bow you carved from the willow wood when you were less than fifteen?"

Tantis smiled. "Yep, finest bow ever made."

Both shook their heads without another comment. The elf grabbed Geoff around his shoulders and easily lifted him into the air. "May Shriak fly with us."

"He might as well," Geoff added. "You are older than he is, so he may learn a bit from the experience."

Laughter rung from the top of the wall, which Geoff thought was welcome to hear. It had been a long time since there had been any such feelings. Tantis resisted further speech but then added, "Watch yourself, Geoff. You have gotten much heavier—or should I say fatter—over the years, and I would hate to drop you."

Geoff shook his head with a smile, and together both men knew they would give their life for the other. There was no flyer elf, short of the princess or her brother, Geoff would rather be traveling with. After a few minutes, they were about midway between the outer wall of Toopek and forest outbreak, and Tantis gently set them on the ground.

Geoff turned to the elf. "Come on, old friend, we shall talk as we go. It has been too long for us."

"Yes, it has."

⊙⟶⟵⊙

Back on the wall, Meris could see the two had landed safely and were walking toward the area of movement. He turned back to Fritz and the others. "If there are any more flyers who would be free to fly support should our friends need it, have them assemble at the front gate."

Fritz nodded. "I shall see what I can arrange." Moments later, he was down the ladder and gone.

To another guard, Meris ordered, "Prepare a party of fifteen that will be ready to charge the trees, and see if we can get some top archers to this side of the wall for the time being." The guard shook his head, and then he too hurried to fulfill the orders. "You may not want this gate open, Geoff, but I'll have a welcoming party ready to provide whatever support you need."

⊙⟶⟵⊙

Geoff and Tantis continued at a swift but cautious pace toward the trees. Their talk had been of the past and all that had happened to bring each to their current place in this war; and although there were moments of good humor, the majority of their conversations

333

left them violently aware of the pain stretched across all of Troyf. Tantis had spent the years, following the Dragon Oppression, recovering from his losses. His entire family had fallen prey to the evil, and he found his own sanctuary on the northeasternmost reaches of Troyf, beyond the canok homeland. He had begun a new life there among those of the forest, a life unaffected by the evils across the rest of the land. However, when he had felt a calling from Elvinott, he knew that his time to mourn had expired. Staying in seclusion did not bring his family back, and should they be watching him now, they would not be feeling pride in their hearts. He knew he was not feeling pride in his heart. He knew he must return and possibly end that which caused his loss so long ago.

Now Tantis found himself in the heat of the war, the same war against the same enemy and with his same friends by his side. As they walked together, however, nothing felt as it did when they were younger. The elf glanced at his companion and no longer saw the draw to adventure burning in his eyes. Instead, he saw the lines of great pain and hardships burnt across a tired face. The elf knew the years had not been good to his friend and wondered if he saw the same in himself.

Tantis refrained from adding any further comment as Geoff seemed content to do the same. His head dropped slightly and then shot up as his ears caught wind of a distant sound. He swung his arm up to halt Geoff, and the big maneth displayed immediate understanding. Tantis searched the tree line, which was now about 300 paces ahead, and his eyes froze on a point near Fritz's original sighting of movement. Pointing his finger to the spot, he whispered, "There are our visitors, I believe there to be four. Do you see them?"

Geoff followed the line to the trees. "I see something, but I can't tell what. It looks like"—he paused then added—"you don't think those are canok eyes, do you?"

The elf stared. "That was my original thought, based on the height and rapid movement, but that color is wrong."

"Just like this whole blasted war." Geoff's voice was stronger but seemed to be driven more on frustration rather than confidence. "What do you suggest we do?"

He let out a sigh then continued to push forward. "It is obvious, canok or not, that they refuse to enter the plain between the forest and the Toopekian boundary, so we have no choice but to come to them."

Tantis knocked an arrow in place. "I have gotten old, Geoff, really old."

"You and me both, my friend. You and me both."

His last statement seemed to drive them ahead, each willing now to admit their certain fears, which their youthfulness had shielded them from in the past, but neither ready to give in to them. Both kept their eyes focused on the activity ahead of them, but with each step forward, they realized that beside one set of eyes, which never turned from their approach, all activity had ceased. No longer were there three or four individuals hidden just inside the tree line. Now there was but one, and that one seemed to be inviting them into the forest.

Geoff motioned for Tantis to stay with arrow ready, and he alone continued forward. The elf knelt down to a knee and kept the small figure nestled in the first few feet of woods locked in his sights. Geoff slowly crept forward while the creature he approached remained completely still. It was not until he drew within about twenty feet before he was certain of the creature's identity, and even then his mind had trouble grasping what he saw.

He waved at Tantis to approach and then proceeded to draw within a safe speaking range. Still holding his club in defense, he said, "Greetings to you. I am Geoff, King of the Maneths and current ruler over Toopek. I must admit that it has been a time period longer than I care to mention that I have looked upon one who appears as you do now, and I would like to understand the occurrence. However, I fear your arrival is one of importance and ask only why you did not approach our city, for you should have known our welcome would have been extended."

The canok nodded understanding. "Let me send my greetings to you as well, King Geoff. I am Mastin, and you are correct in your assessment of my arrival. When you hear me out, you will understand my appearance and why we could not approach. However, time is short, and we must act fast."

As he finished his statement, Tantis arrived, his eyes also showing disbelief. Geoff continued, "This is Tantisolandis Arnolin." The elf nodded greeting while Geoff introduced the canok. "Mastin, you just said *we* could not approach. Does that mean there are others with you?"

"Yes, for some time we have been traveling to Toopek from our homeland to tell you the news of the return of unity among the canoks, but our journey has not been free of obstacles. These forests are overrun with dragon army forces, and to get by certain groups without alerting the entire forest proved difficult. Even now, the three who travel with me are investigating a disturbance and proceeding to lead it away. I remained because I had to get word to you about Schram."

"I understand," Geoff replied. "Let's wait for those you are with and then return to the safety of Toopek."

"No, the others and I are not able to cross this tree-line boundary because of Schram, for lack of a better word. Nor can you cross it to leave."

Tantis and Geoff looked at each other suspiciously, but it was the elf who spoke first. "What exactly do you mean? Why can we not cross it?"

"Before Schram left Toopek, he created a magical barrier, which he intended to be used to defend against the possible event of a dragon attack. We assumed he had created a general barrier over the city, which in time the continually assaulting dragons would break down, and then Toopek would face an unabated attack. Instead, he did something most intriguing."

Mastin seemed most impressed with Schram's work, which gave Geoff a certain security he had not felt for some time. "What did he do?" the maneth asked.

"He created a barrier, but one which is semipermeable."

"What do you mean? It lets something in but keeps others out?"

Tantis added, "And why then would it keep you out? I would think Schram would allow you to enter?"

Mastin frowned slightly at the interruption but continued when he had the chance. "It is semipermeable on magical and emotional standards. I questioned its efficiency at first, but on further discussion with those I travel with, I feel it is genius."

"How does it work?" Geoff asked.

"Any creature free of magic—meaning trolls, goblins, and most dwarves and humans—will cross it freely, whereas any creature that carries any level of magical abilities, no matter how innate, could be prevented passage. What determines whether or not they pass is if they fear what they approach. If they have no fear, as my companions and I do, then they cannot cross without facing the brunt of a tremendous magical power. If they have a fear of approaching Toopek, then they will cross unhindered."

Both looked confused. "Tantis glanced at Geoff and, seeing his expression, shrugged and asked, "What good will it do letting certain ones through?"

"First, it will prevent any magic from being used against Toopek from a great distance because no magic can cross it in that form. Second, it will confuse the dragons on why only certain ones of them can cross, meaning many more could die in the effort of crossing to meet the others. Third, the dragons who will have fear are the young and inexperienced. They are the ones who will cross, and you will meet in battle first. The older and more powerful will not fear this city, and that will keep you safe from their wrath, at least for a time."

"Then, if you tried to cross without fear, you would be killed?"

"Yes, and we would have, had there not been a warning waiting for us as we approached. We assumed Schram would have erected some barrier so we were using our abilities to locate it. When our magic struck it, a message specific for canok magic was released. It explained what I just explained to you and asked our aid to change or just reinforce it. We decided to do the latter, and we will remain here throughout any attack to alter, change, or migrate the magic against any dragon attempts to disarm it. We may only give you a matter of additional hours or days, but perhaps that may provide you the time you need to defeat the attack or escape to safety. We sense a major offensive is building here. The activity around Toopek is intense."

Geoff continued, thinking, then asked, "Could you get through if you wanted to?"

Mastin shook his head. "Yes, knowing how it was created, we could create a void or hole in only moments, but we could never recreate it so precise and specific."

"I understand," he replied. "How is it that you appear as you do now? Are all the canoks back as they used to be?"

Mastin appeared saddened. "There is no longer a division between canoks. We are a nation of one, and for that we will always be in Schram's debt, and all of you fighting this battle together. The only canok you need fear is one known as Almok, brother to one you knew as friend for many years. We do not know how the reuniting of our factions has affected Almok, but we can feel that he remains at the side of the black dragon. Nothing more do we know."

Mastin had not mentioned the name of Kirven in elven fashion to honor Tantis, who still remained beside the large maneth. The canok took a few steps toward both men before adding, "Schram risked everything to return our lives to us. We are here now to do the same."

Geoff replied, "What if Almok joins the attack? Will he not receive the same message and know how to defeat the barrier?"

Mastin remained stoic. "We have felt Almok repeatedly fighting the pull back to our union. He has a dragon half, which he cannot ignore—the same half which his brother fought for all his years. However, we do believe he will not be part of any immediate attack on Toopek, for he is not in this area."

"And what about Schram?" he added questionably.

"Schram has gone with others to try to stop Slayne for good. If he is successful, then any attack here will be short-lived, if at all."

Geoff took a step back and nodded appreciatively to the canok. "Let us hope for as much, Mastin. I thank you for your message and wish you luck in your endeavors. We relish any aid you can give."

Tantis joined his side. "And please express our feelings to those with you as well. It is truly good to see the canoks as one again—" His thought was cut short as he heard the approach of others. "Geoff, a group approaches."

The maneth began to move but was halted by Mastin's voice. "No, it is only my companions and someone they have located. Remember, Geoff, you can cross the barrier to leave, but unless you have a true fear of Toopek, you could not return. Maneths carry a magic within them, one which could prove deadly in this case."

Geoff understood, but he still felt uncomfortable as he too heard the approach of others. The canoks burst through the trees with a wounded human staggering behind them. Geoff hollered, "Reynolds, of all the—"

One of the other canoks cut him off. "There is a large goblin force behind us. You must take the human. He has magical abilities but he also carries extreme fear. He will be able to cross." To Mastin, he asked, "Did you fill them in on the situation?" There was a pause then the canok continued, "Good, then we must be on our way. Geoff, a large force is moving toward your southeastern gate, which is in contrast to the one in our wake. If we are correct in our estimation that the attack was only waiting for Slayne's word, then evidently that word has been given, and in turn, Schram must not have been successful. May your gods be with all of you, and know that we will do our best to assist."

The four canoks exited immediately at a fast pace, which left Steve Reynolds, the Prince of Empor, alone at the edge of the forest. Groggily he stumbled his way toward the maneth and elf. Geoff grabbed his arm and helped him over to Tantis. "Take him to Toopek as fast as you can fly. I will return on foot." He paused and then added as the noise from the forest now grew very loud in the trees, "At a fast pace on foot."

The elf did not pause a moment, and quickly they were putting distance between themselves and the forest. When the goblins first broke the last line of trees, Tantis and the human were well out of bow range, and Geoff was well into the outer limits. However, that fact was of little importance when his blue blood began to spill and he struck the ground. He reached to his leg to stop the pain.

Tantis turned in flight to aid Geoff but was turned back by the maneth's strong voice as he pushed himself back to his feet. "Get the human back. I shall keep moving. Come back if it is possible."

Tantis stared into Geoff's eyes and, although he did fight with the decision, knew the one rule they both lived by their entire warrior life—you never leave one behind. He dropped to the ground and carefully set Reynolds down. The human nodded to the flyer elf one simple nod that clearly said go. And the elf was back to the air.

Geoff ran as fast as he could, but he was severely hobbled by the arrow. A very unlikely shot had landed true, and the trail of blue blood tied back to his leg displayed it clearly. Tantis was flying at a speed he had not met in as long as he could remember. The veins in his wings throbbed from adrenaline and pain, but even through this stress, he knocked an arrow and drew aim on the nearest goblin. From greater than double the length of the goblin's lucky shot, Tantis split its eyes, causing a few nearby to slow their desperate run. He had already let a second arrow fly as the first one struck and another goblin fell lifeless, but their numbers did not seem to be slowing. He measured at least 500 spilling from the forest edge and the movement in the trees behind was constant. Geoff had not looked back to see the number and only continued his jagged pace back toward Toopek.

A second arrow struck the large maneth's shoulder, sending him tumbling to the ground. He tried to turn and continue his trek, but he knew the loss of blood in his leg would not allow it. Instead, he pushed himself up, pulling his club to face those before him with fire burnt into his eyes. Arrow after arrow blew around Geoff, and any that came near he deflected with his club. Tantis had sent all his arrows in return with perfect accuracy, but now his bowfire was done, and he too was drawing back into target range. The first goblin front was only about fifty yards from the maneth, and to his surprise, many were stopping and sending bowfire rather than overwhelming him with a physical attack. He held his club hard, but the goblins were collectively slowing or stopping, and many of their arrows were sailing well above him.

Geoff began scrambling backward, heading toward the Toopek wall but still facing the onslaught of goblins when one of the closest goblin's throat split open from an arrow shot from behind. Geoff swung his head around to greet the scooping arms of Tantis and another female flyer, whom he knew as Kaylis, giving cover. Tantis lifted the maneth up. "Sorry about the pain, my friend, but there is no time to be careful. Grab my bow and we can get out of here."

Geoff grabbed the bow, and as they began to move through the air, the large maneth clearly said, "It is about time. I thought you were going to have me take them all on alone."

The elf reached around and forcibly removed the arrow lodged in Geoff's shoulder. The maneth let out a roar as the pain erupted through his body. Tantis leaned forward and said, "I assume that was your way of saying thank you?"

"Indeed it was, you evil flyer. Indeed it was."

"I thought so," he replied, smiling. "If not, I am sure I could create some other situations that you might want to roar about."

Geoff nodded as Kaylis appeared beside them carrying Reynolds in her arms. "We are out of range right now, but they are still coming. I believe they mean to try to overrun the walls."

"Let them try," answered Geoff's cold, hard voice. "Let them try."

⚬⚬⚬

Tantis set down atop the inside wall, and Geoff immediately began calling out orders. The elf placed his hand on the large maneth's shoulder, "Come now, Geoff. Your city is well prepared. We must see to these wounds first."

The maneth swung his eyes to the outside wall where he saw humans, maneths, and elves busily returning bowfire. He saw Meris running from station to station, securing weak areas with backup bowmen and then continuing around the wall. Geoff appeared torn, but when he looked down to his blood-soaked leg, his rich blue blood working between every joint in his heavy armor, he realized what he must do. "Very well, Tantis, you are correct, but help me to the conference room first. I was to meet Alan Grove there, and if he remains, I wish to speak to him about the Emporians."

Tantis smiled. "I was taking you there anyway. I have medical waiting. Further, that is where the Prince of Empor commanded that I take him."

His voice was smug, and Geoff could tell the elf was not impressed with the Emporian prince. "Yes, that would be Steve Reynolds. Even when he flees for his life like a rat being chased by a tigon, he remains as arrogant as can be." Tantis nodded agreement as he placed, more gingerly this time, his arms around Geoff's shoulders. "Let's go see if we can really make him mad. I

342

think suggesting he take his place along the front wall would be a good start."

Tantis smiled and added, "Why don't you also place him with two of his own *best* bowmen? That would sure be a fearsome defense."

Geoff laughed and then grunted as the pain from the jolt struck him harder than anticipated. Tantis even lost his flight for a bit at the weight shift. They landed in front of the building Geoff had designated for counseling and meetings. It was the largest open building in the city, and it was near the center, providing it the greatest protection. The sudden weight from landing sent another grunt through the maneth's veins, but he showed little on the outside; not so little that Alan Grove, standing at the entrance, did not take notice.

"My god, Geoff, what happened?" he said as he walked over.

The maneth was about to answer until Prince Reynolds, who had also run over as they landed, interrupted. "You fool. You have already taken injury. Is this city so unimportant to you that you would put yourself..."

Geoff stepped forward and crunched the human across the face. "Damn would-be wizard. Sometimes you just need to shut up." Turning to Alan, "I have learned much, which I would like to discuss with you and Pete, if he still remains."

Alan bent down to help the groggy and bloody human prince to his feet. "Yes, Pete has his ships ready to sail and was going to return here after a final inspection. Let's get that bleeding stopped and we'll talk." Grove glanced toward the elf.

Geoff saw the stare and added, "I am sorry. This is Tantis. He is an old friend. He saved both me and the good prince here, but"— he directed this to Reynolds—"no thanks is expected. Tantis, this is Alan Grove. He is commander over the human forces."

They shook hands and the elf said, "I am interested to hear what you have done with all the Emporians. The few I spoke with were quite adamant against bearing arms."

Alan replied with a simple grin, much to the displeasure of the prince he carried by the shoulder toward the building.

"And they believed you?" laughed the elf.

Alan continued, "Yes, the power of persuasion is great. Actually, you helped enforce it as well."

"Me?" questioned Tantis. "I never even met you until a moment ago when we were outside. How could I have done anything?"

Alan smiled again as he and Geoff continued to bandage the maneth's wounds, Geoff taking much less care on his own leg than Alan was on his shoulder. "Well, you were correct in your estimation that the Emporians do not want to fight with bows and catapults."

"Of course we don't," blasted Reynolds. "We do not want to fight at all. We are magicians. We will defeat anyone with our power, not our might."

Geoff shot the human a glare that sent him cowering deep into his chair. He nodded for Alan to continue. "I happened to be speaking with three flyers at the time, so the Emporians had no real idea that this city was not saturated with elves. Furthermore, I don't think many had ever seen many elves, and if they had, definitely not flyers." Both Geoff and Tantis smiled. "When they told me they would not go to the wall to be backup bowmen, I told them that they then would not be allowed refuge in Toopek."

The maneth looked up, surprised. "You didn't. Did Pete put you up to this?"

The sea captain who had walked in unnoticed moments earlier grumbled an interjection. "No, but I'd be mighty proud if I had."

Alan went ahead as if nothing had been added. "I told them if they did not head to the smith and get chest armor and a bow, then I would have the flyers one by one lift them over the walls."

Tantis's large eyes were billowing up with tears. "I can't get over the fact that they believed it." He paused then added, "But that does not explain how I helped the cause?"

"Well, one Emporian was calling my bluff but did so in the most inappropriate way. His comment, I believe, was, 'Ah, I don't believe you anymore than I believe these winged buffoons can really fly.'" Tantis's eyebrows shot up, and a thump was heard as Reynolds's head cracked the table in disbelief. "Yes, I know," Alan continued. "I could not believe it either. But the true response came from Denisilantilis Kleinkis. Do you know her?"

Tantis shook his head with another smile. "Yes, Denisi is a younger flyer, but not lacking in spirit. She follows the lead of Princess Stepha fairly closely. To put it simply, I would never interfere with any of her business."

"Well, I would never call her a winged buffoon either." He could not even keep a straight face as he replayed this part of the story. "She lifted the human by his ears about twenty feet in the air and then began swinging him about like he was a toy." Tears were streaming down Tantis's face. "You should have seen the human's face. I really thought he looked greener than Denisi."

"What happened next?" asked Geoff, as he had neglected his bandaging to better enjoy the story.

"Well, I do not know if he said something to her or what, but I am fairly sure that something along the line of 'So you can fly. You still would never throw me over the wall' was said." He paused, took a deep breath as his audience looked on, with eyes locked on the human and anticipating smiles across their faces, except Tantis, who was actually fearful of what Denisi would do in response to that. "Her next action was immediate and without comment. She cut a straight line at a fearsome pace to the front gate. That is"—he turned to Tantis—"when they saw you taking Geoff over the wall. I guess they thought Geoff was getting the same treatment because according to Denisi, the human began going crazy and demanded to be let down right then."

Geoff smiled. "She didn't?"

"Yep," cried Pete. "Me boys and I saw it all from the harbor. That crazy elf dropped him near twenty feet to the ground. Damn near the funniest thing me boys and I had seen since landing here."

"You should have seen him come running back, asking the whereabouts of the nearest smith. And after the display, all seemed to go fairly smooth. I divided the men up into four regiments and then spread the women who wished to fight among them and sent the others with Greg Stollman. He was going to distribute them throughout various other less dangerous areas."

Reynolds lifted his head. "Some women wished to bear arms?"

He nodded. "Yes, it seems quite a few were impressed with Denisi's actions."

"And she'd be a great role model for them," added Tantis still smiling.

Again Reynolds's head hit the table in disbelief. There were several minutes where little seemed to get done, but soon Geoff recognized they needed to get to business. Alan started inspecting the leg bandage, let out an accompanying sigh, and began to remove Geoff's work and reapply it. Meanwhile, the large maneth retold all he and Tantis had learned from the canoks. He went into detail regarding the force field around the city and the dangers should they stray beyond it. Pete seemed specifically intrigued with the story, but more with exactly where the boundary was in regard to the water.

"I don't know," Geoff replied. "We could not even see the one directly in front of us."

"How I be knowin' how far to go?"

Tantis broke in. "I do not know of Schram other than what elven history has told me and that which I have learned over the last few days, but all my instincts tell me he is wise. I cannot believe he would make this force field too immense as the larger it is, the more areas there are to defeat it. I am, however, certain it will cover the entire city, the bay, and the Tower of Council on the adjacent island. As I understand it, you are set to protect Toopek from a rear assault over the water. We all know that this would be from dragons."

Pete interjected. "I don't be seein' those goblin dogs takin' to any ships against me. It'd be them flyin' beasties."

"Well then, if I understand the premise of this force field, it is a filter not a barrier. Some will cross and some will be prevented. It is allowing us to not face an all-out attack at once. Where the dragons that do not cross are stopped, that is your barrier. Mark it, and stop any that pass."

"Aye, mate, that'd be a right good idea."

Geoff slapped the captain on the back. "You know, Pete, I usually don't have the slightest idea what you are talking about, but as long as you do, I think we are in capable hands."

"If that means you be glad that me boys and I be greetin' those flyin beasties first, then you should know that we are all too happy to oblige."

"Well then, why don't you get back to your fleet and push off? Some of our scouts have seen small boats along the coast, which could be used to smuggle some troops in. Make sure they don't make it."

"It'd be a pleasure," he replied with a bellow. With that, the old sea pirate Schram had originally met when fleeing the Canyon of Icly limped out the door and was gone.

"He is the most disgusting."

"Shut up, Reynolds," said Geoff, testing his bandages by stretching in various directions. He nodded approvingly to Alan and then turned back to face the prince. "Now tell me, Reynolds, what made such a powerful city like Empor come running for cover here?"

Reynolds appeared stung. "We are powerful and faced off against the brunt of their attack for some time."

"How long?"

"Nearly five hours before we began to weaken."

Alan asked, "Is this related to the force field failing the others were talking about?"

Geoff had not heard this information and became instantly more interested. "Yes," the prince replied, "but it was not like the one Prince Schram created. It was made to keep anything from passing, and it worked, at least for a while."

"What happened?" the maneth asked.

"Those you call dragon lords showed up. They were awful in their black hooded robes with their lizard-like bodies showing through. They were clearly very powerful. It took their combined magic only moments before several holes appeared in our barrier. Then, within the hour, the entire force field crumbled. We barely made our escape. Had we not altered our field to move between Empor and here, we would have been cut off."

"And what about Drynak? Has there been any word?"

Reynolds appeared to withdraw even more. "No, I received no message in return, nor did I ever hear from my scouts again."

"That settles it then," said Alan. "It seems your fears were correct."

"What's that?" asked Tantis.

Geoff turned to his friend but spoke to all. "We have no retreat save the water. We fight them here, to the end."

There was a brief silence as each contemplated what was just said and each said their own prayer to their gods. The large maneth, whose body and face had aged beyond its years since first meeting Schram several years ago, rose and spoke with strength only he could possess. "Come, we must man the walls. I must know when and if magic users have breached the barrier. I never realized how important that barrier would be. If they destroy it, we could have two thousand troops on top of us instantly with a mass of magic-wielding dragons breaking their wake. We have got to make a dent in their numbers before it falls."

"Do you mean an offensive into the forest?"

There was no answer.

First Attack

"Geoff," shouted Meris as he looked up from where he helped a fallen human. "I saw you take a pair of arrows in the field. Are you all right?"

"Yes, fine. What is the situation here?"

"It is very strange, like nothing I have seen before. However, I believe we are being successful. You can see all the goblin and troll bodies whereas we have only taken a few injured, but that is all we have faced thus far, just goblin and trolls. It appears to be an all-out offensive, but only by a few groups."

"Have you seen any dragon lords?"

"No, there has been no sign. We have, however, had maybe fifty or so dark dwarves involved in the waves of attacks, but since the last retreat, we have seen none. I am being told the elves have seen massive numbers of DDs mounting along the forest boundary."

Geoff stared across the field but could not see clearly. He saw Fritz moving along the wall a short distance away and hollered to him to come over. Geoff did not give time for explanations before digging into the elf with his questions. "Look along the tree line and describe whatever you can see."

Fritz stared. "I have been inspecting it for the last hour since the retreat. I do not understand it, but still nothing has changed. It appears that about one thousand goblins and trolls are in the fields near the surrounding forest. Immediately within the front tree cover, it seems the forests become completely saturated with dark dwarves."

"Are there any dwarves in the fields?"

At this time Tantis had landed next to them. Fritz answered, "I see a few, but not many. The dark dwarves do not seem to be leaving the forest cover." He paused then added, "Now wait. That is interesting. Tantis, what do you make of that outbreak about twenty paces on the far side of that large goblin party?"

The elf followed his finger. "Good eyes, son. Geoff, why would dark dwarves be affected by the barrier? I know nothing about magic they possess."

"It could be something innate carried down from their distant ancestors. I know that mining dwarves have a magic sense, which allows them to travel mines freely without fear of getting lost. Why do you ask? What do you both see?"

"There seems to be a large number of dark dwarves who attempted to enter but were not successful. They were unable to pass."

Geoff swung his eyes to the area. "Then Schram's barrier is still working at full force."

"I can't speak to the level of working, but it is definitely still acting against some."

He swung back to the elf who had just arrived. "What is our status after the attack?"

"Near as I can determine, we lost only five, all human, but many more were taken injured."

He hollered to Meris. "Have you enough support to hold with those who were forced down?"

"Yes," the young maneth replied. "All has been reinforced, and the areas that were previously most heavily attacked have been loaded with better marksmen."

"Excellent. Keep me informed." He motioned to the elves. "You two, come with me. I have another plan."

ᕙᗯᕗ

Beams of fire burning on hatred shot from Dragon Lord Starland's hand. "Damn that boy!"

Two other dragon lords looked on in a frustrated disbelief. "What could be the secret? How come some can pass and others cannot?"

Lord Starland flashed a stare that caused even the other dragon lords to step back. "Lord Mapes, if you continue to cause me such distress, I shall take out my frustrations on you."

Mapes stepped back toward his counterpart. "I only asked for insight. Your continued swearing has accomplished little in the past hour. By my understanding, you informed Slayne that with dragon support you would have the city under your control and its occupants slaves to Slayne's name. As of now, you have witnessed five waves of attacks, which has left nearly 300 of our troops dead and done nothing to weaken the Toopekian stronghold. You now have less than three hours to keep your word to Slayne. If we do not determine the existence of this force field, then there will be no way to devise a scheme to break it."

Starland's face was as red as human blood. "Nobody, not even you, speaks to me in that tone—"

Lord Sherblade interrupted. "Don't do it, Starland. Lord Mapes is not your enemy nor am I. There is a reason this barrier was made as it is and we must find that secret, but we can only do it together. It will take all our strength."

Starland flashed a glance toward Sherblade and then back to Mapes. "Cross me again, Mapes, and it will take more than Tomas to save you." He swung his arm around again to face the barrier. Through the trees he could see the city he once ruled over. Now he sat unable to even approach it. His voice was low and tone angry. "How long until the dragons reach the tower?"

Sherblade looked toward the sun. "Assuming they ran into no trouble, they should be there anytime."

"Do you think they will be able to pass?"

"No."

"What are we missing?" There was a pause. "We have looked at those who can pass. What have looked at those who can't.

There are no differences. Some trolls can pass, some can't. Do you think with the force of the dragons with us, we can break it? The barrier at Empor was so easy. What makes this one so different?"

"Your son and what he has become makes this one different," replied Mapes. "And no, the dragons would be of little help to break it."

Again Lord Starland sent a deep frown toward the other dragon lord, but then his expression changed, as if something was becoming clearer. "Yes, Schram is the key, or as you said, what he has become. With what I recognized within him when we allowed the elves to return to Elvinott, I have little belief that he is actually my son. However, I do have a strong belief that this is most definitely a complex and impressive force field for the very same reason." He motioned to the others. "Send a message to the dwarven leaders that we are heading along the barrier until it meets with the coast. We must contact the young dragons before they bombard across it."

"Fine, but I don't know what point that will serve. The dragons are determined to destroy those who killed their parents. They will not rest until the humans and all their allies are vanquished from the face of Troyf. They have listened to you on many occasions, but as they draw close to those responsible, even you may lose your authority. Only Slayne can command them now."

"Don't underestimate my abilities, Mapes." Starland had moved to stand only inches from the dragon lord's face. "With Slayne and Almok by my side, this barrier would be of little importance. However, we are not at a point to call for them yet. I will have the power to bring the young dragons before us. Then together we will break the barrier and crush the humans."

Mapes leaned even closer to where his nose nearly touched that of Starland, and the spit from his speech struck the Lord's chin. "Don't be such a fool, Starland. You are Slayne and Almok's puppet. They do not, nor would ever, stand by your side. You stand on a short leash behind them ready to leap at any scrap they toss your way."

"You have spoken your last word, Mapes. Prepare to meet my wrath."

The two locked arms on the other's shoulders. Charged bolts of fire erupted across the clearing. Lord Sherblade and the nearby dwarves, goblins, and trolls all backed away as the two dragon lords threw the mass of their dark magic upon the other. Mapes shoved Starland back and immediately struck the disoriented Lord with a force the likes of which he had never sent before. Starland careened to the side and then hit the ground with enough force to send tremors through the soil.

Instantly he created a barrier of his own, which deflected Mapes's attacks back toward him. Starland pulled himself up, laughing as Mapes fought to hold against the stronger dragon lord's response. "Yes, Lord Byron Mapes, who is the fool now? Your first attack was surprisingly powerful. It is a pity I have to kill you now. You might actually have had a promising future by my side." He was walking toward the other lord who was matching his steps in reverse.

With a last burst of energy, Mapes replied, "No, you are still a fool, Starland." With that he dove to the side and released another unhindered jolt into the confident chest of Starland. His eyes seemed to explode from his head as he was sent careening back toward the barrier surrounding Toopek. He struck it flat, causing the gently darkening forest to suddenly blaze into light. All on both sides of the barrier stared in disbelief and watched the head dragon lord fight to work himself free of the force field's grip. Mapes continued his constant beating, refusing to allow a crevice for his counterpart to claw free from his grip.

However, just as Starland's strength began to fade, Mapes was greeted with a blow of immeasurable proportions. The dragon lord was sent tumbling to the ground, giving Starland the needed opportunity to push himself free of the deadly trap holding him hostage. Mapes wheeled back to face his new attacker. "Tomas, but why?" His voice showed signs of disbelief mixed with anger. "I was doing us a favor."

Lord Sherblade wore an unforgiving stare back. "If I had to make a choice between Lord Starland and you, the decision is simple."

Mapes continued to stare lost at Tomas while Starland slowly made his way over to where the severely beaten dragon lord lay. "Do you understand now, Mapes?" he said with a hiss. "You are the fool."

He pushed himself to his feet though the undefended attack from Sherblade had struck him deeply. He was bleeding internally, and it showed, with blood flowing through his lips and even from one eye. "I understand that I have the power to kill you and would have, had not one of your puppets interfered. I underestimated your pull on the others, but as I speak now, it shall not be my undoing." He issued a short incantation, and immediately he formed into a glowing ball.

"No!" shouted Starland. "I will not allow it." He raised his hand and issued a response that sent several beams of energy into the floating orb of light. Again the forest seemed to erupt with flame and light.

Explosions of immense intensity continued as the dragon lord sent attack after attack into the mist, which, until moments before, had been Dragon Lord Mapes. Starland's lips began to form into a small, crooked grin as his strength gradually returned and he was able to turn even more power upon Mapes, trying to hold his presence before him. Drips of saliva began to flow between his lips while he fed on Mapes's pain, which he could feel returning from the orb. Finally, with a scream which echoed off the mountains and through the forest for miles, Mapes reappeared, his body limp and bloodied. He fell face down in the dirt, motionless for the moment.

Starland walked up to his fallen counterpart and grabbed the front of his hair, nearly piercing his eyes with his long fingertips. Lifting back, he pulled the torn and gnarled face back to where he was looking directly into his eyes. In a voice flowing on nothing but pure power and adrenaline, he raspily said, "You are mine, you detestable, lifeless coward. You crossed the line when you attacked me, and I shall show you no remorse when I take the last bit of life from within you. You are nothing to me."

Mapes stared back, but his eyes were unable to focus on anything. He wished to speak but could not. The pain throughout his body was beyond comprehension. Several of his bones were crushed and he had no ability to move. Only his mind remained intact so he could feel and understand, but not defend. With his last bit of energy, he sucked in his breath and coughed a blood-curdled ball of spit across Starland's face.

The dragon lord screamed and, without another word, grabbed the decrepit body and hurled him toward the force field, knowing the power in the field would tear the remaining life from him, in a display that would show Starland's strength to all those gathered around. However, to the surprise of all in the area, Mapes passed right through as if no barrier were present. Starland and Sherblade stared on in disbelief as his limp body rolled and came to rest well inside the boundary wall.

"How did he cross?" asked Sherblade. "Is the barrier down?"

Starland reached out and grabbed a nearby goblin and threw his distracted body toward the barrier line. The goblin struck the barrier, and brilliant light spread across a wide margin while the goblin screamed in pain, becoming locked in the magical hands. He struggled to free himself, causing the skin on his back to be pulled free before he fell back toward the dragon lord. Starland looked back to Sherblade and replied, "No, it remains." Turning back toward where Mapes now rested, he yelled to the fallen dragon lord. "Mapes, can you stand?"

He lifted his eyes slightly before falling motionless once again. Sherblade moved to stand beside his leader but spoke toward Lord Mapes's body. "Byron, it is me, Tomas. We have treated you unfairly and ask your forgiveness." Starland shot his counterpart a wicked glance. Tomas leaned close to Starland and whispered, "It might be that he can disable the barrier from within. Once we are inside, we can dispose of him without delay."

Lord Starland smiled. "Yes," his voice became louder. "Yes, Mapes, please forgive us. We acted on emotion tied to this barrier and our inability to break it. We—especially me—were wrong. I know only together can we be successful." His voice was soft now, almost as a father talking to a son. "Byron, can you hear me?"

Mapes's body did move slightly but showed little that anything said had been comprehended. Some dwarves had also been able to cross for unknown reasons since first encountering the barrier, and the addition of a dragon lord on the inside sent a bit of a stir among those within the Toopekian barrier. Several went over to aid the fallen lord.

Again Starland spoke softly toward the lord he had brought to his death. "Mapes, we have been successful getting you through the barrier. Our plan worked, but now we need your help." Some of the goblins cheered for the success of getting a lord to cross. "Do you hear us, friend?"

The dark dwarves who were aiding him began to step back as the torn and mutilated face of Mapes lifted up, confused and lost in appearance. "What happened?" he asked to the closest dwarf.

"Mapes," said Starland. "Thank God you are all right."

The dragon lord turned to the voice. He paused a long time and squinted his eyes toward those who held the same appearance as he. Softly but firmly, he replied, "I remember. I remember everything, Starland." He coughed slightly, causing some blood and other solid mass to come up as he doubled over due to the pain in his stomach. "You may say whatever you wish now, but I remember you were trying to kill me by..."

His voice trailed off before he fell face down dead, an arrow protruding from his back. Screams and hollers echoed across the field, and Geoff and his ground troops charged on the surprised dragon forces. Instantly the sky erupted with arrows. Goblins and trolls with some limited support from dark dwarves answered the Toopekian attack.

"Hold them!" shouted Starland. "They are trying to push you outside the barrier."

Geoff heard the order and smiled broadly while motioning a signal with his arm. Suddenly the east gates flew open, and nearly 500 additional troops—mostly maneths and elves—descended onto the plain. Geoff's first group had pushed the unsuspecting goblins into a sudden push forward to hold their position inside the force field, and now his cavalry aimed to pin them between the two.

"Now we move," cried his maneth roar. His forces again lit up the sky with arrows just as his ground force met them in hand-to-hand combat. The dragon troops were little match for the larger and taller humans and maneths. The elves' precision with their bows picked the troubled areas clean, and soon the greatly outnumbered Toopekian force was equaled to its opposition.

"Push them together," the maneth shouted as disorder and chaos started to show in the goblin and troll forces.

Some trolls had begun to flee when Lord Sherblade stepped forward. "Quickly, everyone, fall back."

Starland grabbed his shoulder and spun him around so they each were staring deep into the other's dark face. "What are you saying? We must hold our position. We cannot give up those who have been able to cross."

"Don't be a fool, Starland. For whatever reason, they could enter freely before. There is no reason to believe your son has changed anything so they will be able to enter again at a time we choose. However, if they remain now, we will lose over 1,000 troops and be no closer to entering ourselves. We must pull back while we still have some troops to do so."

Starland stared with fire at the dragon lord who stood stoic and hard. He swung back to the forces then back to Sherblade, whose expression had not changed. Without a word, he issued a disgusted grunt and walked away. A bead of sweat had formed on Sherblade's brow, which he wiped away and then turned to follow his leader. The goblins, trolls, and dark dwarves began to run in a full retreat toward the forest, some even dropping their weapons in the process.

Meris ran up beside Geoff. "Should we pursue or let them flee?"

"We should take them now while the momentum favors our attack but not leave the barrier. Spread the word not to enter the forest. To do so might leave the individuals trapped outside the barrier as we still do not know all of its secrets. We need Schram."

Meris displayed agreement and quickly began to signal as such to the forces but stopped when he heard the sound. He turned to Geoff to see him nearly fall over due to the intensity of the screech. The sound bounced off the walls like a violent thunderbolt aiming to destroy anything in its path. Even the fleeing dragon forces turned in horror back to Toopek to see what could render such a scream.

Meris grabbed Geoff's arm to turn him to face each other. "What in all of Troyf was that?"

The huge maneth locked his eyes on the Toopekian wall and then turned back and stared at the two dragon lords, who returned his gaze inquisitively. "We have been tricked. We have been drawn out like children for treats, leaving our home relatively unprotected and our forces divided.

Meris did not wait for another order or command. "Back to the wall. Toopek is under attack!"

Some of the goblin forces which had attacked the east gate had moved in between Geoff and his army, but they were of little concern as the human, maneth, and elven forces quickly barrel-rolled them into a retreat of their own. Geoff ran with amazing speed despite his injuries but he could not shake the feeling. Was he only racing back to face an army of dragons?

※

Maldor nudged Schram slightly to bring the magician out of his deep sleep. The maneth whispered, "You have been out for nearly a solid day. Never have I seen anyone sleep as such, especially while on the back of a dragon."

Schram raised his head. It is a gift I have been granted through the power held within the staff. I seem to be able to go many days without any rest, and conversely, when time presents itself, I may gain as much as needed."

"Amazing," replied the maneth.

"Not amazing," added Draketon. "Simply a power all dragons carry, for I too have the same ability."

Maldor grinned. "Fascinating, but Schram is not a dragon but the staff was created by one, right? I mean, I do not understand your powers, but a dragon you are not."

Draketon did not reply, only closing his eyes and continuing his flight. Schram smiled a bit and added, "But my powers are focused through this staff, and this staff carries more dragon power than anything."

Maldor only shook his head. "My only wish is that I could capture some of the sleep you seem to find so easily." Just as his statement ended, Maldor's silver hammer began to glow very lightly. Within only moments more, Maldor had entered a deep, restful, sleep.

Schram smiled at the peaceful expression across the maneth's face and remembered all he had learned about the weapons of the Ring of Ku. He looked toward the stars and estimated that if Draketon had been accurate in the time it would take to reach Toopek, then they should arrive there late the following day. He leaned toward the dragon's head. "Draketon, what did you mean when you said "It was an ability all dragons carried?"

There was no reply.

✺

"Perhaps we should land just in the outskirts of their forest and approach on foot. I cannot see that the elves would be altogether thrilled to openly greet a dragon and canok, regardless if they have already received word that the canok sun has been returned, and once again the canok nation walks as one red."

"You are probably correct, Werner," Hawthorne replied. "But I hate to waste the time we have saved with my powerful flight. By catching the winds as we did, we would have an outside chance of alerting Elvinott and then leaving immediately to intercept Schram and the others."

The canok nodded. "I wondered why you were flying as such. I do not understand your relationship fully, but I feel it cannot be so important as to jeopardize our mission here. If the elves see a dragon moving unaffected through their enchanted forest, they will attack at will. Do you believe otherwise?"

Hawthorne gently landed on the forest ground. Her voice carried the same depressed tones, which could be not only heard but seen in her large eyes. "No, I know you to be correct." As she spoke, her body returned to the silky white-skinned human female with her long, soft light-brown hair cascading about her shoulders. She turned back to the canok. "Come, we must hurry."

First Over, Second to Begin

"Close the gates now!" shouted Geoff as he motioned for the guards to move forward. "Throw ladders down to any who have not returned yet. Any flyers, please aid those injured on the field."

"Geoff! Geoff!"

The maneth swung up, searching for the origin of the voice atop the inside wall. "Yes, Alan, what has happened?" he hollered.

"Dragons! Nearly 300 of them at the harbor."

"What's the status?"

Alan showed distress. "The first six passed through the barrier unhindered, but the number seven got caught, and caught hard. In a vicious fight to free itself, it seemed to only get further entrenched. This battle caused all others to halt. After several minutes, number seven fell down dead, its flesh torn from much of its body. Since that, only a few have tried to enter."

"What about the ones that did get through? What are they doing?"

"They have engaged Pete and his fleet."

"How is he holding?"

"Not well." Alan stared back toward the bay after hearing a loud explosion and seeing smoke and fire. "He needs reinforcements." Alan drew his sword and began running along the top of the wall toward the harbor. "Immediately!"

Geoff turned and began filtering through the chaos of bodies, attempting to find Meris. Suddenly, seeing the maneth shuffling guards to various positions, he hurriedly joined his side. "Meris, do you have enough guards to hold should ground forces attack?"

"Yes, we will hold. You take what you need to the harbor. Pete is far undermanned, I can tell that from here."

Geoff slapped his much-younger counterpart on the back, sending a message of approval only the two of them understood. Without another word, Geoff was off shouting commands to anyone within earshot.

Suddenly, surprising to even him, he was off the ground and flying over the inner wall. "You sure know how to add excitement to the day," shouted Tantis as he carried the maneth toward the harbor.

To Geoff, the statement went unheard. His eyes were focused ahead. "By all the gods, how can we defend against that?"

"I don't know, old friend, but remember the past. We have to try."

Geoff stared over the harbor. He watched as nearly twenty ships fought for their lives against eight young dragons, all using their sheets of fire and magic to completely belittle the small vessels. Then his eyes turned to the northern skies, the darkened bodies of hundreds of dragons nearly eclipsing the clear blue normally seen across the water. The hovering beasts were all unleashing immeasurable power against the barrier around the city. The brilliant light emitting from the attack was almost blinding as the barrier somehow was holding.

The large maneth bowed his head. "I remember the past. I remember five dragons leveling my village and all the forests around it. I remember the pain and suffering those five alone brought with them. But this, how can we…" His voice trailed off.

Tantis set the maneth down and then landed next to him at the face of the harbor. Several guards had already arrived, and more continued to fill in behind. They all stared in disbelief at the sight before them. The only sound breaking the dragon's wrath was the hollers of those on the ships. Some screamed in pain, others in fear, and then clearly Captain Pete's wicked battle cry.

The elf leaned close to only allow Geoff's ears to hear. "I remember the pain as well, my friend. I remember holding my mother in my arms as her burned and rippled flesh seemed to melt from her bone. I will never forget." He paused, closed his large green eyes. and then tightened his face into a hard stare. "But this time we are prepared. We have powerful friends, and we must rely on their aid in time. But we have to hold this city until then, and that means destroying those dragons. Three lie dead in the water as a result of the barrier and none, since the last fell, have tried to enter. They are concentrating their attack on the barrier. They know their only chance is to destroy it."

Geoff raised his hand. "Say no more. I know you are correct." He turned to the still-growing army behind him. "I know the situation appears overwhelming, but we have to aid our friends. I can offer no words of encouragement except to do your best. Fight proud, for you are fighting for your right and your children's right to live. May all your gods be with us this evening."

As Geoff looked across his forces, he could see the fear in their eyes slowly change to determination. He knew inside they all still carried some feelings of hopelessness, but he also saw strength and confidence. He felt this giving him power and strength that for a moment had been lost.

"Look!" shouted one of the humans in front, pointing.

Geoff swung his head to see one of the dragons caught by several ropes and spears to Pete's ship. The dragon was flailing wildly, shaking the ship into a crazed frenzy. None of the men on board could get a firm stance to finish the beast. Blood poured from its wounds, but it only seemed to infuriate it further. Suddenly it cried out in pain and fell to the water.

Geoff's eyes fell on his old friend, who was lowering his ancient bow. "That was for my family," the elf said softly, mostly to himself.

Geoff placed his large hand on the elf's shoulder in both an act of praise and caring. "That was a shot like I have never seen before." The maneth leader turned as the men, elves, and fellow maneths all made a push forward. Geoff raised his arms high and released a roar louder than he had ever issued before.

The men answered, and in moments every available ship, raft, or vessel was making its ways toward Pete's fleet and the dragon bombardment. From the shore, archers sent sheets of arrows toward any dragon that drew within range. A young blue turned from the ships and engaged those on land. A burst of fire scored the grounds, sending much of the group to cover while others relied solely on their armor for protection. Geoff and Tantis stood their ground hard as the dragon seemed to center on the two of them. Another burst of flame shot across the shore, and both could feel their skin burn underneath the steel they wore. Geoff could even smell his fur baking to the metal. Tantis issued arrow after arrow, not able to even look and see if any were finding their mark. He was firing by feeling alone, as to look toward his prey would most likely burn his eyes to blindness.

After a second sheet of fire blew across, Geoff turned, trying to time a break in the fire. He lifted his mask from his helm to be greeted with a talon reaching down just in front of him. He shoved Tantis aside and swung his mighty maneth club upward. Contact was made immediately, causing the young blue to jerk to the side out of control. It struck the ground with extreme force while Geoff was pulled down in its wake. The dragon lifted its head and turned to the fallen maneth, revealing a deep gash down its neck where his club had struck and blue blood now seeped freely to the sand. Geoff stared back and saw the beast lock eyes of hatred on his fallen foe. Its neck arched backward as it filled its lungs with fire which, even if it proved to be its last breath, the blue was going to ensure it expelled across the maneth. Geoff pushed himself up, but he knew he did not have enough time to avoid the imminent wall of fire he was about to receive. His only response was to stand tall and stare directly back toward the beast.

Suddenly a whistle caught his ear and then a strange muffled gargle and thump when the dragon fell over dead bearing another elven arrow. Geoff spun around and again saw Tantis lowering his bow. The elf smiled. "And that one was for you, Geoff."

The maneth just nodded in return and gathered his club back from where it had been tossed. They both moved to rejoin the battle over the harbor and were surprisingly joined by Fritz and about five other elves. Geoff looked across the sea, but it was Fritz who spoke first. "Where do things stand?"

Tantis answered. "It appears that over half of the original eight dragons that got through have been killed. However, a much larger percentage of the original fleet has been sunk, not to mention the numbers we have lost in the smaller craft that did not reach the fleet for support."

One of the elves pointed to the side. "Does that still work?"

Geoff followed his gaze and then began to smile a bit. "If not, we will make it work. I can't believe we did not think of that before. It will hold at least one hundred men, is impossible to sink, and, most important, is made of iron."

"Yes," added Fritz. "It won't burn."

"What is it?" asked Tantis. "Will it even float?"

By this time Geoff had already started at a fast pace toward the long-forgotten vessel left to become overgrown with weeds and trees by the shore. Fritz and Tantis directed the nearby elves to remain dug in and send cover arrows against any dragons that drew near. Whatever Geoff's plan was, he would need time to do it. As they reached the site, Geoff answered the elf's previous question. "It is some sort of ferry, probably used when they first built the castle on the island."

Fritz inspected it closely. "By its appearance, it has not been used since then. Its nearly two-arrow length sunk in the sand and mud. Can we even pull it free?"

Geoff ignored the question and proceeded straight to work. "Tantis, carry this end of the rope up and over the lower section of that oak. Fritz, take this rope and join the other elves behind those rocks. When I get into position, I need you all to grab and pull toward the water."

He nodded understanding. There was another explosion on the water, and another of Pete's ships split its mast and was going under. "We must hurry."

Geoff too turned to see Pete's men leaping into the water to free themselves from the fiery ship. His attention to the sea was short-lived as Tantis landed, rope in hand. "Good," the maneth said, taking the rope. "Then, can you take this rope and fly above the ferry? We are going to need all the lift we can get."

"Consider it as such," the elf replied without further comment.

Geoff waved his arm and then all moved to their positions and dug in as deeply as possible. Geoff's rope tightened first, and immediately he felt the pains of his injuries tearing at his muscles. Tantis flew as hard as he could, but it was like pulling against a mountain. When the elves locked their ropes tight, the ferry gave a slight surge.

"Pull!" Geoff yelled as the small movement seemed to drive the maneth. "She wants to come free but the wet ground seems to be holding her down."

Geoff's arms exploded, and he closed his eyes to a tight squint, but the craft still seemed to bite into its resting place. "Please, give me the strength," the maneth whispered before he roared his final push forward.

With the roar, the elves again tightened their ropes, and suddenly the huge iron ferry rocked back. Geoff leaned as hard as he could, offering anything his strong body had left to free the vessel. With a third surge, the front rose high enough to clear the harbor's level, and quickly water rushed beneath it.

The maneth looked back and hollered. "Let it down slowly."

The ferry crashed down hard, causing a large wave to be pushed out. The rear end lifted, with the force of the water freeing it from its tight grip to the land.

They all looked on. "It's floating," hollered Fritz. "I don't believe it actually floats."

He slapped Geoff on the back, with each of them carrying a large smile as if they had already won the battle at sea. Tantis landed. "Yes, but now how do we get it through the harbor? A boat of this weight will gain little from sails, even if we had any."

Geoff pointed behind them to a large wheel device. "That is to hold the tow cable. There is the cable. All we have to do is carry the cable to the identical wheel on the island. Then we will have full harbor access."

"But there are not any ships left to carry it across," added Fritz.

All eyes fell to Tantis. The elf smiled and shook his head. "That is your plan, old friend? Give it to the funny-looking guy with wings?"

The maneth hurried to the huge wheel and, with all his might, pushed it to turn. It squeaked and cracked, but slowly it began to move and loosen. He grabbed the cable and fed it through the tongs in the ferry. Then he turned and nearly fell over as Tantis stood right before him.

Geoff laughed at the surprise, but that quickly faded when he looked into his longtime friend's eyes. The elf reached into his armor and pulled out a small pouch. Holding it out, he handed it to Geoff. "You should keep this. It is a token of the two wars we have fought together."

Geoff pushed the elf's arm back. "No. If now is your time then it is mine as well. Should you not reach your mark, I will be right behind you." He paused then added, "You know, a wise elf once told me never to expect anything to happen, or it probably will." I always thought it was a rather foolish statement, but suddenly I see the wisdom in it." He placed his arm on the elf's shoulder.

"We have a battle ahead of us, but it is one we will win this time, and we will win it together."

Tantis placed his hand on Geoff's shoulder, creating a powerful sight to those who watched. "We will win this one, my old friend."

The elf took the rope and, after replacing his pouch, began a low path across the water's surface. Geoff turned to the others. "We need to keep those dragons away from him, so let's see if we can get their attention."

The elves began sending a barrage of arrows at the four remaining dragons that still were wreaking havoc on the fleet. Geoff replaced his club and removed a special bow designed especially to fit his larger body. He had been carrying it since his return from meeting the canoks at the Toopek boundary but had not yet found the opportunity to use it. Now, however, he was knocking a steel arrow that had been forged custom for his bow. He drew on the closest dragon and let it sail.

The beast screamed in pain as the arrow lodged deep inside its belly. It turned in flight toward the direction of its path to see the small band located on the far shore. The young red, with blood of the same color streaming from several wounds as it flew, made a narrow path directly toward the group. The elves' large green eyes grew even wider while they locked on the dragon's approach. Each was knocking another arrow even before their previous one had made contact, but none were having a grave effect or even slowing the creature's approach.

Geoff locked a second iron shaft into place and drew aim between the dragon's fiery red eyes. Softly, he said, "This one is for you, King McCard." The arrow flew and bit the dragon true to its mark. The beast curled its head down with a gargled screech, tumbling with an explosion of water into the sea and then disappearing under the surface.

A cheer sounded from the other men, maneths, and elves on the shore, and the slew of arrows across the harbor increased as they now believed they could bring the dragons down. Geoff knocked another arrow but was stopped by Fritz's hand on his shoulder. "Tantis is nearly across. He is flying with a pace to match Princess Stepha's."

"Aye, friend." He turned to those along the shore. "Quickly, everyone, to the barge. We will finish this battle in one sweep."

Those who had remained on the banks and some of those from the ships that had sunk, who swam to the safety of the shoreline, came running. Within moments, the barge was loaded, and Geoff stood on the side and pushed while rows of guards grabbed the now-secured tow cable and pulled with all their might. Archers remained at the ready, and slowly the large ferry edged outward, with Geoff leaping aboard as the water deepened.

"All right, let's make each arrow count." Geoff looked across the handful of ships that remained. He saw Pete's own ship bearing down on the largest of the three remaining dragons, and by the appearance of the battle, he would end up the victor. Then he saw the other two sending pairs of magical balls of fire on the deck of one heavily disabled ship. He noticed one of the two dragons was also heavily wounded, but the other, a young red very similar in size to the one Geoff had dropped at the shore, was showing no injuries and providing a fierce fire attack. He pointed at the red. "All aim to that one. First flight on my lead."

Geoff knocked another one of his steel rods and drew on the red. As the barge pulled within range, he released the arrow. The dragon roared and dove toward the water, with the arrow biting through the delicate flesh and bone making up its wing. Suddenly the air was so saturated with arrows Geoff believed it possible to walk across the top of their arch. The red in the water was flailing frantically, but its broken wing would not allow flight. Quickly it was wearing nearly twenty arrows in its back and belly delivered from both Pete's men left aboard the battered ship and the elf and maneth forces on the barge sending the beast to a watery grave.

The other dragon, a slightly larger blue, flashed a glance at the barge and then turned to flee toward the open sea and the wall of dragons that were unable to enter. Geoff lodged an arrow in its back, but it was Tantis who crossed its flight, and with a fatal swing with his sword, opened the dragon's throat, sending it with a crash to the water's surface. It, as well as the large dragon Pete's ship had just brought down, simultaneously sank below the water's ridge; the roars from all that were still alive echoed across the water reaching all those left on shore to roar as well.

⟨∾∾∾⟩

"Fritz, help me pull this boat ashore."

The elf slid over and grabbed the rope ahead of Geoff, and with a final tug, the last boat was safely secured. Geoff fell back in the sand and let out a long gasp. Fritz slapped him on the shoulder and then collapsed beside the large maneth leader. "You did well today, Geoff. You should be proud."

"That is the understatement of the day," added Alan, approaching from a nearby path. "You set a new level today that will be remembered forever."

The tired head of the maneth slowly lifted and drew a short smile. "We did well today, all of us. However, before we begin celebrating, we all should take one more look across the sea." Their eyes followed Geoff's outstretched arm. A short distance beyond the harbor, an endless sea of blackness blocked out the stars, with an occasional burst of energy striking against the shell of protection. "That wall of dragons will not remain separated forever. Soon they will become a tidal wave, one which even this fortress of a city cannot withstand."

It was silent for several moments until Tantis approached. "Geoff, I have accounted for all the flyers and all are well, fielding only minor injuries."

With an outstretched hand, the maneth stood before his friend. The elf gripped his hand tightly. "You acted beyond even your amazing abilities today, my friend," began Geoff. "It is because of you that we all are here now."

The others stood and shared his sentiment. Tantis smiled. "No, we all acted beyond our abilities, and that is what saved each of us." He turned to Alan. "What is the situation on the walls with the wounded and those in the forest?"

All turned for the answer to the question, which had gone unasked for much too long. Alan replied in a sad and remorseful tone. "I am afraid that my news is not as positive as yours. As for Captain Pete's fleet, at least half are severely damaged or destroyed, with at least the same percent of the men unaccounted for"—he paused then added—"although it is believed that many fled to the island and are trapped there across the bay."

Geoff raised his hand and interrupted. "Reynolds, is that you?"

The Prince of Empor made his way to the small group. "Yes. Is there something I can do?"

"I was hoping you would lead a party of your men on a recovery mission across the bay."

The prince seemed stunned to be asked to support what appeared to be a serious mission. His eyes narrowed on the maneth and then a small smile appeared. "I will get a team together at once."

After he departed, Geoff turned back to the group. "Sorry for the interruption, but I just solved two problems. The men will be brought back, and the prince and a group of his men are out of our way for a while. Please continue."

Smiles climbed across all the faces as Alan continued. "As for the forces on the wall, we lost about sixty in our field attack and only ten on the attacks on the wall itself. Since our assault, the dragon forces have seemed content to remain within the trees. I assume that is to our benefit unless they have something new planned."

Tantis broke in. "Have those passed been cared for?"

"Yes, an elven party went through all the ranks. Thank you."

Geoff then added, "I do not think they are planning any attacks until they can disable the force field. As long as that barrier remains, they will not risk separating their forces again."

"How long will that be?" asked Fritz.

"Hopefully at least until Schram returns."

∽✤∾

"Stepha, I cannot believe that it is really you standing before me." The elf fell into his sister's arms. "And you, Krirtie, I am so happy to see you both."

Krirtie replied, "And Madeiris, you will never believe how happy we are to be back in Elvinott, and I am not even an elf."

All smiled and rejoiced in the other's presence until Madeiris motioned to those behind. "Travasis, please escort the guards to the dining hall, for you all must be famished. I wish to have a few moments alone with my sister and Krirtie." The elf nodded and began to move with the others out of the great hall but stopped on the elf king's word. "Also, thank you, my friend, as I am sure I will find out you performed admirably." Travasis nodded appreciatively and then exited with the others.

Stepha caught her brother's grin. "Speaking of which, what was the idea sending guards to help? Have you not learned even now that I am capable of taking care of myself?"

His grin only grew. "I have always known you could take care of yourself, but it was me I was worried about. If Schram had returned, as he was supposed to, he would have had my head for allowing your leave. Imagine the sight, me telling the one person who loves you as much as I do that I sent you, not to mention his other closest friend, to Draag without any support. How do you think that conversation would have gone?"

Both women smiled broadly, but for the elf princess, it was very short-lived. "Tell me, what do you know about Schram? Why did he not return?"

372

Madeiris led the two over to three large chairs in front of the fire pit. After adding another log, he found his seat and leaned back, stretching his legs out to almost reach the now-growing flames. In a soft voice, he began, "I had hoped we would be able to find a few moments' peace before we had to deal with the troubles of the time, but I also realize their importance outweighs any wish as such." He took a brief breath and continued. "Schram did not return as planned, but I suppose you already know that. Instead, several weeks following his departure from our forests, four canoks entered our protected area. However, these were not the white or black canoks you have known for your entire lives. These canoks wore a crisp and brilliant red coat, as they did over 200 years ago. Their presence alone showed that this war could be turning to our favor."

"But what does this have to do with Schram?"

Madeiris showed a slight smile with his sister's impatience. "Well, if you would give me a chance to finish. It seems Schram was the primary force in the return of the canoks of the past. Now these canoks were spreading the word of the change and, to those who Schram specified, relaying a message regarding a change of plans. It seems that with the help of another, they were going to attempt to beat Slayne to his next goal—the Rift Amulet." Both girls looked at each other and shrugged. The king nodded. "I know, for I also had no knowledge of what that meant. It seems that this amulet could be used by Slayne to travel through a wrinkle in space to another world where he could find and obtain a duplicate, or counter, staff to the one Schram carries. If they could gain control of the amulet first, then Slayne's options would have been evaporated, and it would only be a matter of time before he could be defeated, or that was the hope anyway."

The three looked at each other, each appearing pleased with the idea that there was an actual direction in play now. However, one part of the plan clearly left Stepha uneasy. "You said that 'with help of another.' Who is helping him?"

"That much the canoks did not mention, other than a nam—Hawthorne."

Stepha tilted her head, asking a question without actually speaking.

"Until the canoks approached with this information, I had never heard the name. Despite their obvious vagueness, I am certain that they did not question Hawthorne's loyalty. The only feeling I received was one of confidence in both individuals."

Seeing Stepha's expression, Krirtie interjected. "I don't like it either, especially in the wake of all we have learned that is now taking place."

Madeiris's eyes suddenly took on an appearance of worry. "What have you learned?"

Stepha answered. "During our attempt to rescue Maldor, we learned about the dragon army's plan for a massive strike on Toopek—a blitz larger than Toopek, and possibly all of Troyf, has ever seen."

Madeiris rose with two fears instantly burning through him. "Maldor, what happened with Maldor?"

Krirtie shrugged. "As far as we know, he is with Schram."

The elf king look puzzled and Stepha added. "Yes, somehow the magic carried within the hammer was able to connect to a porthole opened by Schram. We were part of it for a time. It was a place consisting of nothing but the darkest and loneliest feelings I have ever sensed. We were attempting to contact Schram through the powers of the Anbari weapons, and during that contact, the connection with the hammer was made."

"That place would be the Realm of Darkness, which is where the canoks said the Rift Amulet was supposedly kept, and their destination."

"The Guardians of Passage control the amulet?" asked Stepha. "Nobody can go there," she added, with fear growing in her voice.

Madeiris could only shake his head. "I understand, but it was the direction they believed they had to go." He reached out and placed his hand on his sister's shoulder. "Now tell me about Toopek. How did you come across this information, and what are the specifics?"

"Jermys overhead a meeting in which Dragon Lord Starland referred to the upcoming attack. We also found out from Lord Meyer exactly the extent of the plan. Krirtie tricked him into explaining Slayne's plan to level the human city and bring it under dragon control. They believed, with Toopek fallen and all the trouble brewing between Feldschlosschen and Antaag, that any opposition to dragon rule would be short-lived."

"Then you know about the Dwarven Civil War and King Kapmann's betrayal to the elves?"

Stepha replied. "Yes, but you are not entirely correct in that assessment. King Kapmann had been organizing aid from a large group of dark dwarves, but they were dwarves who had broken from their race and dragon rule. This party was instrumental in our escape and even now is helping our cause by attacking Draag."

Madeiris stared on in disbelief. "Are you saying that there is a party of dark dwarves on our side?"

"Yes," answered Stepha. "Nearly 600 or 700. However, they are being pushed in every direction, and their only escape, which would free them from bearing arms against miner dwarves or their dark brothers, led them into an attack on Draag."

The elf king paced the great hall until he stopped in front of a small wooden carving that had been created for Hoangis in his memory. Bowing his head, Madeiris issued a short prayer. He turned back to the two women. "There are so many that need our aid immediately, but we must not spread ourselves too thin. I will send a small party to Feldscholsschen to pass the word regarding the dark dwarves, but that leaves Toopek and Draag. Both need elven support in such large numbers."

Stepha moved to stand before her brother, noticing that with each passing breath he took, the more his body seemed to age. She added softly, "You should also know that Jermys has gone to

Antaag. He believes the Hatchet of Claude will help to restore order. As for Draag, most of its troops have joined in the attack on Toopek, which is the main reason we were able to escape. Should we have a choice to make, we must move in force at once to Toopek. It could be their and, in the long run, our only hope for victory. Toopek must hold."

Just then a guard burst in the room. "King Madeiris, two have entered our forest from the north and are using magic to protect themselves from our enchantment."

"Canoks?"

"I do not think so, sir. This magic is different."

Madeiris motioned to the girls. "Come on, we must investigate." To the guards he added, "Organize a large party to intercept. Stepha, lead a dozen flyers to be kept near, but do not approach until contact has already been established."

Both were as quickly out the door as the King's orders left his mouth. Krirtie stayed with the king, and they joined the party already forming at the city's northern entrance to the forest.

Madeiris spoke first. "Halt! Who seeks to enter Elvinott unannounced and shelters themselves so well from its magic?"

A soft, gentle voice answered as they entered the glade. "I am Hawthorne, and with me travels Werner. We require your council, King Madeiris."

The king, puzzled that his name was known, answered as if it had been asked. "I am King Madeiris, and who—"

"And I am Princess Stepha," she interrupted as she landed by his side. She examined the woman before her as if inspecting a thief. Hawthorne stood with only two small cream-colored cloths covering her silky white skin. Her long light-brown hair fell helplessly over her shoulders. Stepha's eyes were then captured by the brilliant red coat of the canok beside the human woman, and suddenly she realized all eyes were back on her regarding her strange interruption. Stepha smiled. "You have been traveling with Schram?"

Hawthorne was intrigued with the elf's behavior and wondered about her relationship with Schram. He had not mentioned anyone that he held in a particular importance since they first met, but she knew he had been tied to someone in his dreams. She wondered if this could be the same elf from so long ago. She stared at the beautiful flyer elf princess and then answered, "Yes, Princess Stepha, I traveled with Schram up until just over a day ago. When we separated, he was well."

"And Maldor?" interrupted Krirtie. "Was there a maneth with you as well?"

Hawthorne smiled at the human woman who was now showing that she was with child. "Yes, Maldor was with him, and he was equally fit, though a bit confused, to say the least. As a young maneth, I am not sure how comfortable he is with magic, much less when he is the victim of unforeseen travel as such. I am pleased to meet you both, Stepha and Krirtie"—turning back to the king—"and may our greetings be extended to all, but time is short and we must act quickly."

Madeiris checked his sister and Krirtie and then appeared pleased that he was to have another chance to speak. "We have begun to organize for a movement of force to Toopek, but I would like to discuss the situation with you before we act. Perhaps your knowledge could take us another direction or allow us to better prepare."

"We will speak, but to help you better prepare, I fear you will not like our words. A battle like one Troyf has never seen is at our door. There will be much loss in the days to come, and the result of which is not known. However, if we do not act, the situation will only worsen, and in the end, all that we know will be lost forever."

Not another word was spoken, and following a very short silence, Werner and Hawthorne began walking toward Elvinott. Madeiris signaled their return, and the elves circled behind the king, who went ahead with his sister and Krirtie to catch the woman and canok. Again, nothing was spoken, but Hawthorne repeatedly caught Stepha's eyes upon her.

Krirtie nudged the elf princess. "You should not be so obvious. She is already aware that you have many questions, especially from your previous display."

The elf glanced toward the warrior woman by her side—the one woman who had known Schram as long as, or longer, than her. "So you think I am being foolish?"

"A little, but she is very beautiful, not to mention the powers she obviously possesses." Stepha frowned at the comment before Krirtie continued. "However, you are as well, and you are the one who wears the ring."

The elf continued frowning. "But you saw the way she reacted when I asked about him. It was as if she had never heard of me and wondered why I would be so inquisitive. What other reason could it be?"

"Well, it could have simply been…" she stopped in midsentence when she noticed Hawthorne was no longer in front of them. Krirtie spun her head to the side. "Hawthorne, you startled me."

Stepha turned in surprise to the woman now right beside her. "Is there something you would like to talk about?"

The woman smiled and then replied softly. "I am sorry to approach so suddenly, but I wish to ask you a few questions, if that is all right?"

Stepha nodded, knowing that the question was meant for her. "As I would like to learn more about you as well, if that also is acceptable?"

Krirtie was listening intently until she realized that nothing more was being said and there were two pairs of eyes upon her. Quickly she smiled, "I am sorry, but I have to speak with Madeiris, so I will have to leave you two alone." After exchanging polite nods, she moved on ahead, the elf king giving her a strange smile when she approached abruptly but then did not speak.

Stepha looked toward the woman questionably. "Am I to assume that your inquiries are in regard to Schram?"

"As I am sure yours are in return," Hawthorne said. Stepha was about to comment but she was not given the chance. "What is your relationship with him?" she asked the elf flatly.

Stepha was stunned by the abrupt question. "You don't mix words. I think that is good." She paused, smiled, and then added softly, "Schram and I have known each other since we were children. We have been in love since we understood what it meant. Recently, when these troubled times began and our lives were again thrown together, we knew that regardless of the differences in our lives, we were meant to be together and sealed our love." Stepha raised her hand as she spoke, showing the Ring of Joining Schram had given her on the Dry Sea of Nakton before he left to seek out the knowledge of Ku. Hawthorne stared at the ring a moment and then back toward the elf. Stepha was uncomfortable with her reaction, or lack thereof, and stumbled over her next statement. "Might I return the question to you?"

"Yes, you may," she responded, "And in time I hope to answer it completely. However, as we now have reached your village, time for this subject must wait. If I understand fully all which is taking place, we have little time to waste before our help at Toopek would be of little use." Both comments left Stepha blank and solemn until Hawthorne lightly grabbed the elf's arm, turning her so they faced each other. "I will tell you this. If you placed the same question before Schram, he would honestly answer that he met me for the first time less than fourteen suns ago in the canok homeland. How can that compete with a lifetime of love?"

Hawthorne hugged Stepha tightly and then proceeded toward the great hall alone, leaving the elf completely bewildered. Krirtie quickly returned to the elf's side. "What was that?"

"I have no idea," she replied. "No idea at all."

⌒▥▥◡

Madeiris looked over the group assembled before him. Forcibly, he said, "If I have heard everyone correctly, then we should move in force to Toopek at once. Stepha should lead the entire field of flyers ahead to both scout for us and offer any immediate aid. I will lead the ground force. Hawthorn, you and Werner are welcome to join us or move on your own, whichever your powers and command see as most beneficial, for only the two of you understand fully where your support would be best utilized."

Werner moved forward to speak for the first time since their arrival. "We will proceed on our own. Our direction will be to Toopek, but our methods of travel may vary from that of your own."

Stepha noticed that Hawthorne seemed about ready to object, but after receiving a stern glance from the canok, she seemed content with his response. Stepha wondered what this method of travel would be and how they planned to go about it. But most of all, she wondered about the strange human woman, her elusive answers, and where she had come from in general. Stepha knew of most of the most powerful humans, and Hawthorne was not a name she had ever heard. Further, Krirtie had lived in the largest human city and she knew nothing of the mysterious woman. What had made Schram trust her so quickly?

Madeiris interrupted the elf's thoughts. "Very well, and I pray for your safety as well as our own. We will follow a direct line to Toopek should your path run similar to our own. With that, we have already possibly delayed too long so we shall leave at once." He turned to everyone. "Please make ready to depart immediately."

After exchanging parting wishes and clarifying plans, the group in the great hall began to disband. Krirtie approached Stepha and her brother. "I wish you all the luck I can give, Stepha. I wish I had wings as well so I could remain by your side. We have been through so much together. Over the last two years I have gone from hating your grip on Schram's heart up to loving you as my closest friend. I never thought that at this point we would have to separate."

Madeiris placed his hand on the woman's shoulder. "Ah, Krirtie, you should never even consider traveling to Toopek. By the look, I can tell you are within ninety days of birth. You must think of your child as well as your home."

"Exactly," added Stepha. "I am certain that when you consider all the facts, your stubbornness will win over, and you will plan a course behind my brother's lead."

Krirtie smiled. "I believe that you are correct in that assessment. However, I don't feel *stubbornness* is the correct word. It should better be described as 'mother's and baby's love for their husband and father and the country in which they wish to live.'"

The elf smiled in return. "Yes, that is what I said, *stubbornness*." She turned to her brother. "We can either lock her under guard here in Elvinott or put her somewhere we can keep an eye on her."

Madeiris began to frown. "I will have no way to protect her. I am strongly against…"

"Let me begin by saying I do not need protection."

Krirtie in turn was cut off by Stepha's raised hand. "Then I suppose it will be up to me to carry her."

"No!" replied Madeiris sternly as Krirtie began to show a slight smile of understanding. "I adamantly forbid it."

"Yes, I agree," said Krirtie. "That would be the only way."

"All agreed then," said Stepha. "We leave at once."

Madeiris began to object again but was silenced by a deep embrace from the girls and a brief exchange of prayers with his sister. As the two left the hall, the elf king yelled, "Fine, now not only will I have a fool magician after my head but a muscle-bound maneth, soon-to-be father as well."

"Relax, brother. Remember, your word is final and you clearly said there would be no way for her to travel by ground with you. This is the only way." Stepha's words and the paired girl's giggles caused a long, drawn-out sigh from the king to be the last sound the great hall would hear that day.

THE BARRIER

"Lord Starland?"

The dragon lord turned to stare blankly at his counterpart. "Yes."

Sherblade hesitated a moment at the obviously agitated response. In a more submissive voice, he asked, "Might I have a word with you?"

Starland did not verbally answer. He only continued his hard stare, his lips pressed tightly together, pushing them almost white in color. Dragon Lord Sherblade let a short period pass until he asked, "I am interested in the whereabouts of our leader Slayne. It was my understanding that he was to oversee the completion of this attack. Would you know anything about this subject?"

Starland spun his head in disgust. "Damn you, Tomas. Do you not have more pressing problems than to labor me with petty questions? I have work to do, as do you. Did I not send you to evaluate our current status?"

Sherblade nodded. "Yes you did, Lord, and it is that job which brings me back before you now. I have been to our fronts and can explain our progress to you in detail, if you desire to hear it. However, it is also this same information that placed my previous question before you. Should I tell you what I have discovered, then I would hope some answers would also come my direction."

Starland whipped his head back. His eyes were fire red and his voice was as ominous as death itself. "What has it come to, Sherblade, threats from you as well? Perhaps you sided more closely with Mapes than I suspected. It shall mean your death should you cross me."

He stepped forward. His tone showed no remorse. "I mean no disrespect, Starland, but if you hear me out, you will learn why my questions must be answered. If you do not, then I am abandoning this attack once my words have finished."

Starland stared unrelenting in return but then seemed to calm slightly. "Speak your mind, Tomas, but know that if I do not hold the same importance in your words, then leaving this room may not be an option for you."

Sherblade did not soften. "As the morning sun begins to shine its light across Toopek on this third day of attacks on the barrier, it is clear that little has been accomplished. Unless something changes its course soon, we will be too weak to ever achieve victory."

"Then what are you suggesting now? Retreat?" Starland's tone clearly showed he was ready to end Tomas's life at that very moment.

"On the contrary. I am saying that if we do not bring this force shield down today, then we will not have enough forces remaining to mount any successful attack on Toopek. For two solid days nearly throughout all daylight, the goblins and trolls and other dragon forces have collapsed on the front wall, and for two solid days, they have been pushed back. Twice they have breached the other wall only to face a thicker inlay of troops along the inside." He paused and then added, "What I am saying is that if Slayne does not come and bring this barrier down so our dragons can begin thinning the resistance, we have only one option."

The dragon lord did not respond before he turned and slowly paced away. Then, with a softer and fading voice, he said, "Slayne had plans which, if successful, would have brought a quick end to all those who resist dragon rule. He was to return here with his new power and quickly return Toopek to my leadership. If something went wrong and he was not able to obtain this new strength, then he was still to return here, and together we would ride on the city. However"—the dragon lord lifted his head and turned back to his counterpart—"he should have been here two days ago."

"Are you saying that you began this attack without his approval?"

"No. I was told that when the city was within our grasp, to take it, regardless if he remained absent."

Sherblade frowned and showed little sympathy. "So, now we have cut our force by one-third and have an emperor who is either dead or unable to return?" He paused then added snidely, "Or perhaps he is too disgusted to return and is seeking out a new empire to insert his rule."

Instantly a bolt of energy shot from Starland's hand and impacted like a rope around Sherblade's throat. The stunned dragon lord lifted one of his long talon-like fingers around the charge, and with a short incantation, it vanished. He stared back to Starland, etching his eyes into his skull.

Starland slowly lowered his hand. "Slayne has simply discovered a secondary plan to put the rebels away for good. He has left it in our hands to secure Toopek, and I suggest we do it."

"Don't try to impress me with your battle cry for support. I give you through today to come up with a plan to defeat this barrier. During that time there will be no more ground assaults without the dwarven troops accompanying the goblins and trolls, and the dark dwarves still refuse to cross the boundary after seeing nearly half of their comrades who attempted instantly meet their death. If you have not come up with a plan that I feel is plausible, then I am ordering the troops back to Draag. Do I make myself clear?"

Starland approached the dragon lord, who held his ground without fear. "I am beginning to understand you now, Tomas. You have always wanted my power. You once desired to be King of Toopek, and now you believe you have discovered a way to do just that. Well, let me make myself clear. Should you decide to give any order without my consent, then you will find that my wrath is unforgiving. Any attempt to return to Draag will be met with your immediate death. You will find that although you have asserted your leadership into the ground forces, they will still answer to me, for I am the leader of the dragons. That fact alone gives me more power than you could ever hope to grasp."

The statements became a test of wills as both dragon lords refused to wither in their beliefs. Sherblade knew that his counterpart had spoken that which was mostly true, but he also knew that to continue any ground assaults would only leave their forces at the bay of the rebel archers. Somewhere, sometime, it was clear that their stalemate would have to end by one of them relenting, but neither were ready. That was, until the large blue dragon—the same one Starland rode at the battle to return the elves to their kingdom—landed in the glade next to them. The blue roared at the confrontation before sending a greeting of fire to make his presence known.

Both dragon lords turned their faces into the flames as if absorbing power from them. The trees and bushes surrounding them seemed to explode in fury and were as quickly silenced. Lord Starland stepped away from his counterpart and approached the huge creature. "Ah, Satrial. I am pleased to see you, my friend. What news is it that brings you in such haste before me?"

The dragon was pleased with Starland's greeting and showed it by dripping balls of fire between its teeth. A second roar burst through the forest before the raspy tongue of the oldest of the young dragons answered the question. "I have information regarding the state of the barrier, which you might find of interest."

Sherblade moved to stand beside the two but allowed Starland to continue the conversation as it was clear the dragon meant only to be speaking for his ears. "Go ahead, my young apprentice, tell me what you have learned."

"I have discovered the field's filtering discrepancies and therefore found why only certain dragons can get through. It is not based solely on magic, as I originally believed, but is rather a two-part defense. It refuses passage to any creature that carries magic within it unless that creature also holds a deepening fear for what it is approaching. Many of the young dragons did hold this fear, and that is why they passed unhindered and also why they now are dead. The creator was simply trying to allow some through so they could defend against smaller numbers."

"What does this mean as far as the barrier remaining intact?" broke in Sherblade, his feelings for the more important issues outweighing his inferiority to Starland and his relationship with Satrial.

The blue turned toward the dragon lord showing deep displeasure at the comment. "I do not trust you have the feelings of my lord. Should your arrogance interrupt me again, I will not delay in destroying all that gives you life."

The dragon lord stared fiercely in return. After several long moments, he turned back to Starland. "Then you shall be in for a test of wills, which you and your lord know you cannot win."

Satrial spun back and brought his eyes down to Sherblade's level. Lord Starland shot a burst, which exploded between them. "Satrial, back. There are more important matters at hand. If what I believe you are telling me is true, then it will not be long before Toopek will face the bulk of our wrath. If this is the case, then after it is over, I will freely grant you your time with my counterpart."

"No, when this is over, then you and I will have our time." Sherblade stepped back from the dragon and locked his eyes on Starland.

Smiling, Starland answered, "As you wish, but know that it would have been to your benefit to let Mapes be successful in his attempt, for you will not be as lucky as he." He turned to face the dragon, who appeared to be smiling as well. "Now, most powerful friend, tell me the state of the force field, and I pray your news is better than that of Sherblade, who screams for retreat."

Satrial frowned. "Never would I offer such a move if it was not your word to do so. As for the barrier, already we have made a cut in the fabric of its lining. We are sending dragons through but slowly making it appear that there is no change in our situation.

They are remaining far back to wait for all to get through and then your word to be given."

"Excellent, Satrial. Spread the word that we shall make several such cuts along the field base in front of each of our main attack forces. Then, when all is in place, we shall crush the mighty Toopek with one fatal blow." The dragon roared again, sending the trees into a wild dance of fire. Starland turned to Sherblade. "Now let me hear your talk of retreat."

"Do you see what I mean, Geoff? It looks different. I would have never noticed myself if one of Pete's men stationed on the Castle Island had not signaled. What do you think it means?"

"I don't know, Greg," replied the maneth leader, his troubled voice clear to the human. "See if you can locate one of the elves. Their eyesight might be able to see things more clearly.

The human, who had become Geoff's right hand when it came to locating individuals, darted off from the harbor. Geoff watched the sky and the mass of dragons involved in a strange rotation throughout it and wondered if the only thing separating the winged army from Toopek would hold until an answer was discovered. He saw that the dragons did not appear to be growing any nearer, but Stollman was correct, they were acting overwhelmingly different. Their constant bombardment against the barrier had ceased, and in its place was an occasional burst that seemed to be more impressive in color but carried less intensity. He wondered what this new direction could mean.

Suddenly he felt a gentle touch on his shoulder. He spun around to greet the soft green eyes of a female flyer. She smiled at his jump. "I am sorry to have surprised you. I thought you heard my approach. I am Denisilantilis Kleinkis, but please call me Denisi. You are Geoff, are you not?"

A slight embarrassed grin answered the young flyer's stare. In a voice uncharacteristic of his rough exterior, Geoff replied, "Yes, I am Geoff, and to date I have never heard an elf approach, especially one from the air, but thank you for giving me the benefit of the doubt." He smiled then continued, "I have heard many stories about you, Denisi, so I am glad we finally can officially meet. Might I also add, I believe those stories did not do you justice. You are truly magnificent." He did not know why he said that, but his mouth seemed like it would not stop. "Also, let me thank you for convincing the Emporian humans to support our cause. Though your methods were slightly unique to some, the end result was perfect."

Now it was the elf who began to blush beneath her green skin, both for the praise regarding her action with the Emporians and Geoff's awkward response and greeting. Denisi was truly beautiful to any who saw. Many even said she exceeded the beauty of Princess Stepha, in a young, innocent way. Her frame was slightly smaller, but her long blonde hair and well-toned body gave her appearance to be much larger than she actually was. Her skin, though elven green, took on a much deeper tone, drawing out an even more mysterious sense. To the strongest eyes, as she approached it was difficult not to stare. To Geoff, it was proving impossible.

Denisi started to speak, smiled at Geoff's continued stare, looked away, and then finally began again. "I am sorry about that exchange with the Emporian. Sometimes I think, I mean I think about, I mean sometimes I think with my bow instead of my head." She paused, took a deep breath, and then added, "And sometimes I just don't seem to be able to think at all."

The two let several short moments pass in silence as their glowing eyes held their own conversation. Then, as if breaking from a trance, the elf asked simply, "What did you need me for anyway? Stollman told Tantisolandis Arnolin that you required an elf's sight to help identify something, but he was detained so I offered to come. What is it I can help with?"

Geoff broke from his daze and pointed with his club toward the sky around the formation of dragons. "What does your elven sight see there? Specifically that group nestled out of formation."

The girl stared at the area briefly and then removed her bow. "I see something that bears closer inspection." With that, her wings danced a bit and she was quickly airborne.

"Wait! All I wanted to know is what…" but the statement was of little use as the elf only increased the distance between them. "Damn elf."

"Ah, don't worry about her. She has proven time and time again that she can take care of herself."

Geoff nearly jumped from his skin, causing the elf right behind him now to laugh. "Tantis! Between you and that damn flyer girl, I am going to fall over dead right on this spot. Announce yourself when you approach, or I am going to cut those wings right off your back."

Tantis continued to smile. "Don't worry about my silent approach. All I did was get your message to come immediately. Because I was unable to leave right then, I informed Denisi, much to her pleasure, I might add, to go in my place until I could return."

"Just what the hell do you mean by that comment?"

"What comment?" Tantis was now beginning to smile more broadly.

Geoff glared at the much-smaller elf. "I can hear your tone. *Much to her pleasure*. Just what does that mean?"

The elf leaned closer. "If you have to ask, then I guess it does not mean anything." His smile held for a short time longer before turning to the sky and asking, "Now, in all seriousness, my friend, what has happened?"

Geoff did not see his gaze and did not actually hear his question. "I mean she was nice enough and all and even appeared to be a fairly strong warrior, but besides that, I have no idea what you are talking about."

Tantis grinned. "Hey, Geoff, I believe you. Now, will you answer my question before I fly up and ask Denisi myself?"

Her name caused Geoff to join his grin. "I asked her if she could see anything different in the action of the dragons. The group to the side is remaining stationary while the other group is moving in that pattern. Furthermore, their attacks on the barrier have, for the most part, ended. She did not offer comment before heading up to get a closer look."

"That really made you mad, didn't it?"

"You bet it…" He caught the elf's grin. "No, it did not bother me in the least." Tantis was nearly beside himself with laughter as the large maneth grabbed his head and forcibly turned it toward the clouds. "Now tell me, what do you see?"

"I see a maneth becoming entranced by a hot-headed female flyer elf."

Geoff threw the elf aside in an attempt to silence his laughter. It failed. With a long-drawn-out sigh, he swung his head back toward the sky. "By all the gods, Tantis!"

The elf recognized the tone in his voice and immediately followed his eyes. Without a word, he had drawn his bow and was joining the maneth in his run to the water's edge just as the young flyer splashed between the white ripples and disappeared beneath the surface accompanied by a wall of fire instantly turning the water's edge to steam in her wake. The sea seemed to catch fire as the dragon's breath lit the harbor with a barrage of shots. Tantis released several arrows into the broad green belly of the beast before Geoff had even retrieved his bow. However, the elven arrows only seemed to entice the dragon's fury. Geoff drew on the approaching creature and let one of his steel shafts fly. A beam of energy struck the arrow in midflight, rendering it harmless into the sea.

The maneth turned with a horrified gaze. "This one carries magic with it and is showing no fear in its eyes."

"Yes," the elf replied. "That means the barrier is most likely down, at least in part."

The two dove behind an outbreak of rock just before fire exploded across the ground in front of them. Geoff was knocking another arrow while Tantis answered the dragon's fire by landing one of his smaller arrows deep within its belly. The creature screamed in rage but was again only slightly affected.

As the dragon circled for another pass with the beat of its wings kicking up dust as if a mighty storm was roaring across the harbor, Geoff swung his eyes to the flying army left in the sky. "The numbers in that mass seem to be growing, but if they are inside the barrier, why do they not attack?"

"Perhaps this one was not meant to attack. The dragon was obviously after Denisi. He might simply have been trying to keep her from escaping with what she had seen."

Geoff nodded agreement momentarily, but his attention was quickly drawn back to the approaching dragon. Regardless of the reasons for the attack, the fact was Denisi was down and the creature now had Geoff and Tantis in its sites. The maneth let Tantis send his arrows first so as to draw the large dragon's attention. Then, as it drew near, Geoff took careful aim and released his next arrow. The rod lodged itself deep within the dragon's tissue, but still it continued its flight. Its head arched back, sending rolls of heat and fire across their cover. The rock itself began to crack and explode, and the intense temperature tore through its layers.

Geoff set his bow down and reached for his club. Tantis laughed. "Put that thing away, my bullheaded fool. It cannot help against this dragon."

He frowned. "I am out of arrows. Between nothing and this club, I choose the club."

"Agreed."

Geoff began to creep out from behind cover to better see the dragon and look across the water for any sign of the flyer elf. "We have to see to Denisi's safety. I will divert the dragon while you move across to help her."

Tantis had heard that tone several times before, and he knew that Geoff could never be more serious or determined. However, one question remained. "Geoff, the dragon may follow you, but you cannot outrun it. What will you do when he engages and you have no cover?"

The maneth stared back without speaking and Tantis understood. Tantis moved beside his longtime friend and the two locked hands, both of their broad shoulders and well-defined muscles expanding greatly in a bond few creatures ever reach.

They watched as the dragon took a wide circle across the harbor and then began an intercept course for the two warriors. Just then, Geoff leaped from behind the rocks and began to run with his maneth club raised high in the air. The dragon reacted immediately to the movement and drew a new line for his now-unprotected prey. Tantis waited until he was certain the dragon's attention was focused and then broke into a lightning flight toward the last area he saw the flyer hit.

Geoff stopped running, giving himself enough time to dig his feet deep into the sand to provide support against the first impact. He gripped his club so tightly that beads of sweat rolled between his large maneth paws. His eyes were locked on the creature when the first wave of fire brought the air to a midday glow. The wind generated from the burst of energy combined with the beast's violent beat of its wings blew Geoff's mane almost straight back. He knelt down and let the flames surge past his brow and dropped his club to his side, ready to swing upward at the precise moment to impact the dragon before its talons could grab his body and rip it to pieces. He raised his club, and the two hit like two planets striking square to each other. The dragon was unprepared for the impact and arched its wings, dropping just out of the maneth's reach, hovering slightly above the water. Geoff roared as blood seeped from his side where the talon had caught the seam between his breastplate and hip. He could feel the pain but believed the wound to be minor.

More importantly, however, he knew he could not defend against this dragon long.

Suddenly the beast screamed, causing Geoff to hold his club directly up. However, his movement was too late, and the dragon hit him with a force like he had never felt before. However, it was not an attack. The dragon was still screaming and flailing its wings wildly. Geoff was pinned underneath part of the creature's side, and from this position, he could see the elven arrow lodged in its neck. He raised his club and swung hard at the place of impact. The creature screamed again and tried to roll its head around to snap its large teeth on the trapped maneth, but the location of the arrow prevented any such turn. Then, without another movement, two more arrows simultaneously struck the creature, and he was silenced.

A soft voice asked, "Geoff, are you all right? I did not see you there, or I would not have dropped the creature so close to you. When it backed up and hovered off the water's edge, it gave me the perfect opportunity to find the most sensitive place to hit—the throat. Any shot lodged deep in the throat has a good chance of knocking out its ability to breath fire."

Tantis approached. "Fine shot Denisi. And Geoff, I have never seen anything like it. Fighting a dragon with a block of wood? Probably not your best idea."

He looked toward Tantis then back to Denisi. "I am just glad you are all right. And thank you for hitting your mark."

The female flyer smiled. "Thank you both for coming after me." She turned and saw Tantis spreading some elven dust across the dragon's body.

Neither answered but Tantis bowed his head just before several voices sounded from across the beach toward the city. "Geoff, Tantis, Denisi, are you all right? What happened?"

Geoff waved. "I am fine. In fact, we are all fine. Thanks to Denisi for dropping this beast so quickly."

Alan, Meris, and Fritz all came hurrying forward, leading a party of human and elven archers. "What happened?" hollered Alan, arriving first to the area.

Geoff began to reply but was cut off by the young flyer. "Geoff sent me up to inspect what was occurring at the barrier when a dragon, who was within the shield, decided my presence was not necessary. After Geoff and Tantis had each wounded it severely, I was able to provide the finishing touches."

Geoff smiled briefly at the response. "Denisi is the hero, let no story from her take that away. However, much more important than that, I must understand what you saw that drove this dragon to so aggressively decide your presence was not necessary." He paused then added, "Or more accurately, decide what you saw should not be told to anyone else."

She took a step closer and immediately her tone turned to one of utmost seriousness. "They punched a hole through the barrier. It is not a large hole, but slowly they are filtering through. I think they aim to slip all of them through unnoticed and then attack in one wave."

Meris broke in. "That confirms our suspicions on the ground. They have found a seam in at least two areas. The goblin and troll forces were trying to hide our view but we suspected something like that was occurring. With this new information, we must assume it to be true."

"Damn!" replied Geoff. "If only the canoks were here, perhaps they could close the holes or even create a new barrier."

"Would it be worth asking Reynolds? The Emporians do know something about such magic." Alan seemed unsure to even ask the question, knowing Geoff's feelings about the human magicians.

"I doubt it. After all, you know how long the barrier they created around Empor lasted. No, there has to be another answer."

Tantis took his eyes from the dragons he had been suspiciously watching to address the group directly. "I believe that our only answer is going to mean preparing for the most violent attack of our lives. Judging by the rate at which the dragons are slipping through and assuming they are going to wait until all are through before they attack, I believe that by nightfall they will have collapsed on the city."

"By nightfall" repeated Meris softly. "Are you certain it will be that soon?"

"As I said, I am only speculating on the rate at which they seem to be moving into position. I can say nothing for certain."

Geoff moved forward, causing the group to circle around him. His voice was strong and commanding. "Meris, pull everyone off the outside wall and bring them to the inside wall. Alan, take those from the inside wall and allocate them among the most secured city buildings. Try to ensure they have line of sight to the walls for our men there who will need their support. The dragons will be fighting with fire and magic, so prepare your troops to the best of your abilities. Also, find Reynolds and see if his people might be able to defend against the dragon magic or slow their penetration." Meris and Alan looked back to their leader surprised by the comment. Seeing their gaze, Geoff added, "These are times when we may leave no stone unturned. If they can even gain us moments, it may be worth it. Now go."

Tantis moved beside the large maneth. "Why pull our force from the outer wall? Wouldn't they still prove useful against the ground forces from the forest?"

He shook his head. "No, I discussed it with Meris and Alan earlier. We will not be defeated by the ground forces, but the dragons present a problem. We have to center our defenses against them. The outer wall will still act as a good buffer between forces. As their troops come over, we will be able to pick many of them off. Those who do make it over will find themselves between two barriers and facing a brunt of arrows. To make a long explanation short, we can't afford the troops on the outer wall and still have any chance against the dragons."

"What is the situation with that mad sea dog?"

"Captain Pete?" Geoff smiled at the elf's description. "He has taken what is left of his fleet to Castle Island. He said he will make his presence known to the dragons in an attempt to draw some of them away from the city. I told him if things get too hot, to save one ship and set sail across the South Sea. He responded simply, in Geoff's best drawl, "I'll not be runnin' from a fight against no winged beasties, lad. You can bet your last pint o' ale on that.""

Fritz, who had remained quiet since arriving, gazed to the sky and then back to his friend. "Tantis, could you carry me to the city center? I have an idea which could prove useful against the dragons, but we must save every minute we can"—he turned to Geoff and added—"with your permission, of course."

The maneth slapped him on the back. "Go. Do anything you can. I will be along shortly, but know I trust your judgment."

Tantis moved beside the elf, and the three exchanged deep, meaningful stares without speaking. Then, the two were off, leaving Geoff and Denisi alone save for a group of archers a short distance toward the water. The maneth waved to the small party. "Spread yourselves among the closest buildings but ensure you have some protection from dragon fire. You will face the first wave. In fact, act not to engage them but provide vision to others of their approach and attack pattern. Do you understand?"

Several raised their swords and bows while cheers of allegiance rang across the water. The group quickly divided and vanished among the first buildings, trees, and anywhere they could find cover. In only moments, the shore had turned devoid of anyone except the maneth leader and the young flyer elf.

"You are a deep and powerful individual, Geoff. When this is all over, I should like to learn more from you."

He was taken by the elf, and although some inner part of him wanted that very thing as well, he had no ability to speak it. He fought for some response because the momentary silence bit him harder than the dragon's talon moments earlier. Denisi had her back to the water, with Geoff still turned toward the sky over the harbor as he watched the continued movement of the dragons. Suddenly, the maneth grabbed the girl and threw her to the sand, drawing his club in the same motion. Denisi instantly jumped back to her feet with bow drawn and arrow knocked before Geoff could even take one step toward the water.

A slew of odd ripples broke the water's surface, with two large grey eyes pushing through first in their wake. The elf adjusted her bow to a direct line between the eyes, but in truth she was completely captivated by whatever creature was slowly becoming known. Suddenly its entire body broke through, placing its size near that of the largest buildings left standing in the city. The creature focused its eyes on the two, and quickly Geoff realized his club would be of no use. "Who are you?" he asked.

The creature stared long at the maneth as if it was inspecting the very particles of his being. "Put away your weapons, one known as Geoff, leader of the maneth and defender of Toopek. For today, I am not your enemy."

Geoff began to lower his club. Denisi whispered, "Don't be foolish. To drop your guard at these times would be…"

She was silenced by the maneth's raised hand. "My club, or your bow for that matter, would have no bearing against a *Physeter catodon*."

The woman's eyes grew even larger. The large creature continued to stare toward the maneth. "Ah, you remember, my young son?" said the whale's deep voice.

Geoff smiled. "I remember stories my father would tell me by the fire—legendary stories about the largest and most powerful creatures in all of Troyf and beyond. But for how you know me, I am at a loss."

"Your father was a good friend, a maneth I shall never forget, as I am sure you understand. I am Khaled, and I am here to speak with you."

Geoff was calmed by the memory of his father, but what exactly this meant was beyond his grasp. He pulled Denisi back to stand by his side and gently helped her replace her bow, which her hands had rigidly locked around. "Khaled, I am here as the time at hand seems to have dictated me to be. But I do not know why you would require my council. Until moments ago, I would have said your existence was just a legend."

"Your confusion, understand it I do. If your worry holds, then let it be said that I come to you through the word of Prince Schram."

"Schram!" Instantly Geoff took several steps forward and a peace engulfed his entire body followed by an energy drawn somewhere from deep inside him. "What is it we need to discuss, and more importantly, will you or Schram be able to help, for his barrier is beginning to fail?"

Khaled narrowed his eyes. "The physeter cannot use force upon any creature free of the water's boundary, and that shall not change unless we alone deem it necessary. We only wish to know if the words spoken by the one called Schram are true."

Geoff was taken by the response. "I will answer anything you ask. What are these words that were said?"

"He declared that on this day the physeter would be free to once again swim the waters without fear of human interference. He said you would be the one to make it law."

If Geoff had anticipated any response, that would not have been it. However, he was pleased that he could answer without question. "I can say without question that from this moment forward, that which you say is law." He paused then added, "But you should be aware that this law may be as such for the time we are able to hold this city and defend against this oppression. Toopek, as well as all of Troyf, faces a danger that may put all life, including the physeters" in peril."

Khaled closed his eyes, and Geoff could feel him probing his mind. "Yes, I learned of this dragon in my meeting with the one called Schram. The physeters have been watching this city for

many tides. Your friends must have been unsuccessful on Cindif."
He paused and his eyes rolled back into his head. "I am sorry,
Geoff, but I must go at once." With that, there was huge splash,
and following a raised tail flipping violently against the water's
surface, he was gone.

"What did he mean by Cindif?" asked the elf, standing
with her arm wrapped around the body of the large maneth—a
position she had taken when Geoff first pushed her bow down,
and she had opted not to move.

"I do not know, but I am more concerned with the fact that
they were not successful. We must go. I always held out that
Schram would be back in time to help, but I must assume now he
will not be. We have to hold this city on our own."

Denisi grabbed the maneth beneath his shoulders as her
wings spread wide. "I may not be the strongest warrior yet, but
like Tantis, I can help move you quickly to where you need to be."
She paused then added, "You have definitely lived up to what I
was told."

Geoff said nothing but did wonder what the hell she had
been told. Then he shook his head and whispered to himself,
"Something from Tantis, no doubt."

"Tantis was one who I asked," she replied, knowing he had not
meant for her to hear.

KHALED'S ULTIMATUM

"Geoff," hollered Meris between breaths while fighting to stop the bleeding from where a broken arrow had become lodged in his leg. "I think that was the last wave. They have pulled back for the night."

"Pulled back for the night?" repeated Tantis between painful coughs of spilled elven blood. "It is two hours till sunrise."

Denisi did her best to support the wounded elf, but the battery of her own injuries left the flyer looking for any safe spot to rest. Geoff ran over and grabbed Tantis in his arms. "Reynolds, get some of your people over here to see to the flyers. We have to keep them healthy. Meris, secure the wall with whatever force you can and get down here. We have to talk."

Geoff set the elf down to the care of several humans who began bandaging him. Then he started for the area Alan and Fritz had set aside to meet. It happened to be a table that had, by some twist of fate, remained in the courtyard to the council room during this first fierce battle and yet was left undamaged. Geoff looked back to where Tantis was being cared for, and the human working to bandage him caught Geoff's gaze. The unasked question was answered with lowered eyes and a short shaking of his head to the negative.

Geoff turned back to meet with Alan when Denisi grabbed his shoulder. The elf pulled her hand away and saw it was now completely saturated with blue blood. The maneth's eyes softened when he saw it was her. "What is it? Are you okay?"

She smiled. "I am okay. I just wanted to thank you for saving me from..."

"You owe me no thanks. You performed admirably and should be very proud. Your marksmanship is unmatched."

"How can I help? We have to see to your wounds."

Geoff clutched his side as a burst of pain screamed through his body, nearly bringing the maneth to his knees. He fought through the surge but it was clear to the elf that Geoff was severely injured, more than he would ever let on. The silence caused by his inability to answer only furthered her conviction to this fact. When he finally began to answer, the elf had already moved beside him to help balance his weight.

She stepped up to whisper to his ear. "Use me for support. I know you must not show any weakness. Too many are depending on you."

"Thank you, but I must go on my own. I will see to my injuries immediately following this meeting."

"I understand," she said. "I will not say anything, but I will remain if you need support. Use me as you need to, and then together we will see to your injuries."

He did not answer but proceeded forward, and with every step, he felt a pain no equal to any he had felt in his lifetime. As he approached the area, Alan rose. "Geoff, are you all right?"

"I am as well as anyone. After only two or three arrows the pain becomes quite intense but not life threatening. No goblin archer is going to bring me down."

Meris approached, limping. "I agree. Those goblins are a pain in the ass, and with that, I will need some help removing this one."

Geoff only shook his head where previously a laugh would have ensued. "Tell me, Meris, you are closest to the ground forces. How do we stand?"

The young maneth released a sigh of his own. "We were holding the dragon army at bay even from the inside wall for much of the early battle, but by the time the dragon forces hit from behind, we lost much ground. There was an onslaught over the outer wall. Much of it has been at least partially destroyed.

There are several avenues needing repair as one only has to jump loose rubble and debris to breach. Then, they began to use the debris for protection to attack those on the inner wall. We had to split our attention between those in our faces on the ground and those at our back from the air. We were simply outnumbered."

Meris was obviously distraught and he rose to move from the table but Geoff motioned for him to remain. "Yes, I know. When the dragons ceased from engaging Pete and our scattered forces mixed throughout the city and turned their attention on your troops on the wall, I feared we would lose everyone. But know one thing, Meris, you did well to hold your position. We held for now, that much shows how well you did. Tell me, what is your current status—or maybe a more accurate question—how many did we lose?"

The maneth did not retake his seat. Instead he paced the table and fought to keep his voice strong. "I am not exactly sure how many I had under my command, but assuming I had about fourteen hundred, then I would say about one quarter are dead or missing and another third are injured."

The elves at the table bowed their head while Alan recited a silent prayer. Geoff simply stared forward in disbelief. "I had no idea we had been hit so gravely."

"Has there been any word from Captain Pete or any of the fleet?" Alan asked.

The maneth leader shook his head. "No. As he had hoped, a good number of the dragons did ignore Toopek and engaged him. However, their numbers were too much for the already-battered ships to handle. After only about two hours, there were few ships left. Since that time, I have seen no sign nor heard any word from any of them."

Again there was a moment of silence. With each comment, the situation was darkening, driving their thoughts toward loss. Geoff was beginning to realize that even the fortress he had built around this city may not be enough to hold against the dragon forces' new numbers. He began to push himself painfully up from the table when Denisi broke in. "Meris, how many of their troops did you bring down?"

The maneth quit pacing and flashed a strange look toward the girl. "I can't be sure. Maybe six or seven hundred before the dragons hit and another three or four hundred after."

"Nearly a thousand," the girl said with a tone full of energy and pride. "And could any of you guess at the number of dragons we can claim victory over?"

Meris placed both his hands firmly on the table but was becoming intrigued by the flyer elf's comments and moreover was liking the raised heads and interest the group was paying her. He did not let anyone else answer as the conversation seemed to be centered on him. "I believe we may have killed ten to twelve, but I believe we injured at least fifty."

Fritz nodded, also feeling the lift in the area, but rather than speak, he let the young girl finish. Turning to the maneth leader with a soft smile twisted in her gaze, she said, "And Geoff, would you argue with my estimates of sixty dragons killed in the city and over the sea and another hundred or so injured?"

The maneth shook his head. "No, I believe that number to be accurate."

"Then don't you see it? We won today. I am certain they planned on owning this city after one attack and they were too beaten to do it. They had to retreat." She paused and turned to the group. "We can hold this city. I am certain of it, but we cannot give in at all now. They have no idea of our numbers or how many we lost. They are spread out and we are not. Do you not all see it?"

"She is right," said Fritz. "Too much has been gained to dwell on our losses. We did hold the city, all of us together held this city. I, like every elf, is no fan of war and death as it goes against our first principle of life, but if we submit to their rule without a fight, then our lives will as quickly end. For that much I am certain."

"Yes!" said Alan.

Meris drew his maneth club and slammed its broadside on the table. "To the end, Geoff, do you agree?"

Geoff rose and slowly made his way over to Meris while a deathly silence seduced the group. All eyes followed his every step as the pain he felt each time his feet struck the ground was carried to each of those in the circle. He placed his hand on the maneth's shoulder and, in a voice which displayed no sign of injury or pain, said clearly, "Don't you have some troops to organize?" He turned to the young flyer elf and gave a stare that told more than any words could ever say before continuing to the maneth. "Our protection is clearly disabled from what it has been. Strengthen it in every area you can and then give me a full report on the status. We have to understand our weakest points so we can be prepared to add support should the next attack strike there."

The young maneth placed his hand back on the shoulder of his leader, creating a powerful sight that, from their current location, a huge percentage of the city could see, causing a slew of cheers and hollers. Without a word to the group, Meris was off shouting orders in numerous directions.

Fritz rose. "I will organize the elves along the wall and inner city. Any flyers remaining I will send to you or Tantis, but I should warn you, our flyers took the brunt of the hit. Many are injured."

"Good," said Geoff. "And thank you. Also, see to Tantis on your way."

"Nobody needs to see to me. I am as good as a 250-year-old flyer elf can be, though I don't see me flying much in the near future."

Geoff swung his eyes to see the completely bandaged body of his old friend. He heard Denisi issue a soft giggle at the sight but Geoff kept his reaction completely composed. Looking at his arms, he asked, "Can you arch?"

"Are you a muscle-bound warrior who fights with a club?"

"I assume that means yes," grinned Geoff, who was actually very glad to see his friend alive. He turned to Alan. "Grove, see that this nonflyer elf is given some new armor to better fit around his wraps. In fact, distribute all the armor we have left to those who need it, or at least have it accessible. Then, help Meris at the wall. I think your aid with the humans will be useful."

"On your word, Geoff." With that, the human who was showing few signs of injury put Tantis's arm around his shoulder, and the two gingerly headed in the direction of the smith.

"Now for you," the maneth said, staring back to the young flyer elf. Her hair slightly matted but, other than that, shined at a time when so much was dark.

"Nonsense," she interrupted. "You are going to listen to me. You are not going to do anything more until we get your wounds cared for. You can't lead if you can't walk. This is not open for discussion."

"There will be time for dressing my wounds once everything is set. For now..."

She reached out and grabbed the warrior at the previous entry point of a goblin arrow and squeezed tightly. The maneth grimaced is pain, roaring as if he had just been grabbed by the talons of a dragon and his body nearly severed in two. Denisi released her hand and said again, "You will get these cared for now, no exceptions. If the smallest person in the room can bring you to your knees, then you are no match for a fight."

The large maneth stared back, this time with fire burning in his eyes. "You know, Denisi, I think I could really start to like you, if..."

"If what?" she asked.

"If, as Meris and the humans would say, you were not always such a fireball."

"I'll take that as a compliment. Now hold still. I have to get the rest of this arrow out. It has broken off at the skin."

The next sound everyone between the city center and the sea heard was a maneth roar followed by the patronizing taunt of an elf successful in her arrow removal.

⟨∞⟩

"Draketon, why have you stopped? It will be near dawn soon, and we could still make it into Toopek before first light if we continue."

"I will go no further, Schram. You have adequate power in your staff to get Maldor and yourself across the water in time. I will remain here until you are ready."

"Ready?" asked the magician. "Ready for what?"

Ignoring his question, Draketon said, "Besides, I could not pass your barrier without weakening it nor could I purposely engage the young dragons in battle. They are my brothers and sisters. I cannot forget my heritage, nor can you."

Schram did not know what to make of the dragon's comments, and the blank stare from Maldor showed the same. He patted Draketon's neck. "Very well, my friend. I shall hope that I will be ready when the time is right."

The dragon closed his eyes and continued to silently hover across the surface of the water. Schram raised his staff and recited a short incantation within his mind. Suddenly, the water immediately beneath them turned solid—not rock or ice, just water seemingly frozen in its place. The two leaped from the dragon's back and, without another word, began a full run with each step they took, solidifying the water in their path, which disappeared immediately in their wake.

Maldor asked as they ran, "How long until we reach Toopek?"

Schram pointed across the sea. "That glow is the island where my parents' castle once stood. We are about one hour out, should we keep this pace."

As they drew closer to the spot Schram had pointed to earlier, he stopped so abruptly he caused the maneth to stumble in his tracks and fall against the magical surface.

The maneth drew his weapon, panting at the pace they had kept. "What? Why have we stopped?"

Schram's eyes were locked on Castle Island, now nearly completely destroyed and burning. The maneth too saw the destruction, but his eyesight was not nearly as clear as the magician next to him. "The shield I created around Toopek is fading. It is very weak." His eyes followed its dome-like shell into the air which, although it was still dark, he could see clearly. "By all the gods!"

"I don't like the sound of that, Schram. What do you see?"

"We must hurry, Maldor. There are several armies of dragons that have assembled inside the shield. They have punched a hole through and now are waiting to attack."

"Judging by the fires across the horizon, I would guess they have attacked already," added the maneth.

Schram stared toward his old home and saw what Maldor saw. A look of horror grew across his face but then slowly calmed. "Then they have held for the time. The dragon army has retreated. We may still have time. Guard your hammer well, my friend, for this shall be its ultimate test. Come, we must hurry."

Maldor roared and fell back in behind the Prince of Toopek. They moved through the force field without issue as Schram created a port, which did not further weaken what remained. In what seemed like only moments longer, they were working their way along the coast of the island, stopping occasionally to lend aid to the few humans who remained alive. An arrow landed near Schram's feet, causing both to stop. The maneth lifted his hammer in defense while Schram motioned to the maneth to calm. "Relax, my friend. If this arrow had meant to hit, it would have."

"Who is approaching at such a pace?" echoed a voice from the trees.

Schram whispered a few words, which caused his staff to glow slightly, lighting the entire area. "Is that you, Captain Pete, you nasty sea dog?"

The one-eyed sea pirate moved from the shadows. "Well, the damn elf decides to finally come back and help save his city, and he be bringing the lion man with him. Where you two been, playin' games and drinkin' ale I'll be bettin ya."

Schram and Maldor approached the captain, and Maldor nearly had to look away when he saw the extent of his injuries. Several wounds spilled red blood, but nothing worse than the welts of burns across the left half of his body. Still, the one-eyed pirate reached out his arms and gripped the human and maneth on each shoulder. "I'd be welcoming you back to your city, but I fear there is not much left to welcome you to."

The maneth, without word, placed his silver hammer against the body of the sea captain. There was a faint glow and then a jolt, which sent both individuals to the ground.

Pete issued a sad laugh. "I guess it don't like the taste of me blood." The maneth stood back up, slightly disillusioned. "Don't worry, boy. I be no worse off than before. Seen many strange things since the first time we all met, but nothing finished me yet."

Schram smiled at the captain's good humor, but as dawn was soon approaching, he knew he had little time for conversation. "Pete, where do things stand? What has happened?"

"Well, me boys and me been dished out a good woopin'. Toopek has faced one hell of an attack, but Geoff done seemed to come out okay. The dragons' been pulled back for two hours now, but I think come sunrise they be comin' back."

"When did it start?" asked Maldor.

Pete thought a minute. "Three days back was the first ground assault, but those had little effect. The big one hit late yesterday. Damn winged beasts come down in force. I don't know how Toopek fared, but we couldn't hold 'em long. I have only two ships left and maybe thirty men who can walk."

Maldor looked to Schram and nodded. The magician stepped forward. "Captain Pete, load up your men and head to the South Sea. Take all the food you can carry, because it is a long journey.

You will come to land, on which you will find a band of elves. Stay with them until you hear otherwise. If Toopek falls, you will have nothing to return to anyway, so perhaps you may be able to save some of your men in the process. You have fought with valor."

"I don't know why you boys keep talking of running. Damn boy, we got us a goodin' here. I don't mean to disobey an order, but me men and I aren't officially loyal to Toopek, so you can't be issuing me any orders. I don't know where this other land across this sea is, but I will go there, in a week or so. For now, I have to prepare my men for battle."

Schram reached his hand out and clasped the captain's tightly. "Pete, from the first day I met you, I did not like you, but I am glad you are on my side. If anyone can cause a problem for those dragons with so few men, you would be the one."

"That I would, Schram, and the feelings otherwise are mutual."

"Then thank you and good luck."

Schram and Maldor began to move toward shore as another sailor approached Pete. The captain asked, "Ships ready?"

"Yes, Cap'n, and we be addin' a little to the second one."

"Good, then let's be given them beasts some of what they been given to us."

Schram glanced back to Pete one last time before dousing his light. Maldor shook his head when the light went down and softly asked, "Do you think he will do it?"

There was no answer. The two began their trek across the harbor, walking across it as before, as if they walked on land the whole way. Pete looked out and saw the two figures on the bay and cursed under his breath. "Damn magic. Whatever happened to fighting with swords and fists, that be a fight I would never lose." He laughed his gargled laugh, "Well, never lose twice."

CWLO

"Fritz, look," said Meris, pointing. "What do you think?"

"I think we should brace ourselves because it is beginning again."

The maneth turned from the top of the wall back toward the city. "Geoff, the armies are moving. Prepare for another attack!"

Geoff waved understanding and glanced back to the southern sky. "Damn! Denisi, can you see the dragons? It is still too dark over the water for my eyesight to penetrate the haze."

"Yes, I see them," she responded. "Some have broken from the pack to investigate what is left on the island, but the majority are remaining in place." She paused and her voice cracked. "No, wait. Meris is correct. It has started once again. They are moving as a group this time, and they are headed straight this direction, toward city center."

The first hollers from archers were heard from their backs at the front wall, but Geoff was too busy issuing signals and orders to notice. There was still a little light, which aided the defenders on the wall against the ground forces but was a big favor to the dragons, which carried a stronger night vision than that of the elves.

Dragon breath lit up the harbor as the first huge beasts met the first slew of Toopekian bowfire. Screams of pain filled the morning air, but time continued to move forward. Geoff launched arrow after arrow into the bellies of the creatures, but unless one did not see them coming, they had little negative effect. A cry of cheers echoed through the streets when the first dragon of the second wave came crashing to the rocks, but the cheer was short-lived as six more were quickly in its wake.

Geoff began to shout orders when he noticed the pattern in the dragon's flight. They were circling in, destroying everything they could, and then pulling out. The waves were coming in repeated fashion and were having a detrimental effect. The ground archers could only take passing shots at the dragons as they raced past. Even those arrows that did hit were single, and any wounds were superficial, but the damage they unleashed on the city was tremendous.

Geoff raced to the largest group of archers. "We must channel our efforts on one or two dragons only. We cannot take them down in a group. I will call out the one we take aim against and all fire goes toward it. Fall back, let's bring them closer to us."

As the second wave began to swing through, huge explosions like none ever before witnessed were heard from the harbor. The maneth leader glanced up but could only see tremendous bright flashes lighting up the whole city. "What in the hell is that?" he said to all around. He could not be sure of their origin or cause but he feared the worst. However, with the first blasts from the dragons, his attention was drawn from the source and back to the flying attack, which seemed unaffected by the activity in the harbor.

"There is one red and one blue," Geoff hollered. "Focus on those two and let's bring them down."

All eyes quickly locked on the dragons he had identified, and when they drew within range, this new strategy seemed to catch the dragons by surprise. Those not targeted flew unhindered across the shore and city, but the two singled out faced a barrage of a full city's attack. The two dragons faltered in flight while a third that turned to defend the other two also took on a fierce attack. The blue's wing got severed and it struck the rocky cliffs hard. Still breathing fire and swinging its talons, those who attacked on foot were quickly thwarted. Denisi moved from the two in flight and took lead on the grounded dragon. As attention was drawn to her attack, a sword bit deep into the beast's throat. Blue blood spilled onto the ground, and the dragon screamed in terror. A second arrow from the flyer made it screech no more.

The two remaining dragons saw the violent death of the other and stretched their talons downward while lifting their wings high, trying desperately to back out of entrapment. Arrows repeatedly shot upward, some striking their mark while others were simply tossed aside. One dragon sent a burst of fire across the archers below. Many screamed as the intense heat melted their armor and singed their skin, creating a smell that tortured those on the ground, but all those who could kept answering the attack with continued bowfire.

Suddenly, one of the dragons turned from its escape and made a direct line toward the rooftop where Denisi and Geoff now stood. Denisi had moved Geoff to this location where he could view nearly all fronts and still be able to aid in the dragon defense from the sea. Now his location had become known. The large red bore down on the building, and with one fireball shot from its mouth, the building exploded beneath them. The flyer elf grabbed Geoff's shoulder, sending a shot of pain throughout his body, which, for the most part, went unnoticed. The two lifted in the air, but with the flames and explosions, their only path took them directly toward the dragon.

Geoff lifted his huge bow and drew a line between the dragon's eyes. A wall of fire encased their bodies as the arrow left his hand. The maneth felt the elf lose hold in the fire and his body began to fall. He tried to locate her but could see noting in the smoke and debris, and his eyes felt as if they were burned closed. He struck a pile of loose rock and fell to the side.

Instantly he was back to his feet, brushing what he could free from his eyes and trying to see where the flyer elf landed, or if she had engaged the dragon in flight. He could hear her cries but was having little success locating her or her direction. Then he saw an arrow fly from the ground toward the dragon still in flight. He followed the arrow to its source and saw the girl trying to push herself up. The sight before him nearly brought him back to his knees. "Denisi, don't move," he shouted as he ran her direction. "Where are you injured?"

The girl's voice was broken and strained, and she was losing much green blood to the ground. "I believe my leg to be broken and maybe one wing. If it is not broken, I know I still cannot fly. However, this is what is causing the most pain." She turned to the side to reveal an arrow lodged deep in her lower back. "I believe I landed on it but I can't be sure."

Geoff reached his arms out. "I will try not to cause more pain, but I have to carry you out of here. We are completely unprotected."

"No, please go. The pain is too great to move and I will just hold you back now." She paused as the pain engulfed her. "Please, Geoff, go. You mean too much to the city."

"I will not leave you."

"Go, before it is too..." Her eyes grew huge and locked on a sight behind them, drawing Geoff's gaze immediately around. The dragon that had attacked them had fled, but the other one had become caught in the bowfire from the ground. It had been wounded but not killed. Now its attempt to flee had brought it directly to the two of them. "Run, Geoff, it is your only chance. Run, damn it."

Geoff retrieved his bow but quickly threw it aside when he saw the string had been burnt through. He drew his large maneth club and held it toward the approaching dragon. "I guess we will see if Tantis was right that you should not bring a club to a dragon fight."

As Denisi hollered again for Geoff to flee, the two forces struck again. The dragon wheeled in a violent fit of pain while red blood poured from its neck. The remaining archers sent sheets of arrows into the creature's midsection, but it now seemed to have only one idea in mind—to destroy Geoff regardless of the cost.

Its flight was obscured and more arrows pierced its skin, but the dragon remained on line. Geoff stood above the elf as she fought to simply stay conscious. The red moved in and the maneth issued a second defense with his large club. However, this time the blow came up short and the dragon reached its long, jagged talons out to grip the maneth's body around the waist. Geoff roared as the long razors bit through his back. The dragon lifted its prey in the air and began to shake him, turning the maneth so he was placed in the line of the archers. All watched in horror as their leader was brutally shaken toward a violent death.

Just as the early morning light exploded across the city, a bolt of energy shot from the ground, and the large red let out a high-pitched, terror-driven screech and released its prey. As Geoff's body sailed toward the ground, a second bolt of energy erupted from below, beheading the creature in flight. The maneth's body fell with increasing speed, and his near-fatal injuries prevented him from even adjusting for the impact. It was only moments before the impending crash when Schram issued another incantation, gradually slowing his fall until his body rested gently on the surface.

Schram hollered at the wall of bewildered eyes. "I will care for him. Prepare for the next attack." Those nearby turned their attention back to the dragons that were swinging for another approach. Schram hustled over to his friend. "Geoff, are you alive?"

"What kind of greeting is that, you blind magician? You will never know how glad I am to see you, but please, see to Denisi, she is severely injured."

"In a minute, old friend, for first I have to try to slow these dragons." He lifted his staff toward the oncoming force and began another incantation. The lead dragon screamed, its guttural agony echoing throughout the city. Its flight lost all control, and in only moments it crashed to the ground dead. The other dragons in this localized assault halted their flight momentarily and stared at the Prince of Toopek.

Geoff looked up from where he still lay and could not believe the ominous sight. Seven dragons hovered roughly two hundred yards from Schram and his staff. All activity between both sides in this area was completely idle. Fighting and terror could still be heard all around the city, the bay, and the forests, but where they stood, nobody moved. "What are they doing?" asked the maneth.

"Telling the other dragons still entering the force field that I am here"—he paused and then added—"and deciding if they can take me."

"Can they?"

Schram smiled. "Still doubting me?" He raised his staff and pointed it not toward the dragons but toward the sky over the harbor. A light as bright as the sun erupted from his staff, impacting the shield and spreading its light like a shell across the entire city. "Let's see if I can't keep any more from joining."

The dragons in the area all turned and began flying back over the bay toward their point of entry through the shield. Cheers rang out from those nearby, but all could still hear the fighting around the city. Swinging back, Schram began stepping over to help his fallen friend.

"They're coming back!" shouted a voice from behind.

Schram swung his eyes back toward the dragons that had fled. However, it was not just those dragons that caught his attention; it was the dragons still coming through the barrier around the city, seemingly still unhindered. Geoff too saw the new movement. "What's the matter?" he asked.

"They have anticipated my magic and created a barrier of their own in the form of a tunnel. It will take me too long to identify its magic and destroy it." His voice became solemn. "I will not be able to stop their entrance into the city."

The dragon attack had stopped, but the dragons were grouping over the bay in large numbers. Maldor ran up and joined the small group around Schram. "I can do nothing unless they engage, and if they all attack at once, I don't know." His eyes turned to his leader on the ground. Geoff? For all the gods, are you all right?"

"Between you and the damn magician asking if I am all right...Let me ask you, do I look all right?" He pointed to the flyer elf. "Please see to Denisi. She took the brunt of the attack and saved me in the process."

Maldor was stunned by his words but immediately went to the girl's side. "I am fine," she said in an angry voice.

The maneth could tell she did not want his help, but he could not leave her completely exposed on the ground. Her leg was clearly broken, and by the damage to her wing, he believed flight was not an option for her. As the elf screamed for him to get away, he slowly and carefully slid his large arms under her small frame and lifted her, taking care not to place any undue pressure on her injuries. Within moments, she was next to Geoff, protected behind some debris. Schram and about five elven archers remained with the group with an elf watching for any attack. As he arrived, Geoff and Schram were deep in a heated conversation, but when Geoff saw the flyer elf, his attention was drawn momentarily to her. She nodded that she was okay, which seemed to appease the large maneth leader.

"We don't have any choice. We fight them here and now, or we don't fight at all and we are done. Is that what you are saying, Schram?"

"Not exactly, my friend," replied Schram, kneeling down next to the maneth and using his staff to draw in the dirt beside him. "The dragons may be able to defeat my magic, but the goblins and trolls will not. If we put all our forces against the dragons collectively, here and here"—he pointed to areas around the bay—"I believe we can hold our position against the dragons. I will take care of all the ground forces." He looked to the maneth. "Can it be done?"

"Yes," said Geoff, now trying to get to his feet. "Maldor, help me to my feet."

The young maneth moved over and lifted his childhood hero to his shoulder. As strong as his voice would utter, Geoff yelled, "Meris, bring all the troops from the wall. Engage the dragons point blank at the bay."

Meris heard the order and looked toward the others questionably. They were holding the wall strong. To retreat now would mean to lose all they had supported and fought to keep. Just before he could question, however, Schram blasted another bolt toward the barrier at the forest. Instantly, the explosions alone sent the goblin and troll forces both inside and outside, scurrying for the cover of the trees. Those inside who previously had been unable to cross back out now ran freely to the woods. The goblin leader struggled to keep his troops moving forward. He raised his sword and charged forward, trying to draw the others in with him. Instead, they only fled fast as his body exploded at first contact with the new barrier.

Meris turned back to Schram and shook his head. Without a word to Geoff, Meris yelled, "All troops pull back. Pull back!"

Just as the troops began filling the lines toward the sea, the dragons attacked as one unified force.

⚬∞⚬

The fighting was the most intense Troyf had ever seen. Schram knelt down beside the large maneth leader. "Remain here, friend. I have repaired your bow, so do not hesitate to use it for cover if you need to. My magic has drained me, I need to rest a moment, or I leave myself and the staff vulnerable. Where is Maldor?"

Geoff took the bow, inspected it briefly, then turned to the magician. "He has joined that front to the west. He fights with incredible ferocity like nothing I have seen before. I do not understand the powers within the hammer he now carries, but if it is as you have said, I shall not underestimate it. Just from our brief contact, I felt a presence the likes of which I cannot identify. It is like how the canok you once traveled with used to talk about what he felt in you. 'Something not as it appears,' he used to say."

Schram stared at the old maneth, whose injuries were still pulling the life from him. "The hammer has many secrets and powers, all of which are just as you have said, not as they appear."

They both stared across the city toward the bay where nearly all the dragons and Toopekian forces were fully engaged in a fierce battle. "We are going to win, Schram."

"What am I missing?" He asked, mostly to himself. He paused then added louder, "Now we have a four-to-one advantage in number of people to dragons, which I suppose makes the sides about equal by my standards."

"What? You have given us a chance? Is that not better than it was?"

Ignoring the question, Schram replied with one of his own. "Geoff, since this all began, have you seen a black dragon or any of the dragon lords?"

"We killed one dragon lord near the forest boundary. The others have never entered to my knowledge. As far as Slayne, we have seen no sign of the black dragon in or around the city. What are you thinking?"

"It means I have been a bigger fool than I thought possible." Schram began running toward the harbor and the fighting.

"What do you mean?" Geoff hollered, trying to get to his feet.

Schram turned back. "I mean that Slayne has little interest in Toopek right now. I doubt this attack is even designed for a dragon victory. He is using this as a diversion to keep me from his true destination. He is going to destroy the one dragon who is powerful enough to bring the true knowledge of the past to the young dragons and use it to turn them against him, the only dragon that could truly defeat Slayne. He is going to attack Anbari."

Schram picked his way through the fighting, lending aid when he could and fleeing when he could not. He arrived at the harbor shore, panting and tired but not willing to succumb to these feelings. He lifted his staff to recreate the magical road across the water when he noticed something strange. As violent as the fighting was, it seemed completely contained now within the city. The water appeared as glass, with the distant fires from the Tower of Council island reflecting off it. Schram swung back to look upon the city, and his overseeing view brought the horror of the reality to his eyes. This battle had become a focal point for the final exchange of bloodshed. There could be no winner here, for that much he was certain.

Then he noticed something else unnatural, or at least without cause. Several times wounded dragons would try to flee the bombardment from the surface, but each time they were denied. In midflight they would strike something that would turn them back. Regardless of what direction they flew, they were boxed in, an experience that sent them into crazed flights of fear and confusion. This, in turn, released massive waves of destruction across the city. Whatever power was causing this trap had misjudged the response, and it was backfiring. Toopek was facing totally uncontrolled and unrepressed vengeance as the dragons fought for their lives to survive. Schram concentrated on the invisible barrier marked by where the dragons were turned. A burst from the staff split the air and arched toward the field. With a deep explosion, it struck the barrier and reflected back. Schram dove to the side as his pulse was absorbed into the sand, changing sections of it into melted glass.

The totally unexpected power in the shield left the magician consumed in thought, and who or what had created such a field was the focus of these thoughts. Then he remembered what Geoff had said. The dragon lords were here. Perhaps they saw the weaknesses in the young dragons and devised this as a plan to keep them fighting, even if it meant their death.

"No," said a deep voice from behind. "The ones you call the dragon lords did not create this barrier, I did."

Schram leaped to his feet and landed facing his adversary. "Khaled, you are here. Then you can help us."

"I will not."

"But why? You can see that what you have done is placing Toopek in greater jeopardy. You have to remove that shield or the dragons will totally destroy the city."

"The humans have never been an ally to the physeters, and it seems now is no different. Toopek's fate is of little concern to me. I must concentrate on only one thing—to return my kingdom to the seas. Anything that might inhibit that movement must be dealt with. That is all I have done."

Schram, the anger clearly showing on his face, knew he could not match powers against the whale. Khaled carried hidden abilities that were beyond his comprehension. He knelt before the creature, who swam with only his eyes breaking the plane of the surface. "If destroying the one city that could ensure your safe return is dealing with your problems, then your knowledge greatly exceeds that of my own."

"No, but your city's war over the sea has already caused the deaths of two physeters. I cannot risk more losses, for there are too few of us left. Your war must remain on land, and that is what my barrier will guarantee."

Schram's heart sank when he observed where Khaled's eyes now pointed. Lying beached in a mess of ship debris was what looked to be nearly a dozen dragons and two huge grey whales. He bowed his head. "Please, Khaled, don't sentence my city to death because of the actions of dragons. The humans and other allied forces here held no part in this tragedy."

"But that is where you are wrong, one known as Schram. It was a human ship that exploded over the harbor. An explosion not caused by any dragon attack, but a human trap bent on drawing the dragons close and then causing their instant death in the explosion. It was the humans who were unconcerned about all life. The death that explosion caused is not measurable. Everything containing life within a tremendous distance was destroyed. Not surprising that no humans fell within its range. That is why I will not turn from my intensions. Humans cannot be trusted."

Schram stared toward the island and knew Pete was responsible. Schram knew the pirate was probably very proud of his actions, not realizing that this act upon the dragons may have sealed Toopek's fate. Schram wanted to plea with the whale, but he was certain that even if Pete had known about the physeter's presence, his actions would not have changed, and Schram was certain that Khaled knew that as well.

His head fell as he turned back to the destruction over the city. Distant cries bounced off the building and he knew each one meant another was suffering. Suddenly, he turned back to the whale, whose expression had not changed. "Khaled, you too are incorrect, or at least in part. You said my war must remain on land. That is not completely true. My war must remain on land or must cease to be a war."

"I do not follow your statement's direction. You cannot end this war."

"You have the ability to separate the dragons from the water. Can you not, therefore, also separate the dragons from Toopek?"

"I could, but will not. For separating your war from the water, I have a reason. For the other, I do not. You must fight your battles, not be protected from them."

"I am not asking for any aid in fighting or to handicap the dragons, I am only asking you to prevent my city from facing what the physeters faced. I must go to face Slayne before Anbari. If I am successful, then the dragons attacking Toopek can learn the truth and will no longer wish for a war. If I am not successful, then things will continue as they were. All I am asking for is the time to save all the races from extinction, not just the physeters. You have to know this to be true. Our races have a symbiotic relationship with each other. If there is total destruction on land, it will in turn affect the water. It is a matter of five days' time. That is all."

"You have three days, no more. If I do not hear back from you then I will remove the separation, and each side will face what it faced before. However, also know that if you are unsuccessful, then your shield around Toopek refusing entry to the dragon forces will also fall, and I will not replace it."

"Understood, my friend, and you know that this will not be forgotten. The physeters will return to freely roam the seas, that much I give you my word."

Khaled closed his eyes briefly, and gradually all the noise from the city ceased. His eyes reopened for one final comment. "Neither side will be able to penetrate the barrier for three days. Now, your time has begun, so be gone."

"Thank you, Khaled. I will not let the physeter down."

Schram had already begun to hurry toward where Draketon rested, and in his mind he heard the words, *I did not do this for you, Schram of Toopek. I did it for another.*

TRUTh BE KNOWN

Stepha signaled the elves to follow and then set Krirtie down, landing beside her. As the band of around two hundred flyers began to gently fill the glade, the captain of the guard began speaking. "As I am sure you have all seen or been told by those who have, it would be pointless for us to attack, for our numbers are just too small to counter such a force. At least 1,500 to 2,000 troops are lying siege to the city, and that does not account for the dragons. It is just past dawn, and Madeiris and the ground forces should be here by midday. We will wait here in the glade until their arrival and then together mount an all-out offensive."

"While Toopek crumbles beneath the weight of the dragon armies?" broke in Krirtie. "I don't think so. I can't just sit by and watch as my home is destroyed."

Stepha turned and stared hard at the girl. "You will have to do just that." She paused and then flashed a look to a nearby flyer. "Kaylis, organize a small party and plan a route to intercept Madeiris. Inform him about the situation and tell him of our plans. Go now, waste no time and ask him to do the same."

The elf understood and, without a second word, motioned to six other elves, and then they were breaking up through the trees. Krirtie moved beside the elven princess. "I will give your brother until midday, and then I am going in."

"Don't be a fool, Krirtie. Besides being with child and very near birth, I might add, you are but one person. What could you hope to accomplish?"

"If it were Elvinott being destroyed, would you not wish to go?"

Stepha remained silent a moment, and slowly her face softened. "I understand your situation, but I still cannot allow you to leave on such a mission. To do so would end your life as well as your child's."

"She is right," added a gentle but strong voice from the side.

The elves in the area jumped at the surprisingly unobserved guest, and many had arrows knocked before they even had a chance to recognize the woman who had so strangely entered their village the day before. Stepha and Krirtie also had jumped at the sound, but it was the elf's bewildered voice which answered. "Hawthorne, but how did you…"

"How is not important," she replied. The woman turned to Krirtie and spoke as a mother would to a child. "You cannot approach Toopek alone, my dear, for it is far too dangerous for even an army to approach, much less only one. We shall wait as Stepha has suggested. It is the correct decision, and you know it to be so."

Krirtie frowned both at the tone and its meaning, but she could not argue the point. Stepha approached the woman. "Might I inquire into the whereabouts of Werner?"

Hawthorne nodded and began walking toward the front of the lines of elves, leaving Stepha behind. "Yes, but you might as well make yourself comfortable as well as tell those you lead to do the same. We will have to wait and grasp every rest we can. It would be foolish not to."

Now Stepha became annoyed by her tone, but again she knew the woman was correct. She gave the order but also placed two groups on watch. Then she moved over and took a seat next to Hawthorne. Krirtie sat near the two but remained far enough away so as not to be involved in their conversation if they did not wish it.

The elf turned to face the beautiful human woman. "May we continue our conversation where we left off?"

Hawthorne smiled and leaned back to rest her head against a tree. Stepha was amazed at the beauty of the woman. There was not a flaw in her appearance from head to toe. The elf wondered how a woman so involved in this war between races could remain so set apart and unharmed. Hawthorne noticed her gaze before answering her previous question. "I am not sure, Stepha. It would depend on what you wished to ask."

"I wish to know how long you would say you have known Schram? You said if I had asked Schram, he would reply fourteen days. I want to know your answer."

Hawthorne sat back up, placing herself face to face with the elf. "In all your time with Schram throughout your entire life, did he ever mention any other woman, be them friend or not?"

The elf shrugged. "Well, of course he talked about Krirtie and his mother, but other than that, no." She paused. "Wait. When I first met Krirtie, she spoke of another girl. Someone Schram did not really know that well or spend time with, but she did say she saw them talking at the forest occasionally. Isn't that right, Krirtie?"

She looked over, pretending not to have been paying attention. She thought, then said, "Yes, there was a girl. I did not know her, and she was not around much. I used to think she was Emporian. She…"

"What do other girls have to do with anything?" Interrupted Stepha, turning from Krirtie back to Hawthorne. "Did you know Schram's mother or this other girl? Is that how you know Schram?"

"No, Stepha, and it is far too complicated to go into now." She suddenly looked very distraught. Her voice broke slightly as she added, "I thought I would be able to tell you, Stepha, and then you could tell Schram, but I cannot. I came back to meet you because I knew I would not have time to tell Schram, and now I can't even find the strength to…" She broke in midsentence and leaped to her feet, disappearing into the woods.

Krirtie and Stepha looked confused, as did many of the nearby elves who took notice to the commotion. The girls rose and began after the woman with a group behind ready to follow. Stepha turned. "No, please remain here. We will be fine. Just stay at the ready." The elves nodded and then the two girls disappeared down the same trail behind Hawthorne.

"What do you think that was all about?" asked Krirtie.

"Again I cannot even offer a guess." The elf replied. "I do, however, aim to find out. I have known this woman now for only a day, and although everything I feel from her is good and worthy, trust her I do not. She is hiding something, and if that something involves in anyway hurting Schram, I will refuse to stand by and let that occur."

"That is something I could never do," said Hawthorne's soft voice from the side.

Both girls jumped, but Stepha showed more surprise both at the statement as well as the sudden lack of emotion across Hawthorne's face. She no longer appeared distraught and confused. Now she was strong and confident. Stepha stopped her run and approached the woman. "It is only a clever and well-traveled human who could create a false trail that an elf would fall prey to. You say that you could not harm Schram, but it is clearly apparent that you have some interest in him."

"Yes, I do have a significant interest in him, as he does in me." Her voice was soft and calm, totally alien to the stress-ridden tone from only moments earlier.

I want to understand that interest. I want to understand how you arrived here before my party of flyers. I want to understand you."

Hawthorne laid her hand on the elf's shoulder. "Relax, my dear girl, I shall tell you. I just could not speak about such in front of the others." Krirtie began to look uncomfortable. Hawthorne smiled toward her. "There is no need to worry. This is meant for your ears as well. Schram has always held the utmost love for both of you, and now it is up to you to tell him the truth."

Krirtie stepped closer. "Excuse me for saying so, but if this is such an important thing to say, should you not be speaking it to Schram yourself?"

Hawthorne bowed her head sadly. "That will not be possible." She paused, then looked back at the girls. "What you are about to hear, you both will immediately believe to be untrue, but please hear the words I say, for my time to speak them is short. I am..."

"In very bad company," finished a raspy voice from the side.

The three all swung around to greet the horrific site before them. Stepha's voice was low and clearly carried her hatred with it. "Lord Starland, I see you have not changed except for the worst. Tell me, what's with the new company? Have you run out of other dragon lords?"

Starland frowned but not as deeply as the scowl Satrial, the huge blue dragon standing next to the dragon lord, wore on his face. Beads of fire and ash dripped from his overlying fangs and landed sizzling on the ground. The elf knocked an arrow but did not release it. Instead she waited for Starland's response. The dragon lord paced a bit then turned. "I knew I was foolish to leave Meyer in charge. The fool has a weak heart for his son. I should simply have killed him so they could be together." His eyes moved from the two girls to Hawthorne. "So tell me, who are you that you consider your life so valueless as to travel with these two?"

"Do you not remember me, Keith?" Hawthorne replied. "We have been through so much together."

All were taken by the unexpected response, but none as much as the blue dragon. He paced uncomfortably about, staring directly toward the strange woman. Starland noticed the action but did not comment on it. Instead, he remained focused on Hawthorne. "I fear you must hold memories I do not."

She continued smiling. "I am Hawthorne, but that also would not waken your memories."

However, it did to the dragon, as it reared its head and released a wall of flames over the woman. Stepha released an arrow in response, drawing a line directly toward the creature's throat. There was an immense flash from the hand of Starland, and both Stepha and Krirtie found themselves on their backs, with the elf's arrow tossed helplessly aside.

"Perhaps this will jog your memory," said Hawthorne's voice from inside the engulfment of flames. Stepha swung her eyes to see the woman standing completely unharmed. However, it was not the Hawthorne they knew. In her place stood another human woman—taller, with more bushy hair. A woman whom Stepha, Krirtie, and Keith Starland knew very well.

"Queen Suzanne?" said Krirtie softly. "How can it be?"

The woman turned, and in a voice no longer of the beautiful woman they had just been speaking with but now the voice of the once Queen of Toopek, who had been missing since the very first attack on the city so long ago, she said, "Yes, but only for a time. I only was queen during the time it was needed"—she paused and curved a small smile toward Starland—"when Schram was needed."

Starland stepped forward. "Yes, now I understand and remember. You are not the queen, for my queen was human. You"—his voice was cold and without feeling—"you are a dragon."

Both Stepha and Krirtie dove to the side as both Satrial and Starland released their most powerful wrath on the body of the queen. The forest seemed to explode into flames. With first impact of their attack, Hawthorne formed into her natural dragon state and created a barrier to repel their anger. Fire shot back toward them, causing the blue dragon to screech briefly as the unexpected heat touched his scaly skin before it was extinguished. Stepha leaped to her feet, and after only glancing briefly toward the magnificent silver and green dragon by her side, she began to mount an attack of her own.

Arrow after arrow, she plunged toward the dragon, but something in their defense made them have little impact. She turned her attack on Starland and let an arrow fly. It struck the barrier dead on but slowly became warped. The arrow's flight was true but the passage was not. Just before striking Starland's throat, it curled at a stiff angle and passed unhindered to the side. Starland simply laughed and continued his attack on Hawthorne, who was beginning to show signs of tiring.

Stepha glanced at Krirtie who was groggily pushing herself to her feet. She wanted to provide her some help, but she knew she could not leave Hawthorne alone to face both of them, especially knowing that if what she said was true, this was Schram's mother. She knocked another arrow and drew at the region a slight bit away from Starland's path. Crossing her fingers, she let the shaft go.

Again, it caught the field surrounding the dragon lord and began to twist. It crossed the barrier and proceeded on its new, altered course just as the arrow before. This time, however, because of Stepha's placement, the altered course turned it toward the dragon lord instead of away from him. Starland turned as it bit through his leg just above the knee. He immediately turned his attack away from the dragon woman and, with one burst, sent a huge ball of energy at the elf. Stepha threw her bow up to shield herself as a reflex, and by some miracle, most of the charge was absorbed. However, she still found herself dazed and near unconscious on her back. Krirtie saw the elf go down and hurried over to provide cover. Seeing the movement, Starland released another charge toward the elf, but this one struck Krirtie, who was racing to protect the elf.

The girl was thrown back with incredible force, falling directly into Stepha's arms. Her rich red blood was flowing across her sides. Krirtie's face was ghostly white, and her eyes were locked open in a cold and lonely terror. Her body was rigid and inflexible, like a branch prepared to break rather than bend. The elf laid the girl to the ground, shifting herself so she could see the wound. Krirtie's armor along her back was completely melted away. Much of her skin was absent or torn. Tears of hatred streaked the elf's face while she violently fought to push the girl's organs back into her body.

Krirtie slowly reached her arm up and grabbed the elf so tight as to turn her green skin blue against the grip. Blood spilled between her lips and teeth as she whispered, "My baby." And then she went limp and her grip was lost.

Stepha lowered her head with tears falling across her cheeks.

The elf rolled to the side, totally oblivious to anything around her. Then she noticed the sword lying to the side. Pushing herself up, she placed on the human woman's back the shiny curved scimitar Krirtie had carried for this entire war. There was an immediate glow and brilliant hum emitting from the sword. Stepha pressed her lips together into a tight smile as her entire face was covered in tears. She could feel the power engulfing the girl like nothing she had felt before. Suddenly, however, the hum ceased and the glow gently faded.

Stepha crawled forward and stroked Krirtie's blood-soaked hair. Her head fell to the ground, and she knew the woman was dead. The elf was beyond rational thought. She was left with nothing but despair. She sobbed, letting all emotions flow. The only sound able to penetrate her new wall of desolation was the faint echo of another's cries. She lifted her head slowly and turned back to the body of her friend.

The scimitar again was glowing faintly, and nestled on its helve was a sight the elf could not believe—an extremely small baby maneth.

"Well, isn't that something? A human bearing a maneth child."

Stepha swung her head up to greet the hard stare of Lord Starland. Behind him sat the motionless bodies of two dragons, one blue and one green. Stepha's eyes showed terror beyond that which she thought possible to feel at one time. She could not speak but only looked on in disbelief. The dragon lord followed her gaze. "Yes, because of you I have lost my mount. When I was distracted from the battle, the one called Hawthorne used the opportunity to attack Satrial. By the time I recovered, my dragon was dead, but Hawthorne was unprotected. I made it slow and painful, as it should be for the mother of my child, and soon will be for you."

Stepha could barely remain conscious. The forest was spinning faster with each word Starland spoke. She lifted her head and shouted out the only thing she was certain was correct. "If it is the last thing I do, I will kill you, Keith Starland. I swear it."

The dragon lord laughed and reached his scaly arm out toward the baby maneth. "Oh, Stepha, you don't even have the strength or power to make me sweat. You and your pathetic group have done nothing that I did not control, and now I even have a trophy." He lifted the baby maneth above his head. "I shall raise him as my own. Slayne will give him power, and eventually he shall take my place as first below the emperor."

Stepha lifted her foot up and slammed it against her arrow, which still protruded from Starland's leg. The dragon lord winced in pain, letting the baby fall toward the ground into the elf's arms. "You do fear me, and my friends."

"You are a fool," replied Starland, removing the arrow from his leg. With death comes obedience. What better way to gain obedience from elves and humans than to kill two of their leaders."

"Like you did Lord Meyer's son?"

"Yes, exactly like killing Lord Meyer's son."

"You took my son's life to gain obedience?" echoed a hard voice from behind.

Starland spun around, surprised. "Meyer, you were instructed to remain at Draag. Your disobedience has not only allowed our captives to escape but brought them here where they have hampered our quick and easy victory. One has even brutally killed my mount, a murder that shall be avenged." His eyes locked on the dragon lord with an expression demanding obedience. "Now, Meyer, have you any explanation for your actions that might make me see my way to only submit my wrath upon the elf and spare your weak-minded body?"

Lord Meyer stepped back momentarily as the unforgiving harshness in his counterpart's voice set fear to his mind. Yet, as he looked across the glade and saw the death laid before him, all his thoughts went back to his son. "I have no such words for you, nor would you rightly deserve any. Slayne murdered my son and then lied to keep me in line. Now you are murdering those who seek to bring about the truth. It was easy for the globes to turn me to the dragon ways, for I always craved to have more power. I was seduced by the opportunity to rule, but a strange power has freed me from my illusions. What I don't understand is why you were so easily turned. You had power. You were the king of the largest human city in all of Troyf. How could you be so weak?"

Starland's eyes became lost for a moment, almost as if a realization seemed on the verge of surfacing. Then, as quickly as it had appeared, it vanished. "Touching speech, Meyer, and it shall be your last." He chanced a quick glance toward Stepha, and with a wink, threw a magical force across her chest. She fell back motionless. "Don't go away, my dear." He turned back to Meyer, then froze. The dragon lord was gone.

There was an explosion with the first impact. Meyer crashed down on Starland like a dragon landing on food. The power released in the attack was immense, and both dragon lords suffered greatly. They tumbled to the ground and then bounced up separated. The strain showed clearly on Meyer's face whereas Lord Starland, although weakened from the blow, remained poised and confident. He issued attack after attack, which drove Meyer back and kept him on the defensive. The few attacks that he could muster were seemingly tossed aside by Starland's laughter. Meyer found himself pinned against a tree, fighting to only delay the inevitable by deflecting his king's violent attempts to take his life.

Starland continued moving forward, stopping only when another step would mean to crush his broken and kneeling prey beneath him. His voice was callous and abrasive. "You are a fool. I could have given you everything—a kingdom, possibly even a world—and you repay me with this. A king has no family, no friends, for to do so would cloud their judgments. You acted poorly, and it cost you your life."

Meyer pushed himself to his feet. "No, it brought me my death, a welcome exchange for my actions. I did have a family, and now I am going to join them." He threw his arms about Starland's shoulder, causing a brilliant explosion of light and fire that nearly sent the remaining trees into a fit of flame. Moments later, however, Starland fell to a knee while Lord Meyer's body went limp.

The dragon lord was breathing heavily as he drew on all his remaining strength to lift him to his feet. He stared down at the lifeless body before him, the dragon-like tail and other appendages already fading. He whispered, "Damn fool, I should have killed him at Draag." His voice began to grow louder and he added, "As I should have done with you as…"

A roll of blood spewed between his lips at the impact of Stepha's arrow to his throat. The dragon lord fell to his knees with his eyes widened in fear. Stepha stepped close and lodged a second arrow into his shoulder, and then another to his chest. Blood was soaking the ground, and still the elf grew closer, showing no emotion save the stoic stare watching the pain before her.

Lord Starland tilted his head up at her when she drew within an arm's length, but his deteriorating body could issue no response or sound. Stepha just watched while he fought to keep hold of any life within his grasp. He lifted one of his hands in the air toward the elf as if asking for her aid. With the tip of an arrow, she pushed the hand away. "Dragon Lord Keith Starland, once father to that with whom I am joined, I do what I swore to do the first day I saw you in Elvinott Forest. Where you go after this day is for those who judge you to decide, but please forgive me that for the first time in my life, I wish for another creature's death." She lifted Krirtie's scimitar, which she had recovered as she approached. "This I do for all those who have died because of your actions, especially my friends. May you find no peace for eternity."

Starland's eyes remained wide and almost pleading. Their confidence was lost, being replaced by an intense terror, not for the impending end of his life, but where the guardians would choose to take him. Moments later, his head rested on the ground completely separated from his body. Stepha remained standing, not shedding a tear nor jumping for joy, but just standing. Her expression was bare and her skin somewhat pale, but the feeling within her was peace.

Schram lifted his hand and placed it on her shoulder. "Stepha, are you all right?"

The girl nearly turned an attack on him in surprise, but his touch soothed her. She fell into his arms. "Oh, Schram, I am so sorry but…"

"I know, Stepha. Please just hold your words, for I see the pain." He paused and just held her in silence for a moment then added, "You were strong in your actions today, and you must remain strong now. You have nothing to be sorry for. Moreover, you should feel proud. You have brought us one more step closer to victory."

"But I could not save our friends."

Schram lifted his eyes to the surrounding area and fell to his knees. He saw Hawthorne lying motionless, and then his eyes fell to Krirtie's lifeless body with a small baby nestled in her arms. The elf gripped him tightly and softly asked, "Schram, how did you get here? Why are you here?"

Schram lifted his head. His voice cracked while he fought back tears. "I was on my way to meet Slayne when we"—he motioned to Draketon, the sight of which caught Stepha by surprise—"felt the battle taking place. I am very sorry I did not arrive in time." He pushed the elf back, made sure she was secure, and gingerly walked over to where the giant green dragon lay.

Stepha stood, walked over, and knelt beside him. "There was a battle. She engaged the blue dragon that traveled with the dragon lord. It was a massive release and exchange of power that left them both dead."

Schram looked up as he touched the dragon's body. "She has life, but it is weak." He placed his staff against the dragon's body and recited a few words.

"Can you help her?"

"I do not know, but perhaps there is one who can. We must get Mi-Kevan. He is the only one who can possibly help."

Schram's mind was becoming clouded, and although Stepha saw his discomfort and confusion, she also knew he must know everything. "Schram, there is more." She motioned toward the far edge of the glade. "Your father struck a violent attack against me, and she moved to protect me. She saved my life, but it cost her much."

His eyes followed her gaze over to where Krirtie lay with a small baby nestled against her. He fell to his knees in despair. "Why does so much have to be taken to win this war? Is it all really worth it?"

Stepha lifted his head to meet hers. Softly she said, "Yes, you know it is." She placed Krirtie's sword across his lap. "She knew it was, and your mother knew it was also."

Schram's eyes narrowed. "My mother?" he spun back to Hawthorne." A tear formed in his large elven-human eyes with a look as if he was grasping for understanding but it was just out of his reach. He turned back to his fallen friend and then back to where Hawthorne's body lay. "I knew. She did not ever tell me, but I knew. I felt it but it was shielded from me."

"Most likely to protect you, my love."

"But how? Why did she not..." his voice trailed off.

The elf princess could feel his pain within him, struggling to stay hidden. "Schram?"

He rose. "Anbari, I have to help Anbari. He is the only one who holds the answers and the one whom Slayne seeks to destroy."

A group of elves appeared with bows drawn from the tree line. Stepha motioned with the palm of her hand. "Halt, for we are safe."

Madeiris pushed through the group. "Stepha! Schram! I am..." his voice quieted when he absorbed the bloodshed before him.

Schram approached the elf king, walking with a strength drawn deep from within his soul. "I do not have time to explain. I need some favors that may seem strange for me to ask, but you must hear them for what they are and do everything in your power to see them fulfilled."

"I understand, my friend."

Schram continued. "Send a party of flyers to seek out the sorcerer Mi-Kevan. He has great healing powers, which twice have saved my friend who was strong with magic. Bring him before the green dragon and ask him to do anything, regardless of the cost, to save her."

It was clear in the elf's expression that he did not fully understand the reasons, but seeing a large red dragon patiently waiting for Schram to finish helped him to do so.

The elf reached for his shoulder. "I will, Schram. We will find Mi-Kevan and bring him to the green dragon." They locked eyes at a level of understanding only two kings—warriors, friends, and brothers—could ever obtain together. "Now, what else would you ask?"

"March your troops to the forest line around Toopek. From this moment on, you will wait three days. If the situation does not change for the better, then put everything into Toopek with the full weight of your troops. However, if the dragon forces retreat, then let them go. Only fight if they attack you."

Madeiris nodded. "Understood." Again he paused and studied the warrior a moment. "Where will your trail take you?"

"I am going to meet Slayne. What happens there will decide our future."

"No," shouted Stepha. "You said you were going to Anbari's. You cannot face Slayne, at least not alone. I will fly with you."

Schram turned and stepped toward the girl he held deep within his heart. "I am going to Anbari's Dominion because that is where Slayne has gone, and I must meet him alone, as it was decided by an agreement made between a dragon and a canok so long ago. You are needed here to stand by your brother's side and lead the elves. I love you, Stephanatilantilis, and I shall always be with you, no matter what happens. We are one, joined as none before, and nothing shall ever break that bond. Trust it, as it may save both of us." He turned to all within the area. "May Shriak fly with you and guard your every step."

Stepha fell into his arms, and they held each other for many moments before breaking. Madeiris reached his arm out again and the two locked wrists. In a strong voice, the elf king said, "May all the gods be with you, my brother. Do not let your thoughts fall to Toopek, for we will hold the city. Focus on your destiny, for any break in thought may be your undoing."

"Thank you, my brother." He stared at Stepha and exchanged thoughts that no words could describe. He walked over to where Krirtie's body rested and knelt down closing his eyes he caressed her blood-soaked hair. He lowered his head and lightly kissed her forehead as a tear dropped from his eye. Saying short prayer, he stood, turned to the large dragon in his wake, and said, "Draketon, are you ready?"

The red dragon stretched its wings, bringing the entire glade into shadow. Stepha moved to grab Schram's side, but her brother held her shoulders and whispered, "Let him go, Stepha. His journey has been decided for him. There is no one on all of Troyf stronger to face this challenge. He has been chosen. Give him your strength now, for it may serve to save him later."

"But it makes no sense. Two are stronger than one. We have shown that since we first started together. He can use my help."

They watched as the dragon broke through the trees, kicking up a wind the likes of which nearly knocked several of the elves to the ground and brought down several limbs as they beat through. "No, this time I believe there is little you could do. Schram has come a long way to reach this place, and only he can decide how it is to continue." The elf turned his sister's shoulders to face him. "And he has made that decision. Now let's do our part to help him here."

She nodded as a tear fell down her cheek. "I will honor his wishes, and yours. Thank you. Madeiris. Our father would be very proud of Elvinott's king."

Madeiris had a flash of pride show through his tough exterior when he heard those words referencing his father. Quickly he pushed them back to hold his stoic leader's pose. "We have much to do. Much life has been lost, and we must aid those who will be accepted. We also must find Mi-Kevan, for I fear time runs short for the green dragon. I do not know the reason, but Schram does not want the green to pass."

Stepha smiled but also held the feelings of urgency. "Yes, we must put everything into finding him and bringing him to the green dragon.

Madeiris stared at the girl and, without speaking, asked the question.

"Because, my brother, that dragon is one you have already met. That dragon is Hawthorne, and Hawthorne is Schram's mother."

Anbari's Dominion
Full Circle

⟨⟨⟩⟩

The land appeared peaceful as the two sailed toward the legendary Black Pool of the South Sea. Below them were no signs of evil, only the mountains, river, and trees that Schram has spent his entire life traveling. However, even as it seemed that all with Troyf was well, Schram knew otherwise. The only reason movements of dark dwarves and goblins were not rummaging across the land was because they had centered their attack on one focal point, Schram's home. Yet, as each moment passed and he and Draketon drew nearer to the Black Pool, he became more certain that the battle of Toopek was but one which was about to take place, and possibly not the most important one.

Draketon's huge red wings beat through the air. Schram heard nothing but his own thoughts, drawing more and more to the home of his greatest master. The powers carried in the staff were reverberating with energy. It was as if the staff was alienating itself from Schram, a feeling which brought fear to the magician. He did not fully understand the staff's power, but moreover, he did not understand his own powers. The only thing he was certain of was that he could not defeat Slayne without the powers of the staff at his command, and for some unknown reason, he was slowly losing that connection.

He gripped the ordinary-looking piece of wood in both his hands, trying to tap the knowledge held deep within its bark. Slowly, it began to respond and calmed the magician's mind. Opening his eyes, he asked, "Is Hawthorne truly my mother?"

Draketon rolled his eyes back. "Do you believe that she is?"

"I do not know. It would explain much but confuse that which was already known."

The dragon shook his head. "What would confuse you?"

He looked discouraged then after a brief thought, said, "I do not understand how she could be my mother, though I feel that she is. She had parents—my grandparents, whom I knew and loved up until they passed, a very human passage. The mother whom I knew, and who was daughter to them, was no dragon."

"Aye, but was your father?"

"No, my heritage with my father is certain, although I learned more about it in the moments before his death than I knew my entire life. I always believed him to be a generous individual who cared more about his kingdom that his actual rule. However, I now know him to be that which he really was—a greedy, power-hungry dictator who would kill anyone in his way, innocent or not, to gain power. I believe that while he reigned over Toopek, he truly wanted the best for the people there, but that strategy was cast aside as soon as the opportunity for more power, possibly without worldly limitations, was put before him. No, my father appeared exactly how he was, a human given powers he did not carry the intelligence to wield. With that, he was no dragon."

Draketon nodded. "Then you are back to your mother. If Hawthorne is not your mother, as you wish to believe, then two questions must be answered. First, why does she claim to be that which she is not? And second, where is the mother you knew?"

"That, my friend, is what I aim to find out, and I suspect that you know more than you are implying."

Draketon sent a burst of flame ahead of their path. "The storm above the Black Pool is upon us. Brace yourself, for the ride will be treacherous." His long mouth turned in an almost smile. "And as for your heritage, I have no answers, only questions."

They descended into the storm without altering their path. Draketon angled his descent along the wind current, and quickly his wings found their true course. It instantly was apparent to Schram that this dragon had made this trip many times in the past. Schram remembered that he could use the staff to help clear their way, but Draketon was moving with pinpoint accuracy already, and with that, he simply held the staff tightly against the dragon's body. He still had strange sensations taking place between him and the staff. He could not determine its origin but he was certain it was there. He focused his mind on the staff, trying to determine whether this was occurring naturally or because of the evil of late, or even if Slayne himself had begun to tap the power from him. His focused mind could not determine a thing. His only known fact was his powers were fading.

They now were drawing near the final destination, and Schram had no idea what to expect on the other side of the storm. They had traveled through the night and partially into the next day, so the darkness they now passed through seemed out of place to the magician and caused an eerie sensation to grow. Draketon held much confidence in Schram's powers, but even he did not know what Slayne might have planned or if it might have happened before they reached the dominion. The dragon kept its eyes forward and prepared an immediate response should an attack occur. He arched his neck in an ominous look of strength, telling Schram they were about to break free of the storm's boundaries.

As the sky had just exploded with light, the winds and rain vanished, to be replaced with the calm and peace of the clearest of days. They both immediately scanned the entire perimeter, but to their surprise, there was nothing there out of place. The water was smooth, with only tiny ripples where a slight puff of air might tickle it a bit. The air was fresh and clean while the sun's rays struck down like a welcomed shower.

Schram indulged the situation a moment before he realized where Draketon was heading. "To the oak tree?"

The dragon's tone was hard but carried a special softness of hope. "Yes, it is the only way in or out."

"Will you be accompanying me, my friend?"

"I will not, though I will be here should you require my aid when you depart, although I think it unlikely."

Schram magically lowered himself to walk along the surface of the water. "You think it unlikely that I will require aid or that I will return?"

"That is for you to determine."

Again Schram was confused by the dragon's lack of answers. He believed Draketon always knew more than he said, but probing into that knowledge only led to more confusion. Schram patted the dragon's neck. "I will be pleased to see you upon my return."

The dragon lowered its head as it sat motionless in the air above the water. "Trust in yourself for what you are about to undertake. The knowledge within you is great and save you it can."

Schram swung back to the dragon who stared at him without emotion. "I know those words, Draketon. Those were the last words my mother said to me so long ago when I left with my closest friend, the canok. How do you know them?"

"The stage is set, and it is now your time to act. If Slayne indeed does wait for you, as you suspect, then you must be prepared for the hardest battle of your life. I know you have faced Slayne in the past, but never such as this. His power is immense and it has only grown, and with that growth, his plans have become defined. If you fail, the world you know as Troyf will cease to exist. Possibly all life in this land, save for the dragons and a handful of those loyal to the dragon, will cease to exist. Slayne's vision is to create a world that will bow down to no other world. He has created a situation where universal domination is within his grasp and only one thing stands between him and possession of it. You, Schram—you are that which is between him and his dreams. He will do whatever it takes to make it a reality. This is not a war for Toopek or even Troyf. This is a war for all worlds, and you are the key to preventing it. Therefore, if you fail, I do not believe you will be pleased to see me."

"Your words are not mixed, are they Draketon?"

He did not answer nor break from his lock on the magician's eyes. Schram lowered his head and began to step toward the tree. Turning back, he said strongly, "I will do my best."

"I know, Schram."

He smiled briefly and then entered the shadow of the Great Oak. He could sense the power still emanating from the tree and could still see a faint aura around the branches, but both sensations were not exactly how they had been during his previous visit. At that time, regardless of how little power he really had, since he was still focusing his thoughts through the Ring of Ku rather than the Staff of Anbari, he still had sensed an immense magical presence. Now, however, although that presence was still there, it had become tainted. He began to worry about the fear growing within him. This, however, lost importance as he realized that he actually did not know how to enter the dominion. Before, he and his companions had had their raft destroyed and had fled to the tree for safety. Once there, they had all blacked out, only to awake later within the confines of Anbari's lair.

He thought a bit more and realized that his only choice was to proceed. However, he did not want to black out this time, so he incanted a short spell to protect him from whatever tries to bring him down. Yet, as he spoke the words, his mind became cloudy, and the environment around him began to dissolve. He glanced back toward Draketon and saw the dragon aimlessly shaking its head sadly. It was then he realized the way in. Any use of magic triggered a trap to pull whoever was speaking it into the lair. Schram tried to stop his spell, but his mind was at the mercy of the powers he had intercepted. He began to sway, dropping his head against his chest. He fought to remain conscious, but he knew it was to no use. His foolishness had sprung one of the most simplest traps, and now his presence would be known to all already within the dominion. If one of those was Slayne, Schram's last conscious thought was one which he knew would be the last of his life.

Schram slowly lifted his head off the dusty rock floor. There was little light in the room, but his eyes quickly adjusted. "Almok!" Schram reached for his staff but found nothing there.

"Remain calm, Schram, for your staff will be back in your possession in moments." The canok, who was brother to Schram's old companion, Kirven, and was the only other canok to have the strange diamond patch on his forebrow, paced back and forth before the weary magician. "I could not allow you to have the staff when you awoke, only to use it on me before you hear that which I have to say. If you refrain from using any magic, you will remain safe. If you do not, then he will know you are here and that I have betrayed him, a thought I know he considered to be a strong possibility."

Schram made no motion other than to sit more comfortably forward to better face the canok who had changed dramatically since their last meeting. Their eyes did not turn from each other as Schram spoke. "Almok, I can see that much has happened since we last met, but if you are asking me to trust you, I cannot. However, should you return my staff to me now, I will hear you out."

"That is all I ask." The canok's large build was equal to that of Kirven's, and when he turned and left the room momentarily, Schram saw his old friend again in his movements. Almok returned, carrying Schram's staff in his mouth. He knelt down and laid it at the human's feet.

Schram lifted the staff and brought it to rest across his chest. "Now, Almok, speak your mind."

The canok took a seat a short distance in front of Schram, and after a short pause, while he searched for the proper words, he began, his voice carrying a stronger and less raspy tone than Schram remembered. "Let me begin by saying I was not certain of my actions even once you had appeared here before me. If I was to have followed my commands, then you would already be dead. However, as you said, much has changed for me"—he paused and leaned forward—"and most of it I do not understand."

"This means nothing to me, Almok, and you know why that is, so discussing it further is not warranted."

The canok appeared slightly annoyed by the interruption but continued without showing it further. "There are certain things that I do know, and these are the things which allow you to live right now." He seemed to struggle with what to say next when Schram did not offer any response. The human relaxed slightly and placed his staff on the ground to his side. He knew he still had no reason to trust the canok who, since they first met, had always been his enemy. But he was also certain that Almok was not lying about one thing; if he had wanted him dead, he would be already.

Almok saw him lay the staff to the side and raised his eyebrows to the action. His breathing became smoother and his eyes even turned slightly softer. He lifted his head again and continued. "When I first met you in that bar in Lawren, I wished to kill you on the spot. I sensed something in you, but I could not place it because of some barrier preventing me. I would have gone ahead and killed you right then, but I was told not to."

"By the hooded figure? One of the dragon lords?" Schram asked.

"Yes. So you do remember our meeting in Lawren as well. The hooded figure was Lord Wayward, and he did not wish anything out the ordinary to occur and possibly jeopardize what we were doing. Though I felt we would face more danger with you alive, I agreed at the time. If I had not and I had killed you, victory would have been within Slayne's reach that first year."

Schram shook his head. "I believe you are right, but what bearing does that have on anything today?"

Almok moved forward again to where he placed himself directly eye to eye with his old adversary. "If I had killed you then, I also would not have ever felt the presence of my mother."

Schram was completely taken by the comment. As if he himself did not have enough problems with his heritage, now one of his most powerful enemies was referring to family, which the canok actually never even knew. Schram shook his head. "I do not understand your meaning."

He backed away and paced. "A short while ago, I felt a strange sensation. It was as if a world I had never known was suddenly revealed to me. I became confused and went to Slayne for guidance. He answered my questions with a spell of obedience. However, the power that called was too great. When my coat began to turn red, Slayne first began to doubt my loyalty. His powers were great, and he used them to hold me in line, but again, my homeland called. I knew if I fled he would destroy me. As long as my diamond patch remained unchanged, I felt that he believed he still had a hand over me. However, when it began to change as well, I knew he would no longer hold any trust in my loyalty. I was becoming more canok than dragon, a thought which I was finding very pleasing. I used my magic to hold my diamond patch the same, but even then it fought against it. As I sit before you now, a coat of red—like those whom I hope to someday call friends—I proclaim that I am a canok, in body and mind."

Schram stared at the canok's soft, red coat and watched as his diamond patch became streaked and then meshed with the rest, becoming lost in Almok's forebrow. He climbed to his feet and stepped toward the canok, stretching out his hand. "Almok, I feel the message you speak is true and with honor. Should your actions continue as such, I am confident your brother would have been the first to welcome you to his homeland, for this is what he foresaw to be possible."

The canok raised his head. "You are one to take huge risks when trusting one whom you always knew to be an enemy. Before this day, I have never wished for anything but your death."

"I know, but now I feel you do not."

"No, but I do not wish for Slayne's either, nor can I hold a direct hand in its fulfillment. I wish you luck in whatever your future holds, Schram, and I thank you for everything you have given the canoks, but especially, I thank you for what you have given me. I am not ready to embrace as friends those I have fought against for so long, but I am no longer content fighting against them either. Perhaps, in time, we will be friends."

Almok turned as if to leave. "Wait, I have only two questions, if you would indulge me?"

The canok stopped. "You have at least earned my ears for two questions."

"Why can I not use magic?"

"You should already know that answer. Slayne cannot detect you unless you draw on the power in the staff. The longer you can go without using it, the closer you may get to him without him learning that I have not followed his rule."

"How were you kept from reading my thoughts when we were in Lawren? I have never understood, and even your brother—my friend—could not tell me?"

The canok lifted his front leg to him. "I also did not understand at the time but have come to learn there were several forces at work. You spoke to the bartender. When I tried to bring that conversation to me, it was not possible. Also, the dragon lord with me was Lord Wayward, father to the girl who sat at your table. Although he was loyal to Slayne's cause, for me to kill his daughter at that time was something he would not allow. He already knew his other daughter was dead, so there was motive to keep me from you from multiple sources. But I felt a strange level of protection from the bartender, a level I have not seen again—until you, that is."

"The bartender? Why her?"

"You were speaking to her, I wished I knew what about."

Schram shook his head, completely lost with the conversation. "Damn, I wished I understood." When there was no reply, he looked up to find that the canok was gone. Quietly he whispered, "Good luck, Almok I pray that you were not lying to me. If so, I am walking into the largest trap of my life."

Schram began to exit the room but then stopped when his eyes caught sight of the wall. He spun his head around the room, taking in the total environment. The room was large and circular with the walls appearing smooth and to be of well-polished marble. The floor was cut from the same stone as the walls, and the ceiling arched in a dome above his head. Yes, he was sure this was the same room he had entered previously with his friends, and now he had but one question. Where was the painting of the long-haired human and the silver dragon he had seen the first time? He gripped his staff tightly and then stepped into the hallway.

The hallways were exactly as he remembered, long and seemingly endless. They wound in every way and left him totally confused as to what actual direction he was heading. He thought a long while about his previous visit to these marble caverns and knew he could not afford the time to travel the massive distance he and his companions had last time, but he did not know exactly where he was going. His first time they wandered aimlessly through miles of mazes before finally deciding to rest for the night. It was during that time Schram had the dream which taught him about the diamond stone and the hidden mirror room, which, in his dream, he used to transfer them to the other passage. He through a moment more and realized that there was no way this entire cavern was carved in marble. It had to be one large illusion that, if one did not have the key to break through, a person could wander their entire lives.

When he came to the next room, he searched it, taking notice to the same smooth marble surfaces and the only other apparent exit on the far wall. Without hesitation, he approached the nearest wall, which was directly adjacent to the doorway he had entered, and touched it. Nothing happened. Schram took a deep breath and turned to leave through what his mind was telling him was the same doorway he had just entered. It was only moments before he knew his mind was wrong.

The walls were no longer smooth but consisted of rough, jagged rock similar to an old dwarven mine. The artificial light, which illuminated the other hallways, was now absent, but Schram's elven vision allowed him to see with near-perfect sight. However, neither of these things, or the fact that the doorway he had just passed through had suddenly vanished, gave Schram the discomfort he was now feeling. It was the bantis staring down at him from the end of the hall which collapsed upon the magician's mind.

It appeared to be the twin of the creature Schram had fought to return the canoks' homeland to them. It was large, reaching nearly to the stalactite-covered ceiling without even stretching its heavily armored neck. Its scales were brown and its two talons gripped the stones beneath it like fingers strangling life from its prey. But since his battle with the magic-grabbing creature before, Schram knew that more than anything he was seeing, even their razor-sharp and pinpoint-accurate tail, their most powerful strength was for magic to be used against them. A bantis will absorb any magic and convert it to power to be used by it instead of against it.

The magician stared at the creature and followed its body all the way along its exterior. This one's tail was huge and already arched in sword-like fashion, poised for an attack. Schram circled his staff slowly, causing a force field to encase his body. The bantis seemed undeterred by this action and locked its eyes on the magician planning its first charge. Like a bolt of lightning, it struck. Schram was taken by the speed, a trait he had not seen at this level in his previous encounter. The style of attack also appeared somewhat different, possibly more experienced, like a master rather than a student. Instead of testing Schram's power and evaluating its adversary at all, the bantis went straight into a vicious physical attack. Schram lifted his staff as a reflex to create a secondary barrier between him and the angle of the creature's attack. The bantis reached its talons out and cut deep crevices into the rock wall to get leverage. In doing so, it shifted its direction completely opposite of Schram's expectations and, his secondary barrier would prove useless. The creature's tail swung with unbelievable speed and accuracy, giving Schram too little time to do anything in defense. The tail struck the initial field he had created, and with a blinding light the bantis vanished.

A bead of sweat slid down his brow, and his long black hair seemed to settle from its flair. His eyes scanned the small cavern quickly but to no avail. The bantis was gone. He lowered his staff slowly and drew a long-drawn-out breath building a small frown across his lips. He remembered the words Almok had spoken to him and shook his head in disbelief. He had been tricked by one of the most obvious traps. In his haste, he had called on the powers within the staff and thus was now certain of two things: Slayne had taken command over the dominion, and the black dragon was aware of his approach—two ideas that left the magician distressed and fearful for what could lie ahead.

The fear generated from the brief encounter seemed to grow with each step he took. Schram now felt the cold sweat trickling down his back, bringing a chill through his body. His legs felt wet and he seemed to be walking in sand rather than on a hard surface, almost fighting to take steps. He had left the previous room via the only apparent exit but had not come to any additional rooms for some time. Instead, he had been led down a dark and damp corridor that, besides the absence of light, had no noticeable sensory offerings. He felt as if he was traveling in some unknown void where even life did not exist, or was not supposed to exist. This feeling for an elf beat him to his core. Even time seemed to be unmeasured.

At a point unknown to him, Schram reached the first room since his meeting with the bantis. He entered it quickly, hoping to either surprise anything that might be waiting in the dark behind its door, or at least act to camouflage the fear and anxiety he was carrying. As he burst through, he was greeted with nothing but an empty room. It was not large or unique in any way. Moreover, it was simply a room, carved from the same rock that appeared in all the halls. Schram's deep breaths echoed back toward him, causing him to realize exactly how his current demeanor must appear. He tried to calm his mind and, in the process, slow his rapid heart. The little effect this had was lost as he exited the room via the only passage available.

He followed the winding corridor for quite a distance, several times coming to new rooms but every time finding them empty. He was not sure which was the loudest, the pound of his footfalls on the rock floor, the constant beat of his rapid, anxiety-filled heart, or the thump as each drip of sweat splashed from his forebrow to the surface beneath. The fear sent chills through his bones. It was not so much the fear of Slayne; rather, it was more the fear of not knowing what, where, or when that anticipation would be brought to fruition. His entire life he had always had someone by his side—Kirven, Krirtie, Stepha, Maldor, and, in some unknown ways, Hawthorne. There was always someone he could lean on for support. Now, however, he was alone.

He arrived at a large wooden door that he remembered from the past. Before, it had swung open on its own and then vanished as the travelers moved through it, leaving solid rock in its place. Schram waited momentarily, and when nothing happened, he leaned his shoulder against the huge wooden planks. The hinges that held it were as large as a maneth's head and more stubborn than a dwarf. Despite all efforts, it would not budge. He looked around the room and then let out a deep, long sigh. He began to raise his staff toward the door when suddenly it cracked like a hot fire and then began to slide slowly and silently ajar.

Again beads of sweat found their way down the magician's cheek and back. He was certain that this whole set of occurrences was simply tests and obstacles arranged by Slayne, but that did not alter the effect it was having and that knowledge did little to calm him. He felt as if he was a token in someone's game and that he was losing badly. He was afraid that if something did not change, he would be in no condition to defend himself when he finally did reach his destination, most likely following the black dragon's plan.

He sighed again as the door crashed closed behind him and then double-latched itself before vanishing into the red rock wall. He peered around the room, which he remembered being in before like it was only yesterday. Remembering his statement then, he repeated it to himself. "I guess I will go this way."

The comment actually lifted his stress slightly as he smiled. Often Schram found that he was more funny than anyone he thought he was, which usually did bring positive feelings to his mind and body. He proceeded through the only doorway and continued traveling down the long hallways littered with rock and debris. This was different from the past, but its importance was probably minimal. Finally, its winding pattern ended, and he could see nearly fifty meters ahead of his path. The corridor he was in gradually grew larger and then emptied into a much more open room, which appeared to be well lit by firelight. The flickering flames caused the various shadows he could see to dance as if they were filled with life. Yet, with each step he took, all he could feel was death and misery. He was familiar with the room he was about to enter because it had served as the site where Schram had been forced to meet in battle with his closest companion in his lifetime, Kirven. Now, however, he was to meet the one creature who was responsible for all the hell that had ravished Troyf for the past 200-plus years. The black dragon's plan had taken that long to turn full circle, and now only one thing stood between its success or failure. Schram sucked in a deep breath and stepped inside.

His staff was immediately drawn to attack and defend when the large black dragon stared down on him.

Destiny

S layne rose from his relaxed and seated position by the fire to turn his burning eyes upon the intruder. The dragon shook his head and in a deep, raspy, and worn voice greeted the human entering his cave. "So, Almok has betrayed me, exactly as I have foreseen he would."

Schram narrowed his gaze on the dragon, and his knuckles turned white on the grip of his staff. "Had he truly betrayed you, he would be by my side right now." He paused, turned a small smile, then added, "He did not betray you. He only lost his loyalty to you when he felt the true calling of his mother." He took a step closer. The anxiety he was feeling while he had approached was quickly fading. The realism of finally being placed at this point vanquished the unknowns, to be replaced with the confidence he held deep within him.

Slayne appeared unconcerned. "Almok's mother was as foolish as any canok I have come across. I gave her the only good thing she ever had, and now the results of that encounter have betrayed me. It is surprising when you remember the one who did remain true to me. Kirven died fighting for me. That must eat at your insides every day, boy."

Schram felt the words hard inside but did not let it show. The truth was, it did always bother him—the choices Kirven made. He always believed that there had to be other options that would have brought about the same result. However, he knew now that none of that made any difference and he had to focus. He could not let Slayne get into his mind, be it through words or magic, he had to protect himself. "Slayne, you as well as anyone know that I never have to defend my old companion, nor would I ever think it was needed. You have, for 200 years, tried to place yourself in a position to rule this world, and I am here now to ensure that you are unsuccessful, just as my companion did when he stood by your side so long ago. You are the one who did not foresee the true course of events. The only thing that 'eats at my insides' is defeating you, now, once and for all."

The dragon laughed. "Well said, Schram of Toopek. How are you going to do this wondrous feat? With the staff?" The black dragon let out a deep laugh, which echoed off the walls and bore into Schram's mind.

Schram sensed that the dragon truly had no fear of the staff. Deep within the creature he felt nothing. He drew a line between him and the dragon. He issued a short incantation and the staff exploded with light. Slayne threw up one of his huge talons and intercepted the charge. Seemingly without a care, he thrust the attack back toward the human. Schram was caught unprepared for this response and the bolt hit him, sending his body to the floor. Schram did not know if the force of the returned magic or the dragon's deep bellows is what actually brought him down, but whichever it was nearly sent his staff flying free from his hands.

Now the dragon took a step closer. "You damn fool. Don't you see that you have no chance against me? I have prepared for your feeble attacks. I am inside the dominion of the staff. I have destroyed its creator and learned its secrets." Schram's eyes filled with horror as he stared back toward the dragon. Slayne smiled. "Yes, yes, I understand now. You did not know Anbari was dead. You could not feel his life fading while mine grew stronger." He moved to the side to clear a passage for Schram to pass. "Go ahead, boy, see for yourself. I can spare the time, for I am in no hurry to become emperor over all creatures."

Schram pushed himself to his feet and began to move toward the pitch-black cavern whose entrance was next to the fire. In his first visit, this room was formed at the base of the Great Oak and was filled with the most beautiful silver vines and white sands broken only by a crystal-blue stream. Schram never took his eyes from the dragon while he backed through the portal, which no light seemed able to penetrate. When he broke the plane of the doorway, however, he was not greeted with the sight he remembered. Instead, he became totally seduced by the lonely desperation brought on by solitude and death.

He spun around and dropped his head as his eyes absorbed what they saw. The silver vines that were present had begun wilting, and their shimmer was already absent. The falls, which gently tumbled downward to fill the stream, had vanished, and now the stream lay dry and barren. The only thing that seemed unaffected by the changes was the white sand path that led to the base of the oak. However, even it was tainted as it now led to something else first. The motionless body of a great silver dragon was placed, with its head against the base of the oak blocking the path. Schram nearly fell to the ground as his elven body fought to accept the death he now witnessed.

"Come to my side, Schram. I have been awaiting your arrival." Schram's eyebrow raised as he realized the dragon had not yet passed, but even the telepathy was weak, showing that death was near.

He hurried to the huge creature's side. "I am here, Anbari. Tell me what it is I can do."

The dragon lifted one eyelid to peer at the young magician. His voice was nearly too quiet and muffled to hear, but he seemed to want to speak directly rather than with his mind's power. "Schram, you have changed so much over the years." He broke off as a small fit of coughing and gasping overtook his voice. "I wish I could be with you to the end, but even I cannot change that which I know."

"Please do not speak of such things. You are the most powerful creature in all of Troyf. You can survive this, and I can help you. I have brought the staff, and it shall return your strength to you as it did upon its creation. Then together, you and I shall defeat this evil upon us."

"No, Schram. I have always known when my time would come. I only hope that I have been successful in changing the circumstances around which it has occurred. You must be the one to face Slayne, as it has been destined for you to do."

Schram's voice became pleading. "But without you, how can I ever defeat him? He has no fear of this staff. He claims to know its secrets—secrets even I do not understand."

"Yes. During my battle, I was forced to reveal certain unknowns to him, which I did not expect him to learn. He indeed is powerful, but there remains an unknown which even he does not expect to turn full circle."

He placed his hand on the dragon's broad neck. "Tell me, Anbari. If there is something which might still lend me an advantage, then tell me what that might be."

"I cannot, Schram, for as a dragon, I know it to be something that must be learned. You cannot be taught that which will give you strength, it must be learned. It must be learned…" he repeated again as his voice trailed off.

"I do not understand, my friend. I have no more time for learning. The time is now."

"The only time I have left must be used to ask a favor of you."

Schram's eyes widened. "Anything. Tell me."

Anbari lifted his head to look at the young man eye to eye. There was a sadness in his voice. Softly, Anbari said, "Please, it is time. Lay the staff across my body."

Schram was reluctant to release his focus of power, but the emotion he was feeling within Anbari made the action almost immediate. He placed the long, seemingly normal branch against the dragon's huge talons so it rested up against his vast neck, reaching across his entire body. Anbari's eyes grew soft and peaceful while his body became more relaxed. Slowly, he became somewhat transparent, and Schram knew he was passing to another existence. However, when he noticed that the staff too was fading, he became immediately fearful. "Wait, Anbari. How can I act against Slayne without the staff? It is part of me."

"Trust in yourself that which you are about to undertake. The knowledge within you is great, and save you it can."

Schram stared on in disbelief while the one creature he respected and admired more than any other gently vanished from this world. His eyes fell down in sadness, but it was more than just the loss of his friend and teacher; it was combined with the loss of the staff. There was no reason for Schram to feel emotional regarding its absence, but he relied on it for all his powers. His worst fear as he entered Anbari's Dominion was that he would have to face Slayne alone, without the powerful silver dragon by his side. Now, even that scenario had worsened. Not only was Anbari going to be absent, but he would no longer be able to draw on his hidden powers through the staff. Schram knew he could not defeat Slayne without it.

"Why did you take my only chance?" he asked softly to the air. "I have gained so much through the staff. I do hold some power within me, but not close to that which I had with the staff. What purpose could this all serve? Why give me the staff in the first place if I am not to use it to defeat Slayne?"

Schram's cries were answered with silence. He fell to his knees and dropped his head to hands, almost already defeated. For some reason, his mind went to the first time he walked without Kirven by his side. The canok had been injured in a battle with a pair of tigons and a small group of goblins after Toopek had first been attacked. He remembered how alone he felt as he and Krirtie continued their trek to Elvinott while Geoff took Kirven to the maneth camp to seek the aid of Mi-Kevan. How he felt at this moment surpassed those feelings. There was nobody left to help him.

Schram, I will always be with you, issued a voice in the magician's mind.

He lifted his head. His cheeks showed the glisten of sweat, and his eyes were deep and red. "I know that voice," he whispered. "I have heard it twice before."

Yes, I have spoken to you when you needed me, but this will be the last time. You have reached your destiny. Now you must find the strength to face it.

"How can I face that which has power so much in excess of my own?"

You must take all that you know, all that you have learned, and call on it like you have never called before. You must be sure in your actions, for anything less and you will be defeated. You have the power, my son, you were born with it."

"Are you my mother?"

There was no reply. Schram pushed himself to his feet and dried his eyes while he thought about the voice he had just heard. Whether it was real of part of his imagination, he had heard it twice before, the last time being before they started their trip to Cindif. He had a feeling of confidence growing within him. Yet when he looked down to his hands and remembered his missing staff, the same barrage of fears engulfed his body. Still, he knew that he could not turn. He knelt down and issued a short elven prayer of life and then retreated toward the room where he knew Slayne remained waiting.

He noticed very little feeling in his knees, as if the joints were totally absent and his body was about to tumble to the ground. Yet he pressed on. The last five steps proved the most difficult. Again, sweat rolled throughout every crevice of his body. He came to a dead stop at the doorway and turned back toward the Great Oak, hoping that something there had appeared and would give him strength in his endeavor. However, before him it appeared as before, a large silver oak whose shine and brilliance slowly seemed to be fading. He shrugged and stepped forward.

"So, you have returned." Slayne narrowed his eyes on the human magician with an intriguing grin forming between his rows of jagged teeth. "The staff? Given back to the fool? Now this is something I did not foresee, or should I say, this is a benefit I did not foresee. Without the staff, a talented goblin could defeat you, boy." He bellowed another deep laugh. "After all this time, after all the loss you have been dealt, you give up, now, in the final moments?"

Schram stood tall before the magnificent creature that towered over him. "It makes little difference what tools I possess or do not possess, for my life dictates that I am truly powerful. My old canok companion, whom you knew to be one of your sons, recognized this to be true, as have many since him. You too shall learn of my true power, my true heritage, before death encompasses you." Schram was not certain who he was trying to convince, but he was pleased with the words he used.

Slayne tilted his head slightly, but it was instantly obvious that he was not concerned with his opponent's strength, words, or threats. "You stand before me raving about powers you have no tie to without a source to wield them from. You are a magician and at times have caused me great distress. However, without the Staff of Anbari or the Ring of Ku, your powers cannot flourish. You know it as well as I. I can feel your thoughts within you. As you stand before me now, you are nothing more than a simple magician and no match for my abilities." He paused and then narrowed in on the magician. "Once I am through with you, I shall seek out your entire group of companions. I will destroy them all, especially"—he smiled with drips of fire now falling through his teeth—"yes, the elf princess. I feel your thoughts for her. Perhaps I will not kill her. Perhaps I will make her the new mother of my next generation of children. Perhaps she will become mine, as is my will." More raspy laughter ensued as Schram felt the hatred build within him. Slayne's laughter subsided and he leaned his dragon head down to meet Schram's eyes. "At least Anbari fought bravely before I crushed him beneath my wrath, and at least you lived to see his pathetic remains vanish to the unknown."

Schram did not turn as he felt the heat of the dragon's breath upon him. He even stepped forward, drawing within reaching distance to Slayne's exposed teeth. "The silver dragon who resided here has, and always will be, the most powerful creature on Troyf. If this was not true, then you would not have spent the majority of your life trying to steal his power. When I defeat you now, your failure will be complete, and his life will live on forever. From the start of this war nearly 200 years ago, you have done nothing but play into his hands."

Slayne spread his wings wide and filled his lungs with air, creating a ferocious sight. The warrior raised a hand up in response as a wall of flame totally consumed his body. The heat was tremendous, and Slayne's laughter filled the room in its wake. Schram looked up from where he had fallen to his back and realized that he was, in fact, unharmed. However, Slayne's face planted right up to greet his made him quickly realize that he could have been.

The dragon's voice barreled through his mind uncontrolled. "I could have killed you just then. You did well to protect yourself from my frivolous attack, but while you were concentrating on it, I could have snapped your frail body in half in only seconds. You are of no concern to me." His voice trailed off and his eyes turned, lifting his brow higher. He continued in a softer voice. "Except possibly as an ally. Join my side, Schram, just as Kirven did before you. Together we can rule all of Troyf and possibly beyond. Under my guidance, your powers can truly grow. You can finally realize your true destiny and your true powers. Those you have fought with will listen to you, they could be turned, we could have a peaceful world led by the two of us. We would be the strongest creatures in the world."

Schram climbed to his feet and his tone showed nothing but defiance. "I could never join you. With you comes hell and hatred, death and destruction. I am not willing to submit those I love to a future such as that. I would sooner die than join you, as would all my companions."

Slayne roared and slammed his talon against the wall and then the ground. "Without me comes death to you and all those with you!" Again he paused and calmed himself. "Yes, your feelings for them run deep. Then join my side and save their lives—it is the only way."

Schram looked down only for a moment. Slayne angled his head and continued. "I feel you question your direction. Perhaps I misjudged the relationship we could have. Perhaps the future might be bright and your friends may live."

Schram turned his back to the dragon and stared into the fire pit. Suddenly he found his mind staring into the fire pit in the great hall at Elvinott. He remembered his life there as a child and then following it up to the present. He spun back around. "No!"

Fire erupted from Schram's hand and briefly caught the dragon by surprise. Slayne retreated a step and quickly recovered, placing a barrier around his body. "You are a fool, boy. I offer you everything, and you spit in my face. You are weaponless and powerless. How can you hope to defeat one as great as I? If I were you, I would pray I make your death quick, though in my mood, I feel I will draw it out for my own pleasure."

Two bursts exploded from under the dragon's wings. Schram defended against the first, but the second struck the human against the chest. His body again flailed across the ground, but he quickly leaped back to his feet and issued an attack of his own. Now the battle had begun. Anything seemed possible as the two fought with only one purpose in mind—to destroy their opponent outright.

The room seemed to be lit with a thousand torches. With each burst of magic of fire released, two more answered its call. Schram was not certain where he was drawing on all his powers, but they were flowing naturally. It was as if this place was bringing out something within him he did not know existed. That is why Anbari wanted him here. That is why this meeting had to be here.

He had developed a fairly inflexible shield about him and could now concentrate his thoughts more toward his attack. With rolls of fire, he engulfed the dragon in flames and then issued the most dazzling and powerful feats of magic he had ever created, but each time Slayne seemed to defend and counter without delay. Schram felt as if he was in a stalemate against an equally powerful opponent, and that battle continued for an unknown length of time. The hours seemed to stand still as the two powerful creatures of magic dealt their most deadly display against the other. Then, Schram realized that his shield was slowly weakening. Moreover, his mind and body was tiring.

He could not determine if Slayne was experiencing the same faults, nor did he have time to evaluate what the black dragon's condition truly was. He concentrated on strengthening his barrier, but now it was taking more of his thoughts than previously required. That in turn took away from the energy in his attacks. His eyes grew hard and he forced his mind to center on his chore, but Slayne's attacks did not seem to be faltering. The dragon even appeared more confident between his violent bursts. It was then Schram began to believe that he could not win.

His barrier collapsed, and the brunt of the dragon's magic was thrust upon his weary and defenseless body. Schram was carried through the air from the first impact and struck the wall with enough force to crack it from the base clear up to where his head had hit. Blood spilled from the wound on his head and between his lips. There was a large, circular burn the size of a maneth's mane across his chest. He slid down the wall and let his head drop between his knees. His exhaustion and the wounds barely allowed him to remain conscious.

Slayne stepped before him. His voice and the stagger at which he moved both clearly showed that he too had grown weary, but he still had more than enough strength to prevail over the humbled human sitting almost lifeless against the wall. "I did not intend to be matched against you for over half a day. Your strength did exceed my expectations." Schram did not—possibly because he could not—respond, but the statement did leave him at a loss. He had no idea the battle had taken the time it had, but also the dragon's ability to move told the human one thing—that he had lost. All Kirven and Anbari and all the others had fought for had failed because he was not strong enough. He lifted his head to stare at the black eyes piecing down upon him. He stared hard at the creature but could make no comment. He could speak no words of strength or defiance. Both he and Slayne knew it was over.

The dragon, though still showing signs of his recent battle, displayed a twisted smile toward the human's weakened state. "Only now do you understand. All those whom you spent your life considering to be powerful, they were only annoyances to me. Anbari was a fool, as you are to follow him. The trail of ignorance goes all the way down to your parents. Nobody shall ever defy me again!"

His comment was meant to further beat Schram, and it proved effective with the exception of one comment. The near dead human-elf-magician lifted his head and raised an eyebrow when he heard the word "parents." Now, he understood what his mother had said to him so long ago, but it was too late.

Slayne saw this change in his expression and took an uncomfortable step backward. "I shall delay no longer. You have defied me for the last time, Schram Starland, Prince of Toopek, and now it is your time to die." He again spread his wings and filled his lungs to prepare one final attack against his already beaten foe, but this time Schram did not see the magnificence in it. He stared back, wishing he had only a few more moments to calm his mind and find those abilities he was only beginning to understand.

The explosion was intense when the fire shot from the dragon's mouth, but the scream following the impact made the first noise almost obsolete. Slayne flailed his head wildly, trying to shake the attached claws free of his throat, causing his final attack to be sent with incredible force directly into the fire pit, sending it into a frenzied blaze. Schram could hardly comprehend what was occurring, but he was certain if he were to mount any defensive, now would be his only chance. He glanced toward Slayne and froze when he saw the dragon calling on his magic to free the rat's four claws from their vicious, penetrating lock on his neck. Black blood seeped from the gashes and coated the rat's fur. Schram gathered all his strength for one final incantation of his own. He knew time was short but this was something that could not be rushed. He heard the rat's body strike the wall and slump to the ground, but already all was in place. His environment began to warp and change, and the feelings within him took on a new level of complexity. He felt his strength slowly returning and a new and untested power flowing within his new body. He lifted his head to stare at the black dragon who only looked disbelieving in return.

"Well, Schram," Slayne said. "I see I should not have delayed, but the outcome will be the same."

Schram lifted his large green wings and stepped toward him. "Yes, I have found my true self. My father, as you and I both knew him, was human, but my mother was not. My mother was joined with Anbari a long time ago and with him, she had four sons. However, without him she had one. Hawthorne was my mother as well as one of the most powerful dragons to have ever lived."

"This changes nothing, boy. I have known dragon magic my entire life. I have honed it, mastered it, in many ways created it. You have never experienced that which you now claim to wield." I give you one last chance, Schram. Join my side or be destroyed."

Schram spread his wings, and to his surprise, he dwarfed the black dragon in size. "I will not join you, nor will I turn." He released a burst of fire, which even exceeded his own expectations. Slayne was immediately put on defense and found himself backing several steps. The black dragon fought as he had before, but the first battle had weakened him. It was his mind this time that was straining to keep intact, and Schram appeared rejuvenated. Slayne had to draw from deep within himself to find the resources necessary to mount any attack. He moved forward, pushing with all he had to break his counterpart's strength, but he could not. Schram used a new reservoir of abilities to shift his attacks and defenses to previously unexplored levels. With one more charge forward, Slayne's defense was broken, and the dragon lay staring back at Schram with a fear-stricken gaze.

Schram stepped nearer. "I was destined to meet you here 175 years before I was born, and now, my destiny is complete. You have failed, Slayne, but in your failure you have caused more death and destruction than any creature in history. For that, I am certain that you shall be punished severely as you pass through eternity. I pray that the guardians will eventually show you peace, for no creature should forever be forced to experience that which the Realm of Darkness holds. May you find that your actions were worth it."

"For a chance to be the supreme power over all creatures," broke in Slayne's raspy and charred voice. "I am certain they were. And the Realm of Darkness fears me, I do not fear it." He coughed, and blood spewed from his lips and nostrils. "But know one thing, boy—my plans have not as yet turned full circle, and your destiny is not complete. You still have not won."

Schram stared down at the fading black creature with hatred flowing through him. He spread his wings one final time and filled his insides with air. In one breath, a dark nightmare ended, and the dragon's head fell down lifeless. Schram did not have to prepare the body for passage. Anbari's Dominion had its own acceptance for the guardians. He only stood back and closed his large green eyes while the dark shadows from beyond slowly engulfed Slayne's motionless body with their terror-ridden screams, and then all sound—and the black dragon—vanished.

The Battle Lives

The adrenaline flowing within him had slowly begun to subside by the time he turned his attention to the motionless rat. He stared at the figure momentarily, hardly able to believe his eyes. Schram pulled his wings back against his huge body and took several large steps toward the spot where he had been thrown. Bringing his huge green head down to floor level, he gently blew across the rat's face. His eyes blinked and head turned while he issued several groggy curses. Then, his eyes locked wide open, and he screamed in a language even foreign to Schram.

"Relax, old friend, I could never hurt you, though I do recall chopping your tail off after our first meeting."

"Schram?" the rat asked hesitantly, his face turning to a suspicious grin. "What the..."

"Calm, my friend. As surprised as you are to see me in this state, I am to see you at all. How did you get here and what happened to you? We all thought you were lost."

"Oh, come on now, Schram. You don't expect me to be giving you—someone whom when I met was human, then elven, then some sort of hybrid magician, only to end up a dragon—any information when I feel this way. My story would fall well short of the thrill of yours, which means my story will have to wait. I do remember the time I was battling two minoks for the right to..."

"Fehr," he interrupted, smiling. "It is truly a blessing to see you again. Come, let's sit by the Great Oak and talk. I have a feeling that it is my story that may fall short of yours, or at least be shorter," he added to himself.

Schram set the rat down at the base of the huge silver oak tree and, after a brief incantation, took his seat next to him, taking his old human-elven appearance complete with long jet-black hair pulled back to a braided tail, which the rat was accustomed to seeing. He let out a soft sigh and said, "I may not be sure of many things anymore, but I do know one thing for certain. You, my old friend, have been eating way too much. Two tigons could share you over three meals and still have some leftovers for a snack the next day."

"Oh, don't you start on me too, you reptile. I heard enough of that nonsense from Krirtie. Besides, it's those fool dwarves' faults. There are the ones who..." his statement broke off when he saw Schram's saddened look. "What happened?" He paused then looked around. "Is it?" His voice trailed off again, fearful to ask that which he did not want to know but could see on the magician's face.

Schram reached out and stroked his ruffled fur. "Much has indeed happened, old friend, and much more is still to come unless we act to prevent it, but first I must know all that you know. There are many things I do not understand, and I have a strange feeling that you may hold some of the answers, whether you realize it or not. I will tell you all that I know and all that we have left to face, but first please indulge me with your tale."

Fehr shifted uncomfortably as he realized from Schram's tone that something grave had indeed happened. He turned to the Great Oak, whose branches and leaves were already beginning to regain their silver brilliance since Slayne's darkness was lifted. He seemed to draw on the power of the tree as if it would give him strength. He spun his eyes back to Schram and began in a solemn voice hardly his own and not his standard storytelling vernacular. "When Jermys and I decided to head to Draag, we had not realized that Stepha and Krirtie would already have begun a journey of their own."

Schram raised his hand to silence his friend. "No, Fehr, I mean from the very beginning. What were you doing in Lawren that first day, and why did you insist on joining our trek to Elvinott? Then, take it all the way to where you became separated from the others only to end up here—in Anbari's Dominion—alone."

Fehr smiled a bit. "Oh, well, if you wish to know all of that, then indeed my story will be equal or better than yours."

He returned the smile. "That is fine, my friend, but make it the short version. All our remaining companions' lives might depend on it."

Fehr could tell from the seriousness in his voice that this was an issue Schram was not leaving open to discussion. After a brief nod of understanding, he continued, still in a somewhat dry tone. "It was many years ago, so many that I cannot even remember exactly, but I was just a few months past my birth, if that should help you understand. My mother had been attacked and killed by some creature in the forest and my father had also died trying to save her. The creature was about to turn on me when a young human female saw the situation and, for some reason, took pity on me. With amazing gifts of magic, she turned the creature in retreat and then took me into her arms. With telepathy, she told me to relax and that she was a friend and would take care of me. She was so beautiful that I could not turn her down, not that I had any method to anyway. She brought me here, the dominion of the one she was joined to, Anbari. I soon learned that in her true form, she was as he was—a magnificent and powerful dragon. Her name was Hawthorne, and she became my mother and teacher. I spent my lifetime here, learning their ways, and languages for that matter, and never once did they ever ask anything of me. There were times which Anbari seemed to have lost everything, but he never turned his back on me, and he always found new strength somewhere. That is why when he asked me for assistance, I could not turn him down, regardless of whether I understood its purpose.

Schram looked down at him. "What did he ask you?"

"He asked me to join you in your trek. He said you would need my aid in certain areas. He told me exactly where to go and how to go about joining, though Krirtie did catch me before I was ready. The rest you probably know. After Jermys and I got the aid from the dark dwarves, we proceeded to Draag."

"Wait a minute. The dark dwarves assisted you?"

His eyes narrowed. "Does that mean you have not spoken to Jermys? Does he remain in Draag alone?"

"No, Jermys is no longer at Draag, and they were successful in freeing Maldor. But I also have not spoken with him directly, and as for the dark dwarves helping you, I am totally ignorant."

"How then do you know of his success, and where is he now?"

"I have spoken with Stepha, and she informed me that Jermys has gone to Feldschlosschen and Antaag to settle a growing civil war. I had heard rumors that King Kapmann at Antaag had begun aiding the dark dwarves and was being overthrown by the loyal Antaagians. Jermys was going to bring order to the chaos, but I will explain that later. How did you and Jermys become separated?"

Fehr resumed his thought. "In the forests surrounding Draag. We were discovered by a dark dwarf force loyal to the dragons. I led them to the river to allow Jermys time to flee. However, I became cut off. I would sooner drown than be a dark brother's dinner, so I said a prayer to Anbari and leaped into the river. The next thing I knew I was waking up here. I do not know how long I was out or how I got here. The last thing I remember is cursing the awful taste of the river water. I got up and walked the passages that I know as well as Anbari himself to find Slayne about ready to put the finishing touches to your pathetic defense. And as for my following actions, I have no explanation other than it seemed like a good idea at the time. Damn black dragon blood tasted like dirt, and he did give me an awful jolt against the wall. I can't see that my attack was worth it, seeing how you had this hidden dragon power and all."

Schram stroked the rat's fur. "On the contrary, Fehr. If not for you, I would have been killed, and Slayne would now be one small step from total dictatorship. You saved all of Troyf." He shook his head. "I cannot believe it, but somehow you are the hero of our world."

Fehr smiled but only momentarily. Although the rat loved storytelling and usually found humor in everything, in the midst of seeing the one he thought of as a father fallen before him, even Fehr knew the times were still indeed grave. His heart sank when he thought about Anbari, but he also felt Schram held more knowledge of his friends, knowledge that was not going to be easy to hear. The rat shifted slightly then added, "I hope that provided you some answers, but now please tell me, what has happened to our friends? I have seen your expression and felt your words. I am more certain than ever that the news will not be good, but I must know."

Schram rose and paced a bit and then retook his seat, this time better facing his furry companion. "Your words did explain much, but I still have many questions. I know of only one who might hold these answers, but I feel that her life is fading fast. We must hurry back to Toopek, for I now must try to do what I previously wished the one who used to own this dominion would do—prevent a war by turning the huge force of dragons back to its old ideals, the true dragon nature. However, you too deserve to know what has occurred in your absence, and although they are words you will find difficult to accept, you must hear them."

Fehr was caught between curses and tears as Schram replayed the hardships they had faced. Even with his newfound strength, the human magician felt the same emotional loss as he forced the words across his lips. He ended with the scene that had taken place just where they were now sitting, beneath the Great Silver Oak where Anbari had spoken his final words.

Fehr looked up with beads of water matting down the fur around his eyes. "We must go to Toopek immediately. We have to stop this war and help Hawthorne. She gave me everything. I must at least..." He did not finish his thoughts.

"Are you up for traveling?"

"I am."

Schram had already changed back into the ominous form of the huge green dragon before he could reply. "Then climb on my back and we shall move with a speed never before experienced."

Fehr did as he was instructed, and moments later they were at the top branches of the Great Oak, breaking through the surface of the water. "Greetings, Schram. You should be proud of your success."

"Greetings returned to you, Draketon, as well you should be for your part in it." The red dragon nodded before Schram continued. "Will you be accompanying us back to Toopek?"

"No, you will not require my aid any longer. However, if you are successful once again, the dragons will need time and a place to absorb what you have shown them. I will meet them upon their return to Draag and offer my aid and knowledge. Should they deem it of value, I can help their transition."

"I am sure they will, if I am fortunate enough to be successful. To convince them of a different truth than they have known since birth, that is a feat that will be difficult."

"Trust in yourself what you are about to undertake. The knowledge within you is great, and save you it can."

Schram smiled at the large dragon. "It sure would have been nice if all of you who knew what was going on had told me about it at some point."

The red dragon smiled broadly. "We did, my friend. We did. You just were not able to hear it until you were ready." The dragon opened his wings wide and began to fly adjacent to Schram. "Remember, the truth is much easier to believe and understand, when it follows a true natural transition. The young dragons have been brainwashed since birth, but that does not mean their actions are consistent with what their hearts truly believe. Dragons are innately peaceful, as I am sure you now understand. Find a way to remind them of this, and you will find your way."

"Thank you for your words, my friend. I have heard them and will use that guidance wisely." They exchanged nods, which spoke more than any words could do, and with a powerful burst of their wings, they broke apart in flight and headed directly into the storm around the Black Pool.

"Hold on, Fehr. I am not as adept as flying as some. This could prove interesting to say the least."

Fehr answered with a deep gulp before the first gale caught his coat, nearly pulling him from Schram's back. Just before entering the storm where all conversation would be lost, Fehr said, "So Schram, now that I think about it, I guess this makes us half brothers."

⚭

"What do you think, Maldor?" Geoff asked, staring toward the sky.

"I think day three of this absurdity is wearing at me worse than day one and two combined. I wished they would quit toying with us and fight directly."

"Aye," said Alan from behind. "I feel like I am being tested to see how mad and crazed I might become staring at an enemy above me but not being able to attack it."

Geoff shook his head. "I wish I had answers, but I do not. Every one of our attacks strikes their barrier and is cleanly deflected, but why they do not attack us is beyond my grasp."

"Perhaps it is because they too are caged?" asked Denisi. Her injuries had been cared for but she was still not fully battle ready. However, she was very pleased to stay right by Geoff's side.

"What do you mean?" asked the large maneth leader.

She moved slightly away from Geoff to face the main group, her movements clearly showing the pain she felt. "I mean that I do not think the dragons have created this barrier between us. If you think about nothing else, what motive would they have to create a barrier that kept us both separated? Their newfound rage before it appeared was having a very detrimental effect on the city. To put if differently, they were winning."

Tantis had arrived just in time to hear these comments. His injuries were extremely severe and still life threatening for the flyer elf, but he too had seen something that he needed to include. "She is right, Geoff. The dragons did not create this. Every morning and throughout the night they try various maneuvers to break through it themselves. They try to hide if from us, but they cannot get through. They are separated from us, the same as we are separated from them."

Geoff stared at his old friend, and after helping him find a seat, he turned back to the group. "Then who did create it and for what purpose?"

Denisi looked up. "Schram? He has grown powerful and he would have the reason. Toopek is his home and he has fought this battle from the start."

Geoff shook his head. "No. He said his abilities had become ineffective against the dragon attack. He did place the barrier around the city, which is to keep the ground forces out, but this one"—he motioned to the air—"is even beyond his talented hand."

"Besides," broke in Alan, "what purpose would he have to keep us isolated as well?"

"So what are you saying then, there is an outsider controlling our fate?" Denisi's statement brought a long silence from those around.

Geoff spanned the faces but stopped on the flyer elf, who seemed to have an idea growing. "What is it, Tantis? Have you the answer to this puzzle?"

His expression was one of intrigue. "What if this is not some violent outsider placing us in a position only to wait for our death? What if it is more a temporary cease of fighting?"

"What?" interrupted Maldor. "So both sides can lick their wounds and be better ready for war to resume?"

"Maybe, but how about if it was not for the war to resume, but peace to be reached?" added Denisi, her tone actually lifting.

Geoff watched Tantis closely as he listened to his flyer counterpart. Tantis turned back to the maneth leader. "Yes. Schram may not have had the power to create the barrier, but perhaps he knew someone who could."

Denisi joined Geoff's side, where she seemed most comfortable. "And if it was an impartial outsider, or even Schram's acceptance of the beauty of life, then that would explain why we too are separated from them. It would not be right for us to be able to destroy them at will. The barrier must be equal. That is the only explanation."

"So let us assume we are correct," Geoff asserted. "What can we do now that might help?"

Tantis shook his head. "If we are correct, then all we can do is wait and be prepared for the worst."

"What might that be?" Maldor asked, gripping his hammer as he spoke.

The elf pushed himself to his feet. "Schram's failure. If he is unsuccessful against Slayne, where he told Geoff he was headed before this barrier appeared, then we must assume the barrier will fall, and we will be facing a more intense opponent than we did before because now their leader will be with them."

Maldor stepped forward. "If we see Slayne, I swear I am going to do everything within my power to introduce him to the pain he made me feel, ending with his violent death."

There was a long silence until Denisi pointed, "You might just have been granted your chance. That blue just passed through the barrier."

All hearts sank as the group witnessed that which the elf spoke. By their deductions then, Schram must have failed. One by one, more dragons began collapsing on the city. Arrows answered their attacks in great numbers, but their efforts on the rejuvenated and strong young dragons were only minimal. Fire again exploded across the city and screams filled the air. Geoff and Maldor led a fierce attack, causing the dragon parties to divide, making their way into two separate battles. The two maneths separated, and each took charge of one of the ground forces' defenses.

Geoff began hollering out orders of retreat when he saw two dragons closing in on Denisi and an injured maneth she was trying to move to safety. "Denisi, two are approaching. Find cover now!"

The elf spun her head to the air to witness the fierce sight. Tears filled her eyes, but she could not budge the maneth, who was unconscious and had become trapped under loose debris. Geoff screamed again and began running to intercept the dragons, but he knew he could not arrive in time. One of the dragons emitted a wall of fire. Denisi saw it and acted just before it struck where she had previously stood. She lifted herself through the air and delivered an arrow, which struck the lead dragon between its huge blue eyes. Geoff had dug in and locked the sights of his huge bow on the same beast. He released a shaft, which bit into the creature's neck, causing it to veer to the side and end its life as it crashed to the ground. The other dragon was caught by the surprise response and veered quickly to the side following a pattern away from the two. Geoff and Denisi both hurried to the aid of the fallen maneth.

Geoff carefully removed the blue helm of the motionless figure, but he knew they were too late. The maneth had been left totally defenseless against the dragon's last attack and the fire had crept between the already-broken metal of his armor. The burns across his body were severe and had already ended his life. Denisi buried her head in Geoff's broad chest, and the big maneth just lowered his head. To himself, so as not to offend Denisi by calling those passed by name, he said, "May you be well accepted, Meris. You were a brave maneth."

"Geoff!" hollered Alan. "Something is happening."

The maneth leader pushed the flyer elf back and turned to the voice. "What?"

"The ground forces surrounding Toopek have still not broken through Schram's barrier and the dragons seem to be slowly pulling back, though I am certain the barrier, which once separated us, no longer exists. Also, there is a much larger green dragon among them that I do not remember seeing before."

Geoff scanned the sky and saw the large green dragon. Turning to Denisi, he asked, "Do you have the strength to carry me closer to where the large dragon flies? Please know, if it turns on us, we have no defense."

She grabbed beneath his arms and lifted him into the air. "Yes, just tell me the path you wish me to take."

"Start there, to the ground where the elves have gathered."

They landed next to a group of elves and humans of which Tantis and Fritz stood at the head. Fritz stared to the sky and then whispered to Geoff. "If we released arrows together, we could probably drop, or at least severely wound, the large one. Most of the others are out of range and it seems to be organizing them—probably for one final attack."

"No," said the maneth leader. "We have little chance if the fighting continues in this manner, but I have a feeling things might change. We will wait this one out until I am sure."

"But what if you are wrong? We will have no chance."

Geoff did not answer. He signaled to all those around to hold their attacks until further direction was given. Then he stared to the sky where it had become darkened by a cloud of dragons, all apparently interested in the action of one of their older kin. He pulled Denisi close to his side and issued a soft prayer.

⁕

"I am Schram, and although you may not recognize me as such, many of you may know my name." He was using both verbal speech and telepathy to ensure that all the dragons heard his words. It was then that three dragons in front, which appeared to be the eldest or the most powerful, moved closer to the much larger green dragon but did not reply or engage in attack. Instead they seemed content to simply separate themselves, making them appear to lead the group in Slayne's absence. Schram took this as a message that he should direct his comments to those three, though all within range should hear his words.

"In my short lifetime, I have taken many forms, from human to elf, but it has only been this last day I discovered my true self. Within me flows dragon blood, a richness that cannot remain hidden. My mother was Hawthorne, one of the most powerful dragons ever to walk Troyf. She was for her lifetime joined to the great silver dragon whose dominion lay within the Black Pool of the South Sea. He was truly the most magnificent dragon this world has ever known."

One of the lead dragons, a large blue, interrupted his comment. "We know of the silver dragon. He is Anbari. He is a traitor to our kind. He sided with the humans and elves when they betrayed and murdered our parents. If I am to believe that he has passed, then I can also believe that justice is finally beginning to be fulfilled."

"You are wrong, my friend, but it is not your fault. Since your birth, you have been taught things—things which in your heart you know cannot be true. Your leader, a powerful black dragon, lied to you to bring about a multi-century plan of aggression, which would assert himself as emperor over the world. For over 200 years he has worked this plan to near fulfillment, and now, on the eve of his victory, I have defeated him. But I will only be completely successful if I prevent you from doing what he has willed you to do. You must hear the truth in my words and recognize what is at stake. The humans, elves, maneth, and dwarves, not to mention goblins, dark brothers, and trolls, are not your enemies and never have been. You have been a pawn playing out a game controlled by one warped mind, but you still have a chance to decide on your own. You can make the choice for life."

"Why should we believe you?" replied the blue. "You are nothing to us."

"You should believe me because you can feel that I speak the truth. You are all dragons and therefore you all carry great powers, but as of yet, you have only just begun to experience the total of those powers. Your leader taught you much, how to fight, how to wield magic, how to destroy and how to hate, but what he neglected to teach you was the most important qualities that make you—us—different from any other creature. Within each of you are strengths, which you can never use against another creature, but rather they serve to only give you and all those around you insight. Your leader did not wish you to gain this knowledge until it was too late, but he has failed."

A younger red looked on with hatred burnt into its eyes. "What is it you ask of us then, to leave here on your word? To run away and hide? I say you are a fool bent on trickery and lies. I wish to hear no more of it."

"Wait!" ordered the blue to his younger counterpart. "I wish to hear Schram's answer to the question. What is it you ask us to do?"

Schram moved in closer to try to give his words more merit. He did not like the direction things were heading. The blue seemed torn and no longer sure, but the younger red had closed his mind to what Schram was trying to say. For him, the decision was made. Even worse, by the reactions of those dragons in their wake, Schram felt the bulk felt the same as the red. He answered strongly. "I ask only one thing, though for most of you it may prove difficult. Search your hearts, your minds. Find that hidden knowledge, for as I have just learned, nobody can teach it to you. This is a quality unique to dragons, and regardless of any teachings bent on keeping it hidden, it cannot be forgotten long.

But you must be ready to accept it, and with that comes accepting the truth."

He paused and then circled back a short distance. "I pray that you hear my plea, for there has been too much killing already. I am going to return to the city. If you continue your attack, then I will know that I have failed, and I hope that some lives may still be spared. However, if you too wish this war to find its end, then know that all will be completely impressed with your strength and insight, and that you will find friends upon your return to Draag, or wherever your paths may take you."

Schram again turned to leave but was halted on the blue's command to wait, which when he turned back, he quickly realized was meant for the red, who was moving into attack from behind. Schram stared hard at the red, who had heeded the warning, but it was the blue who broke the silent stalemate. "I have heard your words, Schram, and will do as you ask. I, as everyone who is beside me now, am a dragon, and as dragons, we do not destroy races without thought or cause. If we find that you have lied and the cause is not just, then our attack will be forthcoming, and my prayers will be following in its wake for any loss of life worn on our hearts. Return to your city now, for we require some time to be certain."

Schram nodded appropriately, and with a quick glance back toward the red, he circled back down to the ground, landing near the harbor. He stepped across the rough sand, which was still littered with debris, and placed his long front talon into the water.

A voice broke the peaceful silence that had begun to engulf him. "What is the matter, one called Schram? Is the ability to fly not as pleasing as you believed it would be?"

"No, my friend. I am simply praying that I was successful. So many lives are at stake. I only hope the dragons will feel the truth."

Khaled lifted his head slightly above the water's surface. "If they do not see it, you should know that I do. I will not allow the destruction of your people. I should not put my race above all others. To do so would make the physeters as guilty as those who struck against us in the past."

Schram smiled between his long rows of teeth. "I cannot rely on you to protect my city. You cannot hold the dragons off throughout eternity, nor can I allow their slaughter while my city remains protected. No, the young dragons have to be made to understand the truth."

Khaled closed his eyes briefly and then reopened them. "Some will learn it, but some remain afraid. In time they will grow to understand and accept that which is the truth." He turned his eyes to the sky where Schram's were drawn to follow.

"I don't believe it."

"Believe it, one called Schram. For you, it is over."

Schram watched as the rows of dragons under the large blue's lead slowly drew a formation leading away from the city. Screams of celebration immediately erupted from throughout the Toopekian streets and harbor leading into the surrounding forests. Schram spun his eyes back to the huge whale before him. "No, for me it may never be over. So much is left to be done and so much has been lost. For my life, I will never forget these times."

Again Khaled closed his eyes. "Yes, memories of past hardships find their way deep within the mind. Let us hope that much has been learned from these past years, enough to prevent other generations from the same mistakes."

"Beginning with the physeters, my friend. Give me one more day to spread the word of the whale's return. From that time forward, the physeters shall swim freely and without fear of human interference. And if any does occur, you come to me for I will deal with the source immediately."

Khaled opened his eyes. "Thank you, one called Schram. We shall not forget." The whale began to dive but was stopped by Schram's expression. "Do you have something you wish to ask me?"

Schram looked puzzled then relaxed. "I only wish to know whom you agreed to construct the barrier for? When we separated last, you said you did not do it for me, but there was another."

Khaled grinned. "No, I said I did not do it for Schram of Toopek, but Schram, son of Hawthorne, did convince me of its necessity." With that, the whale vanished beneath the sea.

He turned to continue to where he knew he must go and was immediately greeted by two large blue eyes. "Schram, I wanted you to understand that we are not the dangerous and rage-driven creatures we have appeared to be."

"I know that, for I am one of you."

"Yes, that is why I wish you to help us spread the word of our true nature. Some of the younger dragons do not, as yet, understand, but they will be brought to that level of understanding. However, I still fear that Troyf will not listen to our words of peace. Just as we refused to accept yours, the other races will still fear us. We will not be free to walk Troyf. We do not wish that to be the case."

"I will spread your word, and know that Toopek will never fear the dragons."

"Thank you. I am Bascom, and I hope we shall meet many times as friends. For now, my prayers do go out for all of Troyf, for not only the dragons, but all races have much to rebuild. Many creatures lost their lives—lives that should never have been cut so short."

"You speak wisely, Bascom. Seek out a dragon called Draketon. He shall help you in ways you could not believe. His insight runs deep and will benefit your cause."

Bascom nodded. "I shall." The large blue dragon spread his wings and lifted his huge body effortlessly into the air. Schram watched as he sailed across the city to the cheers of those below. Then his eyes caught a group running toward the harbor. He smiled their direction, but there were matters much more pressing to be dealt with. He opened his wings and beat a path to where he had released Fehr.

Schram landed in the glade, much to the concerned stares of the surrounding elves. However, since word of the dragon retreat had already spread like fire through a dry forest and the fact that an injured dragon lay in their camp, there was no display of force against him. Schram's eyes shot straight to where Hawthorne had lain and now caught sight of a huge, makeshift tent constructed around her. Standing outside the tent was a brightly robed sorcerer smoking a long, curved pipe, which dipped down almost as far as his beard. Schram took a step forward but halted when he noticed who stood below him.

Tilting his head downward, he met the elf's intriguing gaze. She stared long and hard into his large green eyes before whispering, "Schram?"

"Yes, Stepha, it is I, though you may find it difficult to comprehend."

"No, I do not. For some time I have felt things through you, things I did not understand. For the first time, all seems as it should be."

"You are truly amazing, which is why I have always loved you."

"And I you." She reached her arms around his neck, with his body molding back into his human-elf frame. Pushing herself back, she asked, "Does this mean that Hawthorne truly is your mother?"

Schram's heart jumped. He knew Stepha would not speak Hawthorne's name unless she still lived. "Yes, she is my mother. How is she?"

"I do not know. Mi-Kevan will let nobody but you see her and will give no hint regarding her condition." Schram lifted his eyes back toward the tent where the sorcerer now stood staring back at him. His expression showed little insight, and Schram knew he must go. Stepha stepped aside without comment and Schram slowly moved forward.

When he arrived at the tent, Mi-Kevan said, "I am pleased to see you, Schram. We have been waiting for you. Please go inside."

Schram, still in his human-elf form, continued into the tent. Once inside, he stared at the motionless woman lying on a bed of leaves. Fehr rested with his head across her chest with tears soaked through his fur. He looked up and tried to acknowledge Schram's presence but simply looked away. Softly, without looking toward his friend, the rat said, "I am glad you have returned. She has waited to speak with you." He rose, and after brushing his body against the neck of the large dragon, he gently pushed out the doorway.

Schram moved over and knelt beside the woman. Her eyes opened, and she gingerly turned her head to look upon him. She coughed slightly and he could see she was not well. Softly, she whispered, "Fehr told me. I am so proud of you, Schram."

"Mother, you are the one to be proud of. You have faced more evils and shown more strength than anyone else could ever fathom. I only wish I had known."

She smiled. "I could not tell you. If I had, you would have been driven to discover your abilities too soon. If that happened, you may not have defeated Slayne. As it is, all has become as it should be."

"But you are not well. Can Mi-Kevan help you?"

She again smiled. "My son, you still have much to learn, and in time, you will be brought to understand completely. There are many traits that all dragons strong with magic carry, but there is one that many have wished to be free from. In time you will begin to see things. Their meaning will vary in importance and content, but you will see them nonetheless. This is the future, and do not fear it because much of it can be changed if you act upon it. That is what the one I was joined to did. He saw how the evil was shaping itself and carefully devised a system to defeat it. Each step taken, including your birth and all the occurrences for the two centuries before it, were carefully planned out to create a situation about which the black dragon's evil could be controlled. And with your strength, you made it happen."

Schram placed his hand on the dragon's neck and stroked her scales. "I understand, mother. I understand." He paused and leaned in to be closer to where he could hear her irregular breathing. "What is this trait that so many dragons wished to free themselves from?"

"The ability to see the time of one's own death. It is the sole event which cannot be changed, and my time is arriving, my son. That is why Mi-Kevan cannot help. I am only thankful that I was able to spend my last moments in the company of my son. You have given me the one thing no creature but you could give me."

Schram lifted his eyes to hers. She softened her stare even more. "You let my ears here the word 'mother' from your lips."

"And I am glad I am with my mother." A tear began to form in his eye. "It also lays to rest my question of where my mother disappeared to on that first attack at Toopek. Nobody has seen her, or, should I say, you, since."

Her eyes narrowed, and she felt her life fading. "Schram, you must know one thing more. The mother you knew in Toopek was human. I only asserted myself in her place at two different times. Once for your conception through to your birth, and the second the day I told you to trust in yourself. During those times, your human mother was magically induced to believe all that I was experiencing was happening to her. That is why she knew nothing of her absence. However, if she was taken during the first attack, then she is indeed missing. Do not forget your search for her, for she is your true mother. She always believed you to be her son."

Hawthorne's eyes closed, and Schram fell across her body with tears forming across his face. Slowly, the huge, golden-winged green dragon began to fade and then vanished altogether. Schram did not move for the rest of the day and into the night.

The Future

A morning celebration woke Schram from his sleep. He rubbed his still-wet eyes and knelt across the leaves that served as Hawthorne's final resting spot. He issued a short prayer and smiled when an unknown but not foreign warmth filled his body. He pushed himself to his feet and turned to leave. He emerged from the tent ready to greet the fresh morning but instead, upon opening his cramped arms, he tripped forward, falling face first into the dirt.

Stepha leaped to her feet. "I am sorry, Schram. I must have…"

"Have you been here all night?" he asked, placing his hand against her soft face.

Her eyes dropped downward. "Yes, I thought you might need someone—someone who cared for you deeply."

"You could not have been more correct," he replied softly, pulling her against him. "I love you, Stephanatilantilis."

"I love you, Schramilis."

A quiet voice from behind asked. "Is all well with you, Schram?"

"Yes, Fehr, all is well. We have all lost much, but what we gained has made us stronger. And I have to believe all our companions feel the same, wherever they are."

The rat leaped into their combined arms, causing both to sigh under the sudden weight. Stepha freed one of her arms and scratched Fehr's forebrow. "Well, little guy, I seem to remember the talk of a diet for you. I suddenly believe those words to be sound."

Fehr grumbled and jumped back to the ground. "Won't any of you forget the size thing? For Shriak's sake, did you see Schram's belly when he arrived here? It was as big as a tree. If anyone needs to be thinking about trimming a few, I would not look my direction first. That's all I have to say about that. I mean, really."

"All right, Fehr," Schram broke in. "I think we get the picture. Besides, I think Jermys is best suited to put you on a new eating plan, since you two seem to have taken such a liking to each other."

"Jermys Ironshield?" questioned Fehr in disbelief. "That blasted dwarf has a bigger appetite than a hundred—no, a thousand—tigons. If anyone needs to trim a few pounds, it's that no-good mining fool."

"Schram!" hollered another voice, cutting the rat's raving taunts in midstream as well as halting Stepha and Schram's laughter. "I thought if I found my sister, that you would not be far behind." The two embraced and then Madeiris pushed him away. "I am sorry for your losses. We all feel them greatly but none as deep as you. Know that we are with you."

"Thank you, my brother, but don't let sadness cloud what we have accomplished. The evil has been defeated, and we all are to thank for that."

The elf king placed his hand on Schram's shoulder. "Yes, and you will be pleased to know that I did as you asked. Once the dragons fled, the goblin, troll, and dark dwarf ground forces did not remain long. We gave them free passage back through the forest. We trailed them for a distance to be sure their retreat was final, and I have continually kept scouting parties searching for injured or stray groups who might not know it is over. Most of their directions lead toward Draag or Lake Ozak, but if that will be their final destination, I cannot be sure."

"That is all good news," Schram replied, "but there may be one remaining problem."

"What is that?"

"I have learned that a group of dark dwarves who helped Stepha and the others escape from Draag may still be in the caverns. They too need to be informed of the new situation.

Otherwise, there could end up being more bloodshed where too much has spilled already."

"Consider it taken care of. I will send flyers ahead who will arrive with the returning dragon forces. Word will be spread quickly."

"Thank you, Madeiris. You are truly a great king."

"As are you, Schram, and might I add that your kingdom awaits your return."

"Yes, he replied solemnly. "It is time that I return, for there is much to be done. I would like you and those with you to join me if you are able to leave Elvinott this day."

Stepha glanced at her brother, hoping for a certain reply. When she saw his smiling face, she knew what his response would be. He replied, "Those with me? By all the gods, Schram, I have nearly every elf alive with me. And don't think for a minute that even one of them will miss the celebration that is going to happen."

Schram raised his hand, joining in the smile. "Just a minute, Madeiris. I had no idea your numbers were such. My city might be able to take on a war party of goblins, trolls, and dragons, but allowing a city of elves to collapse upon it, I don't think so."

"Too late, fool. The invitation has been given and accepted. To Toopek!" He motioned to a nearby guard to spread the word, then started hollering and dancing before grabbing his sister to join him. "Come, Schram and bring that fat rat to the party as well, but don't let him stray too far. A goblin might grab him and eat on just his belly for over a week.

Fehr issued a few choice elven curses, which only furthered the group's laughter. They wasted no more time before setting out through the trees toward Toopek. Nearly 700 elves followed their king, princess, and greatest friend toward the ransacked human city. The talk was joyous, and feelings of confidence and success was etched on all their faces. Schram and Stepha walked hand in hand, and although she knew her husband was proud, she also felt his pain for his lost friends and family. She gripped his hand tightly.

⚬⚬⚬

"Well, I don't know where the green dragon went, but I have a feeling he might be coming back soon."

"Ah, Geoff," said Maldor. "You don't know what you are saying. All that dragon wanted was to get a fill of water before joining the other winged assassins and fleeing back to their homeland. You'd see that too if you were not so smitten over an elf."

Alan and Tantis chuckled while Denisi blushed beneath her faint-green skin. Geoff turned red with fire and hobbled over to face his friend. "I suggest you choose your words more carefully, Maldor. I am not, nor have ever been, smitten."

"Oh, yes you have," smiled Denisi happily as she squeezed him from behind, causing the big maneth to smile through his anger. "And I am to see that those eyes never change."

Before more laughter could ensue, Geoff motioned for order. He broke the elf's hands apart, which had become locked about his chest, and turned back sternly to Maldor. "I seem to remember stories of a human woman sending you into a frenzy. Let me think, what was her name?"

"You damn well know her name, Geoff," he answered proudly. "It is Krirtie Wayward, the most amazing creature in all of Troyf and soon to be mother of our child."

Alan stepped forward and rose his mug of ale. "Now there is the best reason yet to celebrate."

"Aye," added Geoff, smiling toward his younger friend. He slapped Maldor on the back with a look of pride across his face as he pulled Denisi close. To Alan, he said, "You seem to be the only one able to rescue an ale."

Alan smiled. "Aye. I found one last barrel left near the harbor, probably unloaded from one of the ships in Pete's fleet. The barrel was cracked, but I was able to scoop about three mugs out."

Tantis placed his hand upon the human's shoulder. "You said three?"

Alan looked suspiciously around as he felt all eyes burning upon him. "What? I was pumped full of adrenaline. Besides that, I was hot and dehydrated. I did not know it was the only ale that survived. How could I have?"

The elf leaned closer. "There is an old elven saying that goes, 'To drink alone is accepted only when everyone drinks alone. To drink alone in company can lead to extreme discomfort.'"

"There is no such saying," sprang in Denisi's confused voice, causing the elf to shoot a glare in her direction and Geoff to whisper an explanation in her ear.

"Well, maneths have their own saying. To drink alone is fine unless you have just won a war and your drink is the only drink in the city. Then to drink alone means that you get stripped down naked and thrown in the harbor."

Alan began shaking his head and taking small back paces away from the group. Geoff smiled and slammed his fist on the table. "Yes!" he exclaimed. "I know that saying. Make it so."

The others cheered except Alan, who fought with every ounce of energy he had left. However, his success was nonexistent as the group quickly stripped him down and paraded him through the city to the yells and hollers of all those in the streets.

They arrived at the harbor with nearly 500 encircled around. Geoff climbed on a nearby crate to act as judge over the crowd. "I stand here now as temporary ruler over this city. Until this changes, it is my sworn duty to oversee that all postwar crimes are dealt with as the law, made up or not, states that they should be." A barrage of laughter and further shouts filled the air. "I therefore ask if anyone has proof of the charges put forth against the accused. Did Alan Grove, once third lieutenant over the king's army and now leader over the human forces, drink the last three ales found in all of Toopek?"

Alan fought wildly, trying to free himself, but the more he seemed to resist, the more he made a spectacle of his nudity. Maldor stepped forward. "I would like to offer proof, oh great leader."

Geoff smiled. "Please, great warrior known as Maldor. What proof have you?"

"I was witness to the accused proudly saying that he did just as you have described. He did consume that last three ales."

"Can anyone else confirm this accusation?"

Tantis stepped forward. "I am Tantis of the elves. I too heard these words. And to add, I believe it was a premeditated crime, though I have no proof of it."

Geoff nodded. "There has been an accusation and a confirmation. Therefore, I regret to say that I have no alternative but to find this rogue guilty and pronounce his sentence of one nude harbor dipping." The crowd went into a cheering frenzy.

"Wait!" shouted Alan. "Am I not even allowed a chance at a defense?"

Almost in unison, the surrounding crowd hollered, "No!" and then continued with their laughter and jeers.

Those holding the human began making their way toward the shore while Alan continued to uselessly resist. Geoff gave the wave to proceed, and they brought his body down to the count of three. Upon reaching two, a deep voice echoed across the onlookers, causing Alan to look hopefully forward. "Just a minute, Geoff. I am not satisfied of guilt."

The maneth looked up with two emotions clearly showing—the thrill to see his longtime friend and true King of Toopek and the fear that his fun may be coming to an end.

"Schram, a charge has been made and sentence must be carried out." There was a pause, then he added, "Please?"

Stepha set him down next to the large maneth where he winked only so Geoff could see. Schram's voice remained hard. "Alan Grove, do you have any words you would say on your behalf."

There was a short pause, and a monotonous silence engulfed the harbor. He answered, "Well, I only…"

"Silence!" shouted Schram. I have weighed the evidence and the words you said on your behalf and find no proof to overrule Geoff's decision. Continue with the sentencing."

A cheer rang from those around, and Alan's eyes turned to pits of fire as he stared back at the maneth and human who could do nothing but fight to keep from falling over. However, when Alan did hit the water, Schram's hysteria threw extra weight against the maneth, whose wounds would not hold, and both tumbled into the waving crowd.

⚬⚬⚬

It was hours later before order was restored to the chaos. The group of companions eventually sorted the situation out and found their way to meet in one of the remaining buildings, which somehow had escaped destruction. Madeiris, Stepha, Tantis, Fritz, and Denisi filled out one corner where Alan, still fuming over the previous "trial," Geoff, and Fehr completed the other side. Maldor and Schram had gone on a short walk together so he could have time to speak to the large maneth about all that had occurred. In their absence, the conversation was joyous and lively, though all still felt the pain of the losses in their midst.

Schram pushed through the doorway, and the room fell instantly silent, with all eyes landing on the powerful figure. Schram raised his hand. "All is well. Maldor shall join us shortly. As you can see, I came across another of our friends. For those of you who do not know him, his name is Werner. It is due to his work and those who travel with him that the ground forces did not break through the barrier. We owe them much."

"For what you brought us, Schram, you owe us nothing. You have returned our lives." Werner smiled and greeted each in the room appropriately. Schram stepped over and embraced Stepha before taking a seat next to her and her brother.

Maldor stepped through the door a short while later. The sadness and loss was well-defined across his face but there was also a certain pride etched into his expression. In his arms he held his child, a large maneth boy who carried a facial grin which could have been given to him from no other than a feisty human warrior girl everyone knew all too well.

Geoff rose and placed his hand on the maneth's shoulder, as he had done so many times before. "It is good to have you here with us, Maldor. It would not be the same without you."

He raised his free hand and placed it on his old hero's shoulder. "For me, life will never be the same again. Yet, with all my friends and my son, Ry-Larson, whom she wanted to be known as Lars, I shall fight through this time."

"We are all pleased to have you with us, Maldor," said Stepha, rising. "Both of you. Now come, let us sit and enjoy this meal together."

They all took places around the huge table. All the chairs were filled, with the exception of one next to Fehr. He had insisted on leaving a seat empty to remember that they were still not all present. They each gave their own thanks and prayers for their safety and the safety of those with them before Schram signaled for the food to be brought in. He had arranged for large mugs to be placed before each of them to symbolize Alan's poor judgment, an act the human found particularly displeasing. The food was piled on each of their plates. Both Geoff and Maldor seemed especially pleased with the portions. Again the conversation became cheerful, and laughter frequently filled the small chamber.

It was about ten minutes into the meal when a loud argument taking place outside the door interrupted the feast. "I don't care if every king in the universe said they were not to be disturbed, I am going in you, stupid human!"

"Jermys!" shouted Fehr leaping across the table, paying little mind to where his feet landed. He struck the dwarf midflight, sending both of them to the ground at a guard's feet.

"It's all right," said Schram, raising his hand to the guard. "He is with us."

Jermys pushed himself back to his feet. "You better believe that I am with you." He spoke directly to Fehr. "And if you ever do that again, you worthless lizard bait, I shall have you skinned and your pelt made into 200 nose warmers."

"Oh, Jermys, it is so good to see you."

"Yes, it is," repeated Schram as he walked to his old friend's side. "I am truly glad you came, though I am not sure how."

The dwarf smiled. "It was the damnedest thing. Antaag and Feldschlosschen had just reached peace, under my guidance of course, when Draketon landed outside our mines."

"Ah, yes. I forgot you two had a deep relationship."

The dwarf nodded. "Yes. After I had done everything in my power to kill him and then upon his death, my hatchet gave him back his life. Well, there is definitely some bond, albeit what bond I am not sure." Schram smiled as the dwarf continued. "He told me to march toward Toopek for a celebration, for the war was ending. We met many of the dragon army ground forces on our way, but they did not wish to engage, so we did not either."

Alan interrupted. "Did you say you were coming here for a celebration?"

"Yes, that is what I was told to expect."

"Then, might it be that you brought a bit of ale with you for the journey?"

The dwarf smiled. "I brought some. Let me think a minute." He paused and looked to the sky as if he was adding in his head. "Draketon mentioned it would be well received if we carried some sustenance with us. Therefore, there are 300 barrels outside the door." He looked toward the group again. "But the way the crowd was acting, probably half are gone already."

All the faces in the room immediately brightened but none as large as Alan's. "Say, Fehr, have you ever heard the saying that if a person is tried and convicted wrongly, then he can so choose any punishment for those who placed that sentence upon him?"

Fehr leaped from Jermys's arms to land on the table. His smile was broad and his eyes danced from Schram to Geoff, both of whom were becoming ghostly pale. "Yes, I do believe I have heard such a law."

"Fine," said Alan. He motioned to Schram and Geoff. "After you two, the harbor is not far." He poked his head out and hollered to some guards.

Schram looked down to Stepha while Geoff grabbed Denisi's shoulder. The elf smiled. "I believe I can speak for Stepha when I say that we would not miss this for the world."

Stepha giggled while guards surrounded the two warriors. Jermys was completely confused but since he just had guzzled his first full mug, he figured he would wait this one out. Alan added, "Schram, I am pleased to see you no longer wear armor, but Geoff, please remove yours. I will let you keep your clothes on until will leave the table. After all, some of us are still eating."

He roared when he struck the chilly harbor water. Schram let out a similar sound with not as much anger carried with it. The group at the harbor cheered for many reasons more than what they watched.

It was not until two weeks had passed before many of the visitors began making their plans to return to each of their respective homes. Schram sat with his friends for one last meal together. All eyes looked up to him while he spoke. "Each of you with me now know that I can never repay you for all the help you have given my city and all of Troyf. From this day forward, I hope that our relations will always be as friends. Werner wishes the same words to be passed from him, and regrets that he was unable to deliver it directly. The canoks, above all other races, have faced the deepest pain these past years, and now their rebuilding requires all their combined strengths. I also wish to extend Toopek's arms should any of you, or those you lead, ever desire our aid. You are all great friends, and you are all always welcome here in Toopek."

Each one made similar comments and exchanges, which left only one statement for Schram. "My final word I wish to extend only to Geoff. I realize that the maneths are at home in the mountains, but if they would wish to live within a city and you be their king, then Toopek is at your disposal."

Stepha looked surprisingly toward Schram but it did not compare to the expression Geoff wore. He rose. "I do not understand, Schram. Will you not remain here?"

"I will not." He turned to Stepha. "I have a life that no longer has its home here. Among the trees and the forests is where I belong. I have always known it." Stepha began to smile. "Also, I have the question of the whereabouts of my mother. Although Toopek is her home, as well as the largest human city in all of Troyf, I know now that humans and maneth can be as one. I will always be present and will offer aid at anytime, but you have led this city through its most dangerous time. You are a worthy king." He gave a gentle sigh then added softly, "And I must locate Queen Suzanne if I ever want this ordeal to truly be finished."

Geoff remained on his feet. "I understand your situation but I hope you understand why I must also refuse your offer. As you said, a maneth's home is in the forest and mountains, and we too strive to be among them. I would gladly offer my assistance should Toopek ever require it, but Maldor and I have a village to rebuild of our own. We"—he put his arm around Denisi—"were thinking of moving out of the deep forests and being closer to Elvinott."

Schram smiled. "I believe you have made an excellent choice, and I do definitely understand your reasons." There was a pause, and his eyes turned on Alan. "Well, since I know you will enforce the laws, do you think you can keep this city together if you were in charge?"

Alan rose. "I won't let you down, King Schram. But I will add that you will always be king and this will always be your city." He turned to Jermys, smiling. "It would also be nice if Jermys would keep the ale coming."

The dwarf belched, causing Fehr to blow a puff of smoke across his face in disgust. Jermys stood, shoving the rat to the ground with a thump. "You get that no-good sea captain of yours to handle the transport, and you'll get your ale."

At almost the same time, they all said, "Pete?"

"I completely forgot about him. He has been stranded on the old Castle Island since the dragons left two weeks ago."

"He is going to be really pissed," said Alan, laughing.

Schram smiled. "Yes, it is too bad it is your job to go get him, for as of now I am heading to Elvinott." Schram rose and took Stepha's hand, and the two of them, followed closely by Madeiris, Tantis, and Fritz, all quickly left with their smiles nearly touching the tips of their pointed ears.

Alan's grin quickly vanished and his eyes fell to Geoff and Maldor. "Don't look to us. You were the fool who agreed to the position." The maneths rose with Geoff, pulling Denisi under his arm, and Lars, who was already walking, leaped from the table to his father's back, and they all pushed through the door before it had even settled since the elves left.

That left the troubled human staring at Jermys and Fehr. The two had been worked down to the far end of the table where their constant cloud of smoke could remain centered over them. Alan stared at the two and then shook his head. "Yeah, right. Fat chance I would even ask." He stomped out of the room with Jermys and Fehr not even noticing that he, or any of the others, had left.

Once out the door, he was greeted with a different sight. A strange hermit-looking human dressed in absurdly bright robes and wearing a beard that would rival Jermys's in length was standing in front of Maldor and his son and speaking in a very aggressive manner. Geoff stood to the side with Denisi. He was still smiling, but by the elf's confused expression, it was clear she did not understand. Alan took several steps forward to better hear the conversation.

"So, Maldor, I told you last time we spoke that I was going to teach you a lesson for talking against me. Well, is it not lucky that I happened upon you now so that instruction may take place?"

"Now, Mi-Kevan, anything I said at that time was clouded in judgment. It was a stressful time. I did not even know what I was saying."

The magician frowned. "Just because I was engaged in restoring Kirven's"—he glanced toward Denisi—"please excuse the reference. It has been a time since I have been in the company of others." The elf nodded appreciatively. He continued. "Just because I was engaged in restoring his powers and strength, that did not allow you to act in such a way. I believe, if memory serves, it began with the phrase 'spell-bounding idiot' and got worse from there."

Maldor shook his head but he knew there was no defense. Two and half years ago, when he had run to get Mi-Kevan to see if he could help the wounded canok, the feud between the sorcerer and maneth had definitely been fueled. Now, it seemed Mi-Kevan was there to make good on his threat, to send the maneth on a little journey.

The magician saw Maldor's concern. "Oh, don't worry, you muscle-bound dolt. I'll be sure and make it possible for you to be back in time for your son's first birthday. I won't let you go much further than the land beyond the South Sea."

Maldor's eyes dropped. He was about to plea for leniency when Alan spoke up. "I don't mean to interrupt, but if I understand things correctly, then you are going to 'send' him somewhere away from here?"

Mi-Kevan smiled and in a satisfied tone, replied, "Yes, far away."

"Well then, I have another idea. It is not far away, but if you mean to cause him hardships, then this is the answer."

Geoff stared disbelievingly across the harbor. "I cannot believe you really did it. Just sending him there was bad enough, but did you have to tie him up and hang a sign around his neck reading 'I was in charge of getting Pete and his men back and I forgot'?"

Mi-Kevan grinned. "Yes, that was a nice touch."

"Thank you," replied Alan. "I figured he deserved it. Give Pete another week over there to dish out his wrath and then we'll send the ferry or another boat over."

Geoff slapped him on the back. "Well, Grove, let it be said that it is never a good idea to get on your bad side, but also know that Maldor's son has witnessed this entire scene. A family vengeance is a rough thing to hide from."

Alan stared at the two-week-old child held in the maneth's huge hands. With a sigh, he said, "Perhaps three days will be sufficient for Pete to cool off."

"Dear boy, you don't know Pete that well."

The New

"I love you, Schram. Will you be joining me soon?" Stepha rubbed her hand over her husband's shoulders while he stared into the peaceful sky above Elvinott.

"Yes, I will, but do you mind if I take a short while longer? It has been so long since I have felt peace such as this."

She smiled and kissed his cheek. "I understand, but I still feel some conflict in your thoughts. Is it your human mother that fills your mind so?"

"Yes, she is there. I must try to find out what happened. If she lives, I must try to help her."

Stepha watched his eyes as they still burned at his loss. She wished she could help but knew there would be nothing she could do now that would help her struggling love. She slid her hand in his and softly asked, "What will you do? Do you believe this is not yet over?"

"I fear that something is left unturned." She lost a bit of her smile, which Schram noticed. "What do you fear? I too see it in your eyes."

"There is one thing which troubles me."

Schram now turned to her. "Please tell me, Stepha. Perhaps together we can find the answer."

"When you told me about all that happened at the Great Oak and about the powers you are beginning to understand about the nature of dragons, one of those traits does not follow with the events."

Schram lifted an eyebrow. "What is it, Stepha?"

"If a dragon knows the time of its death, then why would Slayne have ever felt his plan would be successful? He would have known he was not going to defeat you."

Schram nodded. "And why were his last words 'my plans have not as yet turned full circle and your destiny is not complete' if I was truly the victor?"

She pulled herself in close, and the two held each other as tight as their still-weary arms would allow them to. Without another word, she disappeared through the trees, leaving her husband to roll his stare back to the night sky. Schram leaned back and buried his eyes into the immense darkness. For as long as he could remember, he had never felt as he did at that moment. Even with the unknowns, he truly felt peace and safety.

He was so deep in thought he almost did not recognize the four black shadows creating a rift in the sky as they flew, blocking the stars and causing the air to move under the beat of their wings. Schram leaped to his feet and immediately began a spell of protection until he felt the presence.

The four dragons circled and landed around him in the glade. The largest dragon, a green with silver wings, stepped forward and spoke. "Do you know us, Schram?"

"Yes, you are Cameron, my half brother and the secret behind the powers carried within the Hatchet of Claude. With you are my other half brothers, Aizlan of the sword, Kylscot of the bow, and Kolkmeier of the hammer. I am pleased to finally know you."

"As are we of you, brother. We wished you to know of our separation from the weapons. Our father foretold that once our presence was no longer required, we would be released from the bond. As the times have grown peaceful, that time has occurred."

"I thank you for bringing this news before me. I have longed to speak with all of you but was not sure how to propose to do it."

"We have longed for the same, yet our position was similar."

"Our path takes us to the only home we have ever known, below the storm over the South Sea. We should also say that it is your home as well, should you ever desire it to be."

"Thank you, my brothers, but for the first time in my life, I think I am home."

"We understand and wish you well in your quest for your human mother."

"How did you know?"

"Our mother is very wise. Knowing that you share her and our blood, there would be no other option for you."

"I see that the wiseness of your mother and father has passed to their sons. I wish you all the best."

The blue dragon with golden wings, whom Schram knew as Aizlan, stepped forward. There was a flash at his feet and then a shiny curved scimitar appeared before him. He smiled. "Would you see that Lars receive this sword when he is ready? His mother carried it proudly and gave her life to save her son's. Upon her death, I only had the strength to help one of them. She made the choice, and an admirable one it was."

Cameron interjected. "The weapons will not carry the same strengths they once did, but due to our past presence, there will still be inherent powers that a normal weapon will not have."

Schram lifted the scimitar and held it up as if ready to wield it in battle. "Thank you again. I shall do as you ask."

"Very well," replied Cameron with a smile folding across his large dragon mouth. "We will be off. If you or those with you should ever need us again, you will know what to do." The dragons spread their wings and disappeared into the night. Schram stared at the sword in his hands and could feel Krirtie's presence within it. He was certain her son would do her proud when he was ready to accept it."

Schram pushed the sword into its scabbard, which had appeared on the ground next to it, and then left the glade to join Stepha.

Glossary of Names

Keith Starland: King of Toopek, transformed into Dragon Lord Starland

Suzanne Starland: Queen of Toopek and Schram's birth mother, never seen since the first attack on Toopek

Schram Starland: Prince of Toopek, son to the King and Queen and main character leading the companions against the dragon oppression.

Kirven: Canok, white with black diamond patch, extremely powerful with magic.

Krirtie Wayward: Human friend to Schram, main Companion

Stepha: Stephanatilantilis, princess of Elvinott, brother to Madeiris, son to Hoangis, joined with Schram.

Maldor: Maneth and one of the companions

Fehr: Bandicoot (rat) and one of the companions

Jermys Ironshield: Dwarf, one of the companions, and very close with Fehr

Bretten Ironshield: Dwarf twin to Jermys who betrayed the dwarves and was killed during the final battle in Anbari's dominion.

Geoff: King of the Maneths

Mi-Kevin: Sorcerer, helped save Kirven and lives with the maneth.

Tomas Sherblade: Toopekian Elder who is transformed into Dragon Lord Sherblade

William Meyer: Toopekian Elder who is transformed into Dragon Lord Meyer

Almok: Kirven's twin brother and close to Slayne

Slayne: Evil Black Dragon at the source of the dragon oppression

Anbari: The most powerful dragon, creator of the Staff of Anbari and a source for Schram to gain magical powers

King Kapmann: Dwarf King of Antaag

King Krystof: Dwarf King of Feldschlosschen

View other Black Rose Writing titles at www.blackrosewriting/books

and use promo code **PRINT** to recieve a **20% discount** when purchasing.

BLACK ROSE
writing™

www.ingramcontent.com/pod-product-compliance
Lightning Source LLC
Chambersburg PA
CBHW011934130726
47904CB00014B/2372